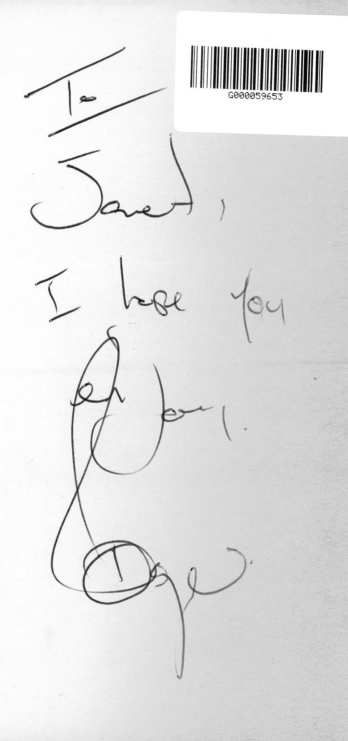

To

Janet,

I hope you

Roger A. Price is a retired detective inspector who had been in charge of a covert unit that received national acclaim for its successes in engaging those who openly sold Class A drugs.

Prior to this, he'd been in charge of the C.I.D. at Preston, having first led a dedicated informant unit.

He also worked on murders, drugs squads, and the regional and national crime squads, often in covert roles across the UK, Europe and the Far East, receiving several commendations.

Now writing crime thrillers, he uses his previous professional experiences to add gritty realism.

Visit the author's website at www.rogerapriceauthor.com

PRAISE FOR
BY THEIR RULES

'A gripping and scary yarn clearly benefiting from your many years of sterling service. Tightly written and structured too with some well devised surprises May I wish you every success'. John Stapleton – journalist and TV broadcaster

'Overall I was singularly impressed by debut thriller, *By Their Rules,* from the pen of former police officer Roger A. Price'. Raven Crime Reads (Top 500 Amazon reviewer)

'*By Their Rules* is former detective Roger Price's first novel and he has put his own extensive experience and knowledge of hunting down big time criminals and the terrifying dangers of working undercover (when each moment is life – or death – on a true knife-edge) to good use, plunging readers straight into a well-plotted, multi-layered story with a neat, surprising twist at the end that will leave them breathless. Excellent stuff – now what about the next one? I for one can't wait.'
Nick Oldham, crime writer

'The author has this novel well placed in the real world. People, places and events are all built around the truth – I believe the author is an ex-cop himself! Impressive first debut that is a well-crafted detective story. If you're looking for a good read to wrap up your summer, consider *By Their Rules* by Roger A. Price'. Sara Knight of the Drunken Druid Review

'*By Their Rules* is as good as it gets. A vivid and persuasive debut novel by Roger A Price'. Book Viral

A New Menace

Also by Roger A. Price

By Their Rules

Roger A. Price

A New Menace

Vanguard Press

A CIP catalogue record for this title is
available from the British Library.

ISBN 978 1 84386 946 7

*Vanguard Press is an imprint of
Pegasus Elliot MacKenzie Publishers Ltd.*
www.pegasuspublishers.com

First Published in 2014

*All characters and events in this publication are fictitious, and any resemblance to
real persons, living or dead, is purely coincidental.*

*Also, many covert tactics are mentioned in this book; some based on real
applications, and some completely fictitious. I'll let the reader decide which are real
and those that are not.*

Vanguard Press
Sheraton House Castle Park
Cambridge England

Printed & Bound in Great Britain

For Candace, Adele and David.

Acknowledgements

To my advance readers who kindly volunteer their time to plough through an early unpolished draft of my work in order to advise on the basics of the story and comment on structure and other issues which need addressing at this earliest stage. It always amazes me what you see, so thanks to David, Chris and Chris, I truly appreciate it.

Thanks to those who having read my first novel, *By Their Rules*, were kind enough to offer feedback; I've been blown away by the overwhelmingly positive reactions, and taken on your comments where I can. To know so many have enjoyed the first book is truly heart-warming, I can only hope you enjoy *A New Menace* as much.

I'm quietly confident that you will, but I'll let you decide.

The books can be read in any order, so I hope new readers enjoy *A New Menace* and go on to try the first.

I welcome any feedback anyone is kind enough to give, and can be contacted via my email address: rapricereviews@aol.com

You can also visit my website at www.rogerapriceauthor.com (which includes links to my Facebook, Twitter, Linkedin and Goodreads accounts) for which I thank Ivor for a professional job and his patience in dealing with me.

Thanks also to family and friends – some near, and some far – for their continued support and interest.

Finally, many thanks to my publisher, Pegasus Elliot Mackenzie, for all their professional work and guidance, from editorial, production, publication and marketing. The book could not have been in better hands.

CHAPTER ONE

John Burrows guessed the next couple of hours would be mundane, tedious even. He was used to CMEs – or Covert Method of Entries, as they were officially called – from his days in the Serious and Organised Crime Agency. And, although he had retired from the cops before it became the National Crime Agency, he guessed nothing much would have changed.

In truth, he didn't really know what he was doing here, sat in the back of an observation van with a rookie. Even though his boss Frank Briers had said, Burrows' secondment here was at the NCA's request – due to his recent knowledge of their target – the fact that he'd been put in the back of a van with a rookie said it all.

"I've never done one of these sorts of jobs before, do they usually pass off OK?" the Rookie asked.

"Usually," Burrows answered, resisting the temptation to check his watch, yet again, "whilst the surveillance team keep a watch on our target as he is stuffing his fat face in the restaurant, the CME team will approach his flat via the rear, and we'll keep the front covered. Just in case an old girlfriend with a key, or whoever arrives unexpectedly."

"How many are in the CME team?"

Burrows sighed, before answering; this guy really was a rookie, he thought. He'd said his name was Brian, a man in his twenties who'd not been with the agency long. He seemed a nice enough guy and Burrows knew he shouldn't sigh – he felt a twinge of guilt; everyone had been a rookie once. "Depends on what the recce showed up the other night. But I'm guessing in this case, there would be a couple of guys to keep the dog happy, a couple of guys to plant the listening devices and the civilian technician to get them past the locks. That's the tricky bit, getting in quickly and switching off the alarm."

"How good are the technicians?"

"They're usually pretty good, recces and intelligence gathered previously gives them all they need to know about the locks and alarms, and then they practice with copies for days before the actual job."

"Must be a bit different though, doing it for real."

"Yeah, that's when the real pressure is on."

Burrows looked at his watch once more, it was 10.45 p.m. and the autumn rain that had been predicted, arrived. It always wound him up how the weather forecasts were spot on when it was bad news, and intermittent at best, when it was supposed to be fine. Though he'd forgive them tonight: rain was good cover on jobs like this, though it did make it more difficult peering through the viewing ports in the side of the van.

They were parked on a quiet residential avenue with grass-fronted pavements bordering Victorian town houses with high inverted V painted weatherboards. Each painted a different pastel colour; it gave the place a real coastal resort feel, which of course is what it was. The street lighting was poor, but fortunately, there was one lamppost right outside the target address.

He noted it had been five minutes since the CME team, using the call sign Tango One, had announced they were approaching the rear of the premises, and he wondered how they were getting on.

"What sort of lock is it on the back door?" the Rookie asked.

"As far as I'm aware, it's just a standard five-lever mortise, after all this is just a rented flat the target uses from time to time for his meetings with the rest of his gang. It's not like his home address back in Manchester; which will be like Fort Knox."

"More like his weekend Southport retreat, eh?"

"I guess you could call it that."

As if the surveillance team leader had been reading Burrows' mind, his radio earpiece burst into life. "Charlie One to the visual, permission?"

"There's no change at the front aspect," Burrows said into his coat lapel, "permission to speak, granted."

"Charlie One to the whole team, update from the Delta team that the target is still in the restaurant having a meal. Charlie One to Tango One, acknowledge the last, and a situation report from you when poss."

Silence.

"Charlie One to Tango One, acknowledge?"

Silence again.

"Visual to Charlie One," Burrows butted in, "maybe you're parked too far away and they aren't picking you up, I'll try, we're only a hundred metres away."

Charlie One agreed and Burrows tried raising the CME team Tango One, but received no reply. Something was wrong.

Burrows suggested to Charlie One that, as they were the nearest, he would slip out of the van and do a walk-past at the rear to see what was going on. It was a ground floor flat; the property had been converted into several apartments. It had a rear yard accessed from a secluded alley, and intelligence checks reported that the other flats in the building were currently unoccupied. They were summer lets; Southport for all its charm wasn't the place to hole down for the winter.

Charlie One told Burrows to go ahead. So he asked Brian to stay vigilant whilst he slid out of the side door to the van, the one facing away from the target premises. Glad to be out of the van, Burrows stretched his large frame as he stood up straight. He was in his fifties and getting too old for cramped obs vans, he thought. Though he kept himself in shape, sitting in obs vans had always been a back-killer.

As soon as he was away and heading towards the end of the block, he checked that his own communications were working OK. Brian speaking as the 'visual', said he was loud and clear.

The weak street lighting was low and helped Burrows stay unobtrusive as he kept to the shadows, pulling up the collar of his leather jacket as he walked. Once he turned the corner at the end of the row, he felt relief at being out of sight, and quickly made his way down the unlit back alley. He counted the rear gates until he was sure the next one was the target address. The gate was open, and he waited a couple of metres away, catching his breath as he listened intently. Nothing.

He checked his watch; it was now eleven. Fifteen minutes since the Tango team announced their arrival at the rear. Setting his radio to whisper mode – which amplifies quiet speech – he tried to raise them again. No reply.

Something was very wrong, there was no way they wouldn't be able to hear him from this distance. As stealthily as he could, Burrows tiptoed to the edge of the gate, and slowly peered around its jam. It took a moment in the subdued light for his eyes to adjust. It was even darker than in the alleyway, at least the passage had some ambient light at each end of it.

He took a step in as his vision attuned. Then he saw them.

CHAPTER TWO

Four bodies. All lying on their backs on the concrete floor. They were all trussed up and not moving. The back door to the premises was wide open, but with no sign of life from within. Burrows rushed to the nearest man, and as he leaned over him, he could see gaffer tape over his eyes and mouth. He ripped the tape off and the man's head just lolled from side to side. He didn't react to the removal of the tape.

Burrows quickly checked for a pulse. There was one, albeit slow. He was alive, but unconscious. Thank God. He checked the other three, all the same. All four had their hands tied behind their backs with plastic handcuffs. He couldn't do anything about that now, he'd need a knife to cut them free, so he concentrated on removing the gaffer tape. That done, he caught his breath for a second and crouched down as he whispered into his lapel.

"Burrows to the DI, urgent."

"Charlie One receiving, go ahead, John."

Burrows was just about to speak further when he heard a noise coming from the direction of the back door. He spun around as he jumped to his feet, ignoring Charlie One's repeated attempts to raise him in his earpiece. A golden Labrador trotted towards him, tail wagging. Burrows breathed out heavily.

"Charlie One to Burrows, respond. What's going on?" Burrows' earpiece pleaded.

"Wait one, Charlie One," Burrows replied.

He quickly put the dog back into the ground floor flat and closed the back door.

He then brought Charlie One – Detective Inspector Nigel Crabtree – up to speed on what he had found. There was a long pause after Burrows finished speaking as Crabtree was obviously taking in what Burrows had said. He'd barely taken it in himself. Then Charlie One replied, he told Burrows that he was sending a people carrier down the back alley to get the four men. Then added, "Where's the technician, the locksmith?"

Burrows felt sick, amid the chaotic last few minutes, he'd failed to notice that there was no sign of the technician. "I'm sorry Charlie One. He's not in the yard. Maybe he's legged it."

Charlie One responded with several attempts to raise the technician over the airwaves. No reply.

"Burrows to Charlie One, I'll check the house."

"You'd better be quick, John, we've just heard from the surveillance team's leader – Delta One – the target has finished his meal early and is preparing to leave. He could be on his way back to you."

This was just getting ridiculous, Burrows thought, still not able to comprehend exactly what had taken place here in the last twenty minutes. He rushed to the back door knowing he had no time for stealth now as he opened it and entered. The dog sat in the corner of the kitchen, just raised his head and gave a solitary wag of its tail as Burrows raced inside. He'd seen the layout of the flat during the briefing earlier that evening. A one-bedroomed, ground floor flat with a kitchen and lounge. It only took him a minute to search the place; there was no sign of anyone. He left the way he had entered and closed the kitchen door behind him. The last of the four unconscious CME team was being loaded into the rear of the MPV parked across the rear gate.

One of the MPV crew gave Burrows a quick nod as he re-entered the back yard from the kitchen.

He gave Charlie One a quick update over the radio as the MPV drove off.

"The rest of the teams are out searching the adjoining streets for him," Charlie One replied, "but I suggest you get out of there sharpish. Delta One has just confirmed that the target is mobile again and he's headed back your way."

Burrows acknowledged the last transmission as he ran down the back alley the same way as he had entered. It was about a hundred metres to the end where it joined the street. He was halfway down it when his earpiece crackled again.

"The target is confirmed back towards his H.A. approximately two minutes away."

Burrows' heart rate quickened, as did his pace as he ran and slid on the uneven damp cobbles, made more treacherous by a coating of wet leaves. He skidded to a halt as he reached the end, cursing the sound made with grit underfoot, just as the observation van came into view. Thankfully, Brian must have seen which end of the alleyway Burrows had entered by, and guessed he'd leave the same way. The van pulled to a halt and Burrows jumped onto the front passenger seat.

"Cheers, mate. You timed that well," Burrows said.

"Had to guess which end, I couldn't get in on the radio to ask. It's gone mental. And to make it worse, the Delta surveillance team have come onto our channel."

Burrows nodded as he listened to the continuous radio chatter. The target had just entered his street from the opposite end. Time to go.

They spent the next two hours with the rest of Charlie and Delta teams looking for the technician. Ian Townley was his name. A small man in his thirties who had his own locksmith business but was contracted to work part-time, as required, for the National Crime Agency. So, as such, he was not a casehardened operative, but a civvie on an earner. And that was part of the problem. Whatever had happened in that back yard had been quick, unexpected and undoubtedly scary. They were working from an assumption that he had somehow thwarted his assailants and legged it into the night, and was probably cowering in fear in a doorway somewhere. But after two hours, there was still no sign of him. Charlie One had said that his mobile phone kept ringing straight to answer machine, and that there was no sign of life at his home address in Preston. One car had been sent there and told to remain outside until further notice.

Delta team had followed the target back to his flat, he had gone in, and all the lights were now off. Two of their cars had been told by Charlie One to remain static there, and cover both front and rear approaches to the property. The rest of both teams were then stood down by Charlie One and directed to the Liverpool office for a debrief. It would be quicker than going back to their base in Manchester.

At this time of night, it would only be a forty-minute journey to the Liverpool Branch Office of the National Crime Agency. Burrows had been there many times before when it was owned by its predecessor, the Serious and Organised Crime Agency. He'd been a detective sergeant on SOCA at its Lancashire Branch Office before he'd retired about eighteen months ago. That was before he'd joined the secret Special Projects Unit, run by his old SOCA boss, Detective Superintendent Frank Briers. He'd just finished his first job with the SPU and was nearing the end of a month's break when Briers had asked him to act as a liaison officer on this job. But as far as this current team, headed up by DI Nigel Crabtree, were concerned, Burrows was still retired and not working for anyone else.

He'd never met Crabtree before, and got the impression that he didn't really want some ex-DS on his team. Burrows had tried to act circumspect, so as not to upset anyone. But knew he could be of help, due to his recent dealings with their target. It was someone he'd come across on his first SPU job. Jonny Moon was one of Manchester's nastier villains.

He and Brian sat in silence on the short journey into Liverpool, and he spent that time musing as to what had really gone on back in Southport at Moon's flat. It was obvious to him that they'd been expected, but how? And where was the locksmith Townley?

CHAPTER THREE

Twenty minutes after arriving at the nondescript office block on the outskirts of Liverpool city centre, Burrows had grabbed a brew and sat at the back of the briefing room next to his new rookie mate Brian. The rest of the Charlie team shuffled in and took a seat. Then DI Nigel Crabtree entered the room and stood at the front. He was in his forties, six feet tall and slim. An older man whom Burrows didn't know, but guessed was Crabtree's boss, joined him. He had the halo of importance that some senior officers just naturally seem to exude about them. Crabtree was in smart casuals whilst the other man was wearing an expensive suit.

"First of all, for those who don't know him, allow me to introduce Detective Chief Superintendent Gary Ray," Crabtree said.

Ray just nodded, and Crabtree continued. "Secondly, the four men from the CME team have been taken to a military hospital not too far from here, in order to avoid unwarranted questions that NHS medical staff would no doubt ask. And I can tell you that all four will be OK. They are still out of it, but uninjured. According to the doctor treating them, they had been rendered unconscious, probably, with the use of chloroform or something similar. So, obviously we won't know more until they are awake."

"What about the locksmith guy?" a voice asked.

"Townley, yes, I was just coming to that. We've no idea. We suspect he's legged it and got himself away. That said, we can't understand why his phone's turned off. Anyway, as of ten minutes ago, we have an authorised live cell-siting set up with his service provider, so, as and when he turns his phone back on, we should get an idea of where he is."

Crabtree then said he wanted to go through the observations log for Charlie team staff, sign it off by all involved and then go through the earlier intelligence briefing to try to work out what had gone so disastrously wrong.

It didn't take long to go through the log, as there wasn't much on it. Observations had commenced earlier in the evening, the target Moon had left the flat alone and been followed by Delta team. Charlie team had maintained a watch on the flat whilst the CME team had approached via the rear, and that was pretty much it. It should have been a straightforward job to enter and place the listening devices in the lounge.

The intelligence case justifying their actions said Moon used the flat at weekends, and sometimes during the week, to hold meetings with other criminal associates. It was thought he was planning a major drugs importation, but the details were sketchy. Their authority to plant the bugs was limited to the lounge as that is where he was assumed to hold his meetings. If it later transpired that he did all his dirty talking in the kitchen, then they would have to apply for fresh authorities and go through the whole process again. It would be a pain in the backside, but that was the balance between the intrusion into someone's private life, and the operational need to gather the intelligence.

"According to the intelligence brief, Moon was supposed to go for a meal, where he was due to meet 'someone of interest'. He indeed went to a local restaurant on Lord Street in Southport, but did so alone, and met no one whilst he was there. The Delta team are of the impression that he left suddenly to return home," Crabtree said.

"Why's that?" one of the team asked.

"Because he took a call on his mobile and then got up straight away and asked for the bill." Crabtree answered, before turning to face Burrows. "John, have you any historical gems of info to add?"

Burrows ignored the dry undertones before answering, "I think the whole thing was a set-up from start to finish."

"Well, I'm not sure about that, as far as we know he just had some security we weren't aware of who took our guys by surprise," Crabtree answered defensively.

"Well I am," Burrows answered, "he goes out alone, turns all the lights off. Goes to a restaurant alone, and returns suddenly after a phone call taken shortly after our guys are attacked. And when I got there, it was obvious the alarm was turned off as the back door was left open for his pooch to wander about if it'd wanted to."

Crabtree didn't answer. Burrows knew what he'd summarised made sense. He also knew it suggested a leak. There was no use edging around the subject.

Detective Chief Superintendent Ray stood up and invaded the silence. "As unpleasant a suggestion as John's is, it is one that we will have to consider. If only to rule it out. So, before anyone leaves this room this morning, I want you all to hand in your personal mobile phones for scrutiny. And if any of you have a problem with that, you'd better have a good reason why."

No one said anything.

Then Crabtree's own mobile rang. It was probably an update from the hospital, or from the Delta teams still out there, Burrows thought, as he watched him take the phone from his pocket and look at the screen before answering it.

But, he didn't just glance at the screen as you do when wanting to see who is calling; he seemed to stare at it. Burrows could see the slapped expression on Crabtree's face as no doubt did everyone else in the room, before he put the phone to his ear. He didn't speak, just appeared to listen, intently.

After thirty seconds or so he said, "But," shortly followed by, "Hello, hello," before he took the phone away from his ear and just stared at the screen once more. The call had obviously ended. Crabtree then glanced at his boss before turning to face the room. "That was Townley, or should I say, Townley's phone. It appears he's been taken."

"Taken. What do you mean taken?" Ray asked.

"Taken, as in kidnapped," Crabtree replied to a stunned audience.

This really didn't make any sense now as Burrows struggled to understand what exactly was going on. Crabtree then took a further call a minute or two later, which apparently had come from Townley's phone service provider. It said that Townley's phone had been turned on for a minute, during which time it had pinged a phone mast which suggested the handset was currently headed south on the M6 near to Birmingham's infamous 'spaghetti junction', from where its carrier could take one of several motorways in different directions. A good place to use the phone, Burrows thought.

Crabtree then continued to elaborate on what the caller had said. That *they* knew the NCA was going to Moon's flat, and why. That no one had been hurt, and it would remain that way as long as they – the cops – followed instructions. They apparently told Crabtree to pull his surveillance off Moon, and that Moon should not be approached in any way. They also told him to get some sleep and be prepared to receive a further call mid to late morning.

CHAPTER FOUR

It was almost five a.m. by the time Burrows was dropped off outside his central Manchester hotel. He'd chosen it because of its proximity to Piccadilly railway station; he had come up from London by train, not expecting to be in Manchester more than a day or so. Brian said he'd collect him at eleven a.m. and Burrows thanked him; at least there was time for a couple of hours' sleep. It was still dark but the roads were starting to get busy.

Fortunately, Burrows had only known of Crabtree's investigation for forty-eight hours, so Crabtree agreed he could keep his mobile phone – though he still checked the call log before letting him take it. But Burrows knew the only two people he'd called were the rookie Brian, and Frank Briers. He'd have to bring Briers up-to-date on what had taken place, but he'd get some sleep first.

By ten thirty a.m. Burrows was up, showered and dressed, perched on the end of his bed with a brew in one hand and his phone in the other. As far as the local DI Nigel Crabtree was concerned, Burrows had retired from SOCA eighteen months ago before moving to Thame in Oxfordshire where he now lived. Detective Chief Inspector Frank Briers, his old boss, had been seconded to the home office and promoted to detective superintendent. All true, plus Briers had offered Burrows' services as he had first-hand knowledge of Crabtree's target

Jonny Moon. Burrows had told Crabtree that Moon was the last person he'd had dealings with prior to retiring. The last bit wasn't quite true; Burrows had had dealings with Moon a month ago, albeit for only a short time.

What Crabtree didn't know, and Burrows obviously did, was that Briers now ran the operational wing of a secret government department known as the Special Projects Unit.

The prime minister set up the SPU to take on the country's worst villains; once they were deemed too hard to do by conventional methods of investigation. Burrows had been brought out of retirement by Briers, who'd partnered him with ex-MI5 Intelligence Officer Jane Lee.

Burrows was the team leader with a designated call-sign of Alpha, Jane was Bravo, and Briers was Zulu. Though he liked to think that Jane and he were equals really, he wasn't one to pull rank unless necessary, never had been.

All this had taken place little over a month ago and Burrows and Jane had faced down their first target, a dangerous and vicious criminal called Shonbo Cabilla.

Although Cabilla and his team had been their focus, Moon had not. To be fair though, Moon was only an associate of Cabilla who had let him use some of his premises in the past, and assisted with the odd favour. But in Burrows and Jane's endeavours to trace Cabilla, they had paid Jonny Moon a visit at his Trafford Park base in Manchester.

That had ended up with Moon giving them the address of one of Cabilla's premises in London, and although it was out-of-date, it had helped lead them to Cabilla. Moon was certainly no grass though, he'd only found his tongue when Jane shot him through his hand. That was just over four weeks ago, and was why Briers had sent Burrows up to liaise with Crabtree's team.

Burrows knew he didn't really have much to offer, certainly nothing of any great value that Crabtree didn't already know, so he suspected his boss Briers was just being nosey on hearing the name Moon, and wanted Burrows there to get the inside track.

Burrows rang Briers' number and he answered on the second ring, "Hello, John, I'm on my own so you can drop the call-signs," Briers said before Burrows could call him Zulu.

"OK then, Frank. I've got an update for you, but you ain't going to like it."

Burrows then iterated the events of the previous evening as concisely as he could and paused whilst he took a sip of tea.

"They've kidnapped a civilian locksmith, and then issued threats to the police? Am I hearing you right?"

"'Fraid so, Frank. Albeit at this stage the threats are implied, but it takes some beating doesn't it? In all my time in the cops I've never heard of any villains who'd dare to try and pull such a stunt."

"Nor me, John. The utter temerity of them, unbelievable."

Towards the end of the call, Briers asked Burrows to stay in Manchester for a while longer, to go to the midday briefing to see what the update is and to ring him later. Burrows asked why, as this was not strictly SPU business. Even thought he had only done one job with the SPU, he knew that before any job went live, it started as an intelligence case, which was considered by an executive of three. This executive consisted of the Home Secretary, the DPP and the head of the NCA. Burrows knew that the group had no chair and that all three had to answer yes to two questions: Was it in the public interest to take executive action against the named target in the intelligence case? And was it against the public interest *not* to take executive action?

This check and balance ensured they only targeted those who really deserved it, and to make certain, that by taking action they didn't make matters worse. All three had to answer yes to both questions – a 'Yankee, Yankee' as Briers called it and even then, the prime minister had to ratify the decision. So, with all that considered he'd politely pointed out to Briers, "This is a million miles away from a 'Yankee, Yankee', Frank. Are you sure you want me to hang on up here?"

"You're right of course, John, this is not really in your remit, but as the executive are not considering anything at the moment, and Jane is away training, I'd like you to stay a while longer. I must admit I am intrigued as to who Moon is working with. And what they are up to? Aren't you?"

It was as Burrows thought: Frank was being nosy, but he had made a valid argument. Burrows was astounded by the kidnap, and would love to know more. "Fair point, Frank, I'll go to the midday scrum-down and give you a bell later." Burrows ended the call and looked at the time: it was 10.55 a.m., time to head for the lobby.

As he waited in reception for Brian to arrive, he thought about his partner Jane. On hearing Briers mention her by name, it reminded him of how much he liked her. Though he had only known her for a few weeks, they had got on well. It's amazing how quickly you can get close to someone when you are working in a dangerous, fast-moving operational environment.

In fact they had got on a little too well on their last job, something they had both decided to put on a shelf in order to stay focused. Something they had both agreed on, at the time; though he wouldn't mind finding a ladder. Then he heard his name and looked up to see his lift approaching.

CHAPTER FIVE

Jonny Moon couldn't help grinning to himself as he re-entered the flat. Did that idiot in the Vauxhall Vectra, who had followed him from the restaurant, really think he hadn't noticed him? He'd toyed with the idea of going for a bit of a drive on his way back, just to keep these National Crime Agency fools on their toes for a bit, and for the sport of course, but he was under strict instructions himself.

The first thing he did do was to check on his dog, but she was fast asleep in the kitchen. He knew she wouldn't have wandered off, in fact he'd left the kitchen door open on purpose; to stop those police clowns in their tracks for a moment, focusing their attention on the open door whilst his men attacked from the shadows. Though, he was surprised to find the door now shut. Must have been his men; the cops would never had got that far. Just shows who the real professionals are.

Five minutes later, he turned off all the lights and headed to bed. He pulled the new phone from his inside pocket, the one the waiter at the restaurant had handed to him under his bill. Even though he was not expecting a call until 10.30 a.m., he switched it on nonetheless, just in case the game changed and they needed to contact him. It was safe to leave on, he knew the phone was clean, unregistered and only used once. The cops knew nothing of it, even though it had been passed to him right under their stupid noses.

It took a while before Moon could settle properly, his mind buzzing with the evening's events. And then his attention wandered back thirty years to his youth. He was still the same weight as when he was eighteen; he'd always been as slightly built, as he was short. Which was why he used to be picked on at school, it is how he got the nickname, 'The Vicar', not helped by his youthful looks.

It was around the time of his eighteenth birthday that he realised his lack of height, build, or mature looks, didn't actually matter. What mattered was how far a person was prepared to go; and after years of pent up humiliation and frustration, it all came tumbling out one night when he met one of his old school bullies in his local pub. He hadn't seen this guy since he'd left at sixteen but remembered all too well the fear and anxiety this guy made him suffer, as all the horrors of his last few school years came flooding back to him.

He was with his mate in the pool room of his local in Wythenshawe; two other guys he vaguely knew were on stools waiting their turn at the table. They all knew Popeye, at least by reputation if not personally, when he entered the room. 'Popeye', what a stupid nickname, Moon had always thought. It was typical of his old school nemesis' arrogance to call himself suchlike.

All he said to Moon was, "Hi, Vicar, haven't seen you around since school. Been choir singing lately?" Then Popeye laughed at his own pathetic attempt at humour and glanced around the room daring the two on the stools not to laugh along. But as he passed Moon and his attention was momentarily on the others, Moon spun the pool cue in his hand so the thick end was away from him. He then struck the back of Popeye's head with as much force as he could muster, catching him squarely where the top of his spine and the back of his head met.

The pool cue snapped in half as Popeye hit the floor face down. He groaned, but didn't move. Using his foot, Moon flipped him over onto his back and could see that Popeye was either heavily stunned or unconscious. He couldn't believe his strike had been so effective. He felt elated, released, reborn even.

He picked up the broken pool cue by its heavier end, the end that had done the damage so far, and thrust the broken jagged tip into Popeye's right eye. Fluid and blood burst forth from the ruined eye and Popeye awoke screaming in what must have been unbearable agony.

As he sat up and put both hands to his damaged face, Moon bent down towards him. "That's for all the years of grief and pain you gave me, and if you ever speak to me again I'll pop your other eye, Popeye." He then stood up and sniggered at his own sick joke before he addressed the room, "And if any of you grass me up to the filth, I'll kill you. Do you understand? I'll kill you all." He realised how unhinged his voice now sounded as the three bystanders – including his pool partner – all nodded furiously.

He then turned back to Popeye. "You and me are square now, but if you say a word then I'll be back to finish the job." And with that, he turned and fled taking the pool cue with him.

He'd left that pool room a different man, he felt liberated by his outpouring of aggression, felt as if he had truly come of age, even if his soul had started to wither and die. And from that day on, he was never frightened of anyone again. He surrounded himself with like-minded muscle and soon built up a reputation of someone not to be messed with. Someone who knew no boundaries and who would exact outrageously disproportionate responses to any slight, or otherwise deemed lack of respect.

His nickname 'The Vicar' had stuck, now for far more sinister reasons. A nickname he now enjoyed for its negative undertones.

Back to the present, he mused at how he'd built up a successful criminal empire in Manchester, and had a comfortable lifestyle, though he was tired of playing continual hide and seek with the cops, SOCA, and now the National Crime Agency. But if this new job came off, he could probably disappear somewhere warm and go legit.

He'd never actually met the man he was working for, but he knew of him, and he had a fearful reputation. Not that that bothered Moon: as far as he was concerned half of it was probably no more than urban myth. He knew, as evil as he could be was nothing compared to some of the stories he'd heard attributed to him. Though he knew very well how useful such underground legends could be when it came to underwriting one's authority. He just felt a little uneasy, working with someone he'd never seen. He pushed these thoughts from his mind and concentrated on the job they were pulling, and the rich returns in store on completion.

The next thing he was aware of was the mobile phone ringing in an ascending ringtone as he stirred from his sleep, he glanced at his watch it was 10.30 a.m., the guy was certainly punctual. He sat up before answering. "Yeah."

"Everything's going to plan. So far, so good. I rang that skinny, irritating cop in the early hours to tell him we had their locksmith."

"Crabtree?"

"Yes, that's his name. I told Crabtree to expect a further call later this morning."

"Do you think he believed you?"

"Well, I rang him on the locksmith's phone. That should have done the trick. I also told him to pull all surveillance off you."

"Hang on, I'll check," Moon said, as he put the handset down and pulled on a dressing gown before looking around the curtains at his front bedroom window. Returning to his bedside table, he picked the phone back up. "Yeah, the idiot in the Vauxhall Vectra's gone and I can't see any other unfamiliar cars."

"Good, but I want you to check properly."

"OK, I'll get dressed and take the dog for a walk, and double check."

"The number on your screen is my new sterile phone number. But don't use your new phone other than when speaking to me. Then the filth will never be aware of these two numbers."

Moon could feel his anger rising, who did this guy think he was talking to? Some two-bit punk amateur? He chose to let the remark ride; he was probably only being careful, thinking out loud. "Yeah, yeah I know."

"Good, well once you're happy they've gone as instructed, you can head back to Manchester. I'm going to ring Crabtree around twelve, so if you see anything you're not happy about, can you let me know before then?"

"Will do." And with that, they both ended the call, and Moon headed towards the kitchen to make a brew. He'd calmed down now, but he didn't like being talked down to. That said, this job would be a one-off, they wouldn't be working together again.

CHAPTER SIX

It was one p.m. before the briefing at the Manchester office was now due to start, it had been put back due to operational developments. All of the Charlie and Delta surveillance teams were present, the hum of chitchat ended abruptly as Crabtree, and Ray entered the room. Burrows could see neither looked to be in a good mood as they bristled business-like into the room. He had been waiting nearly an hour for the briefing to start and with about thirty people in the room; the temperature was starting to get uncomfortable. They squeezed past Burrows as they made their way to the front, and Burrows couldn't help but notice the sharp acrid smell of Ray's aftershave; it smelled spicy; more flagrant than fragrance. At the front, Ray plonked himself in one of the two forward facing chairs, and Crabtree stood as he addressed the room. He started by going over all that had been said a few hours ago, mainly, Burrows guessed for the benefit of the Delta team, who had probably just been helping out last night as this was clearly Crabtree's and Charlie Team's investigation.

At the conclusion, he thanked Delta team and then stood them down. As soon as they had all left the room, Crabtree continued, telling them all that he had pulled the Delta team's surveillance off their target Moon, as instructed. A few murmurings of apparent disbelief rumbled around the room.

"That's enough of that," Crabtree said. "As long as these thugs have got Ian Townley, we have to tread carefully. His safety is now paramount. Everything else, including our investigations into Jonny Moon, comes second. We can always pick up where we left off when this is all over."

"Does this mean we're ending all surveillance on Moon?" one of the team asked.

"It does for now, until we have a chance to properly evaluate the risks. I've no need to remind you all that we are in unchartered territory here, so we have to act carefully."

More murmurings, but this time with a tone of understanding.

"We have applied for an urgent warrant of interception on Townley's mobile, which was signed by the Home Secretary Bill Dwyers only a couple of hours ago. I'm probably not supposed to tell you that, but I want you to know that we are doing what we can, so when I say all investigations into Moon must stop, then stop they must, and when you leave this room you will follow my orders and what I have just told you stays in this room."

As the murmurings grew in positivity, Burrows realised what Crabtree was doing. He was correct; he shouldn't have divulged the presence of the phone tap – or lines, as they called them – even to his own investigation team. But by telling them this, he was obviously hoping to ensure compliance with his request to cease all investigations. Detectives were never good at being told to drop things, especially in emotive circumstances.

They would also know that if they did anything that was seen by Moon or his associates then he might say something about it, which could be picked up by the interception and get back to Crabtree. It was a clever ploy, Burrows thought.

Burrows knew that an urgent request for interception was only granted in extreme circumstances; such as when life was in danger and it was needed over the next twenty-four hours. He also knew that the authorisation would have to be reviewed, and if no useful intelligence had come from it, then the authority would be cancelled, and the interception would be switched off. Interception of someone's phone was one of the gravest intrusions into someone's private life, so was very rare, and the rules surrounding it were very strict.

Crabtree then closed the briefing but asked a smaller group of four, including Burrows, to wait. Burrows felt a bit sorry for Brian the rookie as he got up to leave; he said he'd wait for Burrows in the canteen.

Crabtree waited for the last of the others to go before he spoke. "OK, here's the deal. What I've just told the rest of the team isn't strictly true. We have got a line on Townley's phone like I said, but I'm in no doubt it won't be used again, that is if it hasn't already been ditched."

"Why's that?" one of the others asked.

"Because the kidnappers rang me an hour ago from a public phone box in Birmingham. I reckon they only used Townley's phone initially, just so we'd know they had him."

"That makes sense," Burrows said.

Crabtree took a seat before continuing, "I've asked you to stay behind, John, because we don't have a current phone number for Moon, so we can't get a line on him until we do. I was hoping you may have access to a recent number."

"I have and you're welcome to it, but I'm sure he'll have binned it after his dealings with me."

"I'm sure you're right, but we have to try. Anyway, what exactly where your dealings with Moon?"

"Sorry, Nigel, I'd love to tell you, but can't. All I can say is that it was nothing that connects in any way with your job."

"Fair enough, but let me know if anything on your job becomes relevant."

"Will do," Burrows replied.

"Does this mean – we are still investigating?" one of the others asked.

"You can bet your pension on it. No one tells the National Crime Agency what to do, especially not some pond life dreg," Crabtree answered.

Crabtree then went on to explain what had been said in the earlier phone call. How the bad guys had demanded surveillance lifted from Moon, which he had done, to appear to be going along with them. How they had said they were conducting business with Moon and that they expected that to be concluded in two weeks' time. That Crabtree was to cease all operations against Moon whilst they completed their affairs, and that if he did, then Townley would be released unharmed.

"This is unbelievable," said a detective sergeant called Henry. Adding, "How do we even know that Townley's still alive?"

"They put him on the phone, briefly, it was definitely him, and he is clearly very frightened," Crabtree answered, "and they told us they know everything we are doing."

"Unfortunately, it looks like you were right, John," Ray said, speaking for the first time, "which is why we've asked you to join our inner sanctum. You are from outside with no prior knowledge of our investigations, so we know you are clean. We are going to have to be extremely cautious from here on in."

"Well, I can understand why you told the rest of team about the interception on Townley's phone, but if we do have a mole, then the bad guys will no doubt soon know about this," Henry said.

"I had to tell them something Henry, and it's like John said, they will no doubt have ditched Townley's phone already, so a line on it will be useless," Crabtree said.

"Well, we have one thing going for us, when this is all over, Moon won't be too hard to find and we can just lock him up for being involved in the kidnap," Burrows offered.

"That's the other thing, John, they also said that even though they were doing business with Moon, he didn't know anything about his flat about to be bugged, or what had taken place in his back yard, or even that Townley had been snatched. The voice on the phone just said, Moon was told to go for a meal and not to come home until instructed. They say we can't prove anything against him as he didn't know anything," Crabtree said.

"Do we believe them, boss?" asked Henry. "I mean, they could just be saying this to protect Moon, and ultimately themselves."

"The thing is, we just don't know Henry, but I can promise you we are going to find out," Crabtree finished.

CHAPTER SEVEN

Tony Bentine enjoyed the lifestyle his criminal acumen afforded him, already a wealthy man by conservative means; he would soon be rich by celebrity definition. He was only forty and when this next job came off, he would be able to go anywhere, and do anything he wanted, whilst still young enough to enjoy himself. He wouldn't have to take risks again, not unless he wanted to. He nodded at the waiter. "Kalimera," he said, as he headed to the quiet corner of the taverna he usually aimed for.

"Good morning," the waiter mirrored in English, continuing, "your usual coffee?"

"Yes please, Sanos."

Bentine loved this taverna as it faced over the square in the centre of Hanioti, a picturesque bustling centre of the resort. It was his favourite part of the Kassandra peninsular, in his favourite part of Greece. Autumn was still very warm here, without being too hot, though it started to get a little rainy from here on in, but still one of his favourite times of year. He'd spend the winter here as he had the last few years, and although this place used to be full of Brits, they had been replaced with Serbs, now. Bentine didn't mind, it added to his anonymity.

Another reason why he liked this taverna was the wi-fi, unlike most of the others around the square. He could get his laptop out and sit there doing business all day if he wished, and it would only cost him several coffees and some food. Sanos delivered his drink together with a small bottle of water before walking away as Bentine's phone vibrated on the table. He looked at the caller ID before answering it.

"Everything all right? I wasn't expecting to hear from you just yet."

"It was as you suspected. They are continuing to investigate the locksmith's disappearance. Although they are keeping it low-key."

"Quit the gags, and just tell me."

"Sorry, couldn't resist it. OK, Crabtree has told all his staff that they're dropping all investigations, but they're not. He has assembled a small team of four, including some retired DS called Burrows. John Burrows, ex-SOCA. Anyway, they have tapped the Locksmith's phone, but expect it to be a waste of time. They're trying to get a current number for Moon's phone, which is where this Burrows bloke comes in."

"How do you mean?"

"Well, this Burrows supposedly had dealings with Moon about eighteen months ago, and albeit, that's a while ago, Crabtree thinks he might be able to help, background knowledge and such like."

"Should I be bothered about this, Burrows?"

"Not just yet, but I'll monitor things from this end. He's already suggested that they have a leak."

"We expected that, but are you sure you can't be compromised?" Bentine asked, with a hint of concern.

"No worries, I'm watertight," the caller said.

"OK, we'll move to stage two straight away and I'll await your feedback from their reactions," Bentine said, before ending the call.

He took a sip of his coffee as he mused over the conversation. It was to be expected Crabtree wouldn't heed the initial warnings; the cops were not used to being in this position, but now he'd move it forward. He checked that he still couldn't be overheard, before dialling a number. "Can you speak?" he asked, as the call was answered.

"Yeah, I learnt it at an early age," came Moon's voice in reply.

"Why is everyone a comedian today? You're supposed to be a professional. I meant are you free to speak?"

"I know, I know. It's not just you Scousers who have a sense of humour. You just think it is."

Bentine knew Jonny Moon came highly recommended, not least for his violent nature, which was an asset, but as time went by, he was starting to find the man more and more irritating. He sighed expressively before continuing, "Let's get back to business. It's time to go to stage two. As we suspected, the bizzies have failed to heed the warning."

"What did Crabtree say? You know, when you told him to back off whilst you finished your business."

"Not a lot."

"I bet his face was a picture."

"I bet it was, but he needs to learn a lesson, so it's over to you."

"No probs."

"Let me know when it's done."

"Yeah, yeah, I know," Moon replied.

Bentine wasn't sure whether his growing dislike of Moon was cultural or not. There only be thirty miles separating Liverpool from Manchester, but the two cities had always been worlds apart. The Mancs always thought that Scousers were just jokers and conmen, who had an inferiority complex because their city was smaller. Scousers thought the Mancs were just a bunch of big-headed idiots who were jealous of the Scouse wit. But he would only have to put up with him for the rest of this job. One bonus though, was that they were in no way connected. Scouse and Manc villains just didn't work together. "One last thing, Crabtree has apparently got some retired cop by the name of John Burrows working for him."

"So?"

"Well, this Burrows claims to have had dealings with you eighteen months ago. This is why Crabtree has him in his inner circle. Is there something you are not telling me? I thought you'd not had any face-to-face dealings with the bizzies since you were a kid."

"I haven't, and I resent the implication," Moon replied, loaded with aggression.

"I'm not accusing you of anything; just asking."

"Just as well then, and to answer your question I've no idea who this Burrows is, but I'll find out."

Bentine ended the call, but before he did, he told Moon to be careful, not to draw attention to himself, just to sort stage two out. He could tell Moon seemed a little upset, but that was Mancs for you, not happy at taking orders from a Scouser.

He waved Sanos over and asked him for a beef stifado, it was time for lunch, after which he'd head for the beach.

***

Moon knew that Bentine had rung Crabtree to issue his demands as he'd received a text from him earlier saying, 'call has gone in, ring you later'. But when he'd rang just now to fill him in proper, the last thing he'd expected was to be told to go to stage two. He didn't know where Bentine was getting his information from, but he obviously had a well-placed source. He'd taken the dog for a walk earlier and, happy that there were no filth still camped outside his flat, he'd made his way back to Manchester. He'd checked under his car first and around the wheel arches and couldn't see any tracking devices. He'd also pulled a few anti-surveillance moves on his return journey – going around roundabouts several times to see if the same car followed him round and round, and that sort of thing – but had seen nothing, so headed back to his new Trafford Park address. He hired industrial units to use as a base but kept moving premises every few months, just to keep the filth on the back foot, he knew they often had a look at him. He just made sure they never saw anything.

Going over the conversation he'd just had with Bentine, he'd be glad when payday came; it was proving harder than he'd imagined working with him; cats and dogs rarely went together. He'd hold his temper, for now. After all, this was a one-off.

Anyway, who was this Burrows character? Probably some analyst type desk-jockey, he thought. He knew he'd had no dealings with cops for years, not face-to-face, that was for sure. Anyhow, he'd ask around, just be on the safe side.

He grabbed his car keys and headed out of his unit to travel the short distance to where Townley was being held. Time to check on his guest; and then time to go to stage two.

CHAPTER EIGHT

At the end of Crabtree's briefing, Burrows found a quiet corner to ring Frank Briers to request Moon's old phone number. When Burrows met Moon, it had only been a month ago, but Moon hadn't known he was one of the good guys. He and Jane – his new ex-MI5 partner – had paid Moon a visit in the guise of fellow villains. They knew he'd historically rented out premises to Shonbo Cabilla, who was their target. It was simply a good place to start their search. Burrows recalled how their meeting had not gone to plan, and but for Jane's timely intervention he'd have been in big trouble. Anyway, he'd rang Moon on his private mobile to set up that meet, and all Moon had seemed to be interested in was where he got his number from. So, he was in no doubt the number would no longer be valid.

Five minutes after his initial call, Briers rang him back to confirm that the number was dead. That covered, he then brought Briers up-to-speed after Crabtree's meeting.

"The audacity of these people just gets worse," Briers spat, "telling Crabtree to pull his surveillance was bad enough, but telling him to cease all operations for two weeks whilst *they* conduct *their* criminal enterprises, is beyond belief."

"For them to be so daring, Frank, the scam they are about to pull must be a big one. Probably drugs," Burrows said.

"I wouldn't call these cowards daring, but I know what you mean. And I agree it must be something big they are planning. Just so you are aware, the Home Secretary Bill Dwyers is hopping mad about this. He became aware of it, when he signed the warrant of interception for the tap on Townley's phone. He's called a meeting of the executive tomorrow to see if this isn't something the Special Projects Unit should get involved with. He's asked George Reed, the head of the National Crime Agency to get an official update from his staff so when they sit down with the DPP, they'll have all the available intel."

"Do you think this job will come our way?"

"Not sure it really fits the criteria at this stage, John, but we'll have to see. Keep me informed of any updates you get and I'll feed them into Bill Dwyers before he meets with the other two tomorrow."

Burrows said that he would and they ended their call. He and Jane had been contracted by the executive of the SPU to sort Cabilla out a little over a month ago, and although it had been their first job, it had been the SPU's first job too. But it was all still new he guessed, and open to change. But, even if the executive sat properly in session, and agreed a 'Yankee, Yankee', they would still need the prime minister's approval to go operational. As far as Burrows could see, after this was over, the cops could pick Moon up easy enough and that would lead hopefully to the shadowy figure that kept ringing Crabtree.

Burrows went to give Crabtree the bad news about Moon's phone number, but was able to give the name of a few associates from memory. The names of two of his ex-minders, and a bloke called Mathews who used to hire out premises for Moon to use. Crabtree said he'd give them to Henry, the DS, as he was doing all the intelligence and background checks surrounding Moon. Crabtree also told Burrows that the four guys from the CME team had fully recovered, but could add little about their attackers. There had been at least four of them, all dressed in black with balaclavas on, and all had struck with great speed.

Sounds like a professional team, Burrows thought. And he was starting to wonder what real use he could now be to Crabtree, who he'd noticed had dropped the attitude when talking to him.

Then Crabtree's phone rang and as he pulled it out of his pocket, he looked at the glass screen and said, "No caller ID, all quiet please," before nodding at a guy sat in the corner who had a small table in front of him piled up with electrical kit. There was just Crabtree, Henry, Burrows and this other guy in the room. Henry rushed to the office door and locked it. The guy with the technical kit pressed some buttons on his equipment and then told Crabtree to go ahead. The phone had only been ringing for about ten or fifteen seconds but it felt like an age to Burrows before Crabtree finally answered it. He appeared to listen for a few seconds before saying, "I don't know what you mean. Wait, er no, er look, I've pulled the surv…" Then he pulled the phone away from his ear.

Burrows noticed the technical guy was now wearing headphones, and all eyes went to him as he spoke, "I got it, but it's through a voice distortion device like the last call."

"Location?" Crabtree asked.

"This is weird," the technical guy said, as he checked his equipment, and looked up before continuing, "It says Gdansk in Poland, unknown number. The last call said a Birmingham phone box. I don't know how he's doing this, but it looks like he is somehow bouncing the phone signal all over the place. Perhaps he is using a satellite phone of some kind. I'll have to make some enquiries. Perhaps speak to GCHQ, see if they can help. This looks above my level of expertise."

"As you've probably guessed, that was our mystery man," said Crabtree as he turned to face Burrows and Henry, "he said that we've failed to follow out his instructions. Said that he knows we've continued our enquires. Said that because of our non-compliance there will be consequences. Then the line went dead."

"How the hell does he know this?" Burrows said.

"That's what I'd like to know," said Crabtree.

Burrows was only too aware that three sets of eyes were staring intently towards him.

CHAPTER NINE

Moon had rung ahead before he approached the address; just to make sure there were no filth about, for whatever reasons. He didn't want connecting to the address. One of his two men there, Phil, said it was clear. There had been two PCSOs doing a leaflet drop in the area, but they had moved on. Not that it bothered Moon; PCSOs wouldn't know who he was. But it told him his men were being alert, and that pleased him. The address was an end-terrace house with rough ground at its gable end, with the next three houses on the other side being empty. He'd taken out a six month let on the place, though they only planned to use it for the next two weeks or so. Bill, the other guy at the house, had sorted it all out using false papers.

Having driven past once to satisfy himself all was well, he parked his Jag on the rough ground at the side of the house, and entered via the rear yard. Inside the kitchen to greet him were Bill and Phil. Brothers, in their forties, both as big as each other, though Moon could tell them apart, he always thought they were both ugly and didn't spoil a pair. But they had worked for Moon for years and he trusted them both. "How's our guest?"

"A trembling wreck," Phil answered, "we've had to put him in one of those white paper suits the filth use."

"Where are his clothes?" Moon asked.

"Bagged and binned down the council tip, couldn't stand the smell no more after he'd finished with 'em," Phil answered.

Bill just nodded. Moon had often noticed that when the brothers were together, it was usually Phil that did the talking. He never knew why, as far as he was concerned they were both thick. No matter. "Have you fed him?"

"Just given him water for now. Thought we'd let him settle down a bit more before we fed him; in case it went straight through him again. I've only got one paper suit." Phil answered.

"Where did you get that one from?"

"It was Bill's; he kept it after he got nicked for that rape charge last year. The one you got sorted for him."

Moon looked at Bill, who was grinning now, obviously very pleased with himself. Anyway, it seemed obvious that Townley wasn't giving his men any problems, not that he'd expected him to. After all, he was just a locksmith from Preston. He wasn't filth and he wasn't a villain.

Moon told Phil and Bill to take him to see Townley, and he followed them both upstairs to a rear bedroom. Outside, they each pulled on a balaclava and then Phil went in first and switched the light on. Moon entered, followed by Bill. It was a small room with a single bed covered in bin liners, by the centre of an inner wall. Handcuffed to a chain, which was in turn handcuffed to a metal ring in the wall, was a small man in his thirties. The crumpled white paper suit was far too big for him. And he looked terrified. He sat up on the bed as they entered. Moon noticed that the only window was covered with black bin liners and the floor was bare boards. There was no other furniture in the room.

He warned the man to behave, and told Bill to remove the gaffer tape from over his mouth. The man yelped as Bill tore it off.

"So, locksmith. How long have you been burgling decent people's houses on behalf of the filth?" Moon enquired. Townley didn't answer, so Moon slapped his face hard. Townley cried out.

"Don't you dare disrespect me," Moon said.

"It's only the fourth job I've done for them. Look, I'm really sorry; if you let me go I promise I'll never do work for them again. And I'll not say anything about you guys. I swear it."

"Listen, Townley. As much as you deserve to be here, simply for doing what you do, there is more to it."

"I don't understand."

"You don't need to. It's just that we need to ensure the filth do as we ask for a couple of weeks, and you're our insurance policy."

"Two weeks. Oh, God, no."

"Ish. That's if everything goes to plan. Then you'll be released. Trust me, you'll be out of here as soon as it is possible. I don't want my men inconvenienced any longer than absolutely necessary. But I'm going to need you to behave yourself."

"I'll not give you no problems mister; I just want to get out of here. And you can trust me on what I said before. I'll say nothing."

"Oh I've no doubt about that, or else my men here would have to reacquaint themselves with you up in Preston." Moon said, noting the added fear apparent in Townley's eyes, when he used the word 'Preston'. "Yes, we know everything about you, so you should remember that," he finished.

"Yes, sir, I will."

"There is just one problem we have though, Townley. That head pig you were working for…" Moon said, pausing.

"Crabtree," Townley said, filling in the void in an apparent effort to please.

"Yes, Crabtree. Well, he must be either very stupid, or a little hard of hearing. See, we need him to listen to what we are telling him, so we need to send him a little incentive. Just to make sure he does as he's told from now on. And I need you to help."

"Yes, anything, do you want me to record a message or something?"

"We're not jihadists you cretin," Moon snapped, his temper rising in an instant. He was going to leave it to Phil and Bill, but the snivelling little man that Townley was, had annoyed him again. He'd do it himself, for the fun of it.

"Look, Townley. We need them, and you, to realise we are serious. If you're lucky, the message we send Crabtree should do the trick. But as far as you are concerned, think of it as a fine. A fine for working for them in the first place." Ignoring Townley's confused expression, he turned to Bill who was by the door. "Tape this idiot's mouth up again."

When done, he added, "Now go and get the bolt cutters."

CHAPTER TEN

"Wow. Hold it right there, guys. I know I'm the newbie here, but I'm here at your request, don't forget that," Burrows said.

Crabtree loosened his stare and said, "He's right. Let's not get paranoid, Frank Briers offered John's services here, and I would trust Frank Briers with my life."

"I'm also retired, and only here as a favour to Frank," Burrows partly lied.

"OK," Henry said, his demeanour softening.

"Good, now maybe we can think this through calmly, because they do seem to be remarkably well informed," Burrows added.

"All right then," Crabtree said, "let's check all our phones since the one o'clock briefing, and let's do it together."

Burrows knew he was the only one to leave and then re-enter the room since Crabtree's briefing, Henry had remained in the room throughout, as apparently had Crabtree. The examination of all the phones revealed nothing, and the only call Burrows had made was to Frank Briers to get the historical intel on Moon. Both Henry and Crabtree exposed their call logs and the few calls that had been made by them were easily explained.

The technical guy was then brought into the equation; Crabtree had called for him to set up soon after his earlier briefing had finished, he willingly showed Crabtree his phone anyway, and it was clear it hadn't been used. Crabtree added that the technical guy had not been briefed on the job, he'd just been asked to link up Crabtree's phone to record incoming calls and to try to trace the incoming number and location. Happy he was still none the wiser, Crabtree let him go, but warned him about speaking to anyone with regard to the call he had just heard. He willingly signed a need-to-know document, which threatened him with dismissal if he revealed what little he did know.

He said that the equipment was now set to automatic so, wherever Crabtree was when he received his incoming calls, the kit would at least record them, if not locate them. The tech guy said he would make enquires with GCHQ at Cheltenham to see if they could offer any help, and then report back.

After he'd left the room, Henry spoke first, "Why don't you get an urgent 'line' on your phone, boss? Like you did on Townley's."

"No need, Henry. If one side to a telephone conversation is aware that it is being intercepted, i.e. me, then the authority required drops from home secretary to assistant chief constable, and our deputy director of the NCA has already given his consent. Hence the reason for the tech guy being here."

Burrows asked where the other two guys from Crabtree's inner circle were. The other two who had been present at the meeting. Henry interjected that they were both his DCs; Ian and Mark, and that he would trust them with his life. Burrows said that he didn't doubt it, but suggested he should get them back here, so they could check their phones and ask whom they may have been chatting to. Perhaps they had gone for a brew in canteen and been overheard, he offered.

Crabtree agreed and rang them both, telling them to get back to the briefing room straight away. He came off the phone and said they were both still on the premises. They chatted through the ramifications of the phone call whilst they waited for Ian and Mark. Henry suggested the villains might have technical help.

"What do you mean?" Burrows asked.

"Well, if we're all clean, then they're getting their info from somewhere. This room could be bugged for all we know."

"But that would mean this office building is compromised, not just from the point of view of putting a bug in here, but from the fact that this is the Manchester Office of the National Crime Agency, the location of which is supposed to be a secret. God, it gets worse," Crabtree said, grabbing a chair.

Burrows knew from his time with SOCA, and with the National Crime Squad before that, just how much care went into selecting nondescript office buildings for the cops to use. All had a covert identity, under the assumed name of some business or other, and the prospect of the whole building and its real use being blown was not a pleasant one.

"Well how would they know about the building?" Henry asked.

"Don't forget they knew about the CME at Moon's flat in Southport, before we tried to do it. I think John's right, we have a mole, and if it's not one of us five, then we can only assume the mole has planted a bug in here somewhere," Crabtree said, adding, "so let's be very circumspect in what we say, at least until we can get this place electronically swept."

Burrows and Henry nodded, and then Crabtree wrote something down on a piece of paper and passed it to them both. It read, 'As soon as Ian and Mark are here, and I satisfy myself of their integrity, we will relocate to somewhere else that only I know about. At least then we can run operations from there.' Burrows and Henry nodded again and passed the note back to Crabtree.

Mark was the first to arrive, and Crabtree took him into the corridor to speak to him. Five minutes later, both walked back into the room and Crabtree beckoned him and Henry over. They followed him out of the briefing room and to his office, which was on the same floor, and once inside with the door shut he spoke. "It was as we thought before. Mark and Ian went straight from the briefing to the canteen, which was where they both were when I rang them. Mark's phone hasn't been used since the briefing and he says Ian's not used his either. I've also checked his story with the canteen manageress and she confirms their presence as Mark has said. No offence, Mark."

"None taken, boss, under the circumstances."

"Where is Ian then?" asked Burrows.

"He went for a leak; I'll text him that we're now in the boss's office."

Five minutes later, in walked Ian carrying a shoebox, he placed it on his boss' desk, and said, "I just came out the gents and Sally from the front desk grabbed me. Said this had just been hand-delivered by some tramp. Apparently, the tramp said he'd been given twenty quid to deliver it, and that he 'didn't know nothing' and then he legged it."

All attention turned to the white shoebox on the desk. Burrows could see that its lid appeared unfastened and loose. On the top of the lid, written in black marker pen, were the words, 'Last warning, Crabtree. Or you can guess what happens next'.

All of them just stared at the box in silence; Burrows examined it as closely as he dare. What if it was a bomb? He wondered. Then, as if stealing his thoughts, Henry broke the impasse.

"Well, it's not a bomb, that's for sure."

"How do you know?" Ian asked.

"Because bombs don't generally bleed," he answered, pointing to a small dark stain on the side of the box that appeared damp.

And with that, Crabtree grabbed the lid and flipped it off. They all looked inside and in unison recoiled in horror. Burrows realised he was looking down on a severed, human big toe.

CHAPTER ELEVEN

Burrows spoke first. "Look, Nigel, this is starting to get serious—"

"Serious? Serious? I'll kill them. Who the hell do they think they are?" Crabtree interrupted.

Henry and the two DCs Ian and Mark just stood staring at the grisly appendage, as Burrows continued. "What I mean is, this is now going up to a whole new level, and I'm thinking that there is little more I can offer to help with regard to my knowledge of Moon."

"Sounds like you want out?" Crabtree said.

"I do. I don't know what more I can do. And if I'm going to bail out, then now, before you relocate to your new operating centre, would be as good a time as any."

Burrows knew he had to get himself back to London and see his boss Frank Briers, not only to brief him, but he really did feel that he had outstayed his use. As unsavoury as things were, this was now a reactive investigation and probably not something the Special Projects Unit should be getting involved in.

"I suppose it's easy to forget that you're supposed to be retired, and giving up your own time just to help as a favour. I've started to think of you as part of the investigation team."

"I'll take that as a compliment."

"You should, but just one question before you go."

"Sure, what?"

"Is Moon capable of doing this?" Crabtree asked, as he looked back towards the box on his desk.

"Definitely," Burrows answered, "the man's a vicious bastard with no conscience."

Burrows then wished them all luck, and Crabtree asked Henry to drop him back at his hotel.

On the journey into central Manchester Henry didn't speak much, but Burrows could tell he was deep in contemplation, so left him alone, until he spoke first.

"You say you dealt with Moon shortly before you retired, about eighteen months ago?"

"Yeah, that's right."

"Well, I've been doing all the background and intel checks, as you know, and I can find no record. In fact, the last official interaction with Moon was many years ago over some violent assault," Henry said, before turning to look directly at Burrows.

Burrows felt the pressure of the question. He knew it had only been a month since he'd met Moon, but that had been as part of the SPU job, when he'd met him as a villain. And in any event, he had only done so in order to get to Cabilla, who had been their primary target. He knew he'd have to be careful how he answered Henry, give him something that was plausible to keep him happy. He paused deliberately before he spoke, "I think I can trust you now Henry, after all you have trusted me."

"Go on."

"Well, there would be no record of an investigation eighteen months ago because I was undercover, into Moon, but looking for someone else," Burrows partially lied.

"Right, OK. That'd explain it, I suppose. How did that go?"

"I wasn't deployed to Moon for long as our job went off in a different direction. Like I say, Moon wasn't the real target." This seemed to settle Henry back down. Burrows knew he had pretty much told him the truth, just lied about the timings, and more importantly, whom he'd been working for. It was the lesser of two compromises to let Henry think he had an inside track on an undercover job – albeit an old one – to keep him away from the SPU. He knew that only eight people knew of their existence, and it was paramount it remained that way. As the conversation ended, they drew up outside the hotel and Burrows wished Henry good luck and thanked him for the lift. In truth, he was glad to get out of the car before Henry's suspicions kicked off again. Now, he was out of the way he'd soon be out of mind; it was the right time to leave.

After checking out, he made his way on foot to Manchester Piccadilly to catch the next train back to London. He had thirty odd minutes to wait, so made his way to one of the station cafés to ring Briers over a coffee. He choose Starbucks near the front aspect, they had a few tables and chairs outside on the pedestrian area, always a good sort of place to make phone calls out of earshot. After briefing him, he took a sip of his beverage as Briers replied.

"OK, John, thanks for that. Look, you may as well head straight home, and I'll see you in the Pimlico briefing room at 2.00 p.m. tomorrow. Jane, as you know, has been training up the new boy Steele, and I'll get them both in for then."

"Why's that, Frank, are we not done here?"

"Not sure yet. There may be a need for us to get involved covertly, but we can talk more tomorrow." And with that, they ended the call and Burrows turned back to his coffee.

As he waited for his train, he felt a pang of sorrow at leaving Manchester. He had been gone a few years now in reality, although he'd only made the permanent move after he'd retired from SOCA. Whilst he was still part of the Lancashire branch of his old firm, he'd kept two addresses, one in Thame and a flat locally. It was handy when deployed as an undercover officer; it didn't matter where in the country he was working, he'd have a base not too far away. But over those years he'd become established in Thame, so decided to settle there when he left the cops. After all, he was divorced with no kids and both his parents were gone, so there was little to keep him there, though this trip had reawakened his fondness for the town. Perhaps, he'd move back one day.

Then his mind moved back to what Briers had said, about 'getting involved covertly'. He'd have to wait until tomorrow to find out what he meant.

CHAPTER TWELVE

Jane had enjoyed the last two days. Even though it was Steele who had done most of the hard work, she had spent the last month lazing about and was glad of the opportunity to claw some fitness back. She wondered how John was getting on up in Manchester, and hoped the NCA job into Moon had come off: he was bad news. She wondered how his right hand was doing, since she had put a round through it only five weeks ago. She smiled to herself as she reflected.

"What are you smiling at? It's me doing all the hard work," Steele said.

She looked up, and was about to answer when her phone rang. Looking at the screen it said 'Zulu Calling'. "Hi, Frank, how are things."

"Good thanks. Look, how are you two doing down there?"

"We are just about done. Larry's fitness is good, and his weapons training is easy; he's a natural."

"I was hoping you'd say that. Can you get yourselves back from Essex for a briefing tomorrow at two, at Pimlico?"

"Sure, is there a job on?"

"Not certain yet, I've just spoken to Burrows and he's on his way back from Manchester. There have been developments; he'll brief us properly tomorrow afternoon."

And with that, they ended the call. She turned to Steele, she was impressed with what she'd seen him do over the last couple of days. He was ten years younger than she was, in his early thirties, so fitness hadn't been a major issue. He'd also been a U/C – undercover operative – before he'd had to leave the cops, so was astute too. He was of mixed heritage as his mother was Turkish and his father was white. It gave him a great look, which Steele said widened his appeal as a U/C. Jane reckoned it would widen his appeal with the ladies too. Facing him now, she said, "Well, Larry, it looks like you might be about to put the last two days' training to the test." She then filled him in on what Briers had said.

"OK, Jane, that's great, but can I just make a point?"

"Go on," she replied, not sure what was coming.

"I know I've only just joined the SPU, and am untested as far as you and Burrows are concerned, not to mention the boss—"

"Forget it, Larry," Jane interrupted, "John and I only did our first job a month ago when we met you."

"I know, Jane, it's not that, it's the fact that on that job, I was supposed to be undercover for the National Crime Agency into Mackey, Cabilla's right hand man, before I got myself lifted by them, when they suspected me of being a grass."

Jane remembered how she and Burrows had suspected Steele of going over to the dark side, until he helped them at the end. "Look, I know we had our reservations about you, but that job's over now," she added.

"Yeah, but I'm only with you now because I ballsed up, got in over my head, and had to leave the cops because of it."

Jane moved to the bench outside the training facility's front door, and Steele followed. It was obvious he wanted to get things off his chest. Their location was an old converted farmhouse in rural Essex, now owned covertly by the military. Surrounded by established trees, it was quite private.

"What you'll soon learn, Larry, is that you've been conditioned over the years operating as a police undercover."

"I don't know about conditioned," he replied defensively, "the whole point of being undercover is that you have the freedom to engage the bad guys on their level."

"You think so, but you don't. In the cops you're still stymied with rules and regulations – the ones you found yourself breaking on the last job, leading to you having to leave the cops."

Steele started to nod slowly.

"It's because of that that Briers offered you the chance of joining us, don't you see?"

Larry was nodding more now, and Jane could see a light of understanding starting to emit from his eyes.

"I realise the SPU is well secret, and off the books, but are you saying we have no restrictions?"

"Yes, once a job has the PM's approval, how we achieve the aims and objectives are pretty much up to us. The bad guys don't have rules and regulations holding them back, so why should we?"

"I get it now, really get it." Steele said, smiling.

"Liberating feeling, isn't it?"

"Sure is. I was just bothered as I'd messed up – by police standards – that Burrows and you would think me a dickhead, and now it looks like we may be going operational I just wanted to, you know…"

"Say no more, Larry, you've got nothing to prove, and Burrows will be cool with you too. I'll pass on our little chat if you like."

"Cheers, Jane," Steele finished.

"Right, let's get our stuff together and get back to London, it looks like we may have a busy day tomorrow."

***

Tony Bentine lay back on his sun lounger as he gazed out across the Aegean Sea. It was a beautiful afternoon and the sun was shining. In the distance, he could see Sithonia, the second of Kassandra's peninsulas. His mobile phone on his occasional table rattled as it started to ring, spoiling the moment. He picked it up and saw who was ringing so he took the call.

"Yeah."

"It's been done, stage two."

"Excellent. How's the patient?"

"He'd be hopping mad if he wasn't chained to a wall."

"Why the crap gags all the time? It's not impressing me."

"Sorry. OK, no the patient's OK, proper shit scared, but OK."

"What about Crabtree's response... hang on a sec," Bentine broke off as a North African man walked straight towards him. "Before you ask, no I don't want to buy some hand-fucking-carved table; I'm on a beach, so fuck off."

Bentine watched the man quickly leave before continuing his call. "OK, carry on."

"Sounds like you're having fun."

"Just tell me, and don't bother with any beach sellers' type jokes."

"From what my men can see, he seems pretty much housebound in that office he thinks no one knows about. Have you had any feedback from your channels?"

"Well, he's gone mental, and talked about moving to a secret location. And that Burrows character's fucked off back to London."

"Do you think he'll listen and quit meddling now?"

"He'll have to. He'll be given no choice. He'll be told to back off for two weeks or until we tell him otherwise. You'll have to be ready when this is over."

Bentine picked up the irritation in Moon's voice as he answered.

"I know that, you don't have to remind me. Once this payday comes in, I'll be long gone. And no matter how hard Crabtree and his piglets come after me, they won't find me."

Bentine ended the call and lay back on his lounger; things were going OK, nearly time to get started.

CHAPTER THIRTEEN

John Burrows arrived at Pimlico in plenty of time. The office was like any other 1970s block in the area, nondescript with a rough concrete façade, which had seemed so popular back then. Having cleared the entrance he made his way to the subterranean-level briefing room. He wasn't sure who would be present; he knew Briers and Jane would be there, and probably the new bloke Larry Steele. But as for the executive, he wasn't sure. He knocked on the heavy steel door, which was opened straight away by Briers who quickly slid through it, closing the door behind him.

Though a few years older than Burrows, Briers never looked it. He stood up ramrod straight, as usual, and looked immaculately dressed; this time in an expensive blue wool suit. Only, his greying hair hinted at his age, though it was less so than Burrows', which he'd always thought of as unfair.

"I thought I'd give you a quick heads up before you go in. Jane and the new guy Larry are obviously here," Briers started.

"How's he doing?" Burrows asked.

"Jane says he's ready. I appreciate you've not had much chance to assess him yourself, but there will be time for that later."

Burrows knew that Steele had done a lot of undercover work when he'd been in the cops, so wasn't over worried, after all Briers had picked him, which spoke volumes. He was young – in his early thirties, but had been a detective sergeant like himself, so was no fool. He also had a great look; being of a mixed heritage background, which gave him a wide appeal. He would be able to ham it up from either of his parents' backgrounds. "Well, if Jane says he's ready, then he's no doubt ready. Who else is in the briefing room?"

"Well, that's why I wanted a quick word before you came in; the executive are all here. I thought it was only going to be the Home Sec Bill Dwyers and the head of the National Crime Agency – George Reed – but, the DPP Susan Jones is here as well."

Burrows had only met them once before, and that was when they did their first 'live' job for the SPU. It was said then, that it would be exceptional if they ever met again. Once the executive had all agreed action against an individual, and the PM had ratified it, Frank Briers became the go-between with them and the operational team. So their presence not only ramped up the pressure, but also meant it was getting serious. "We just need the Prime Minister himself, and we'd have a full set."

"Well, you're lucky, John. The PM was going to attend but had to cancel at the last minute, but Bill Dwyers will brief him later. But, just so you know, they are already pretty much in the picture, as George Reed has briefed them. He'd asked Crabtree's boss to keep him informed."

"That'll be the detective chief super, Gary Ray."

"Yes, that's him."

"Wasn't he suspicious that the head of the NCA was taking a personal interest in things?"

"Don't think so, he said he'd not overdone it, just asked to be kept abreast of developments as it was one of their contractors who'd been taken."

Burrows nodded, as Briers turned towards the door and they both walked into the room.

In the centre of the room was the circular briefing table with the three executive members sat around. To his left was the coffee machine where Jane stood with Larry Steele, her athletic frame highlighted as she leaned back against the table. Burrows knew she was in her forties but she didn't look a day over thirty. Jane and Steele nodded at him before joining the others by the conference table. Briers formally did the introductions, as much for Steele's benefit as for any other reason, and then asked Burrows to give them a précis of his trip to Manchester. When he finished, he opened the floor for questions.

"We've had the briefing on Moon after your last job, is there nowhere you or Jane can think of that he might be using to keep the locksmith fellow?" asked the head of the NCA.

Burrows turned to face him; Reed was a small man in his late forties, but with an unnervingly piercing gaze. "As you are no doubt aware sir, from your updates from Detective Chief Super Ray, I've given over the historical addresses we had and they've all been searched and are apparently empty now. He's the sort of bloke who moves around fairly regularly as a matter of security."

"Hmm," he replied, as he sat back in his chair.

"As elusive as Moon can be, he's indigenous to Manchester; after this is over, he shouldn't be too hard to track down."

"I've no doubt, but that's not the point."

"If you don't mind me asking sir, I'm not sure I understand the point, well not from the SPU's point of view. As horrendous as this job is, isn't it a job for Nigel Crabtree and his team to sort out by conventional investigative means?"

Reed opened his mouth, but before he could answer, Bill Dwyers who was at the other side of the table spoke. As all eyes turned towards him, Burrows couldn't help but be impressed by the sheer presence of the man. He was in his mid-fifties and of only average height and build, but there was an aura about him that far surpassed his previous military service. "The point, Mister Burrows," he started, emphasising the word 'Mister', as if giving John false standing, "is that these bastards are not going to be permitted to set strategy. The day we cow and tail to the common criminal, is the day we should all just raise white flags above our heads."

"I meant no offence, sir," Burrows said apologetically, "I just thought as we had no leads to go on, and the fact that they are obviously well-informed, it may be safer to do as they ask, at least until we get Townley back, and then we or the NCA, can go after them with all resources."

Speaking for the first time, Susan Jones the DPP put her hand up towards the home secretary, as if to silence him before he could speak. She was of similar age to Dwyers, but very small and petite, though her voice projected an image of someone twice her size. "Before you blow your blood pressure sky high again Bill, allow me to explain." Turning to face Burrows, she continued. "The executive have sat in session on this issue because we feel this poses a significant threat to the safety of our communities. Never before in the UK has a criminal element had the audacity to kidnap a cop – or agent acting on the police's behalf – in order to ensure compliance, so that they may continue whatever further criminal enterprises it is that they are doing.

"If we allow this to go ahead unchecked, albeit for all the right reasons, i.e. the safe return of Townley, then we will open the floodgates. And make our police vulnerable to future such occurrences."

"Thank you, Sue," Bill Dwyers said, before continuing, "if you take it to the extreme, what is there to stop any villain nicking any cop off the street and then making demands whilst they hold them. The police would lose all authority. No, we need to stamp on this, and in so doing, send a veiled message to those in association with those involved. To ensure this never happens again."

George Reed was the next to speak. "To finish off, executive action has been agreed, and the PM has given his approval. We should leave now," he said, addressing Jones and Dwyers. "And let Frank Briers give his operational team their instructions."

All three of the executive then made their way out of the room and once the steel door had sprung shut, Burrows sighed and relaxed. Briers told them all to grab a coffee and he would explain further.

A few minutes later, the four of them were back around the table when Briers went on to explain. He told them that Crabtree had indeed been told to stop all investigations, and his boss Ray was keeping a close watch on him to ensure compliance. That way, the bad guys would get to know through whomever their source was that he was doing as instructed.

"Any idea how Crabtree's team have been so badly compromised?" Burrows asked.

"Unfortunately not, Crabtree is rightly incensed by it." Briers answered.

"I bet he's none too happy at being told to back off either," Burrows said.

"He's not, but he knows there is nothing he can do, he's on a tight leash held by his boss. So as from now there will be absolutely no activity from the NCA, and the bad guys will be free to finish off whatever it is they're doing."

"I'm starting to get the picture now, Frank," Jane said, speaking for the first time.

"Well, as you can see, there is a sort of power vacuum in place for the next two weeks. The cops are all back in their box and we've got the head of the NCA on our executive to ensure that."

"Which no doubt leaves us free to roam without fear of stumbling over the NCA," Jane added.

"Exactly," said Briers, "your instructions are simply this. Find and release Townley, and then remove this organised crime group, permanently."

"By organised crime group, I'm guessing you mean Moon and whoever he's working for?"

"I mean anyone and everyone involved, or in your way. Moon, Moon's partner in slime, and anyone else you deem an operational risk. Clear?"

Burrows and the other two answered, "Clear," in unison.

CHAPTER FOURTEEN

Having finished his call with Moon, Bentine checked that his area of beach was still empty before dialling another number, which was answered after a few rings.

"Hi, Tony," the recipient started, "how are things at your end?"

"Under control. Crabtree's at stage two and we have our two-week window, or longer if we need it."

"Brilliant. I'm loving this tactic."

"Never mind that, how are things progressing at your end?"

"Well, as you know the cargo left Sihanoukville over three weeks ago and was reloaded onto an ocean going container ship in Singapore. Both the customs officers there and back in Cambodia have been paid off, no problems."

"And you've had no comeback since?"

"No, the people over there have got the whole Gulf of Thailand well and truly sorted. It's a route we can use again, if you want."

"Let's get this one home first. Where is the ship now?"

"It passed the Cape of Good Hope about three days ago and is currently travelling up the west coast of Africa. She's expected in Southampton in seven days' time, weather permitting."

"Good. Have you got the driver sorted?"

"I've got a good one I've used before in London. He doesn't know anything other than to be ready for a driving job in about a week. He'll meet you in Southampton the day before the ship is due to dock. Has your man Moon got the buyer ready?"

"He says so."

"I know I'm just the transport man in all this, but are you happy you can trust Moon?"

"As far as you can trust a Manc, I suppose. But he's giving nothing away about the end-user, so we're stuck with him."

"You can't really blame him for that, I guess."

"I guess. Anyway, you can tell me the name of the boat now?

"Yeah, it's the MV Nirvana, but with respect, don't try and follow its progress; you'll only leave electronic footprints. I'll keep you informed of where it's up to."

Bentine knew his contact had paid a member of the crew to give him regular updates via a sat phone, so there was no need to check the vessel's progress by conventional means, no matter how tempting it was. He had to remain professional. And with several hundred containers on the ship, there was virtually no risk of compromise from the crew member; only Bentine knew the container's identity number.

"Understood, keep me informed and we'll speak soon." Bentine said, ending the call. He knew the last leg of the journey via road from the port was going to be the riskiest. And he didn't really like the idea of only meeting the lorry driver the day before. But, he'd just have to trust his contact, for now anyway.

***

Moon walked back into the end-terrace house's kitchen to see Bill filling the kettle. "I'll have a coffee, Bill."

Bill nodded back as Phil walked in from the hall, "Hi, boss, did the tramp do the delivery OK?"

"Yeah, no probs. I paid some chancer fifty quid to pay the tramp twenty quid to deliver the shoebox. So, even if they ever found the tramp again, which will never happen, as they all look alike, there's no link back to us," Moon said, as he sat down at an old red and white Formica table. Phil joined him, followed a minute later by Bill with three cups of coffee.

Moon took a sip, then, "How's old nine-toes upstairs doing? Has he stopped bawling yet?"

Both brothers laughed, and Phil answered, "He's just about calmed down now. He thinks every time one of us goes to check on him, it's time to lose another pinkie. I've told him he'll be OK if Crabtree gets the message."

"I spoke to Tony Bentine earlier and he says Crabtree's being put on a short lead, so we should have no further interruptions. You can tell Townley that if you want, might make him easier to control."

"Will do, boss, though he's got no arse for a fight," Phil said.

"I can see that. Make sure you keep changing the dressing too. We don't want the idiot catching an infection and dying on us."

"Bill's just changed it five minutes ago. He's in charge of that."

Moon and Phil both turned to face Bill as Moon said, "Never had you down as the nursing type." Bill just grinned that stupid one front-toothed smirk of his, and Moon and Phil laughed again.

Moon finished his coffee and told both men that things were now progressing as planned, and with luck in seven or eight days' time it would all be over, and they would be all the richer. As he stood up to leave, Bill spoke.

"Prossies," he said.

Surprised by Bill's rare speech, "What do you mean, prossies?" Moon asked.

"I'm going to spend my share on prossies."

Moon just glanced at Phil and shook his head slightly as he went through the back door, wholly unsurprised by Bill's explanation.

Moon connected his phone to the car via Bluetooth and put a call into his buyer, whose identity he had gone to great lengths to protect, and not just from Bentine. Jack Jones was a formidable man, with a reputation every bit as fierce as Moon's, he knew; but they went way back. "Hi, Jack, it's me. Thought I'd bring you up to date as I fight my way through the traffic. How's it going?"

"Fine, Jonny, fine. Are there any developments?"

"I just wanted to reassure you that everything is now going to plan—"

"Is that twat Crabtree behaving now?" Jones interrupted.

"Yes, the present in the shoe box did the job, and I've just left the ex-ballerina and he's not going to die on us or owt."

"I wouldn't give a shit if he did, that's your end of things. What about the cargo?"

"It's past the point of Africa, and everything is being monitored, all ways up."

"I'm glad you rang, as I've been thinking about what happens afterwards."

"Well, Jack as I told you before, I'm going to do one, good and proper, and there is no way the filth can link us together. I've been very careful."

"I'm sure you have, Jonny, but it still bothers me. The filth will be after you and everyone else they can identify; big-time. I know you say you've covered everything, but think about it."

"What do you mean?"

"I mean – without insulting you – they have never been rubber-dicked like this before; being held to ransom. We're in new territory and that Crabtree will be after revenge once it's over. Let's face it; you've made him look a right tool."

Both men laughed before Moon spoke, "What do you suggest we do different?"

"Insurance policy," Jones replied, "take out some extra insurance and let Crabtree know how the policy will expire if they come after us."

"I don't think even Crabtree will be able to stop an investigation once it's over, it'll probably come from way above him."

"Fair point, but he can be our eyes and ears, slow them down or fuck 'em at best, give us the heads up if they start to get too close, at worst."

"Yeah, I don't suppose it would do any harm. But how do we get a twat like that to play ball? He's one of the straight ones."

"I'll leave that to your own leprous imagination," Jones finished. And both men laughed again before ending their call.

CHAPTER FIFTEEN

Burrows was finishing off his telephone conversation with Briers whilst Jane drove. It was the day after the briefing at Pimlico and it felt good to be working with her again. Whilst she kept her eyes on the road, Burrows kept his peripheral vision on her. With her brown hair tied behind her head, she was a strikingly attractive woman.

It had been good to catch up with Larry Steele over a drink the night before, but he couldn't help but feel a little pleased when Briers had asked Steele to stay in London, whilst they sought Moon out. Steele's disappointment was obvious, it was his first job with the SPU and he clearly wanted to make a good impression. Briers had told them that recently; one of Moon's historical mobile numbers had been reactivated, ringing the same number in London and one abroad. They had no intel on the foreign number but had identified the London one as a public phone box in central London. Moon's phone had since gone dead again, but it was a lead.

Depending on what Burrows and Jane turned up in Manchester, Steele might be needed to react at short notice in London. Or so Briers had reckoned. It actually made sense, but Burrows was glad to be with Jane on his own, for now anyhow.

"What did Briers have to say?" asked Jane.

"Just that he's got Steele housed near to the central London phone box, should we need him to cover it."

"He didn't look too happy at being left behind to babysit a phone box."

"I know, but who knows how this will pan out, he might end up in the thick of things down there, and we are the ones out of it."

"I guess. Anyway, what do you think of Larry?"

"Yeah, he seems OK. And if you say he's up to it then that's good enough for me."

Jane pulled off the M6 and started heading towards Manchester. The last time they came up to Manchester they had booked into a hotel near the airport and had decided to use the same place again. May as well reduce their exposure to a minimum, they'd figured.

It was a little over a month ago when Burrows and Jane had come to Manchester looking for Jonny Moon. On that occasion, they were after someone else, and thought Moon may be able to help them locate him. Things hadn't gone exactly to plan, which was why Jane had to shoot Moon through the palm of his right hand. They got the information they were after but he'd sent two of his goons after them. And that hadn't ended well for the goons. No, as and when they did find Moon, he wouldn't be over his namesake to see them again.

"We'll have to be real careful," Jane said, as she swung their car into the Hotel's parking area.

"I know that, Jane, but how else can we hope to flush him out?"

"Not sure. But we'll be like a worm on the end of an angler's hook. And it does make one a tad nervous."

Burrows just grinned in reply as she parked the car.

The Britannia Airport Hotel was actually in the Wythenshawe district of Manchester and not at the airport, though it wasn't far away and it had good access to all the motorway networks. Burrows noticed the temperature was a little cooler than London, but the sun was out and it wasn't a bad day in all. They had booked a twin-bedded room on the journey up, citing Burrows' 'bad back', which was consistent with what they had said last time. Burrows knew how important it was to appear the same, so as not to raise any interest in them from the hotel staff. The greyer they could be, the more easily forgotten they were. And they would each have their own bed to sleep in; more's the pity.

What he hadn't told Jane was what Briers had read to him over the phone. The details of an article that was to appear in tonight's Manchester Evening Telegraph. He thought he'd leave that gem until she read it. Prior to setting off from London, Briers had told them that the North West Counter Terrorism Unit based in Manchester had an agreement with all the editors of the regional newspapers. They could approach them at short notice to have anything put into the papers; usually coded messages of some sort, for operational reasons. It meant that the editor may have to pull a story, or postpone one to make space, and not all of them were overjoyed to do this, even if it was in the national interest.

Jane knew about the tactic from her time with the security service, it was a common enough ploy used by MI5 over many years. It was where the counter terrorism units got many of their ideas from, MI5 and Special Branch. But what Burrows hadn't told her was the exact contents of the message.

He was surprised though that so many editors agreed to do this, often at such short notice, as they had various conflicting commercial pressures to contend with as well. But Jane had explained that the papers were always well compensated for their cooperation, even to the extent of potential lost revenue from advertisements that might have been pulled as well.

By the time they had checked in and made themselves comfortable, it was after three p.m. so Burrows said he would nip out to a local newsagent to get the paper. Jane said she would stay and man the phone should it ring. Burrows had told her that a particular mobile number was to appear in the paper, and that he had put the relating pay-as-you-go SIM card in an old handset, not that either of them expected a response that quickly. They didn't know whether Moon read the paper, they were just hoping that someone connected to him did, it was worth a try.

***

Jonny Moon parked the hire van on Sunnybank Road in Bury. A mixture of pre-war and more modern built residential properties on the outskirts of Manchester. The address he was interested in was one of the more modern built houses at the top of a hill. It was a modest sized detached residence with an Audi A4 parked on the drive.

He could hear Pill moving about in the back of the van. "Keep still, will you, before some passing brat hears you." The gnarled scar tissue in his right palm was driving him mad today, and that wasn't helping his temper.

"It's not that comfy in here you know."

"Stop moaning: it won't be much longer, if our info is right she'll be leaving to collect her piglets soon. Look, I'm going to pull past the address so you can get a clear shot out the rear windows."

Moon then drove up to the address and turned left into a side road opposite the property. He pulled over and stopped the engine, the rear of the van now facing the front of the address. He carried on looking via his door mirror. "As soon as she comes out of the front door I'll shout you. Make sure you get a shot of her before she gets into the motor. And make sure you get the house in the background as well."

"I know, boss, I have done this before," said Phil indignantly, "remember it's my brother Bill that's the thick one," – Bungalow Bill to his mates, as he had no upstairs, not that many dare say it to his face – "I'm Phil, remember. Anyway, what about the piglets?"

"We'll not follow her there in case she clocks us. We know which school they're at; we'll just get there before her. Wait, the front door's opening, Phil, go for it."

Phil didn't answer but Moon could hear the camera's shutter clicking away. As soon as he saw her getting into the driving seat of the Audi, he fired up the van's engine and set off briskly. "Hang on, Phil, till we get to the school."

"No probs, boss."

"Did you get the shot?"

"No worries, boss, I've got several good ones. All showing her face, the motor's number and the house."

"Nice one, Phil, I never doubted you."

Ten minutes later, he parked the van outside a local high school, and watched the Audi arrive a couple of minutes later. The woman got out and greeted two teenage boys as they slumped towards her and the car. One was aged about thirteen and the other slightly older. Moon could hear Phil's camera clicking away again. He picked up a copy of tonight's Manchester Evening Telegraph from the dashboard and opened the pages to give him a bit of cover, especially considering where they were parked. There were so many pervs around nowadays; he didn't want to attract attention.

"I've got good shots again," he heard Phil say as he watched the Audi drive past them.

He would give it a couple of minutes before they did one. "Nice one, Phil, we'll let her go then I'll drive around the corner and you can get in the front." He turned back to the paper and opened it again to see a half page advert on page three. He was drawn to it, as it was an unusual place for a half pager.

'Bonnie and Clyde seek a reunion with their old friend Jonny. So sorry we all fell out, hope your hand's feeling better. Please ring us on the below number', the words set in large font filling half the page.

Moon stared in disbelief as his scar tissue started to itch again.

It was over a month ago that those villainous bastards he'd nicknamed as Bonnie and Clyde came to see him, they were after an address for an old mate of his. He'd arranged a meet with them on the ship canal towpath, but the bitch had got the jump on him and shot him through his hand. He'd sent his two best men to London after them and they both came back in body bags. He'd then put his feelers out amongst all the villains he knew, both in the north, and in London, and no one had ever heard of these two. The thought of getting his hands on them again was too good for words. But he knew he had to be smart, they had obviously come to finish the job, whoever they were.

CHAPTER SIXTEEN

"Hope your hand is feeling better," Jane read aloud, before bursting into laughter. "If there is any chance of flushing him out, then this is it. He'll be apoplectic."

"That's the idea. Glad you like it."

"I do. If intrigue doesn't get the better of him, the piss-take surely will." She remembered his face the first time they met when she'd had to shoot him through the hand. Though, to be fair he was threatening to have her raped, so deserved all he got.

They chatted through the possibilities of what to do when Moon or one of his cronies responded to the advert. They didn't want to become too easy a target. But they had to concede that Moon would probably think that they had come to finish him off, so would have to think of a way to reassure him. One thing was for certain, he'd finish them without a second's thought if he could. So, they came up with a rough plan between them, which was only frustrated by the fact that the phone didn't ring. They stayed in the room, even ordering room service so as not to be in public if Moon did call.

During the passing hours, they watched TV and Jane mused over what happened between Burrows and her on the job they did the month before. They sort of ended up in bed together, but decided to park any feelings until after the op. Since then, neither of them had mentioned it again and Jane was unsure whether it was just a one-off. She couldn't help glancing at Burrows when he wasn't looking; he didn't look his fifty years, and had a masculine profile with high cheekbones and a strong jaw. She was unsure what to do or say, so she decided to do and say nothing, for now anyway.

They decided to go down to the hotel bar for an hour or so as Moon hadn't jumped at the chance to ring them. Perhaps, he hadn't seen or been made aware of the article, or perhaps he was biding his time. They eventually returned to their room at midnight as the bar closed. Burrows suggested they turn the phone off: he said if Moon rang in the middle of the night, then he would be doing so to gain an advantage; ring them when they were asleep to disorientate them. And in any event, as much as they wanted Moon to take the bait, Jane said, it would make them appear needy, too keen, jumping up to answer the phone in the middle of the night. No, Moon was one of those people who loved to have control of any situation. Burrows agreed and he switched the phone off.

Jane awoke first, and was up and showered before Burrows stirred. She was glad the room had twin beds as it saved any embarrassment, but was equally unhappy that it had as well. She turned the pay-as-you-go phone on whilst waiting for the kettle to boil. No messages, or text alerts.

Over breakfast, they discussed what to do next. Jane recalled when they first came to Manchester on the previous job. They got Moon's phone number from a man called John Mathews, he was the legitimate name used by Moon to rent out commercial properties on behalf of Moon and no doubt many others. That way, it kept the criminals' names away from any of the buildings they used. Mathews was just a small man on the fringe who laboured away under the auspice of being a businessman.

Though, they did have to cajole him into giving up Moon's number, they had been true to their word; and had not told Moon whom they had got it from. Maybe that would buy them some credit.

"Why don't we go and see Mathews, he might have an address, or an up-to-date number for our Jonny?"

"That's not a bad idea, Jane."

"Or, we could maximise our time. I'll go and see Mathews, and you could drop in on Detective Inspector Crabtree and his boys, on some premise, and see what they're up to?"

"Now, that's also a good idea. But do you want me to come with you to see Mathews, in case he kicks off?"

"No, I'm fine. He was no problem last time. And if he blanks me, and reports straight back to Moon, that's also fine."

"Yeah, that would send his interest and temper sky high, knowing we were actively searching for him."

That agreed, they left the hotel and Burrows drove to Manchester Ringway Airport. They'd need two cars now, so Burrows said a rental from the airport was handy, and a place where they wouldn't be noticed. Jane used one of the fake set of IDs Briers had given her when she'd signed up. She used a fake passport as well as false driving licence to give the impression she had just arrived by jet. It was all good cover; even when you didn't need it, you never knew when the added attention to detail would pay off.

By late morning, they parted; Burrows headed for the Manchester Branch Office of the National Crime Agency, and she was off towards Trafford Park to see Mathews. She'd also hired a sat nav with the car and soon recognised the area of Trafford Park as she neared her destination. It was a modern single-storey commercial building, steel with windows at one end and a small car park to the side. She drove past once to refresh her memory before parking up in a nearby layby. She noticed the same Jag that Mathews had previously used parked in the same bay. Last time they came, they'd flushed Mathews out of his office on a pretext, followed him and then took him at gunpoint to a disused warehouse for a little chat. This time they had already decided on the direct approach.

Five minutes later, Jane was on the car park facing an up-and-over door, which was next to a normal one set in the metallic sidewall. She dialled the number for the premises and recognised the receptionist's voice, who put her straight through.

"Mathews."

"John, it's an old friend here and I'm stood outside. I just want a little chat. Promise. No funny business like last time, and before you slam the phone down, remember we never gave you up to Moon. We kept our word."

A short silence followed by, "YOU—"

Jane interrupted, "Five minutes with you, in your office. On your own turf. Then you'll never see me again. I promise."

She had decided not to issue any threats like before. Trying the more congenial approach. A further pause, then.

"You've got a real cheek, after you took me at gunpoint and then left me locked in the boot of my car."

"Yeah, but we did ring your office and tell them where to find you," Jane said, trying to sound as feminine as possible, which wasn't easy when you are talking about locking someone in a confined space at gunpoint.

A further pause, followed by.

"OK."

Two minutes later, and she was in Mathew's office. He was as she remembered; a portly man who looked unkempt and unhealthy for his middle years. She carried on the softly approach by apologising for their harsh attitude last time, justifying it by saying the people they were after were not very nice.

"I suppose you think Jonny Moon is a pussycat do you?"

"I know he's not, but we never said where we got his phone number from."

"Well, I am grateful for that at least, but I did get a visit from him." Mathews said, before going on to explain.

Apparently, Moon had visited several people once his hand had been repaired by some backstreet GP. He said he was happy with Mathews, but to be on the safe side he was ending his relationships with all his sub-contractors.

"What does that mean?"

"It means I'm now down £250 a month."

Jane knew that Mathew's only job with Moon was to be the official name on any properties he wanted renting, and to front-off any enquires that might come, whether legitimate or otherwise.

"What do his other sub-contractors do?" Jane asked.

"He has loads of people like me, doing all sorts on the fringe. He's a careful bloke."

Do you know his current whereabouts or have any links or phone numbers for him?"

"No, and if I did, I wouldn't give them to you."

Jane then reached into her jacket pocket, and saw Mathew's eyes widen as she did. "Relax," she said, as she pulled out a bundle of bank notes from the operational funds Briers had given her.

"There's two grand there, to help offset your losses," she said, as she threw the elasticated wad onto Mathew's desk.

She watched him, as he quickly scooped the money into one of his desk drawers.

"What now?" he said, with growing confidence in his voice.

"Now, I walk away. I'm not here to threaten you this time. But, there is another two grand here, if you get a sudden recall," she said, as she pulled a further bundle from her other inside pocket. Keeping it firmly in her right hand, she could see Mathews' eyes shrivel with obvious greed. She'd stopped halfway to his office door. Seconds passed, nothing.

"OK, I'll be off then," Jane said.

"Look, he's sacked me, so I'm out of date. But I do know a boozer he used to use."

"Used to use? Let me guess, I give you a further two grand, and when I get there, no one's ever heard of him?"

"Oh they will have heard of him all right, and if you were a Manchester villain, you'd know it too," he replied.

"Why is that?"

"Because he's been shagging the landlady Carol for years. Just don't know if he still is. Loads of people will know this."

"Good," Jane said, throwing the second bundle onto Mathew's desk, "that way, no one will know it's come from you then."

"The Hope on Eccles Old Road, in Salford. And I don't want to see you again, no offence."

"You won't," Jane answered, as she turned and left.

CHAPTER SEVENTEEN

"Remember me telling you about those two bastards?" Moon spat at Bill as he joined him in the front of the van.

"What two?"

"These two," Moon said, as he threw the newspaper along the dashboard, still open on page three.

"Fucking hell, boss," Phil said, as he read, "what do you reckon to it?"

"It's obviously a trap, but I need to think it through. I want those pair of twats so bad; but we'll have to be careful. Once I come up with a plan I'll ring them and set up a meet. But first, we have work to finish here."

Moon drove back to the end-terrace house where Bill was entertaining Townley. Having entered, he told Phil to get the photographs uploaded onto his laptop and then to download them onto a clean pen-drive. When he'd finished, he had a look at them. Phil had done a good job. This eased his temper a little before he put a ski mask on to go upstairs to check on their guest.

"How's the little creep been behaving?" he asked Bill as they climbed the stairs.

"No probs, boss," Bill replied, through his usual inane grin.

True enough, Townley was curled up on the single bed holding the chain that fastened him to the wall as if it was some kind of comfort blanket.

"You keep behaving, and this'll all be OK," Moon said.

Townley peered back at Moon through his wimpy eyes, "When can I go home Mister? I've told you, I'll not say owt to no one."

"Like I said before, just two weeks, maybe sooner if things go to plan. Just sit tight and behave."

"You're not going to hurt me again, are you? I am behaving, and I've got a wife and kids who must be going out of their minds with worry."

Moon walked closer, and punched Townley hard in his face, knocking the back of his head into the wall. "What? Like that you mean?"

Townley just yelped and said nothing. Moon couldn't stand the weak bastard and the pleasure of hitting him lifted his mood further. He turned and left the room, and as he made his way downstairs, he savoured the moment when this job was over, when they wouldn't need Townley anymore. He'd originally planned to let Bungalow Bill and Phil deal with him, but he might do it himself, as a treat.

***

Burrows wasn't sure whether Crabtree would be in or not, but decided not to ring ahead. He may be in, but busy in a meeting or suchlike. Whereas, if Burrows was waiting at reception, Crabtree would no doubt find a few minutes to spare. He didn't have to wait long. After ten minutes, he was ushered into Crabtree's small office next to the briefing room where Burrows had been a few days earlier.

"I can only give you a few minutes, John, but to what do I owe this pleasure?"

"I was just up here visiting a sick relative, so I thought I'd pop in and see how things are?"

"Nothing serious, I hope?"

"No, as it turns out thanks. Pity it wasn't whilst I was up here the other day. Anyway, I was just wondering if you've got the locksmith back? And, as I was in the area…"

"Sore point, John. I can't really tell you anything, but in short, no. And, I've been told to drop all enquires for at least the next two weeks."

"That's bad form. Sorry to hear it. I take it you're no nearer to knowing where Moon is then?"

"No, the enquires with GCHQ to try and trace the calls I received came to nothing. Apparently routed through several countries and publically owned servers."

"What, like internet cafes?"

"Yeah, that sort of thing, libraries and even piggy-backing off commercial servers as well. Notwithstanding any security that was in place."

"Sounds quite sophisticated," Burrows added, before a thought occurred to him. "Look, Nigel, I'm going to be around for a couple of days, so if there was anything you wanted me to do, sort of off the books, in order to find Moon, just let me know." This way, he could keep a line of communication open with Crabtree, which could prove useful, plus it might help him and Jane find Moon themselves.

Crabtree didn't answer, but Burrows could see him wrestling with the idea, before he spoke. "It's a nice offer, John, but I'm in enough shit as it—" He was interrupted by his mobile ringing.

John plonked himself in the office chair on the opposite side to Crabtree's desk whilst he took the call. He heard him answer, then go quiet. Then saw him go white. Then he gawked at Burrows, before reciting his email address. Took the phone from his ear and collapsed in his desk chair looking frightened. Burrows was about to ask if everything was OK, when he heard Crabtree's desktop announce the arrival of mail. Burrows said nothing as Crabtree frantically worked the wireless mouse on his desk. Then he stared at the monitor with what looked like a mixture of terror and confusion on his face – almost childlike. Then he spoke.

"That was Moon. And he's just sent me an email," Crabtree said, before spinning the monitor around so Burrows could see it.

Pasted onto a blank email message – which Burrows noticed came from a Hotmail address – were three photographs, one after the other. The first was of an attractive brunette climbing into an Audi saloon. The second, of the same woman stood outside what looked like school gates. And the third, of the same woman greeting two teenage children dressed in school uniforms.

"Shit, Nigel. Are these Townley's family?"

"No, John. They're mine."

Burrows was stunned. Did this bastard Moon know no limits? Even in the old days, villains knew where the lines were drawn, and so did the cops for that matter. An unwritten rule existed which neither crossed. But this guy was off the scale.

Crabtree explained that Moon had told him the photos represented insurance.

"Insurance for what?"

"Just to make sure I stick to the agreement and do nothing over the next two weeks or so."

"And nothing more?"

"No," Crabtree answered.

Burrows wasn't sure, he felt that Crabtree said no a little too quickly. Almost defensively. It gave him the distinct impression Crabtree was holding back on something. After all, they already had Crabtree under control, so why send the email?

Then Burrows had an idea. Even though the incoming email was from a Hotmail address, which anyone could access without having a contract with an internet service provider, he might be able to locate where it came from if he was quick. He lunged out of his chair and hit the return button on the email.

"Hey, what are you doing?"

"Trying to link the email back to where it was sent," Burrows explained, but seconds later, an automated service email arrived from Hotmail saying that no such person existed at the domain of Hotmail.com.

"Bloody hell, that was quick," Burrows said. He explained that the sender had registered himself as John Smith. But by the time Burrows had tried to return the email to him, the sender had de-registered himself.

"Thanks for trying, John," Crabtree said, "but it would have no doubt been an internet café or something, and he'd have been long gone by the time we got there. But worth a go."

"So, what are you going to do now, Nigel?"

"I'm going to take you up on your offer. But it must stop between you and me, and for heaven's sake, tread carefully. And do nothing without my say so. OK?"

Burrows knew that if he found Moon, then Crabtree's problems would be over. It would lead to Townley's release and Moon's disappearance. He just wished he could tell Crabtree, he liked the guy's nerve.

"Agreed," Burrows answered, "but where do I start?"

"There's a pub in Salford. I don't know its name, or where it is exactly. But the landlady is called Carol. Moon used to have a relationship with her, but I don't know whether he still is."

"Have you checked licensing?"

"Yeah. There are no landladies or landlords' partners called Carol in any boozer in Salford. We figure, as it came from several sources some time ago, it's correct intel, but this Carol is probably just a barmaid working on a cash-in-hand basis. It was one of the active actions we had to trace her and the pub. But that was before the investigation was stopped."

"Do you know how many pubs there are in the city of Salford?" Burrows asked as he rose from his chair.

"Lots, I know."

Burrows told Crabtree he would ring when he had something, said his goodbyes and headed for the stairs.

CHAPTER EIGHTEEN

Back at the Britannia hotel, Burrows couldn't wait to tell Jane what had happened. She was already in the room when he walked in. "We are looking for a landlady come barmaid called Carol. She's close to Moon and works in a pub in Salford somewhere, but I don't know the name."

"I do, it's the Hope on Eccles Old Road."

Burrows turned to face Jane who was perched on the end of the bed, grinning. "I think you'll find that's one-nil, Mr Burrows."

She'd done him again. But he didn't mind, she was a first class operative as far as he was concerned. He laughed, and then they briefed each other with their respective reports.

"How do you want to play this?" Jane asked.

"I'm not sure if I'm honest. What if Moon is in the pub? It's not the ideal place to come across him and he knows what we look like, so as soon as we enter, he'd clock us and get the drop on us."

"Give us a minute," Jane said, before picking up her overnight bag and going into the bathroom.

Ten minutes later, she reappeared now wearing a smart blue skirt, high heels, and a red jumper. Gone were her jeans and sweatshirt, as was her dark brown bob, now covered with a long blonde wig. He barely recognised her.

"So, what do you reckon?"

"Brilliant, all those years you spent at Five were clearly not behind a desk."

Jane gave him a playful kick, before he added, "It'll be dangerous though Jane, so I suggest you wear a body mic and I'll plot up outside in case it goes tits up."

"Agreed."

They both made their way to their car and Burrows opened the boot and unlocked the gun safe hidden below the carpet lining. They each drew a SIG Sauer P226 9mm handgun together with a full clip of ammunition. Burrows was already wearing his lightweight shoulder holster and quickly put his weapon away. Jane slipped hers into her handbag and after checking no one was around, slipped her ballistic vest under her short puffa jacket. They each had a gun safe at their respective homes and Frank Briers' instructions were clear; when not armed for operational reasons, their guns had to be in one of the safes. Even so, Burrows had parked the car, which was fully alarmed, on the car park under a light, and within view from their room.

They got into the car and headed out. The sat nav took them to the junction with Lancaster Road and Eccles Old Road, in Salford. The boozer was a huge place at the junction with entrances from both roads. It was raised several feet above road level, with a car park at the rear. Burrows drove around it a couple of times before parking in a side road.

"This won't be easy," he said, "the place is pretty big. As soon as you approach the bar you will be on display, and it'll be impossible to take in all areas at once."

"Don't worry, even if Moon is in there he'll never recognise me. Don't forget I'm asking about Carol, not Moon."

Burrows felt his cheeks redden a little, was he being overprotective? "Yeah sure, but wear your body radio anyway, it's in the glove box."

Five minutes later, they parked at the rear of the pub and Burrows watched as Jane tottered towards the Lancaster Road entrance.

"Radio check?" he heard Jane whisper as she approached the steps that led to the door.

"Loud and clear. You receiving me OK?" Burrows said.

"Yes, yes," came the response as she started up the steps.

Burrows turned the car's covert radio loudspeaker off and continued to listen via his radio earpiece. He could hear Jane opening the pub door, which was immediately replaced with an assortment of loud music and chatter, the place sounded moderately busy. He checked his watch; it was seven forty-five p.m.

**

Jane could see that the place was close to full, probably a mixture of afternoon drinkers, who appeared the more worse for wear, and the early evening crew, who looked fresher. Two environments coexisting. The in-house speakers were playing a loud tune she didn't recognise, and two men at one end of the bar were shouting at each other. It didn't look like trouble, but could escalate.

She made her way across the large room to the bar and could only see one barmaid serving who seemed preoccupied with the two men quarrelling; no doubt keeping a close watch in case things got worse. As Jane glanced around, she saw another member of staff, a bloke, collecting empty glasses. Both looked in their twenties, possibly students she guessed. She mumbled towards her shoulder, where her radio mike was under her jacket, that she was approaching the bar, no apparent dramas. She heard no acknowledgement in her earpiece, but a few moments later, it crackled inaudibly. She assumed it was Burrows replying, but she couldn't make out the words due to the noises from the bar washing over her.

On seeing her approach, the young woman behind the bar walked over to her. "What can I get you, love?"

"Half of lager please, and I wonder if you can help me. I'm looking for Carol, been told she used to work here."

"Sorry, love, me and my boyfriend," she said, motioning towards the glass collector, "have only worked here a few weeks. Don't know about the staff that left."

Jane was about to ask for the landlord, when the barmaid added that the boss was away all day and wouldn't be back until tomorrow. The two old boys at the other end of the bar were swearing at each other now, and the barmaid cut away and made straight for them, telling them to either calm down or leave.

"Maybe I can help you? Who're you after?" came a gruff voice from behind Jane. She spun around to find herself facing a middle-aged man with a huge beer belly, shaved head, and a noticeable deep scar running across his forehead. It was an old scar and looked like a deep crease. "Sorry?" Jane asked.

"Wasn't ear-wigging love, just waiting to get a pint and heard you asking about Carol. 'Fraid she left ages ago. More's the pity; she knew how to pull a pint, unlike these kids they have here now. You a mate of hers, like?"

"Yeah, yeah," Jane answered a little too quickly she thought, having been taken aback a little. "Erm, she was an old mate and I moved away and we lost touch. Just passing through, thought I'd look her up, that's all. No big deal."

"Well, I'm not sure where she went to when she left, but let me ask a couple of the regulars. See if they know."

The shaven headed man then turned without waiting for a reply and walked over to the two guys who had been arguing. Two or three minutes passed, and Jane could see the three seemed deep in conversation. At least the two old boys weren't kicking off now. She was starting to get impatient and shouted across that it didn't matter, but thanks anyway. But the man shouted back that one of the older men may know where Carol moved onto, and to hang on a minute whilst he tried to recall. She smiled back as nicely as she could, feeling the pressure to stay, and not appear impolite.

But after two or three further minutes, she walked up to the three of them and said she really had to go. Thanked all three of them.

"Sorry, love," the shaven headed man replied, "these can't remember which pub she moved to, sorry."

She thanked them again and turned to walk towards the door. She caught a look in the shaven headed man's eye, which started to unnerve her. No matter, she was going now, and she whispered into her mike that she was coming out as she pushed the door open. She was glad to be outside as she walked down the steps, glancing up to relocate their Mondeo as she headed towards the car park. It was only when she neared that she looked up properly.

The driver's door was wide open, and Burrows was gone.

CHAPTER NINETEEN

Burrows watched intently as Jane climbed the steps and entered the pub. He heard her say she was heading towards the bar. He muttered an acknowledgement as he squinted against the car park lighting, one lamp near to him seemed to be shining directly into his eyes. A knock on his window made him jump. A large man in his thirties or forties, hard to tell exactly, stood in silhouette with the offending light behind him. Burrows wound his window down, wondering why he hadn't noticed him approach.

"Yes, mate—" was all he managed to say as the man grabbed Burrows hard around his neck with both hands, his thumbs pressing on his Adam's-apple. Burrows' hands instinctively shot to the man's wrists, as he struggled to breathe. The man squeezed even harder as Burrows strived to make a sound in a vain effort to cry out. A mouse-like whimper was all he could manage.

He was aware the passenger door opened, as the sound of passing traffic grew louder behind his head. He then felt the unmistakable impression of a gun's muzzle pushed hard into the base of his skull.

"I'll tell Phil to let go of you, so long as you don't make a noise or do anything stupid. Nod if you understand?"

Burrows nodded.

"And keep your hands on the steering wheel, or I'll have to shoot you here and now. And that would be a shame. It would spoil my fun. Nod again."

Burrows nodded as he felt terror replacing shock. The fear ran up his spine in an icy blast as he recognised the voice. He did as instructed, and as he heaved in clean air, he felt Phil's hands relieving him of his gun, and taking his mobile phone from the top of the dashboard. He turned to face Jonny Moon in the front passenger seat with a Glock handgun pointing at his ribcage. He noticed that Phil had disappeared but soon returned in an old white transit van. He pulled across the front of Burrows' Mondeo, got out and then slid back a side-opening door. Burrows was bundled into the rear of the van closely followed by Moon. It had only taken two minutes to lift him, quickly, quietly and with no fuss.

Burrows knew now was not the time to be noncompliant. On the plus side, the big oaf that Moon called Phil hadn't searched him properly, after taking his gun he obviously saw his mobile on the dash and looked no further. In Burrows' other pocket was the 'Moon' phone, which he managed to slide under the driver's seat as he was regaining his breath. He'd also managed to dislodge his radio earpiece and noticed it fall onto the driver's seat as he got out the vehicle.

He didn't want Jane ringing him on either of the phones, only to compromise herself. There was just a chance that Moon hadn't seen her, or if he had, he'd not recognised her. And, if they had seen the earpiece, they might start to question who they thought he was.

"Does Bonnie know you're shagging that blond?" Moon asked.

Bonnie and Clyde had been Moon's nickname for them when they met him on the last op. He was just grateful Moon hadn't recognised Jane. At least she was safe for now. He didn't answer Moon. No point.

"Have it your way, dickhead, for now. But you will talk to me later, whether you want to or not."

***

Jane scanned the car park, no sign of Burrows or any other vehicles. The Mondeo was alone with the driver's door open. She looked towards the exit in time to see the tail lights of an old white transit van disappear into the night traffic. She didn't see its number plate. She ran to their car and saw that the ignition key was still in place.

Then it clicked. Bastards. She ran back into the pub only to find that the two old boys and Mister Helpful with the creased, shaven head had all apparently left in a hurry through the front door. She ran after them.

They'd been a diversion and now they were her only link to whoever had taken Burrows, though she had a good idea. Out front, she couldn't see them. Then she saw a white van, similar to the one that had left the car park, screech away from the kerb a few metres away. It must have picked them up. A car behind sounded its horn and flashed its lights, having been cut up by the van. That split second of extra illumination gave her a clear glimpse of the rear number plate. It was a 51 reg ending ZZA. She committed it to memory as she ran back to their car.

Moments later, she drove out of the car park, right, and then to the traffic lights which were on red. She powered through them, turning right into a cacophony of angry horns. There was no sign of the van but she accelerated hard along Eccles Old Road. All the while trying to raise Burrows on the radio, assuming he still had his body radio kit on, but all she got back was static. She checked the glove box to find his body kit in there, he might still have his earpiece, but without the body kit, she knew it was useless away from the vehicle.

She soon reached a major roundabout with the M602 and realised the van was long gone. She carried straight on towards Trafford Park in a vain hope she'd come across the van parked up. When they had first come across Moon, he was operating out of a rental unit in Trafford Park, but they never knew where. And, as Trafford Park was the size of a small town, she realised her quest was hopeless.

She pulled over to ring Frank Briers in London and take some instructions. After ending the call, she headed back to the hotel. Her adrenalin replaced by fear; she knew what Moon was capable of. Briers said he would have someone work on the part registered number and that she should sit tight at the hotel. He also said he would get Steele on the road, and he should be with Jane in about three hours.

As she sat musing what had happened, she had a thought.

When she put her phone down, it was all clear. She'd rang the pub asking after Jonny Moon, only to be told he was there earlier but left in a hurry with his mate Phil. They must have seen them arrive, just happened to be in the boozer when they turned up. They knew there was an outside risk of this, but wouldn't have expected Moon to clock them on the car park. She also realised her disguise had probably saved her. After all, she shot Moon through the hand to get the information they had previously sought. She was the one Moon would have preferred to get hold of, she was sure of that. She also knew she had to come up with something, and fast.

She spent the next ten minutes searching the car. She found Burrows' earpiece, which she had been sat on. As Burrows hadn't been expecting to go on a foot follow, he must have been listening to the radio via the car kit. At least all the body-radio gear was safe; it would destroy Burrows' legend of being a villain if Moon found surveillance equipment on him. She also found the Moon phone under the driver's seat, but couldn't find Burrow's work phone, which was a worry.

Back in the room, she rang Briers to update him, "Thanks for that Jane. But as a precaution we've already sent a destruct virus to his smartphone."

"How's that work?"

"It'll destroy all data on the phone and SIM card. Contacts, call log, texts, browsing history, the lot. It'll just look as if the phone's knackered."

"Handy bit of kit."

"Yeah, it's only recently been developed. Your old colleagues at Five are having great fun with it; apart from its use as a disruption tactic, if they have a target with two phones, one dirty and one clean, but they can't ID the dirty one to put an intercept on it, for example. They can now zap the clean one, forcing the target to use the dirty one for social calls, and ID it that way."

"Sounds good. Does John know about this new kit?"

"Probably not unfortunately, but at least he's safe from compromise, from the phone anyway."

"Yeah that's a relief," Jane said, adding, "What do I do if Moon rings in on the 'Moon phone'. The number we put in the paper?"

"Stall him, until Steele's with you, and then go get the bastard. But remember your brief, find Townley and then eliminate Moon."

Briers said his usual 'ciao' at the end of the call, and Jane changed back into her jeans and took the blonde wig off. She went downstairs to grab some food before Larry arrived, and to think through her next move.

CHAPTER TWENTY

No sooner had they set off, the van screeched to a halt. Moon had sat next to Burrows up near the driver's compartment on a long bench attached to the side of the van. There was one on each side and it reminded him of the old Black Maria police vans in the days before cages, and health and safety. The back doors opened and three men jumped in closing the doors behind them. Moon shouted at Phil to 'go' and then turned to the three men. Two were in their sixties and one in his forties. The younger one looked a handful Burrows thought; with a shaven head and a nasty wide scar across his forehead. He guessed they had come from the pub, and he just prayed that Jane was all right.

"Nice one, I'll sort you out with a drink later on. Any dramas?" Moon asked.

"No," answered the youngest man, "we just kept her talking like you asked. I had to rope these two old buggers into it, but saw the van leave the car park just as she was leaving. Couldn't have been timed better."

Burrows listened intently to crease-head. It sounded like they let Jane walk out the back way whilst they'd shot out the front. He breathed out. Hadn't realised he'd been holding his breath whilst listening. At least Jane would be OK. If not a little confused. But Burrows knew how resourceful she could be.

"They'll be a drink in it for you two as well," Moon said. Both men nodded in silent reply. "But for now, we'll have to drop you three off round the corner."

After a short detour into a side street to drop the three men off, they were soon back onto Eccles Old Road. It was only then that Moon moved along the bench seat a little, taking the muzzle of his gun from between Burrows' ribs.

"Fuck me," Phil shouted from the front, "that bird of yours hasn't wasted any time having your car away. It's in front of us."

Seconds later, both Burrows and Moon lurched forward as Phil swung the van violently to the right. Obviously, getting out of Jane's rear view before she spotted them. She must have made ground whilst they were dropping crease-head and his chums off. But Burrows didn't hold out much hope, Jane would no doubt be concentrating hard on the traffic ahead, not behind. At least it suggested that she had seen the van leave the car park, but whether she got the registered number or not was another question. He knew he was running out of options and the sudden manoeuvre Phil had done followed by the slight unseating of Moon and himself was an opportunity.

As both men were thrown back onto the bench, Burrows used the distraction and head butted the left hand side of Moon's head as hard as he could. Then he ran at the rear doors. He'd noticed that when they had dropped the three men off, Phil had opened the doors from outside. Now, he knew why as he approached them. The interior handles were missing. Shit. He upped his speed and threw himself at them shoulder first with all the strength he could muster.

The doors held and threw him backwards into the van. He tripped as he fell, turning and landing heavy on his front. Before he could get up, he felt a hard heavy thwack at the base of his skull. "Pistol-whipped," he thought, before a second heavier blow. Then he passed out.

***

Jane checked her watch for the umpteenth time; it was just after eleven p.m. Then she jumped at the knock on the hotel bedroom door.

"Jane, it's me, Larry."

Having closed the door after letting him in, he said he had some news but needed the bathroom first. She watched him as he made his way across the room. In his early thirties, the ex-detective was of average stature but with a huge personality. She liked Steele. But she liked Burrows more, and was growing increasingly worried.

Re-entering the bedroom, Steele said, "That's better."

"Thanks for that," Jane said, sardonically, "but what's the news?"

"Whilst I've been driving up here, Frank Briers has been working on that part-registered number you gave him. Something, something fifty-one, ZZA."

"And?" Jane said, standing up.

"Well, there are several white Ford Transit vans that could fit, but only one in Manchester. PD 51 ZZA belongs to a Carl Denton, who spookily enough, lives in Denton on Collins Road."

"Where's Denton?"

"East Manchester. Come on get your coat."

Jane remembered that before joining the Special Projects Unit Steele had been an undercover officer from Manchester. This was his back yard. En route, he filled her in on what they knew about Denton, which wasn't much. He was a plumber by trade, but was suspected of running an illegal taxi service with his van, specialising in ferrying stag parties around the city. He had some known criminal associates, as he went to school with many, but hadn't had his own collar felt.

Forty minutes later, they parked up on Collins Road with a view of number thirty-two. It was a short terrace street with garden-fronted residential properties. And parked outside the front was Denton's van.

"Is it the one?" Steele asked.

Jane confirmed that it was. It had the same graffiti on the rear doors, 'Man City are shitty'. Steele pulled a face when she explained. He was obviously from the sky-blue half of the city. The trouble now of course was what to do? She reckoned that Moon had simply called in a favour in borrowing the van, which had probably been close to the pub when she and Burrows first approached. As bad luck would have it. And it was no doubt back with the owner, Denton, may know little else; just that Moon borrowed it for an hour or so.

"He may have an idea where Moon took it?" Steele said.

Jane had to agree it was worth a shot, however thin the chances. There was little point in being subtle now.

"If we go in heavy, although that is to be expected, won't Moon wonder how we've traced the van so fast? Allowing for the fact that as far as he's concerned you saw the full reg number."

Steele had made a good point. Then Jane thought back to when she and Burrows first made contact with Moon. They did it on a mobile number Mathews had kindly given them, but Burrows claimed he'd bought it from a bent cop. They could run the same scam again. She explained this to Steele, before they both checked their weapons and got out of the car.

Bang, bang, bang, for the third time before it brought a response. Jane could see an upstairs light go on before the bedroom window opened to reveal the naked torso of a man in

111

his forties, who appeared jaundiced as he leaned out into the glow from the yellow street lamps.

"What the fuck do you two want?" the man shouted.

"Not to have to kick your door in, when we only want a quick word," Steele shouted back, in an emphasised Manc accent.

"You the filth?" the man asked.

"No, Denton, we're not. But you'll wish we were if you don't open this door, now."

Jane could see the man react to hearing his name. This was their plumber-come-taxi-driver. He shot back inside and two minutes later, they were in his hallway.

"You lent your van out earlier. We just want to know where it was taken to," Jane said, speaking for the first time.

Denton made the expected denials before Steele pulled his SIG Sauer handgun from his shoulder holster and stuck its muzzle into Denton's fat gut, pushing him flat against a wall. Denton's eyes gawked in disbelief.

"Look, I'll cut you a deal. We've no beef with you," Jane said, trying her best to sound northern. Well, less southern, at least. "Moon doesn't need to know where we got the address from. We know he borrowed your van to move someone, we just need to know where."

"But, how—"

"Because she clocked the number of your van, and a nice bent cop was good enough to give us your address," Steele interrupted.

"So, if you don't want to see your own lard splattered across the hall, give," Jane demanded.

Denton said that Moon had rung him whilst he was working on a job near the Hope in Salford. Said he wanted to move some merchandise at short notice. Said there was a 'oner' in it, no questions asked. Denton said he didn't ask too many questions, as Moon wasn't the sort of bloke to say no to. Jane saw Steele push his gun further into Denton's gut, when he asked him where Moon kept his 'merchandise'. Denton spat an address out, he said it was where he'd got his van back from.

He wasn't a real villain, Jane thought; just liked the idea of being one. Before they left, they advised Denton of the consequences of warning Moon. Reminding him that they wouldn't tell Moon where they got the address from, so he would only be outing himself. And Moon would no doubt take disloyalty very personal.

Denton said they had no worry on that score. He was clearly as scared of Moon as he had been of them. He added that he didn't have Moon's number anyway. If Moon wanted the van, he just rang him with his number withheld. Jane believed him.

CHAPTER TWENTY-ONE

Jane looked at her watch as Steele pulled into the quiet terrace side street. It was after 1a.m. and the roadway was devoid of traffic or people. They had agreed to allow themselves one drive past the property; being seen once was never a problem, but the same car driving past twice was always a risk. Even at this time of night.

The house was as Denton described, an end-terrace, which looked run-down. It had rough ground on its gable end, and the two adjoining properties the other way were bordered up with steel shutters.

"This must be it," Steele said.

"Yeah. The speed Denton described the property after he gave us the address was too fast to be a lie."

"I agree. It was as if he was desperately trying to convince us he was telling the truth."

"Well, we'll soon find out," Jane finished.

Steele parked their car farther down the street out of view from the target address. Steele switched the interior light off so it wouldn't illuminate when they opened the doors. They both slipped out slowly, holding the door handles up whilst they closed the doors, releasing them only when the doors were in place. Fortunately, there were not too many streetlights around, and nearly half were smashed anyway. Arriving at the gable end, they took a moment to listen. Nothing. Curtains drawn upstairs and down, and no lights were visible. A wooden side gate at the rear end of the gable wall was ajar. Steele slipped past it first before nodding for Jane to follow. The back door was a half-glazed UPVC sealed door with a Yale type lock.

"Piece of piss," Jane whispered, as she pulled a small black plastic wallet out of her jacket. "The difference between Five and the NCA is that the Security Service teaches us how to do this. Safer than hiring the likes of Townley."

"Do you think he's here as well as Burrows?" Steele whispered back.

"Makes sense," Jane replied.

"What do we do if someone's disturbed?" Steele asked, with what Jane could tell was a hint of trepidation.

"We go in fast and hard," she answered, before turning her attention back to the door. She opened the case and pulled out a couple of picks, which she always thought looked a little like Allen keys. The second one slid in easily and after a couple of seconds fiddling, she asked Steele to hold the door handle in the up position. She fiddled again and the lock clicked. Steele pushed the door open as Jane replaced her picks.

They both drew their weapons and slowly entered the property. The kitchen was basic, with an old Formica table and chairs to one side, with a small gingham pattern that took her back to her childhood. Jane led the way into the hall crouched down with Steele pointing his gun at full height over her shoulder. That way, if there was a contact, they could both get a clear shot off.

They cleared the empty front room and turned their attentions to the staircase, which had an old multi-coloured carpet on it. Threadbare in its centre with the most tread at its edges. Jane pointed to the edges, and slowly placed her feet one after the other at the stairs outermost ends. One at a time, one-step after the other. Steele nodded his understanding and followed suit. Wooden staircases were notorious for creaking, and at this time of night, every sound seemed amplified. The least worn part was always at the edges as signified by the carpet ware. It was also, where the steps were at their strongest. No guarantees, just the best bet.

Jane was at the last step when her right foot started to elicit a noise. She stopped, and slowly lifted her foot off the stair, straining to hear if anyone was rousing. Silence. She breathed out slowly and missed out the penultimate step, standing up straight on the landing, shortly followed by Steele.

There were three doors leading from the landing area, two were wide open and one was shut. A rear-facing bedroom. She nodded at one of the open rooms and then at Steele. He turned towards it, as she headed to the other. Her room was empty, as it had appeared from the top of the stairs. She glanced back at Steele and his nod said the same. The both made their way to either side of the closed door. Waited and listened. She heard nothing. Steele shook his head. Jane realised that whatever they were facing would be in this room.

"Time to go noisy," Jane whispered in Steele's ear.

He pulled back from her, nodded, then with his left index finger he pointed at his chest and then put it up in the air. He would go first, she realised he was saying. Jane stood back to give Steele room and raised her pistol in a two-handed grip.

Steele rocked back on his heels slightly before lunging forward. Jane saw his left hand grab and turn the circular door handle at the same time his right shoulder hit the door. It burst open and crashed into an inner wall. She saw Steele duck and dart to his right, his gun back in his hand. She dashed in and to the left. They both slid to a halt. Then silence, as they took in their surroundings.

There was no one there. Just an empty single bed pushed up against a wall with a metal ring screwed to the brickwork through the plaster. If Burrows and Townley had been here, then they were obviously too late. Then she noticed a small amount of blood staining on the mattress and her heart sank. She took a closer look, the mark was darkening. Darker than un-aerated blood. Old; certainly not new. Then she remembered the shoebox incident with the toe that Burrows had told her about, and relaxed a little. So, Townley had definitely been here. At least this suggested he was still alive, and if he was still alive, hopefully Burrows was too. If only to act as bait for her.

She turned to face Steele, saying, "Come on, Larry, let's get out of here." But before he could answer, she nearly fainted in shock. The phone in her left hand pocket let out its shrill ringtone. Recovering, she pulled it out and just stared at it. It was the Moon phone.

***

Burrows could hear a voice in the background. Talking to itself. It became clearer, louder. He realised he was coming around, realised he had been out. Then he remembered and opened his eyes. Now alert. He couldn't see anything, realised there was a hood over his head. He was propped up against a wall, then the pain in the back of his head hit him, he remembered it all. He kept still as he tried to take in his environment as best he could. Let them think he was still out of it. The voice was Moon's and he was obviously talking into a phone. He listened intently.

"Right, bitch, wakey-wakey I'm answering your stupid ad. But you're no longer in control. I have Clyde, but it's you I really want. So you have a decision to make; do you leave me to play with your boyfriend until I get bored and kill him, or do you do the honourable thing, and do a swapsy. Don't talk, just listen. I'll ring you at ten and tell you where to meet me," Moon said, before obviously cutting the connection.

Burrows realised what Moon was up to: he wanted both of them. Then he heard a further ringtone, and listened again.

"Yes, Tony, I can hear you. Why do people ringing from abroad always assume they can't be heard? You could be ringing from next door and it wouldn't matter," Moon said, followed by a pause.

"Keep your hair on Scouse; I'm only winding you up. Yeah… no probs… sure. Anyway, how far away is it…er, got that; Tuesday, OK, Southampton, OK," Moon said followed by a further pause. "I know it's gone one in the morning, you rang me, remember? In a bit, laters," Moon said, before ending the call.

Then he heard footsteps, the lights went out followed by the sound of a door shutting and a lock turning. Tuesday was in four days' time, far less than the two weeks that had been mentioned, and Burrows now knew where Moon's business was going down. He had to get himself out of here, and before Jane did anything heroic in nine hours' time.

CHAPTER TWENTY-TWO

Jane pulled the phone from her ear and pressed the red icon, then looked up at Steele. "No prizes for guessing who that was."

"All I know is that I nearly messed myself, when it rang."

"Too much info, Larry. But I have to admit the timing was spooky."

"You don't think he's got this place under obs do you? Playing with us?"

"It's possible I suppose, but no, I think he'd have challenged us, especially after what's just been said." She repeated the conversation.

"Why wait until ten? It's obviously going to be a trap. One he knows you'll not be able to resist," Steele offered.

"I don't know, but let's get out of here."

En route back to the hotel, they talked through what had happened. Jane told Steele she was impressed with him at the house.

"Thanks," he replied, "bit nervous going in, if I'm honest. Being an ex-undercover officer is a bit different to what we did back there. Just a pity they weren't there."

"Well, there is one thing for sure. I'm not going to sit around and wait for Moon to ring back."

"Sure, but where do we start looking?" Steele asked.

Jane didn't reply at first, and then she had an idea. "How far is Trafford Park from here?"

"Not too far – why?"

"Well Moon has obviously decided to take no chances after snatching John, and decided to move Townley at short notice. Regardless of all his beef with us, it's Townley that really matters. He's the insurance that's keeping the NCA at bay whilst they do whatever. John and I are just a personal distraction."

"So?" Steele said.

"So, he's pulling in favours at short notice. I know it's a long shot but maybe he gave his old friend Mathews a call. He's got a big enough commercial unit to stick John and Townley in."

Doing a U-turn in the road, Steele replied, "It's defo worth a try."

***

As Moon was locking the door, he was aware of someone behind him.

"Everything OK in there, boss?" A voice asked.

He recognised it as one of his men, but before he could answer, the man continued.

"Sorry about before, but I had to say something. I proper shit myself. And I had to give 'em something just to get shot of them."

By now, Moon had turned around and was facing his man. "Will you calm down, you did the right thing. I'm not mad at you. We couldn't have taken them on there and then. There'd have been armed filth crawling all over us in minutes. Not to mention a blood bath that would have led straight back to you, and then me." He started to walk away from the locked door before adding, "Clyde was out of it throughout, and still is. I gave them time to get to the address before I rang, so now they'll be clueless."

"But what if they come back here after more info?"

"We'll be long gone by then," Moon said, before adding, "And, Carl, for fuck's sake, put a shirt on and cover that fat gut of yours."

Moon walked down the stairs to the kitchen to make a brew, turning his back on Carl Denton he allowed his expression to default back to a snarl. He was a good liar. He'd sent Phil off in Denton's van to take Townley to a new address. It wasn't safe to remain at Denton's for too long. It had only been a temporary measure. The same problems would arise as with the last place. People start to pay attention. That was the problem with using residential addresses, especially terraced ones. Everyone's a nosy fucker. Coming to Denton's hadn't turned out such a good idea; it had nearly all gone to rat shit. He wasn't sure whose Clyde's two mates were who had come to Denton's looking for him, though one was possibly the bird from the pub; he'd ask Clyde about that later. He'd also noted that they still had a good contact in the police.

Moon recalled when Clyde had first rung him several weeks earlier when he was after his old mate Cabilla. He'd said he got Moon's mobile number from a bent cop; that's something else he'd ask Clyde about later. Then he heard the van outside, time to move Clyde and get out of here. He'd told Phil to move them one at a time whilst Clyde was out of it, safer that way. He washed his cup, before wiping it clean with a tea towel. He wiped the cupboard door and everything else he'd touched and put the tea towel in his pocket before meeting Phil in the hall.

"Any problems with the wimp?" Moon asked.

"No, piece of piss. The little twat's gagged and chained in his new home."

"Right, let's square things with Denton, and then grab Clyde, and get out of here."

Phil went upstairs to get Denton, so Moon could pay him for his trouble. Whilst waiting, Moon prepared to leave by wiping some more surfaces he'd touched before putting the towel back into his right-hand leather sports jacket pocket. Then, he pulled a Glock 17 handgun from the left-hand pocket. He liked the gun, the cops used a similar one and he reckoned if it was good enough for them, then it was good enough for him. Though his had a different barrel fitted; it had a threaded end onto which he screwed a silencer, which he'd taken from an inside pocket.

CHAPTER TWENTY-THREE

Burrows had no idea how long he'd been unconscious, or where he was. As the mists cleared, he tried to remember as much of what Moon had just said as he could. The first was obviously with Jane using the phone number they had set aside for Moon, the one they had put in the Manchester Evening Telegraph advert.

So, Moon wanted to do a swap. As if? He knew Jane wouldn't fall for that. But why wait until ten. He clearly had other things to do first.

The second call was more interesting. He'd referred to the caller as 'Tony' and 'Scouse'. Mentioned 'Tuesday' and 'Southampton'. This could only relate to their main business. The reason why they'd taken Townley in the first place. And what of Townley? Where was he now? But more pressing, how was Burrows going to get out of here?

He was on the floor up against a wall. His hands tied in front of him with what felt like plastic, and he had a bag over his head, which felt like plastic. He could feel his hot breath rebounding off the inside and condensing on his face. His biggest advantage now, he realised, was that they wouldn't know he'd awoken. As his thoughts fully cleared, he heard voices followed by a set of footsteps coming up the stairs. He tensed. Then he heard more voices, nearer, and two sets of footsteps walking away from outside his room. They went down the stairs. He relaxed a little.

Then he heard a commotion, raised voices and Moon saying, "OPEN THE FUCKER'S MOUTH."

This was shortly followed by silence. Then, two sets of feet back on the stairs again, coming his way. He tensed once more.

The steps stopped outside his room and he heard a key turn in a lock. The door opened and he slumped his shoulders. Playing dead.

Then, Moon's voice, "Looks like the twat's still out of it."

"Do you want me to give him an alarm-kick?" said the other voice, which Burrows recognised as the van driver.

"No, Phil, he'll probably kick off, and we've made enough noise in this quiet back street for one night. Go and get the van and back it right up to the front door, and we'll carry him straight into the back of it. We'll be gone before we cause too much of a stir and we haven't got to struggle with this twat then."

A few minutes later, and the van driver Moon called Phil was back. He could feel himself being manhandled and went as limp as he could. There was a lot of huffing and puffing, as he was hoisted up horizontal. One set of hands had his feet and the other set were under his arms. They carried him along the landing and down the stairs feet first. He considered having a go on the stairs but chose to wait.

In the hall, they dropped him onto the floor from what was probably only a few inches but it felt from higher. He had to stifle any noise as pain shot across his shoulders.

He heard the front door squeak open followed by a metallic clang.

"Fuck," Phil said.

"What?" Moon asked from behind him.

"Parked the fucking van too close, can't open the back doors wide enough. I'll have to pull the van forward a touch."

"Well hurry up will you?"

Burrows heard the van doors being shut and a scrapping noise that sounded like Phil squeezing between the front of the house and past the van's rear.

He listened intently, heard a door bang followed by the van's engine firing up.

When he'd been dropped, he'd landed with his legs bent, knees up. His feet were near enough flat on the floor. He had purchase. Now or never. Using that purchase, he sprung to his feet, and blind, he crashed backwards hoping he'd catch Moon, as he pulled the plastic toiletry bag from his head.

Spinning around, he saw Moon staggering backwards, just managing to keep his balance. Shock chiselled into his face. He saw Moon's right hand head towards his pocket, noticed the large lump of gnarled tissue in the centre of his palm, courtesy of Jane.

Burrows kicked Moon hard in his groin, and as he howled in pain and bent in two, his damaged hand dropped the heavy silenced handgun he was trying to pull awkwardly from his jacket pocket.

As Burrows bent in a race with Moon to get the weapon, he heard a gun's loud report and the smashing of glass behind him. Phil.

Burrows grabbed the weapon by its suppressor, no time to spin it around and get a hold of it properly. No time to trade shots with Phil. He darted for a door to his left, which he hoped, was the kitchen. It was. He was halfway through the doorway when he heard a second shot embed itself in the wall just past his head. Then he tripped and fell over something. A body. A fat bloke on the floor with the back of his head missing.

Burrows just managed to stay upright as he tumbled over the corpse. He got hold of his gun properly now and fired two shots in quick succession back the way he'd come. Should buy him a few moments' respite. He heard the unfamiliar 'phutt' 'phutt' as the suppressed rounds left his gun.

He grabbed at the rear door handle praying it would be open. It was. He heard a commotion behind him as he flung open the door and felt cool refreshing air hit his face. Risking a glance back, he could see that Phil had made the same mistake he had, but he had lost his balance falling to the floor. Partly helped by Moon running into the back of him. In different circumstances it would have been comical, but now wasn't the time for humour.

Burrows was glad of the precious moment's advantage it would give him. He was across the open back yard in seconds and leapt over a short wall finding himself in a traditional Victorian back alley. He headed to the shortest end, about fifteen metres away. Turning the corner, he saw red dust explode from a shattered brick in front of him. He ran towards the street where the house fronts faced, hoping it would provide some cover, and deter Moon and Phil from getting too public. Then he heard sirens.

Good news and bad news. Good in so far as it might stop his pursuers. Bad, if he was caught with a silenced handgun, which had a fifty-fifty chance of being responsible for the removal of the back of the fat guy's head in the kitchen.

He daren't throw it away he might still need it, and anyway, his DNA would be all over it. He reached the end of the street, and noted its name was Collins Road; it joined onto a major urban thoroughfare. He still had no idea where he was. The sirens were getting louder. He glanced back down Collins Road as he turned onto the main road. Half the other houses' lights were on now.

Scanning his options, he knew he had to evaluate the greatest of the two threats: Moon and Phil. Take cover and assess. He jumped behind a four-foot high garden wall. Fortunately, the houses adjoining the main road were pre-war semidetached with large gardens. Burrows took cover behind the wall and was sheltered from the house-front by a large oak tree.

Catching his breath, he heard a diesel engine scream out of Collins Road onto the main road. It was going away from him so he glanced over the wall to see the rear of the van from the house accelerating away. First threat over. Now the second.

He knew the cops' first thoughts would be to assess the risk at the address. They wouldn't know who, or what, was still inside the property. Or, whether any guns were still inside the house. He also knew that one of the first things they'd do would be to throw a cordon around the threat at a safe distance. The junction with the main road being an obvious choice for one end of it. Time to go.

He jumped over the wall, and down the next side street on his right, adjacent with the rear of Collins Road. He had just turned the corner when he saw a succession of police patrol, and armed response vehicles screech past the road-end under heavy braking as they approached Collins Road.

He'd made it, just. Time to keep going. Now he felt the bump on the rear of his head kicking in again as his adrenalin started to subside.

CHAPTER TWENTY-FOUR

Jane watched Steele as he expertly put their car through its paces on the highways and byways of Manchester's suburbs. Both she and Burrows were good behind the wheel, but Steele had the edge. He was a good-looking bloke with a complexion that just wasn't fair on a man; due to his mixed heritage. This had no doubt widened his appeal as a police undercover officer.

She was enjoying his company and had no doubt that he'd fit in well with their little team, bringing additional skills. But as her mind wandered, she couldn't keep her worry about Burrows away for too long. She'd only known Burrows for seven or eight weeks, having been brought together by Briers for their first job on the Special Projects Unit. "Shit – Briers…" she thought.

"I'd better bring Frank up to speed," Jane said to Steele. "He's not going to be happy."

"I'm just glad I'm driving," Steele remarked.

Two minutes later, Jane closed the connection on her phone and turned to face Steele. "Frank says he'll delay telling the Home Sec about John until morning. Says he wants an update by eight. We have until then to get John back. If not, he wants to know what our engagement tactics will be when we arrange to meet Moon."

"Any ideas how to play that?" Steele asked.

"Not a clue. You?"

"Let's just hope he's at Mathews' unit," he replied.

Jane's phone started to ring again. She guessed it was Frank Briers ringing back until she looked at the screen and saw a Manchester number. Moon? She pressed the green icon but didn't speak. After a short pause, "Thank God. Where are you?" Jane said, turning to meet Steele's inquisitive gaze and mouthed the word, "Burrows." She listened some more, then said, "We're mobile en route to try Mathews' gaff. Yes, we. Larry's with me. Stay put we'll be with you as soon as."

She quickly filled Steele in. Burrows had escaped, just, apparently, and was ringing from a public phone box in Denton. She recited the address of the box's location, and Steele did another U-turn in the road.

Whilst Steele navigated his way to Denton, Jane put a further call into Briers to give him the good news.

"Denton?" Briers asked.

"Yes, why?" Jane asked.

"Well, we are just getting some news from the GMP wires about a shooting and murder at a house in Denton, Manchester. If its Burrows related, get him to call me once you've picked him up," Briers said, before ending the call.

Thirty minutes later, all three of them were back at the hotel. Jane had managed to cut the PlastiCuffs off Burrows before they entered. Steele booked in separate and then met up with them in their room.

Burrows finished briefing them both, after which, Jane added, "Looks like the gunshot injury through Moon's hand came in *handy* again," she said, grinning.

"Is that the best you can do?" Burrows said.

"You've got to *hand* it to her, at least she's trying," Steele added.

"You too? It's going to be a long night."

Jane felt her cheeks reddening somewhat. She was being a bit girlie, but she couldn't hide her relief that Burrows was back safe. Steering the conversation back, she faced Burrows and asked, "What about Townley? Could he still be at Mathews' place? We were on our way there when we got your call."

"Don't think so. I heard Moon make a comment about not being disturbed once they were 'out in the sticks'. So I'm guessing they've taken him somewhere rural; which could be anywhere?" Burrows answered.

After further deliberation, they decided to get some sleep and look at things anew in the morning. "What if we get no more leads on where they are keeping Townley?" Jane asked the room.

"Southampton?" Steele asked, as he stood and turned towards the door.

"Well, at least we know Moon's going to be there on Tuesday," Burrows said.

"Have you two any idea how big that port is?" Steele added. Jane just shrugged, as did Burrows.

***

Burrows was up early the following morning, considering the day he'd had yesterday. It was before eight and he glanced across to the second single bed to see Jane still fast asleep. He wanted to be up early to catch the morning news on the TV. Depending on what he saw, it might dictate policy. He flipped through the channels until he found one on a regional news slot. It was all about the fatal shooting of a man at his home in Denton, Manchester. The anchor cut to a reporter at the scene interviewing a local from two doors away. An elderly woman said she had seen some to-ings and fro-ings the previous day, but hadn't taken much notice. The reporter continued, saying that although gunshots had been heard in the early hours, which had woken local residents, who had alerted the police, no one had been seen running away. When the police eventually entered the property, they found the body of the householder who had suffered fatal gunshot wounds. It appeared that the assailant or assailants had then stolen the man's van to make good their escape, registered number so and so.

It then cut back to the anchor in the studio, who said that unconfirmed reports had just come in to say a van had been found ablaze up on the moors above Oldham, sometime within the last thirty minutes, and it is not yet known if the incident is related. The programme moved onto the weather and Burrows muted the sound before putting the kettle on.

So, they were obviously nowhere near Oldham, that's for sure. Burrows guessed they may have had Townley up there somewhere; perhaps at an old farm building or the like, but after what went down in Denton, he was pretty sure they would be on the move again, and no doubt had Townley with them.

Burrows was relieved that apparently no one had seen him fleeing, but he had grabbed the kitchen door handle during his escape. Thinking back, he recalled the handle was brass and had a decorative uneven pattern hewn into it, so he was confident no fingerprints could be retrieved, but it wouldn't have taken much sweat transfer to leave his DNA.

He rang Frank Briers to voice his concerns, and felt reassured by what he was told. As he ended the call, Jane stirred and sat up.

"I thought I heard voices," She said.

"I was just on to Frank; looks like no one saw me last night. I was bothered about the kitchen door handle but Frank has hacked into the GMP Crime Scene database, and it says the kitchen door handle had been wiped clean. Looks like Moon or his mate must have grabbed it too, and then covered their tracks before leaving."

131

"What now then?" Jane asked.

Burrows told her about the news bulletin and the burning van and finished by saying, "I'm going to take a shower, and then I reckon we should all head back to London. I feel as if I've pushed my luck to the max already."

CHAPTER TWENTY-FIVE

Burrows glanced at his watch as the three of them left the hotel, nine thirty a.m. – they should be back in London by one-ish. Jane had a small flat in Milbank, central London, and Steele had taken out a short term let on a flat in Fulham. As he lived in a cottage in Thame in Oxfordshire, he suggested that Jane travel with Steele. He couldn't help but feel a little deflated, but he knew it made sense.

Over breakfast, they'd agreed to head to their respective addresses to have a few hours down time and then meet up the following morning at the office in Pimlico. Even though it would be a Saturday, Briers would be there to debrief them. There was nothing to be gained by staying in Manchester now, and they only had until Tuesday to get to Southampton and find Moon and this 'Scouse Tony' as they'd started to refer to the other guy as.

They agreed to stop at Hilton Park Services on the M6 near Birmingham, and Burrows was about half an hour away when his phone rang. He answered it via his Bluetooth, it was Crabtree; he'd forgotten about him.

"John, it's me, Nigel. Can you speak?"

"Yeah, go ahead, mate, I'm on my own."

"How did you get on in Salford?"

"Yeah, did a few boozers but couldn't find anyone who knew of a barmaid or landlady named Carol," Burrows lied.

"Well, never mind that now, have you seen the news this morning? A shooting in Denton."

"Yeah—" Burrows started to say, before Crabtree continued.

"Well, that bastard Moon has got something to do with it. The bloke killed was a known associate of his. Not that we'd ever prove owt if he was responsible, the place had been wiped clean and he'd be false alibied up to his neck, no doubt."

"I saw on the news about a van on fire over Oldham way. Was that connected?" Burrows asked.

"Yeah, it was the deceased's van, a burnt out shell along with the barn."

"Barn. What barn?"

"There was an old barn nearby also torched. The local plod are writing that off as kids, but I know it must have been where Moon was keeping his head down."

So, that confirms it Burrows thought, that is probably where Townley was taken. He was as sure as he could be that Townley was now with Moon, and on the move.

"I could do with you working the pubs and clubs around Denton, see if you can't pick up on some local gossip," Crabtree asked.

Burrows had to be careful here, he didn't want to say he was going back down south, he didn't want Crabtree getting frustrated and breaking his embargo. "Look, I'm just out on an errand, I'll give the pubs a go tonight," he lied. "Bell you tomorrow, yeah?"

"Yeah," Crabtree answered.

"You stay put, Nige. Leave it to me."

"OK, will do. Tomorrow then," Crabtree said, ending the call.

Over coffee in the service station, he told Steele and Jane about Crabtree's call.

"He's got a point you know. It might be worth doing the local bars, and even go on the knocker purporting to be from the press. Might turn something up," Steele offered.

"I'm glad you said that," Burrows said.

"Why?" Steele asked.

"Well, I'm too hot at the mo. Just 'cause no one's come forward doesn't mean I wasn't seen legging away from Collins Road last night," Burrows added.

"And, I'd be no good with my southern tones. Not in the local working men's clubs that's for sure," Jane proffered.

"OK, I'll go back. It makes sense; I've only been there a day," Steele said.

They all headed to the cars at the outer edges of the car park. Steele took his gun and shoulder holster out of Burrows' car boot together with a spare magazine from the floor safe. They said their goodbyes and Jane jumped into Burrows' car, throwing her holdall onto the back seat. Burrows couldn't hide an inner smile to himself as they meandered towards the exit.

***

Jonny Moon ended the call and turned to face Phil who was driving, "I can't stand that Scouse prick. He really thinks he's something. Says he's on his way over. Says he'll meet us the day before; introduce us to the driver."

"Well, after this job's over, boss, you won't have to put up with him again," Phil offered.

"I know, but his holier than thou attitude gets on my tits. I know he's bringing the cargo in, but without us, he'd have no buyer. And, I'm not too happy about using a driver I don't know."

"I could do it, I've got an HGV licence, Class One," Phil said.

"I know, I suggested that to him, but he insists on using his own man. It's like he doesn't trust us."

"I suppose; if I drove we could just nob off with the stuff, in theory."

"That's what the Scouser said, but I said he could have rode shotgun. But, no, that's too much risk for him."

The muffled groaning and banging started up again, prompting Moon to add, "And as for that annoying turd in the boot, he's pushing me to the limit."

"What do you intend to do with him, when it's all over, boss? I mean, won't it be better to honour our agreement with the filth?" Phil asked.

"You losing your bottle?"

"No, am I fuck, but I thought you'd changed your mind; said it would bring too much grief after us if we off-ed him?"

"I'm only winding you up, I did say that, and it is true. But there may be another way," Moon said, as the embryo of another plan started to excite him.

"How do ya mean, boss?"

"I'll tell you later. Look, we can't keep going around the M60 all night, head towards Preston, I've a mate there who'll put us up for a day or two, no questions. The last thing we want is for the filth to give us a pull with Twaty in the back. I'll bell your half-brained brother to join us, once we get there; I've got a little job for you both." Moon finished and then told him the address.

He couldn't be sure, but he thought he saw a look of distain flash across Phil's face when he insulted his brother, Bill. He'd let it drop, but Phil had better remember his place. Then he calmed a little, he was probably being over-prickly after what Bentine had said to him. Especially the bit he hadn't relayed to Phil. The bit about Denton. Bentine knew about the fatal shooting, which was no surprise as it would be all over the news, but he'd asked if it was anything to do with him. He'd denied it of course, and asked him why he thought it was? Moon tried to recall the exact words Bentine had then used: 'because I know Denton was a mate of yours, I just hope you're not drawing attention to yourself with some petty squabble, whilst we're doing business'?

Cheeky twat, Moon thought. Who the hell did that Scouser think he was? But more worryingly, how did he know that Denton was an associate of his? This guy was certainly well connected, and that worried him.

CHAPTER TWENTY-SIX

Burrows had politely declined Jane's offer to stay at hers overnight when he dropped her off in central London. It would have saved him a journey back into the Home Counties, but he didn't want to end up in an awkward situation like last time. Not whilst they were operational, sadly. But he was glad to sleep in his own bed, and awoke surprisingly refreshed, and was grateful for a change of clothes.

Having endured the traffic back into London, which was bad, but not as bad as a weekday, he arrived at Jane's flat at nine thirty a.m. By ten, they had parked in the SPU's indistinct office underground car park in Pimlico. It was the same as all the other government offices in the area, dirty concrete and no windows on the ground floor.

At ten past, they entered the subterranean conference room via its secure door. Frank Briers was already there at the round oak table, a steaming coffee in hand. They each grabbed a brew from the machine in the corner before joining him. Briers had once told them that the table where the executive of the Special Projects Unit met, was round to signify that there was no chairperson; each vote was equal. And the Home Secretary, head of the National Crime Agency and the Director of Public Prosecutions had to all agree; firstly, that it was in the public interest to take action, and secondly, that it was not in the public interest *not* to.

He knew that was to ensure that they were not creating more harm by taking action, than by not. Echoes of the Iraq war had sprung to mind, though Burrows had never voiced as such. Regardless, the Prime Minister had the last say, and that was good enough for him.

Taking his seat, Burrows asked, "We're not expecting the Executive today again, are we?"

"No, John, relax. I know this is only our second op, but once the job comes to us, once operationalized, we, or I particularly, never see them again. I just keep the Home Sec briefed on the phone and he does the same with the PM," Briers answered.

"We're a bit like knights of a modern-day round table?" Jane said, smiling.

"I don't seem to recall any females in King Arthur's day," Burrows added.

"Look, you two, keep this banter for when you're out in the field, can we get down to business," Briers said, bringing the meeting to order.

As they each sipped their coffees, Burrows and Jane brought Briers fully up-to-date with the events of the last day or so in more detail than phone conversations would allow.

"What about Steele? Have you heard from him this morning?" Briers asked.

Burrows said that he hadn't, explaining that Steele would have been at it, in the pubs until late. Adding that when he took his phone off charge this morning there was a text on it sent by Steele in the earlier hours.

"Anything?" Briers asked.

"Afraid not. It just said, 'No luck. Will ring you later.'"

"OK, then down to business, we need to sort out a plan of action for Southampton. Though, it'll be tricky with the amount of container traffic coming into that place by the hour. And we don't know for sure what the commodity is exactly," Briers said.

"Must be drugs?" Jane added.

"You'd think so, either cocaine or heroin is probably the best bet," Burrows said.

"Must be a huge amount to warrant all the risks that Moon and his cronies are taking. They probably see it as a 'one-off and retire' type of job," Burrows said.

"Well, if that's true, at least we know we are looking for something sizable. But the best bet is to pick up on Moon and stay on him," Briers said.

"That's not going to be easy," Burrows added.

Briers went on to explain that overnight he'd had some help from the Home Sec, or Jane's old mob at MI5 to be exact. Their technical support unit had turned out and were installing, what appeared to be traffic flow cameras on all routes into Southampton.

"I know the ones you mean," Jane interjected, "they're the tall slim blue ones aren't they?"

"Yes," Briers answered, "you often see them on motorways at busy junctions."

Burrows knew the ones they were referring to, Briers continued to explain that, as they didn't know what vehicles Moon or his mob would be using, normal ANPR – automatic number plate recognition – cameras would be of no use. So he'd called a favour in from 'Five'.

"That's the beauty of your old firm," Briers said, turning to face Jane, "they never ask any awkward questions. Unlike our old mob," he finished, turning back towards Burrows.

"So, what do these cameras do then?" Burrows asked.

Briers said he'd let Jane explain whilst he refreshed his coffee.

"Facial Recognition Systems, FRS, they zoom in on the occupants within a vehicle in a split-second and capture the facial features, which are then checked against a database at Thames House."

"Are they any good?" Burrows asked, knowing how unreliable police kit could sometimes be.

"The best on the market," Jane answered, "but nothing's fool proof."

"What if there's an obstruction?" Burrows asked, as Briers wandered back towards them.

"Once the camera locks on to part of a human signature it hunts until it captures the face. If it fails, it transmits to the next camera down the road its partial data and that one takes over. A row of three is usually enough."

"Impressive stuff," Burrows finished, as Briers arrived. Then a phone rang. Briers removed his mobile and put his hand up to hush Burrows and Jane. Briers listened in silence, then thanked the caller and ended the call. As he turned to face them, Burrows could see the puzzlement on his face.

"As of ten o'clock this morning," Briers started, whilst glancing at his watch, "twenty minutes ago, Ian Townley walked into Preston Central Police Station's enquiry desk. Dishevelled, frightened, and limping; but alive."

Burrows and Jane both stared back at Briers, opened-mouthed and speechless. This really didn't make any sense. Or did they have it all wrong about Southampton? Was that something else? Has Moon completed whatever business it was he was doing? Or had Townley managed to escape? After all, he is a locksmith. As Burrows was digesting the news and its possible implications, Jane spoke first.

"What's he saying?"

"Well, it's early days, the first job was to let his family know he's safe, and then the local CID have taken him up to the nearest hospital to get his foot treated," Briers said.

"Yeah, of course, sorry," Jane said.

"But the early indications aren't good. He's obviously been frightened to death; he's already told the detectives that they can ask all they want, but he's saying nothing. Other than to say he's making no official complaint about what's happened to him. And he's also told them not to bother him in the future for any other 'simple' lock picking jobs."

CHAPTER TWENTY-SEVEN

Tony Bentine had spent the day on the beach, again, and looked fondly over the Aegean Sea towards Thessaloniki as the setting sun cast its orange hue across the gentle ripples. Nightfall came early at this time of year but the autumn sun was still pleasant. Especially compared to his native UK; which was where he was headed the following day.

Normally he'd have gone home for a light tea before heading out to the town square for the evening. Hanioti was quiet now that most of the tourists had left for the season. There were still a few tavernas open, and he enjoyed taking money from the locals over the card table. There weren't many Brits who stayed on over winter, and those that did, were pleasantly unsocial; either too old to come into the square of an evening, or too grand to get involved. On the northern end of the resort were a number of large self-contained luxury apartments, all set in their own grounds from where the occupants rarely ventured out. A few were Brits, retired bankers and the like, but the majority were Russian or Serbian, who turned their homesteads into mini-Eastern Bloc abodes.

Bentine was the only foreigner who ventured out in the closed-season evenings, and he liked it that way. The guys he drank and played cards with often enquired as to his means, and he would simply tell them he was a businessman who worked from home. All he needed was a phone and an internet connection; he just preferred that home was in Greece and not England. Everyone accepted this, apart from Stavros, a local shop owner, he was a nosy bastard, but he could handle him.

He'd just entered his apartment when his mobile phone rang. Looking at the screen it said, 'Manc Calling'. He wasn't expecting a call from Moon, what the fuck did he want? He sighed, as he pressed the green icon to accept, "To what do I owe this unexpected pleasure?"

"It's all right for you out there sunning your tits off, whilst I'm doing all the graft over here and freezing mine off in the process," Moon started.

"It's not about that Denton shite, is it?"

"No. And anyhow, how the fuck do you know I know Denton?"

"The difference between Scousers and Mancs; Scousers are always one step ahead," Bentine couldn't resist saying; he knew that would wind Moon up.

"Well, you've got that one wrong this time. And your sources aren't as efficient as you think they are," Moon said.

"What do you mean?"

And then Moon told him. He could barely believe what he was hearing. Moon had let Townley go.

"WHAT THE FUCK DID YOU DO THAT FOR?" Bentine asked.

Moon blithered on about how whinny, Townley had become, and how it was tying his men up, blah, blah, blah.

"I don't suppose you now consider yourself compromised in any way do you? Or had that not occurred to you?" Bentine asked.

Moon tried to explain to him that Townley wouldn't say shit. Just how he could be so certain, Bentine wasn't quite sure; though he knew Moon had a fearsome reputation.

"No villain in Salford would dare cross me," Moon said, "They all know me."

"Does this extend to locksmiths from Preston?" Bentine asked.

"I should think so, now I've removed one of his pinkies." Moon replied, his cynicism clearly seeping through.

Moon had gone on to suggest that the filth would now be fooled. Bentine took a deep breath and asked how? He explained that they might see Townley's release as a sign that they had concluded their business. Job done and game over. They might think that Moon and whoever else was involved were now long gone. He said that he was currently in Preston and was about to head to Southampton, so after the business was properly finished, he would have no reason to go back to Manchester.

Bentine was controlling his anger a little better now, as he knew he had to, whilst still dealing with this moron, but couldn't resist a further jibe. "So you won't have to go back to Manchester for any loose ends or anything?" he asked.

"No. Once the exchange is done and we get paid, I'm off." Moon answered.

"Well, I suppose that's a plus then; not having to visit Manc land again."

"Cheeky twat," came the swift reply.

He could tell he was starting to get under Moon's skin, and smiled at the thought of his contorted face on the other end of the phone. Moon then said that Bentine should give him more credit and respect. He said that he'd put some extra insurance in place. Bentine was hardly listening, as he mused over the developments. Remembering about the threat to that copper, Crabtree. The photographs of his wife and kids. That should ensure safety for the next couple of days. After all, he was flying to the UK the next day, and they would be all sorted in a couple of days thereafter. He just wished Moon had kept hold of Townley a while longer.

To be honest, he still didn't fully understand why Moon had let him go. Was he losing his nerve? Sometimes those who shout the loudest, shit the most, he'd always thought.

Returning his focus to Moon, he said, "Anyway, I'm catching an early flight from Salonika in the morning, so will be in Southampton by late afternoon."

"Didn't you hear what I just said?" Moon moaned at him.

"Yeah, I should give you more credit. Anyway, what did you mean about extra insurance?"

"That's what I'm trying to tell you, for fucks sake. I'm looking at it now."

"Looking at what?"

"Susan Crabtree. The wife of Detective Inspector Nigel Crabtree. As of an hour ago, she is now our guest till the job's over."

Bentine couldn't believe what he was hearing for the second time, "What? Don't tell me you've fucking well snatched a copper's wife now, instead of Townley." He didn't wait for an answer; Moon would know the question was rhetorical. He just told him to make sure no harm came to her, and not to do anything else, and he meant, anything, until he saw Bentine.

As he ended the call, he could hear the twisted glee in Moon's voice. Not doing business with him again was now not enough. When this job was over, he'd have to make sure no one else did business with Moon, ever again. Even if it meant failing to discover whom Moon's buyer was. This guy was becoming too much of a risk.

CHAPTER TWENTY-EIGHT

"I take it that Crabtree is on his way to Preston, to de-brief Townley? Whether he wants to be spoken to or not?" Burrows asked.

"Not sure, John, but you'd expect so. We might learn more then. I'm glad you've still got your link into Crabtree; we might need it," Briers answered.

"Don't forgot Larry," Jane added, "he's up in Manchester if we need to re-deploy him."

Burrows was about to add something, when his own phone rang. Glancing at the screen, he said, "Crabtree," to warn the other two before he took the call.

"Hi, Nige, I was meaning to call you; I'm afraid I've nothing to report back on."

"Where are you now, John?"

"I'm still in Salford," he lied, but fearing Crabtree was about to ask for a meet he added, "but I've really got to head back down south this morning."

"That's fine, John. Look, I don't want to sound ungrateful after all your efforts so far, but I was ringing to ask you to back right off; so you heading south is ideal."

Trying to think what Crabtree would expect him to say, Burrows asked, "Why's that, Nige? Have you found Moon?"

"No, more's the pity. But there have been developments."

Crabtree then went on to explain how Townley had been released, and wasn't speaking to the local detectives. In fact, he'd specifically warned them not to send Crabtree or any of his team to see him. Moon had obviously scared him out of his wits.

"I suppose, the toe removal didn't help any. But he's your only possible link to Moon, isn't he?" Burrows said.

"He is, but don't forget the photos, John. I can't take any risks with my family."

Burrows felt a wave of sorrow flood over him; he couldn't image how much pressure those photos of Crabtree's wife and kids had placed on him. "Do you think he's finished his business now he's let Townley go?"

He didn't get an answer, Crabtree said he had an incoming call from his wife and cut the connection. Burrows brought the other two up-to-speed, whilst he poured another coffee. Then he took a second call from Crabtree.

Two minutes later, Burrows ended that call and turned to the other two. He explained that Crabtree's voice was desperate as he pleaded with Burrows to promise he would leave everything alone and head off back south.

"Why didn't he stress it like that in the first call?" Jane asked.

"Because the interrupting call wasn't from his wife. It was from her phone, but not from her," Burrows said, noting confused looks on Briers and Jane's faces. "It was Moon calling to tell him he has now snatched Crabtree's wife, Susan, as a replacement for Townley."

After a short silence Briers spoke. "This is exactly why the executive of the SPU authorised this job; once these bastards get used to snatching cops or police employees – or their families – off the streets, there will be no end to it."

"Well, the only key we have is Moon himself, and we know he'll be in Southampton by Monday at the latest. The shipment is due in on Tuesday," Jane reminded them.

"Yeah, today is Saturday, Frank, so if we are in Southampton by tomorrow at the latest, we should be ahead of Moon," Burrows said, before adding, "Do you want me to get Steele to head up to Preston, see what he can find out? I don't suspect Moon will move Crabtree's wife all the way down to Southampton. He'll probably leave her with his goons. We know he has at least one with him; I met him in Denton's hallway, remember."

"No, too dangerous; if Moon catches wind of someone sniffing about, he'll think it's Crabtree and we'd be putting his wife Susan at risk," Briers said.

"And don't forget, Moon has friends in the force," Jane added.

They each took a five-minute break, before returning to the circular table with yet more cups of coffee. Briers had rung Steele and told him to get back to London with all haste. It was heading towards lunchtime now, and it wouldn't be until Sunday afternoon at the earliest before Five's technical support teams had the facial recognition cameras operational on the approach roads to Southampton. Briers said he wanted all three of them to be in Southampton by mid-morning at the latest.

"Steele should be here by early afternoon today, so why don't we all head off then, and wait until the cameras go live?" Burrows asked.

"Well, once Larry's here, I'd like you to squeeze a quick little job in," Briers said, as he turned to face them.

"What, in the middle of an op at a critical juncture?" Jane asked.

"This'll only take a couple of hours, and I'd like you to take Steele with you," Briers said.

Burrows was as surprised as Jane appeared, but Briers was adamant. He said the executive had approved the job; it had two yeses. It was in the public interest to take action, and not against the public interest by the taking of that action. It had also received the approval of the PM, apparently. When Burrows tried to push Briers on what it was, he said he would brief them once Steele had landed. Suggested they used the next couple of hours to freshen up and grab some spare clothes, for what would no doubt be a busy few days ahead. Briers also reassured them that it would 'only take five minutes' and it was important that they were seen to be able to sort out quick problems as well as the major ones. "The size of the problem does not affect the principles which apply to what we do," he had said.

Burrows rather understood what he was trying to say, though Jane still looked a little nonplussed. But he wouldn't be drawn further, said he'd meet them back here at three o'clock. And with that, he turned and left.

"Sounds intriguing?" Jane said, after Briers had left the room.

"Certainly does, especially as we are in the middle of something else. I guess we'll have to wait until Larry arrives to learn more."

They both then stood up and headed for the steel door.

CHAPTER TWENTY-NINE

Having first gone to Jane's flat in Millbank, Burrows drove them to his cottage at Thame in Oxfordshire. Jane reckoned she had been to Thame sometime in the past but couldn't remember when. It was a pretty market town and she enjoyed seeing where John lived, though by the state of the place it was obviously a bachelor pad, and then some. After a quick shower and change, Burrows reappeared with a holdall of clothes; neither of them knew how long this job would take from here on.

He then drove her to a large car park in the town centre, whilst he called into a local Chemist for some toiletries. When he returned to the car, he started banging on about the old council buildings in front of where they'd parked. Something about the curved sandstone lintels over the windows. She had forgotten about Burrows' obsession with architecture. On the last job she'd collected him from outside Paddington railway station and received a lecture on London's first underground rail line. "What's a lintel?" she asked. And on watching him take a large intake of breath before replying, realised she had made a tactical error in asking.

"Sorry, am I boring you?" Burrows asked, several minutes later.

"No, not at all, now it's my turn. Have you heard about the new anti-wrinkle cream?"

Burrows laughed, seeming to take the hint, as Jane added, "Well, I'm going to need it if you don't stop talking about frigging brickwork."

They both laughed this time, and the rest of the journey passed less painfully. It was nice to take an hour or two out and empty the mind, Jane thought. Burrows had said in the past, that was often when he got his best ideas, and she could see why. She was also enjoying his company again, even if he did go on about bricks and stuff. She wasn't sure where it would lead. Recalling on the last op how, after a long and arduous day, mixed in with lack of sleep, adrenalin and alcohol, they had ended up in bed together at her flat. Not very professional, she knew. Then she wondered some more whilst taking in the Oxfordshire scenery.

It was two forty-five p.m. when they entered the subterranean briefing room at Pimlico. Larry was already there nurturing a coffee. The aroma smelt good, so she headed for the machine in the corner. Salutations over, they were all seated at the circular oak table when Briers walked in. Jane noticed he was more casualty dressed. It seemed strange to see him in anything other than his pinstriped suit; it took an edge off his authority.

"Sorry, Larry, that you haven't had chance to get your breath back, but time is against us," Briers said to Steele.

"No probs, boss, it was a straight run down from Manchester."

Addressing them all now, Briers continued, "The Executive agreed a job yesterday, and before you say anything, I know we are in the middle of a serious op, but this won't take long."

Jane and the other two acquiesced with nods and Briers carried on, "the PM thinks it is important that the SPU take on little jobs as well as the bigger ones.

"A low-level toe-rag causing havoc on a housing estate is just as big a problem for the people living there, as anything else. More so in reality, as far as those affected are concerned."

"I hear where you're coming from, Frank, but there must be thousands of such instances. If we get involved in these jobs, surely we'd be doing nothing else."

"Potentially true," Briers answered, "but in most cases, the efforts of the Safer Neighbourhood Teams are effective in sorting out these problems. Don't forget our remit; we only take on jobs where there is no prospect of achieving the desired effects by normal means."

"Yes, I know that, Frank," Burrows answered.

Suddenly conscious that Steele hadn't been with them long; Jane turned to him, and explained how the Executive worked.

"Thanks for that, Jane," Briers said. "And in any event, it does no harm for us all to remember that." Briers said.

Jane could sense that Burrows felt unhappy about this job, notwithstanding the wider moral essence behind what Briers had said. They were each given a narrow manila folder marked 'Top Secret' and 'Eyes Only'. She settled down to read the intelligence case, opening the front cover. The first thing she saw were two colour photographs; one of a young man apparently aged seventeen, and one of an elderly man; with the most hideous bruising and swelling to his face. Both his eyes were closed, one cheekbone was lower than the other, and there wasn't an area of skin that was not coloured yellow, blue or black. She recoiled a little, glanced at the other two, who seemed engrossed, and then read on.

Albert Finlay was aged seventy-nine, a widower of five years, who lived in a small terraced house on the fringes of a large housing estate in Newham, East London. This latest beating had only happened a few weeks ago. One of his cheekbones was broken during the attack, which took place in his home. The police were able to get the photograph whilst he was in hospital, otherwise they would possibly never have known about it. The problem with Albert was he steadfastly refused to make a complaint. The police knew that over the last few years, a local yob named Derek Hixson, and his gang had made poor old Albert's life a misery. The problem being that when Hixson first targeted Albert, he dutifully made a complaint to the police. Hixson was arrested and charged with anti-social related crimes and taken to the local Juvenile Court; where he was acquitted. During the trial, Albert became suddenly vague when giving his evidence, and the fact he was only partially sighted gave the defence lawyer an easy job in casting doubt on the identity of Albert's tormentor.

Burrows spoke, breaking Jane's concentration. She looked up as he addressed Briers.

"As bad as the result at court was, why wasn't that the end of it?"

"As you'll see when you read on, it was only the start. The poor bloke has had to suffer years of torment, rubbish thrown into his garden, obscene behaviour by his front window, in fact every conceivable act of anti-social behaviour you can imagine, including drug dealing right outside his front, which usually resulted in needles being left behind."

"And you are telling us that plod can't sort this out?" Steele asked, speaking for the first time.

"It's not their fault. Because Albert is too frightened to report anything to the police, they don't know about most of it."

"I guess you can understand that, after what happened the last time he involved the authorities," Jane said.

"Absolutely, they have picked up on bits and pieces of info, but every time they visit Albert to try and get to the facts and elicit a complaint they can act on, he won't even let them into the house," Briers said.

"What about neighbours?" Steele asked.

"The local cops routinely go on the knocker, and no one has seen or heard anything," Briers said.

"I guess they are all scared of this gang," Jane said.

"Yes, and the fact that if all the grief is at Albert's door, then it's not at theirs," Burrows added.

"A bit cynical, John, but probably true. Alas, it seems to be the way sometimes nowadays," Briers said.

"What about a proactive approach?" Steele asked.

"The cops have tried that, they have had Hixson in the nick several times with his parents for a little chat, but he just laughs at them, and his dad asks 'where's the official complaint?'"

"Bastard," Burrows said, adding, "but he's seventeen now, so an adult in the eyes of the law."

"Let me stop you there. They've tried that, getting a grip of Hixson on his own, now they lawfully can, but it's too late. He just laughs at them. He's no fear of authority; he knows Albert will never complain."

"I know it's not the answer, but what about rehousing Albert?" Jane asked.

"The council can't force him anywhere, he's living in his own house," Briers answered.

All three read on and when finished Briers took the files from them and fed them into the crosshead shredder under the coffee machine table, before turning to face them again.

"One question, Frank," Burrows said, "How come we are getting all this information available to us now, considering the old bloke won't complain and the neighbours are all turning a deaf 'un?"

"Don't know, is the short answer, but the intelligence is pretty detailed as you've just read."

"I think the answer is in the last paragraph," Steele said, continuing, "it says that the rest of Hixson's gang don't want anything to do with the old man, but are all scared of Hixson. Says that Hixson makes them do stuff, but that none of them have ever hurt Albert. Hixson reserves those pleasures for himself."

"I noticed that too," Jane said, "it's as if Hixson's gang want free of him, but can't."

"That's why the brief's so detailed I reckon. Someone's taking a huge risk here," Steele added.

"What do you mean?" Jane asked.

"I reckon one of his gang has turned informant," Steele finished.

"Nice one, that makes a lot of sense. So, if Larry is right, Frank, why can't the cops pursue Hixson, now they have a live intelligence feed?" Burrows asked.

"Had," Briers said. "The info suddenly dried up around the same time one of Hixson's gang had an unfortunate accident and fell down his stairs breaking an ankle."

Jane groaned aloud, and saw Steele's and Burrows' heads drop a little.

"Still think this job is beneath us, or we haven't got time to squeeze it in?" Briers said sarcastically.

"Point taken, boss," Burrows answered. Jane noted he used the word boss rather than Frank, showing due respect to the point.

"So?" Briers added.

"So, let's go get the bastard," Burrows said.

"Just so we are clear," Briers said, as he was gathering his papers together, clearly preparing to leave, "this requires a non-lethal option. Even a non-serious injury option. We are better than he is. Just make sure he never bothers Albert Finlay ever again."

CHAPTER THIRTY

Bentine swore under his breath on feeling the cold air blast as he walked out of Southampton's Central Railway Station. He headed for the taxi rank to take the short ride to his hotel, which was only a mile away. Glancing at his watch, it was just past three p.m., he'd made good time. Though he was missing the Greek weather already. Once at the hotel he'd sort out a hire car. It would have been a lot easier to grab one from Heathrow, easier than taking the train; but he was a cautious man. Flying into Heathrow left one 'footprint', and the hiring of a rental left another. Always better to put some distance between unavoidable markers, then if the authorities were tracking him, it would be a lot harder for them to make the connections. Not that he thought for one minute that they were looking at him; after all, he lived abroad off the radar, it just paid to play it safe. It was why he'd never been caught.

After checking in, he'd sort out the car and then make some calls. He'd already rung that idiot Moon to tell him he'd arrived. He wouldn't be seeing him until the following day, or even the day after – Monday – so, that was a blessing in itself. It gave him time to scope the place out, and meet the driver his contact in London was sorting, probably tomorrow. Then his mobile rang and the screen just said 'London', which he knew meant his contact there. He took the call. Apparently, the contact had heard from his man on the MV Nirvana; everything was on schedule; the ship would arrive on Tuesday as expected.

"What about the driver?" Bentine asked.

"Yeah, he'll be with you by Monday at the latest," his contact answered, with what Bentine thought was hesitation.

"Everything, all right on that front?" Bentine pushed.

"Absolutely," the contact answered, sounding more confident, "just don't like saying too much on these things. Are you staying where you said you were going to stay at?"

Bentine said that he was, and the contact said he'd arrange for the driver to meet him there, but he'd give Bentine a further call when he knew exactly when. Ending the call, Bentine lay back on his king sized bed to consider the conversation. Was there a problem with the driver? If not, why didn't he give Bentine a confirmed time and date then? But he shook it off, he knew his man in London was usually reliable; he probably didn't want to give too much detail in one phone call when he can do it in several; safer that way, just in case anyone was listening. Bentine could appreciate the caution and decided to go and try out the hotel restaurant.

**

After Briers left the briefing room, Jane suggested they sort out tactics and get on this job straight away. Burrows agreed, and they grabbed more coffee. Jane suggested to Burrows that it might be good for Steele to take the lead on this one with her, and Burrows could supervise separately. "After all Alpha, you are the team leader," she said playfully.

"It's all right for you being the alpha male," Steele said, "but, it's no fun for me being a right 'Charlie'."

Burrows agreed, of which Jane was glad, it would help Steele prove himself to John, not that he needed to, but she recalled their conversation after he'd finished his induction training.

Fortunately, all three of them knew the London Borough of Newham quite well from their previous lives. Set in the East End, it had undergone a substantial facelift over recent years. Not least thanks to the 2012 Olympics and Paralympics being held at Stratford, which was part of the borough. It was fast becoming one of the new places to live and work and substantial investment and regeneration was ongoing.

Jane knew that the estate where Hixson lived in Stratford – the Carpenters estate – was one of the beneficiaries; Newham Council together with the University of Central London were spending vast amounts on the area, Jane knew this from reports she had read in the local papers. "It said in the intelligence brief that the Hixson family used to live in one of the tower blocks that are highlighted for demolition," Jane said.

"Yeah, and looking at the map on my smart phone, he has been re-located with his parents just around the corner from where Albert Finlay lives," Burrows added.

"We've got this job at just the right time," Steele added, "poor old Albert's problems are obviously about to get even worse."

Burrows said he would head off first in the Mondeo and cover the Hixson address for any signs of activity, Jane and Steele should take the Vauxhall Insignia that Briers had given Steele, and have a ride past Albert's address. They would stay in radio contact. Jane suggested that they did an area search if there was no sighting of Hixson whilst Burrows kept the home address warm. That agreed, they all headed towards the underground car park.

As Jane and Steele reached the Vauxhall, she suggested she drive, and then explained why.

Steele nodded, saying, "It may take a few hours to find Hixson though, he's probably still in his pit from last night's anti-social activities."

Jane just raised her eyebrows as she climbed into the drivers' seat. She drove the short distance to Victoria Embankment and headed east, keeping the Thames to her right. It was only a few miles before they reached the East India Dock Road, which took them onto the A13 Barking Road. Finlay's address was on an estate to the left. Many of the terraced houses were on short streets all linked on the north side of Barking Road. The sat nav finished the journey for them, and they drove past number ten, of what appeared to be a quiet side street full of pavement fronted terrace houses. Some were red brick, and some had cladding on their fronts. Unfortunately, number ten had cladding, well part cladding, and part worn back to the original brick; unfortunate, as the part facia provided an excellent writing surface.

At the end of the road, they pulled over to survey the plot. "Did you see the graffiti?" Jane asked.

"Some of it, pretty bad," Steele answered.

They drove past again, more slowly this time. Jane could see that some of the graffiti has been painted over, only to be re-sprayed on with fresh obscenities. 'Free blow jobs here. Call any time after midnite' read the largest one in bright red paint against the off-white background. "The illiterate moron can't even spell midnight," she muttered aloud.

As they reached a side road junction Jane saw a woman in her forties struggling with two bags of shopping. She looked local. Jane had an idea; she pulled over and told Steele to hang on a minute as she climbed out the car in front of the approaching woman. "Sorry to bother you," Jane started.

Slightly stunned, the woman stopped and looked up at her.

"We are looking to buy a house in the area," she said, glancing back towards Steele in the car, whom she'd noticed had now dropped the drivers' window. Turning back to the woman with the bags, she continued. "We hear it's an up and coming place to be, and a good time to buy at the right price."

The woman didn't answer, as if waiting for a question.

"And we really like what we see, but couldn't help noticing the graffiti on the outside of number ten. I was wondering if you lived round here and—"

"It's a great place to live," the woman interrupted, "it's just that the old guy who lives there has some problems with some local boys."

"Oh right, can't anything be done to help him?"

"Oh no. No one gets involved; it's not anyone else's business. Anyway, some folks say he done stuff to bring it on himself. I gotta go."

Before Jane could speak again, the woman was off down the street. She climbed back into the Vauxhall and turned to Steele. "You hear that?"

"Yeah. No one gives a toss. And I've noticed something else."

"What's that?"

"Number ten is the only house with graffiti on it."

CHAPTER THIRTY-ONE

"Contact, contact, contact," Jane's radio earpiece burst into life with Burrows' northern tones, "Alpha has eyeball with the subject, he's leaving his H.A. and is walking east generally in the direction of the victim's address. Beta, Charlie, receive the last?"

Jane acknowledged for them both, and they listened intently to Burrows' commentary over the next ten minutes. He had left his vehicle and was now shadowing Hixson on foot. Steele, was following on a map on his smart phone, and had confirmed to her that Hixson was heading their way. They stayed where they were, parked up on the opposite side of the road, about twenty metres past Albert's address, each using their door mirror to get a view to the rear.

As Jane saw a figure in the distance approaching she swivelled in her seat to get a better view. Still using the seat's headrest for cover, she looked through its open centre and could see a figure nearing. She could also see Burrows thirty or so metres behind him. Confirming this with Burrows, Jane took over the eyeball and watched as Burrows did an about turn and headed back to collect his car. She and Steele would take it from here.

As the figure approached, the person Burrows said was Hixson came into clearer view and she could recognise him now. They would wait until he passed, and then Steele said he would take up the foot follow. She would shadow him in the motor.

Jane watched Hixson as he drew closer to number ten; saw him turn to face the house. No doubt, the bastard couldn't resist admiring his graphic handiwork. But then he stopped, turned and walked down the short path to the front door. She prepared to get out and go after him, thinking he was about to barge his way into Albert's home and do God knows what.

"Wait one," Steele said.

Jane peered, and could see that Hixson wasn't banging on the door or anything; he was fumbling with something between him and the door. Then she saw him lean back slightly, whilst appearing to hold and touch the centre of the front door.

"He's holding the letter box open," Steele explained.

Dread coursed through Jane, thinking he was about to put a lit match or similar through the hole. Then she saw it. He let go of the letterbox and stood further back, whilst he finished urinating over the outside of the door.

"The dirty little bastard," Jane spat.

She watched Hixson shake before he put himself away, and then carry on walking down the street towards them.

"Ready?" Jane asked Steele.

"Damn right," came the reply.

Hixson passed without giving them a second glance and turned right onto a further side street. As soon as he'd turned the corner, Steele leapt from the car and started walking behind him. Jane drove up to the junction, but waited before going further, she could just see enough. The road was almost identical to Albert's but longer. At its end, on the junction with Barking Road, was a large supermarket. Jane waited for more distance between them before she turned into the road proper. She saw Hixson and then Steele cross over onto the same side as the supermarket.

"At the next back alley," Steele said via her earpiece.

"Yes, yes. I'll move up," Jane responded.

"Alpha to the eyeball permission," came Burrows' voice.

"Go ahead," Steele said.

"I'm making ground. Mobile, two minutes away, if you need any help?"

"Keep coming, John, but I should be OK," Steele replied.

Having turned the corner Jane was catching up, but slowly, she didn't want the car engine to startle Hixson, who was now about ten feet away from a back alley. Steele upped his pace. He was closing fast.

As Hixson reached the alley he started to turn around, but Steele was right behind and shoved him hard with both hands, sending him flying from sight into the back entry. Jane drew the car to a stop across the back of the entrance and reached across to open the rear nearside passenger door. She looked up to see Hixson pick himself up off the cobbled floor, a started, but hate-filled look on his face. Steele moved towards him, partially blocking her view, and then stopped. Something was wrong. She jumped out of the car and could see the two men facing each other three or four feet apart. No one was speaking. But Hixson was clearly pointing a small black handgun directly at Steele. She hadn't expected this.

She ducked down using the car for cover, made her way to the boot, and opened it. She'd lost her view down the alley, but was more concerned about getting to the gun-safe in the boot where Steele's handgun would be.

Then she heard a cry of pain, and it wasn't from Steele. She raced around the corner to see Hixson bent double with both hands holding his crotch, whilst Steele was picking up the discarded gun.

"Are you mad?" Jane said.

"Replica," Steele answered.

"You hoped."

"I could see the end blocked off," Steele finished.

Jane was still amazed, but just nodded as Steele used a set of plastic cuffs on Hixson.

"You've got it all wrong pig," Hixson said, adding, "I had just found that lying in the street. Was on my way to your pig shop like a good citizen, innit. When you grabbed me, which by the way is assault man, I was trying to hand it over to you as I knew you was a pig, innit."

Steele then slapped Hixson hard across the face, saying, "That's an assault. And I'm not a pig, *innit*."

Hixson didn't answer, but suddenly looked less sure of himself than he had a moment earlier. Steele asked her if the boot was 'secure'. She took that to mean the gun-safe, and said that it was. Burrows then appeared, and between them, they dragged a non-compliant Hixson to his feet.

"You making a big mistake, man. You don't know who you disrespecting," Hixson said, moments before Jane covered his mouth with gaffer tape.

The men bundled Hixson into the boot of the Vauxhall, and Steele re-joined her in the front. Burrows following on behind, they turned right onto Barking Road and headed east towards the North Circular Road.

CHAPTER THIRTY-TWO

"That was pretty brave of you back there," Jane said, as she drove.

"Nah, I could see that the end of the barrel was plugged," Steele answered, with added gusto.

"Even so, it could have been a shadow you were seeing at the end of the gun, as opposed to it being blocked off."

"Now you tell me that," Steele said, grinning, before dropping his smirk and shouting at the muffled banging noises coming from the boot. "Shut up you noisy bastard or I'll knock you out."

The banging stopped.

"Be careful, Larry," Jane whispered. "I know you were shouting but he obviously heard you."

"Fair point," Steele said, "silent running till we get there."

Jane nodded as she drove towards the Motorway. They had initially planned to take the M11 up to Epping Forrest in Essex, but later decided they could do with somewhere nearer. Steele had found a place between Stratford and Enfield, just off the North Circular. There were a number of reservoirs there, and one of the smaller ones called Banbury Reservoir was very close to the main road, ideal for their purposes.

It wasn't long before they were off the main drag onto a county road called Folly Lane, which Jane thought was quite an appropriate name. It had fields on one side and the reservoir on the other. It was like being in the country but without leaving

London, which meant housing estates wouldn't be far away, so they would still have to be careful.

***

Moon drove the Land Rover Discovery he'd borrowed into the deserted farmyard in Beacon Fell. A country parkland situated a few miles from Preston, out of the city and up in the hills. It was on the edge of the Forest of Bowland, an area of outstanding natural beauty. Moon knew the place had been designated a Country Park since 1970 – he used to visit as a teenager in the early seventies. He picked the spot; as he knew it would be quiet at this time of year, save for the odd rambler.

He parked up next to the caravan and saw the curtain twitch as he approached. By the time he'd got there, Phil had opened the door for him.

"How's our house guest, or should I say caravan guest," Moon quipped.

"Good one, boss. Yeah no probs," Phil replied.

"And have you kept your brother's perverted hands off her?" Moon asked.

"He's been good as gold, he wouldn't," Phil answered, with what Moon discerned as a mixture of defence and annoyance.

"Good, keep it that way," Moon finished, as he climbed the step and entered the twin wheeled-based caravan.

At the end, on the window seat, he could see Susan Crabtree looking pensive. She was an attractive woman in her thirties who would be very attractive but for the fearful look on her face. She had been crying and her mascara had run down her face making her look like Morticia from the Addams Family. He scolded Phil's brother Bill who was sat next to her, and then turned to face her. "I'm sorry this idiot hasn't let you freshen yourself up, we are not barbarians, well not with coppers' wives anyway; some of us aren't that dumb."

"Look, I don't know what's going on but if you let me go now, I swear—" Susan started to say.

Putting his hand up to silence her, Moon continued, "Look, it's complicated; we just need you to travel with us and behave for a couple of days at most and then it'll be over. Trust me; no harm will come to you if you don't kick off. It's not you we're interested in."

"A couple of days. Oh my God," Susan started to say before putting her hand to her mouth. She started to cry again.

"Fucker keeps doing that," Bill said, which took Moon slightly aback as he rarely spoke to him when his brother Phil was there.

"Shut up, Bill," Phil said from by the door. "Look, boss, we'll take real good care of her now. In fact, now I'm back, I'll stay in here with her and Bill can drive."

"Good idea," Moon said. He wished he'd thought of using a caravan when they'd lifted Townley, it made far more sense. It also meant they could take the hostage with them to Southampton. He could keep a tighter control on things this way.

He then told Susan that they'd start travelling through the night and through most of Sunday. They would park up for a couple of nights, but by Tuesday night at the latest, it would be all over and she would be free. She looked crestfallen when he told her this, but once she got over the shock, he reckoned she'd be more amenable having a fixed timescale in her head. A time and date to count down toward.

He knew it was one thing nicking a DI's wife, but he didn't want to have to hurt one. They'd be coming after him big-time, as it was, no point making the posse bigger than necessary.

Ten minutes later, the Land Rover was hooked up to the van, with Bill driving and Phil in the caravan with Susan. Moon was following behind in a Nissan, hired with a stolen driving licence provided by his mate in Preston.

He'd spoken earlier to Bentine, who had arrived in Southampton, and spent most of the conversation moaning about the weather. He'd be glad when he wouldn't have to put up with that Scouser any more.

CHAPTER THIRTY-THREE

Jane helped Burrows walk the struggling Hixson from the boot of the Vauxhall over towards the reservoir. Steele said he'd join them in a minute. The place was ideal, with a high privet hedge masking Folly Lane, and then open ground to the reservoir. They had even found a small track, which led from the road and took them behind the screen of trees, which was where they left the vehicles.

Burrows ripped the gaffer tape from Hixson's mouth and told him to be quiet or he'd put it back on. He then stood behind him and Jane stood to one side as Steele caught them up. It was Steele's gig so neither her nor Burrows spoke again. She noted Hixson was a big lad for seventeen; he looked older. He was wearing the usual uniform of his generation; a hooded grey top and jeans, which had the crotch somewhere between the knees. At least if he broke free, he wouldn't be able to run too far, she thought.

"Right Hixson, you've got some explaining to do, and it had better be good," Steele started.

"Don't know you man, and don't know what beef you're 'aving whit me. But this an't right, innit."

"First up, cut this pseudo-Caribbean crap. You're as white as baby shite and probably can't even spell Caribbean," Steele continued.

Ignoring Steele, Hixson started to answer, "You badly disrespecting me now—"

Steele slapped him hard across his face, leaving a red handprint on his left cheek. "I said cut the crap. Anyway this is about *you* disrespecting Albert Finlay."

Hixson had lost some of his swagger, but tried to deny knowing Albert.

"You know Albert. It was his letterbox you pissed through earlier."

Hixson didn't answer but Jane noticed him shift from one foot to the other. He'd be wondering how they knew.

"In fact, the way I have it, you and your gang of other baby shites have been making old Albert's life a misery for some time now."

Jane saw Hixson's eyes widen slightly before he answered, "OK, but what is it to you?"

Steele then told him their prearranged cover story. That Albert Finlay was his uncle, that Steele – using the name Eddie – had been away at Her Majesty's pleasure for a few years and was now back in town. And he'd be calling in on Uncle Albert from time to time to check up on him. He also told Hixson that if anything at all happened to Albert or his property, he'd consider it Hixson's fault and come after him.

"But what if some other dude does stuff?" Hixson asked in a voice that Jane noticed had lost all its arrogance and with speech that sounded nearly normal.

"Tough. You'd better make sure no one else bothers him then, hadn't you? If you are such a big man on the street, that shouldn't be a problem."

Hixson didn't reply. Then Steele reached behind him and pulled his Glock handgun from his waistband. Jane now knew why he'd been delayed in joining them. With his left hand, he took Hixson's replica from his jacket pocket. He briefly pointed them both in Hixson's face before throwing the replica into the reservoir.

"Next time, you'll get the real one in your mouth," Steele said, as he inched the gun nearer the trembling Hixson's face.

Then as if he'd read Jane's earlier thoughts, he said, "You're a big lad; someone told me you're only seventeen. How old are you?"

"Twenty-three. Look, mate. You've made your point and I get it, no problems," Hixson said.

Jane also got it; he'd probably been lying to the police about his age for years. The longer they treated him as a juvenile, the better, no doubt.

Steele finished off by warning him what would happen if he went to the cops. He then cut the plastic cuffs and told Hixson to run and not to look backwards. He didn't need telling twice.

"Nice job," Burrows said.

"Thanks, John. I've got to tell you how much I enjoyed that; after twenty years in the cops being stymied by all the rules and regulations," Steele answered.

"More fun, and hopefully more effective," Burrows finished.

As they walked to their cars, there was no sight of Hixson. After a quick de-brief, they decided to head back to Pimlico. Jane said she would put a quick visit into Albert. Less threatening a strange woman knocking on his door, than a man, she explained.

"I get that, but is there any need?" Burrows asked.

"No point in removing the threat, if poor old Albert doesn't know about it, and is still living in fear," she said.

"Nice one, Jane. Larry and I will see you back at Pimlico."

Jane nodded at them and then got back into the Vauxhall. On the journey back to Stratford, she mused at what she'd say to Albert, that was if he'd let her in. But she'd needn't have worried on the last score, as she pulled up opposite she could see a senior aged man she recognised as Albert Finlay at the front of his house. He'd just finished whitewashing over the last lot of graffiti.

He glanced up as she approached, and Jane saw a sorrowful emptiness in the man's eyes. His cheeks were hollow and his shoulders slumped. The old cardigan he was wearing was swinging in the breeze, probably thirty years old, she thought. And now thirty years too big for his shallow frame.

As she neared, Jane put the warmest smile she had on her face to defuse the obvious growing concern on Albert's.

She told him she was from the council and would only need a couple of minutes of his time. He told her he would listen as she was here but that he needed nothing. He was clearly still very independent.

He then looked around, fret lines returning to his brow, "You'd better come in my dear; I don't want no one to see me talking to no one from the council."

Jane followed Albert into his modest front room which had an old armchair and two-seater settee on opposite sides of an eighties coffee table. The curtains were closed, which Jane thought odd. Albert invited her to take a seat as he slumped into the armchair. They sat in semi-shade, the only illumination coming in from the hall. Looking around she noticed a set of glass doors leading from the lounge into a dining room. The rear curtains were also drawn.

Having settled, Jane told Albert she was not from the council, and then quickly reassured him on seeing his fret lines deepen once more. She told him the story of Derek Hixson's visit to Banbury Reservoir. Albert said nothing, looked confused. She told him the story again. Then he spoke.

"But why? Why would you do this for me?"

"Because it's what we do. We don't work for anyone official, we just right a few wrongs, because some of us care," Jane answered as best she could. She wanted her story to be credible, but had to remember operational security, didn't want to give too much away. She carried on, telling Albert about his new nephew 'Eddie', and if he had any further problems he just needed to mention Eddie's name.

She looked deep into Albert's countenance, and could see he wanted desperately to believe his problems were over. She reassured him again, and then made a decision, which she wouldn't be telling the others about; she wrote down her mobile telephone number on a scrap of paper and gave it to Albert. "If you ever get any more problems from Hixson – which you won't – then just ring that number and ask for Eddie," Jane said.

Albert took it and looked like he was starting to believe all that Jane had said. He looked up at her as she rose from the sofa, "What's your name?"

"Just call me Eddie's friend," Jane answered.

"No, I'll call you my angel. Cause that's what you are."

Jane smiled back at him, and saw Albert's face grin for the first time since she'd arrived. Possibly, the first time in a long while.

"Do me one last favour, would you my angel?"

"What's that Albert?"

"Open my front curtains will you. I haven't had them open in five years. Had to shut out what was out there. Now I don't have to any more."

By the time she reached the window, they were both crying.

CHAPTER THIRTY-FOUR

Bentine finished his soup and sandwich before returning to his room to freshen up. It was early yet, just after five, but he thought he would take a stroll whilst the town was busy with rush hour traffic. It would be less obtrusive that way. He'd return to his room later before heading out for the evening. He had his coat on this time as he moaned to himself about the cool air blowing up from the port.

He knew that the port of Southampton was a huge place, with terminals for cruise liners, roll-on roll-off ferries, as well as container ships. Before having a bite to eat, he'd grabbed a town map from reception. The easiest way to the Western Docks would be to take a cab the couple of miles or so up Mountbatten Way; but again he was concerned about footprints, and couldn't be bothered hiring a car until the next day. He'd get the hotel to arrange that. He also thought it was good to get your bearings, and know different ways to and from places. All good security. He'd noticed on the map that there was a train station at Millbrook, which was a mile down the line from the Central Station he'd come in via, perfect.

He walked to the Central Station where he jumped onto a local train to Millbrook. Then, after a ten-minute stroll at the other end, he was nearing the Western Docks, a huge container terminal that must handle thousands of containers a day, he thought. There seemed to be a constant stream of wagons going into and out of the main entrance. Brilliant, their solitary container coming off the back of the MV Nirvana would be as rare as a comedian in Manchester; he laughed aloud at his own humour.

Deciding he'd seen enough, he started to walk back to Millbrook station when his phone started ringing, looking at the screen, he saw it was his mole in Manchester, the one Manc he trusted, he answered the call.

"You settling in OK?" the Manchester man said.

"Fucking freezing, but no worries. How's things at your end?" Bentine asked.

"Sorted. Better than sorted. The man is behaving better than I would have imagined."

Bentine knew he was referring to DI Nigel Crabtree, avoiding saying his name. He'd be astounded if it was any different, knowing that idiot Moon had snatched the bloke's wife. But he was surprised his mole didn't think the same. "How do you mean?"

"Well, I know the toe-in-the-box gag did the business; putting him back in *his* box. But as you know, the previous owner of the toe is now training for the Rio Olympics, yet our man's no appetite to go after the toe-cutter. Reckons he is, but it's all superficial. In fact, he's doing fuck all."

This told Bentine two things; firstly, Crabtree hadn't told the caller about the threatening photos he'd received; and secondly, he'd said nothing about his wife disappearing. All good news.

"Good, look there's another threat hanging over him which should buy us the few days we need," Bentine said. He knew he had to tell his mole something.

"Oh right," the Manchester man answered, slowly.

"I'm not keeping you in the dark; it's just safer you don't know the details. But at least if he's behaving, it'll mean you don't have to, risking showing yourself," Bentine answered.

The caller said he understood, and was OK with that. Said he'd still keep a close eye on him nonetheless. Bentine sweetened the man up by saying he'd 'wire the usual into the usual'. Ten grand should keep him happy. He ended the call.

"'OK with that,'" Bentine muttered aloud. Why did every one think they had a right to know everything? They forget who the boss is sometimes, he thought as he made his way back to the station.

He stopped a minute later on seeing a park bench on the pavement and took a seat. Whilst he had one on him, he'd remind someone else who was boss, and pulled out his phone and rang 'London'. It rang for ages, and he was about to disconnect, when it was answered, the delay angered him. "Don't fucking rush will you?"

"Sorry," came the reply, "I was just—" his contact started to say.

"Never mind that shit, can you talk?"

London said that he could, so Bentine carried on, "I'm getting bad fucking vibes from you. I want to know when your driver will grace me with his presence. Or don't you actually have one? And don't bull me; I'm not in the mood."

There was a pause before London answered. He swore to Bentine that he had the man sorted, but he'd been on another job, which was why he hadn't been able to confirm things when they last spoke.

Bentine bollocked London for not being upfront and then said he expected the driver to be at his hotel at 3p.m. the following afternoon. He added that he expected a text from London within half an hour confirming this with the bloke's name. "You got all that?" he finished.

"Yeah, yeah, no probs, sorry," came a nervous reply.

Bentine then ended the call without pleasantries and carried on his way. It was time to get all these idiots in line, the job was about to get very real, and he wouldn't allow any fuck-ups caused by unprofessionalism; too much at stake. London had done good arranging the ship transfer from Sihnoukville to Singapore, but he was using established contacts that Bentine could have used if he'd been bothered, but the way London had gone on about it had wound him up. After all, Bentine had sourced the purchase of the goods and at the right price in the first place. London's job was facilitating transport, no more.

Thirty minutes later, as he walked into his hotel lobby, his phone vibrated in his pocket. He pulled it out and read the text, 'Sorry about messing you about, boss. Meant no disrespect, 3pm tomoz confirmed. The geezer's name is Gerry'.

He texted back, 'That's better', and then smiled to himself, before dialling a further number; someone else he knew in London.

***

Jane walked into the Pimlico briefing room to see Burrows and Steele already there, they had a coffee waiting for her.

"How did it go with Albert?" Steele asked.

"Good, I'll wait until Frank arrives, save me repeating myself."

Moments later Briers arrived and joined them by the table, he stood, as there were only three chairs around it. Both her and Burrows remained silent and let Steele brief Briers on how the job had gone.

When he'd finished, Burrows said, "He did a top job, Frank," smiling at Steele, "that little shit Hixson won't be bothering Albert again anytime soon."

"Excellent. Still think the job was an unnecessary distraction, John?" Briers said.

Putting one hand up in resignation Burrows answered, "Fair play. You were right. The exec were right. Needed doing, and took no time at all."

Jane then told them all about her visit to Albert – leaving out the fact that she's given him her phone number – finishing off with the curtain remark, which brought repeated tears to her eyes.

"That's great feedback, Jane," Briers said, "I'll make sure the PM as well as the Executive get to hear that little anecdote."

Moving on, Frank then brought them up-to-date on the main job, which effectively meant nothing. He'd had enquires made in Southampton, which told them very little; there were numerous container ships coming in and out the port all the time. He said that the Western Dock was the likely destination for any incoming commercial vessel, and on the plus side, the town itself wasn't very big from a point of view of locating Moon.

"Trouble is, we still don't know what the commodity is exactly, "Burrows said. "We are assuming drugs, and as good a guess as that is, it could be coming in as luggage off a cruise ship as easy as from a commercial vessel."

"I realise this, John, that's why out best chance is to find Moon and then stay on him wherever he goes," Briers answered.

"Any news on the facial recognition cameras?" Jane asked.

"Bit of a delay, but should all be operational by tomorrow."

Briers then told them all to go home and grab some sleep before heading for Southampton in the morning; he'd ring them if anything changed.

"Save you going back to Thame, John, you can crash at my flat in Fulham if you want," Steele said.

Jane was about to offer Burrows the same at her place in Millbank, and couldn't help but feel a little disappointed, when he accepted Steele's offer. Though she did catch a half glance in her direction as they all stood to leave.

CHAPTER THIRTY-FIVE

Burrows was glad Steele had offered to put him up, not just to save any embarrassment by staying at Jane's – he was sure she would have offered – and to save him the drive home. But it would give him the chance to get to know Steele. They had a lot in common, even though there were twenty years between them; they both hailed from the North West, had both worked for the cops in Manchester, and had both been undercover officers.

Burrows was in Steele's Insignia, having transferred his kit from the Mondeo that Jane had taken. He'd suggested they all meet up during the evening for something to eat, but Jane had said she planned a microwave meal, bath, and an early night. It was true they had an early start tomorrow. Steele pulled up outside a block of newly built flats in a side street off Fulham Palace Road. "They probably pulled down a perfectly sound lot of Victorian terrace houses, to make these cardboard blocks," Burrows commented.

"Kip in the car if you prefer," Steele replied with a grin.

"Sorry, Larry, I'm not dissing your gaff. I just prefer the older architecture."

"No worries, it's not my gaff, it's only rented. But I hadn't realised you were a closet Sir Christopher Wren fan."

Burrows laughed, as they climbed out of the car. He kept watch whilst Steele emptied the boot safe and ten minutes later, they were putting their weapons into the newly installed floor safe under the fridge in Steele's kitchen. His flat was on the first floor, which added to the security.

"That'll leave a nice hole in the floor when you leave here," Burrows said.

"No doubt Frank will fix it, he seems to sort most things," Steele answered.

"Yeah he's a top bloke; I've known him many years. Used to work together on the Squad, back in the day," Burrows answered as they each made their weapons safe. He noticed Steele had a Glock 17 pistol whereas he had chosen a SIG Sauer P226 semi-automatic service-issue handgun. His held nineteen rounds against Steele's seventeen, but the Glock was still a very good choice of weapon he thought.

Having washed and changed, they decided to go out and grab a curry and a few beers, before getting back at a reasonable time. The next few hours passed easily for Burrows, and he was enjoying Steele's company more and more. The feeling appeared mutual. Over the meal, Steele kept asking Burrows when he reckoned the curry-house had been built. Also, did he prefer older women as well as buildings? Trying to fight back, Burrows asked what interests Steele had, obscure or otherwise.

"The Blues is about all I can think of, especially the older stuff, you know the old Delta Blues," Steele answered.

"'*I woke up this morning... der der de da,*' what, stuff like that?" Burrows said.

"Heathen."

They argued over who was paying the bill before they agreed to go halves and then made their way back to the flat. It was just after ten Burrows noticed as they got in. Steele offered him a nightcap and when Burrows asked if he had any whiskey, the craic started again.

"Sorry, John, that's an old man's drink. Everyone drinks vodka nowadays, or hadn't you heard."

"All right you cheeky git, that'll have to do, but I'll expect a fine malt next time."

"Next time—" Steele started to reply when his mobile interrupted.

Burrows wasn't paying too much attention as Steele took the call, until he saw a change in him. Suddenly, Steele's face had stiffened; there was an aura about him, his diction changed, even his accent flattened; it sounded bland. Burrows recognised what he was seeing and kept quiet. He could see Steele going into another persona as the conversation lengthened. He listened attentively.

"No, mate, I'm good, sound. Not heard from you in a while. Been slopping out, mate?" He heard Steele say, confirming what he thought.

"No not heard from Mackey in over a month. No one has, probably got nicked," Steele said. A pause.

"Well, after that last job, it proper put the shits up me, know what I mean. So I've jacked it in." A further pause.

"Yeah, yeah, look I'm just a driver man, not that I'm not grateful or anything for the graft, but, but—". An interruption, then.

"OK, calm it, I'll hear you out. Yeah, I'm on my own, go on," Steele said, as he turned to look at Burrows.

Burrows nodded at him to assure Steele he understood, and would keep quiet. Two or three minutes passed, Steele listening and only spoke to add the odd 'OK', and 'go on'. Then Steele finished the conversation by saying he needed ten minutes to think about it, and then he'd ring him back.

To Burrows, this was good tradecraft. It sounded like an old contact from Steele's undercover life was ringing him to prop him for a job. He knew that Steele's legend had been that of a bent wagon driver, which was how he'd got into Mackey on his last job. That was how they'd come across each other. Steele had been undercover into Mackey, and Jane and Burrows had been deployed by the Executive of the Special Projects Unit into Mackey and his boss Cabilla.

Burrows assumed Steele had asked for a few minutes to give him thinking time, normal sort of procedure. It would also give him a chance to ring his old controller to see if they had a U/C wagon driver who Steele could recommend when turning the job down.

Coming off the phone, Steele said, "Well that was interesting," as he headed back into the kitchen returning with the vodka bottle. He topped them both up before speaking. It was as Burrows thought, an old contact in London, of all places, was propping Steele for a driving job. Was offering him ten large ones, but he had to be available straight away, hence why the man needed an answer quickly.

Burrows knew that Steele had to be careful, he may no longer be a U/C but he still had his persona to protect, in order to protect himself. 'Once a U/C, always a U/C' his old welfare officer used to say; he knew that even when retired they had to be careful. They never knew who they'd run into in the future. In Burrows' case, there were areas of south London he'd rarely venture into again.

"Are you going to try and find someone else to pass it onto?" Burrows asked.

"Well, that was what I was thinking, you know, rather than just put him off, but…" Steele let his words hang.

"No, Larry," Burrows snapped, "you work for us now, there's no going back. You're not even a cop any more, let alone authorised to act as a U/C. And we are in the middle of a major job, if you hadn't forgotten."

"You don't understand, John. I know all this, of course I do. But this is different," Steele said raising his hand to stop Burrows interrupting, which really pissed him off, until he heard the rest.

"The man wants me to drive a container wagon," Steele continued. "And he wants me to drive it from the Western Docks in Southampton."

CHAPTER THIRTY-SIX

Burrows stopped himself, and just stared at Steele for a moment before speaking. "When?"

"Next Tuesday. He's paying well over the odds, and he sounds desperate."

"And you have to ring him back in ten?"

"Yeah."

"Why the rush?"

Steele said he didn't know. They both poured another drink whilst mulling over what had happened. Steele suggested the man had been let down at short notice.

"He's probably ringing all his contacts," Steele said, "which is probably why he needs an answer straight away. If we leave it too long, he'll no doubt bell someone else who'll only be too happy to grab the job, and we'll have lost our opportunity."

"You're right, Larry. Look, you ring him straight back and say you'll do it; we can always pull out later if need be, and I'll bell Frank."

Burrows went into the bathroom and closed the door. He rang Frank Briers and spoke quietly so as not to interrupt Steele in the lounge. Briers agreed that they should grab the job before it disappeared, but that Steele should demand a meet with his old contact before the actual job. It would give him a chance to understand more of the details, and Burrows and Jane could follow the bloke away. He also warned them to be available to pull out if need be, as the facial recognition equipment would be going live by late morning. All that agreed, Burrows returned to the front room, quietly, as Steele was ending his call.

"How'd that go?" Burrows asked.

"Brilliant. He is one relieved geezer. He says I've to meet the top man at a hotel in Southampton at 3p.m. tomorrow, and not to be late, this geezer is not someone to piss about, apparently."

Burrows then filled Steele in with what Briers has said.

"Already sorted," he answered, "I've arranged to meet my contact at ten o'clock tomorrow morning."

Burrows was impressed, "Top job, well done, mate," he said, before adding, "anything else?"

"Just one bit of extra info," Steele said pulling a quizzical expression, "for some reason, he says that when I meet the top bloke, I'll have to call myself Gerry."

By seven o'clock the following morning, both men were up and Burrows was making a brew whilst Steele finished his shower. He was starting to regret the last couple of vodkas, hoping a strong coffee would bring him round a little quicker. He answered a knock at the door and let Jane in. He'd rang her last night to bring her up to speed, and could tell she had had the early night she'd planned; she'd sounded groggy when he rang her, and she walked into the flat all bright and breezy. No matter, if the coffee didn't work, the adrenalin of the job would do it.

Steele's man said he wanted to meet him at Heston services, which was between junctions two and three on the M4 motorway heading out of west London. It never ceased to amaze Burrows how often villains used motorway services for meetings or to exchange contraband, usually drugs. That said, the old bill weren't much better; the number of times he'd met U/Cs, or snouts – when he was handling informants – at service stations.

In fact, in some areas it was probably the forces of good and bad that kept the remote ones afloat. Burrows obviously wanted to get the team there well in advance of ten a.m. to give them chance to clean the plot and sus it out. He didn't expect Steele's contact would have any reason to be wary – after all, it was he who rang Steele, and he who named the rendezvous – but it was good tradecraft to take precautions.

Soon after 7.45 a.m., they all left Steele's flat. Steele took the Insignia and made his way to junction one at the start of the motorway, where he said he'd await a call from Burrows who was with Jane in the Mondeo.

He and Jane would approach the service station and carefully check it out. Steele's man obviously knew neither of them, and as it was Sunday morning, the place shouldn't be too busy.

By 9.20 a.m., they had scoped the place fully, and were both happy that no one was loitering about. Fortunately, the place was indeed quiet, so they chose a table in the corner of the main restaurant and called Steele to come onto the services.

After a quick chat, Steele picked a table with only two seats and waited with a brew. Jane said she would choose a table nearby, where she would be able to see Steele's face, but behind anyone sitting opposite him. Burrows then made his way outside to the Mondeo to cover the approaches to, and exits from the car park. The Insignia was parked as close to the service station's main doors as possible with the keys above the sunshade. As soon as the meeting was over, Burrows would follow the man away, and Jane would back him up in the Insignia. Steele would have to jump a cab to the nearest tube station and make his way back to Fulham.

At 9.50 a.m., Burrows saw a shabby brown hatchback pull up near to the service station main door. An equally shabby looking man in his thirties got out and headed towards the entrance. He noted the car's number plate. It was the third such arrival in the last twenty minutes. The first two had been innocent. He passed on the description of the bloke to Jane via his covert radio. "Scrawny build, short dark hair, white, only about five foot five tall, wearing blue jeans and a grey hoodie."

"Yes, yes, Alpha. Confirming Bravo has visual on the man, and can affirm that he's our subject. He's seen Charlie, and is heading straight to him," Jane replied in his earpiece.

Burrows quickly changed the position of his vehicle so he had a good view of the hatchback and was in a good spot to take up the follow on it. It also put him in a different position, just in case the scrawny man had noted his vehicle on his way into the services. Which he was sure he hadn't.

Ten minutes later, and his earpiece erupted in a series of rapid clicks. He knew it was Jane warning him that their subject was leaving the restaurant. Burrows started the Mondeo's engine, watched as 'Scrawny Man' left the service station, and headed straight towards his car. He didn't look around, but was walking with purpose. Burrows watched him get into the driver's seat, start the engine, and start to manoeuvre out of his parking bay.

In his peripheral vision, he saw Jane calmly stroll out the main doors and get into the Insignia. Burrows would wait a few moments before starting to follow Scrawny Man. He watched, as he made his way off the car park towards the exit road; Burrows didn't want to be too close to him from the off, after all there was only one way he could go. He watched the Hatchback slowly make its way towards the exit road passing a parked lorry as it did. Burrows started to move forward. As soon as Scrawny Man turned right onto the main exit road, and out of view, he would accelerate to join him. That way he would only appear in his rear view as they entered the motorway entrance lane.

But as soon as he'd started to roll forward, Burrows jumped on his brakes, and shouted into the radio for Jane to wait. Scrawny Man had passed the goods vehicle and a blue Honda Accord pulled out from behind it, only a few metres away from him. It had two men on board and Burrows saw the passenger point at the hatchback. It was amateurish, showy, and done with no finesse. But Burrows was certain of what he saw; someone else was following Scrawny Man, and they looked like trouble.

CHAPTER THIRTY-SEVEN

Jonny Moon followed the Land Rover and caravan out of the farmyard and towards the M6 at Preston. He'd told Bill to keep to the speed limits to avoid any unwanted attention. He'd hired the black Nissan to keep him separate from the others; if they did get a pull from the filth, he could put his foot down and avoid the drama. How Phil and Bungalow Bill fared would be their lookout. It wouldn't harm him any; it wasn't as if the filth didn't know he was involved, he just needed a couple more days to put this job to bed and he would be off. No one would find him again. Well, not on these shores. He decided to drive through the night, to keep the risks to a minimum. None of the vehicles they were using were linked in any way to either of them, so hopefully it should be OK.

By the early hours, they had reached the outskirts of Bristol on the M5, having stopped at motorway services on the way. When he'd checked with Phil, Susan Crabtree seemed to have calmed down. He'd told Phil to try to get on with her, befriend her if he could; it would help keep her calm. Plus he wanted her awake during the night; he planned to park up during the day, and arrive in Southampton during the early hours of Monday. That would give him plenty of time to meet Bentine, and sort out this driver issue. He still wasn't happy having to use Bentine's driver;

he wanted the chance to meet him before Tuesday and satisfy himself.

They pulled off the M5 onto the M4 before they hit Bristol and headed towards the Cotswolds. He'd told Bill at their last stop to turn off the M4 and head north on the A429 towards Malmesbury where they could pull over and find somewhere suitable to wait the day out. According to the sat nav, that area was only about ninety miles from Southampton, which would make the second leg a short jaunt by comparison to the first. If they found a secure enough place, he might even base the caravan there, whilst he conducted all the business in Southampton.

They travelled north along the A429, which was a remote country road, notwithstanding its A class status. It had no footpaths with high privet hedges on both sides. Moon noticed a break in the hedge where a farmer's gate hung in pieces and called Bill back. They could park up in the field behind the hedge, at least until they found somewhere more permanent. It would do for now though. Behind the hedge would be out of view from the road, and it was very dark with no streetlights for miles. Though they would have to be gone before first light brought out any nosy farmer, but at this time of year, that meant they had hours yet.

Once parked and settled, Moon considered whether he should leave Bill with the Crabtree woman, albeit for only a short while, whilst he and Phil looked for somewhere better to hole up. The alternative meant taking Bill with him, which he didn't fancy. He spoke to Phil, who assured him that Bill would do as he was told.

"He behaved himself when he was guarding Townley," Phil pointed out.

"Yeah, but he didn't want to give him one. Or did he?"

"Steady on, boss, fair play. You know he's always been loyal and obedient."

Moon relented, but to be on the safe side he told Bill to stay in the Land Rover and keep his eyes peeled. He then spoke to Susan Crabtree and explained what was happening. He apologised as he tied her hands to the table, which was fixed to the floor of the caravan. He then gagged her with a tea towel, but before doing so, told her the alternative was to have Bill babysit her. She said she was more than happy to be bound and gagged.

Moon checked his watch before getting back into the black Nissan; it was just after four, plenty of time until sun up. Bill jumped into the passenger seat and they slowly made their way towards the gateway. Moon kept the car lights off until they were back on the road.

Thirty minutes later, they found the perfect spot, even if it was in the dead of night. They had turned off the main road at random onto a single-track lane called Common Road, and after a further random turn, they came to a narrow T-junction of two minor country lanes. There was no hedge opposite the junction where some young farmer had no doubt ploughed his tractor straight across whilst coming back from the local barn dance pissed up, or whatever it was they got up to in these parts. But 100 metres across the field past the opening was a small crop of trees.

Moon had sent Phil on foot to recce it. On his return to the vehicle, he said it was a dense clump of trees with a gap on the blind side big enough to drive their vehicles into, and be out of view. It was only to while away the daylight hours, as they'd be gone by nightfall tomorrow, so on hearing Phil's description, Moon agreed, and they headed back to get the Land Rover and caravan.

On arrival back at the field, Moon checked his watch; it was 4.40 a.m., still plenty of time to move everything and be settled before it became light.

He'd turned the lights off whilst still on the road and checked that there were no vehicles approaching. There weren't; in fact, he hadn't seen any since they first arrived. Moon then carefully turned right onto the uneven surface of the field and headed back to where the other vehicles were. He drove slowly as his eyes were still adjusting to the total darkness, but took his time, he didn't want to run into them. After a minute or so, they hadn't come across the Land Rover or the caravan.

He could barely see beyond the Nissan's bonnet; if anything, it seemed darker than before.

It was no use, he pulled up to get out and have a look; he must have veered off in the wrong direction. He turned off the interior lamp before getting out so as not to further blind themselves. Outside he could see a little better but not by much. "Can you see where the fuck they are?" he asked.

"Can't see fuck all, boss. We must have passed them."

Moon agreed, and they both got back into the vehicle. Moon said he would have to turn the car headlights on, just to get their bearings.

"You'll probably spook Bill if you do that though," Phil said.

"I'll turn them off again once I know which direction to head in. Even your brother should realise it's us by doing that. And anyway, we'll be on in him seconds. Once I know which bloody direction to go."

Phil just nodded as Moon turned the dipped beam on and swung the car around in 360-degree circle.

He saw nothing. The field was empty.

CHAPTER THIRTY-EIGHT

"Where the fuck…" Moon started to say.

"We have got the right field, haven't we, boss?"

"Of course we have. Look," Moon replied, pointing at the grass in front of them. In the car's headlights, he could see the disturbance to the turf where the Land Rover and caravan had been. Turning to face Phil, he could see he'd clocked it as well.

"Perhaps the bloody farmer's wet the bed and moved Bill on thinking he's some tourist taking the piss?" Phil asked.

"Well, why the fuck didn't the daft twat ring us to say so, then?"

Phil didn't answer him. Then another thought hit him. "What if the local filth has come across them? He wouldn't be able to ring," Moon said, not wanting to think this as an option, as unlikely as it was. He thought, here they were in the dead of night in the middle of nowhere, hidden from the road, how the hell would plod have been able to come across Bill and the woman?

One thing was clear; if they had, then they would just have to do one, and leave Bungalow Bill to his own luck, whether he was Phil's kin or not, there would be nothing they could do. But it would put pressure on the next forty-eight hours though; with no bargaining ploy, the full weight of the nation's police would be after them big time. Did he tell Bentine, or not? That was another problem. The Scouser would do his nut.

"What if Bill's been nicked?" Phil asked, as if reading his thoughts.

"He's fucked then, I don't know what you'd expect us to do about it?"

Phil didn't answer him; he no doubt knew the answer.

Moon then told Phil to do a quick recce in the Nissan's lights, on the off chance that Bill had managed to get rid of his phone in the dark before being lifted, but he didn't hold out much hope. The phones they were all using were untraceable pay-as-you-go, but the call register would lead the cops to the numbers being used by Phil and Moon. They would have to ditch them and get new SIM cards as soon as the shops opened. Moon handed Phil his phone and told him to write down the few numbers that were in them before they ditched them. He was happy that even Bill would have nicknames against the numbers in his phone, as did he. For example, he had Bentine in as 'Scouse Twat'. "Whose numbers did your brother have in his phone?"

"Just you and me; As 'Boss' and 'Bro'," Phil answered.

"Well, let's be grateful for that at least then. But let's be careful. If he's a good boy and keep's stum, we can expect to receive a call from the cops on some bollocky pretence to try to establish who he is," Moon said, as he accelerated hard along the main road back towards the M4. He knew Bill's prints and DNA would eventually identify him to the cops, but that would take time. Especially, as it was five a.m. on a Sunday morning. Or so he hoped; it would give them a head start before the filth joined the dots.

Then, as if on cue, Phil's phone started to ring. He'd finished researching them, and had put both phones into the centre console. Moon could see it was Phil's that was dancing around, and he jumped in before Phil could pick it up. "Let it ring to voicemail."

Phil nodded and Moon placed it back into the central console as it carried on ringing. It seemed to go on forever, and was starting to irritate when it fell silent. Moon pulled over into a layby and killed the lights. He was about to reach for it when it beeped to register that a message had been left. The momentary start meant that Phil got to it first. "Go on then, but play it back on loudspeaker," Moon ordered.

Phil orientated the controls of his phone and the message stared to play. But it wasn't the cops. It wasn't what he'd expected at all. It was Bill's voice. Relief surged through him on hearing Bill's inane tones greeting his brother. At least he hadn't been nicked, and if he had been moved on, it didn't matter now. Moon could simply redirect Bill to where they were, and then they could all head to the clump of trees they'd found earlier. All this flooded through Moon's mind in an instant.

Then he listened to the rest of the message. He could barely take it all in. The dozy half-wit had done a runner. Said he didn't want paying for the job. Cheeky bastard. Said all he wanted was to play with the copper's wife for a few days, and then he'd do one. Said to Phil, to tell the boss not to worry, 'cause when he'd finished having his fun he'd get rid of her where she would never be found.

Moon was stunned into temporary silence before he turned to face Phil, who now had his head in his hands. "Brother or no brother, I'm going to kill him."

***

Bentine had finished his fried breakfast and headed back to his hotel room. He would have time to kill until he met the driver his London contact had arranged for him. He'd told 'London' to make the meet for three p.m. He now wished he'd made it sooner.

No matter, he could always have another wander down to the Western Docks if need be, not that he thought there would be anything else to see.

At least the weather was more settled today, and according to the TV, it would reach a mild twelve degrees centigrade in the southwest; whoopy-do. He wondered what the temperature would be back in Hanioti. Probably a pleasant twenty-four or five degrees. The sooner this job was over, then the sooner he could get back to warmer climes. And the sooner he would no longer have to work with dickheads like Moon. He needed to arrange a hire car, or get that gormless looking twat on reception to do it, then he could have a ride around and familiarise himself with the immediate area. He'd never been to Southampton before; didn't reckon on coming back anytime soon either.

Using the room phone, he told the gormless one to sort him out with a car in the next hour or so, he wasn't bothered what kind; just something mid-range and comfortable. He'd just put the handset back in its cradle when his mobile started dancing around the bedside table. Bentine checked the screen to see who was ringing before accepting the call. "Yeah, what've you got?"

"We're behind him now—" the caller started.

Interrupting, Bentine said, "Careful what you say. I know we are both using clean SIMs but you never know."

"Don't worry, it's me you're dealing with now, not the twat I'm referring to."

"I know, I know," Bentine said apologetically.

"As I was saying. We are close, and I don't think he's spooked, but it's only a matter of time before he is. Even he'll work it out eventually."

"What did he do?" Bentine asked.

"I'll ring you on the other one in a sec, with that," the caller answered.

Bentine was impressed with his tradecraft. He knew that meant his man would update him on where the bloke had been on a different phone. Even if the filth were listening in, they'd only hear part of the conversation.

"What do you want us to do with him?" the caller asked.

"Cancel his contract. I was always going to ask you to do that; we no longer need his services."

"On it now," the caller replied, before the line went dead.

Bentine leaned back into his beside chair as he smiled to himself; he only wished he could be there to watch.

CHAPTER THIRTY-NINE

Burrows didn't recall seeing the blue Honda Accord when he'd recced the car parks earlier, and nor had Jane when he asked her. It looked as if it had arrived after the meet with Steele had started. He wondered why they hadn't gone into the services to see whom Scrawny was meeting, if they *were* there to tail him. He asked Jane what she thought.

"Depends on what their brief was? Perhaps, they didn't know he was due to meet Larry. Perhaps they thought he was just making a pit stop," Jane offered.

It was a fair point he thought. If they – whoever they are – were following him from A to B, then it would make sense to wait on his parked car. They probably thought he'd just stopped for a piss and a coffee. But who were they? He was sure they weren't professionals, well not professional good guys that's for sure.

He waited until both the brown hatchback that Scrawny Man was in, and the blue Honda Accord following him – too closely – were off the car park and out of view before Burrows went after them. Once on the exit road, he just caught a glimpse of the Honda's taillights as it passed the petrol station, he hung back.

By the time he was in the acceleration lane he could see the Honda 100 metres ahead and right behind the hatchback. He pulled into the first lane, matching their speed, which was about fifty. There were two further cars between them, so he had good cover. He could see Jane in the Insignia in his mirrors three or four cars further back. They were headed west towards the M25, and after about two miles, Burrows' phone rang. It was Steele.

"You've got company."

"Thanks, Larry, but we've clocked them," Burrows said, quickly bringing Steele up-to-date, before adding, "but how did you know?"

"I've just taken a call from the guy I'd just met. He's well freaked out. Wanted to know if I'd been followed to the meet. After I managed to convince him that I hadn't, he double freaked, and then told me to watch my back, before saying he was going to ditch. Then rung off."

Burrows told him to stay at the services for now and then he spoke to Jane over the radio and told her to move up closer. As he accelerated to close his own gap, he saw junction four signs ahead. At the countdown markers, he had one car between him and the Honda. Jane was right behind him now. Burrows slowed to thirty, and as he did so, the hatchback did a last minute swerve across the hatch markings onto the junction exit road. He was spooked all right. The Honda went with him, blatantly, only just making the turn in time.

Burrows and Jane made the exit look normal and were about thirty metres behind the Honda when it suddenly put its foot down and drew level with hatchback. As it matched the hatchback's speed, Burrows saw an arm extend from the front passenger window. It spat fire, as the hatchback accelerated out of the danger zone. This was completely unexpected, something else altogether. The Honda went after the hatchback, with all efforts of remaining covert long gone; it was now a pursuit.

The two vehicles ahead took the first exit from the roundabout at the end of the slip road, which would lead to the A4 Bath Road. As Burrows reached the junction, he was held momentarily. He took the first exit with Jane up his tailpipe. He spoke quickly to her and she said that she too had seen the gunshots.

"What are we going to do?" she asked.

"Well, we can't just watch a murder; we'll have to stop it." Burrows knew this would be easier said than done, as both of their weapons were in the boot safes.

Up ahead he could see the busy roundabout junction with the A4, but no sign of the vehicles. He accelerated hard, and then had to stamp on the brakes as he approached the give way line. Fortunately, the way ahead was clear, so Burrows came off the brakes and hit the roundabout at thirty. He was just about to take the first exit onto the A4 when he saw the back of the Honda as it slewed around the roundabout taking the second exit; an effective straight on. Heading straight towards Heathrow Airport.

Then, at the last minute the Honda veered left, east onto a perimeter road and out of view. He wasn't sure if the two hoods in the Honda knew they were behind them now, or not. They should be, but they seemed so intent on chasing Scrawny Man, they might not have clocked them yet; or so he hoped.

Burrows followed, with Jane close behind him. Over the next few minutes, he constantly lost sight of the Honda as the road meandered around the eastern boundary of the airport. Then as Burrows skidded around a right-hand bend, he saw both vehicles parked at odd angles on a large grass verge. The front of the hatchback was right up to a perimeter fence, which led onto tree-lined fields, which were obviously airport property. There were no houses around. Both cars were abandoned with their doors open. It looked as if Scrawny Man was making a run for it, and had used his car bonnet to get over the eight-foot fence.

At least it would give him and Jane the chance to tool up. The only problem being, that there was no sign of Scrawny Man or his pursers.

Quickly, Burrows and Jane put on their ballistic vests and drew their SIG Sauer P226 9mm handguns, with a spare magazine of ammunition each. Then Jane straightened up the cars and closed the doors, so as not to attract attention, whilst Burrows went to work on the fence with a pair of bolt cutters from the boot of his Mondeo. It would only take a minute to cut through and would be safer that way. He'd noticed that the top of the fence had razor wire across it and apart from possibly injuring themselves; it would no doubt leave fibres from their clothing and other evidence including their DNA behind.

As soon as they were both through, Burrows heard two rounds being fired from a small calibre handgun over to their left in a clump of established trees. But he heard no scream. Jane had obviously heard it too as she drew her weapon and they both ran towards the noise. Reaching the edge of the trees Burrows stopped to listen and beckoned Jane to do the same.

Then he heard voices.

"Nowhere else to run now," said a London accent, which seemed very close.

"Look, man I've no idea what the grief is here but if Tony's sent you then this is all sortable." A scratchy voice in a similar accent replied.

"That's the man who met Larry," Jane whispered into Burrows' ear. He nodded, and indicated that they should split up. Jane nodded back and then headed into the bush as Burrows went to his right along the edge of the trees, toward the voices that appeared to be close to a clearing.

He walked slowly on the edges of his feet being careful where he put them. The trees were quite dense, but after a few metres, he came to a halt behind a wide oak tree and things came into view.

Scrawny Man was backed up against a tree in a small clearing, breathing heavily and looking pasty. The two men from the Honda were facing in, both with their leather jacketed backs to Burrows, which was good. Both had a handgun in outstretched arms pointed at Scrawny, which was not so good.

The man to Burrows' right spoke; it was the same voice as before. "Nothing personal, mate, but your contract has been terminated."

Burrows saw the man's gun arm tense and movement on his index finger's knuckle. Decision made. Burrows fired two rounds as he saw Scrawny Man's eyes widen in a mixture of terror and confusion.

One round did leave the man's gun but it flew wildly high as he fell dead to the floor. A blend of blood and gore flew from exit wounds in his chest and sprayed across the face of Scrawny Man.

Burrows then turned his attention to the other man who had spun around and was taking aim at him. The assuredness in his actions, not appearing spooked in the least, as he turned to face down Burrows had all the sign of a professional, ex-military Burrows thought. All this flashed through his mind in a millisecond as he adjusted his own aim to the man's central body mass. He knew it was going to be close. Like a wild-west gun draw.

Time had slowed to a crawl as Burrows took aim; he was still pulling his own trigger when he heard the report of another's weapon. He'd been too slow he thought. Waiting for the pain to hit. But it didn't. Instead, flesh flew from his assailant's face as his skull disintegrated. He'd be dead before he hit the ground.

Burrows looked up in surprise, coated with relief as he saw Jane walk from behind a tree. She lowered her smouldering gun as she appeared from the shadows.

"That was close, God, that was close. But thanks," Burrows spluttered, as he started to calm.

"That's another one you owe me," she smiled, before turning to nod towards an ashen looking Scrawny Man, and continued. "But what are we going to do with him?"

CHAPTER FORTY

"Give me that phone," snarled Moon, as he snatched it from Phil's open hand. He quickly pressed redial, and then waited for the ring tone to start. It didn't, it rang to voicemail. Calming himself, to hide his blossoming rage, he spoke in placid tones after the beep. "Look, Bill, I know I've not always been that easy on you, but we have a problem here. I need you and the copper's wife back with Phil and me. I'm not angry with you, honest," Moon lied, "but, I'm happy to cut you a deal. Bring the woman back to the field before it gets light, keep your hands off her until this job is sorted, then we can all go our separate ways, and you can have the woman, and do as you like. Please, ring straight back when you've heard this," Moon finished, before ending the call.

"Do you mean that, boss?" asked Phil.

"Perhaps not at first, but maybe now I do. Why should I worry after the job is over? After all, her presence is only to our advantage now. We could even let her ring hubby just to keep everything cool."

"I know he can be a liability, boss. But he is my brother, and like you say, after the job is over we are all going our separate ways anyhow."

Moon was genuinely feeling calmer. This could work. Get Bill back with the woman without kicking off and do the deal. He keeps his hands off her until the job is over, then does as he likes with her in lieu of money. More dosh for him and Phil. And the extra dosh will be a good incentive for Phil to keep his cretin of a brother in check.

"Look, Phil, you ring him back and tell him I mean the deal. I'll even split the extra cash with you so long as you keep him onside."

Phil grinned as Moon mentioned splitting Bill's share of the money. He smiled inwardly; obviously brotherly love only cut so deep when money was involved.

Phil then rang his brother and left the message. Moon and Phil stayed in the layby and waited. Ten minutes passed, before Phil's phone kicked back into life again, but this time he got out of the car before answering it. Moon let him go but opened the passenger side window so he could hear.

"No, I'm on my own, he can't hear," Phil said, as he turned to face Moon, who just nodded, as Phil went on to explain the deal.

"Yep, straight up, no come backs, but it'll cost you your share, and you'll have to wait till after the job before, you know…" Phil said, letting his words trail off.

There was a long pause, before Phil waved at Moon and then gave him a thumbs up sign. Moon then shut the window to keep out the cold night air. Two minutes later, Phil was back in the motor.

"You're being straight aren't you, boss?"

"I'll not lie and say I'm not well-fucking annoyed at him Phil, but, yes I'm being straight. It makes sense all round."

Phil then explained that he'd told his brother where the crop of trees was, and that he'd said he would see them there in half an hour or so.

***

"You don't have to do anything with me, honest. Look, I've no idea what's just happened, but thanks, I think. I hope," Scrawny Man spluttered as he wiped the gore from his face.

"Relax," Burrows said, "you're in safe hands, for now. But someone wanted you dead."

Scrawny just nodded as he continued to clean himself with his handkerchief. Burrows quickly searched both bodies. Both were clean, pros, apart from the first man who had a cheap pay-as-you-go mobile in his left hand pocket. Burrows researched the memory; it had only called one number, and had only received calls from that same phone. It also had one sent text message to it, sent twenty minutes ago: 'Will complete shortly and confirm in ten'.

Burrows showed this to Jane before showing the number to Scrawny Man.

"Oh fuck. That's Tony's number," he said.

Scrawny went on to quickly explain that Tony was just some big dude who lived abroad, and paid Scrawny for the odd errand, and to be his London-based contact. He explained about Tony being in Southampton and wanting a wagon driver for a job on Tuesday. His only involvement being in providing the driver, which he'd finalised only this morning. A bloke called Gerry who he'd just met at Heston services on the M4.

"Why would he want you dead?" Jane asked.

"No idea, honestly. Probably didn't want to pay me the ten big ones he'd promised. I should have known; it sounded a lot for a driving job. Too good to be true. But who are you guys?"

Burrows didn't answer Scrawny as he checked his watch; twenty-five minutes had now passed since the dead man had sent his text. Tony would no doubt be wondering what was going on.

"Just hired hands," Jane said, "sent to clear up some mess," she glanced towards the two dead men as she spoke. Then she added, "It's just lucky for you we chose today to do it."

Burrows walked over to Jane and after a brief exchange, she walked up to Scrawny who started to cower. She told him to relax as she wiped down her gun. Both Burrows and Jane were wearing surgical gloves, and Scrawny Man looked on bemused.

Burrows watched Jane put the gun in Scrawny's hand and then grasped the outside of his hand, pushing his fingers onto the weapon before letting go and gingerly taking the gun back from him. She slipped it into her coat pocket before turning back to Scrawny, who was starting to look worried.

"Relax; it's not what you think. Well, it won't be if you behave," Burrows said.

Jane then explained to Scrawny Man what she had just agreed with Burrows. They would let Scrawny go and he should count himself extremely fortunate today. His instructions were clear. Disappear, say nothing about the events of today, and don't try to contact Tony or the driver whom he'd met earlier. In fact, never contact either of them again.

"Yeah, absolutely, no probs. But why did you do that?" he replied, nodding towards Jane's pocket.

If you ever speak to anyone about the events of today, then this gun – the murder weapon – to use police jargon, will find itself delivered to a local police station. See where I'm going with this?"

By the look of horror on Scrawny Man's face, Burrows could see that he'd caught on.

"Yeah, yeah I get it," Scrawny said.

Burrows then told him to use the hole he'd cut in the fence, and to make sure he wiped the top of the fence in case he'd left any fibres. The man nodded and was gone.

By the time Burrows and Jane got back to their car, the brown hatchback had left. An old newspaper, presumably from Scrawny's car, was on fire at the foot of the fence and grass around it was quickly catching alight. He'd certainly got the message. Burrows was also sure they had covered their own tracks adequately.

Five minutes later, Jane had driven them around the corner and pulled over. Burrows took the baddies' phone out of his pocket, and as discussed with Jane during the short drive, he started typing a text message to Tony: 'Confirming completion', remembering the phrase the dead man had used in his earlier message, 'sorry about delay in replying. No problems'.

Within a minute, a reply came back, 'Gud. Fees will be paid into your a/c, now destroy handset'.

Burrows showed Jane the response.

"At least we have a head start now. No doubt this Tony and Moon are going to come together," Jane suggested.

"I guess," Burrows said, before adding, "let's go and collect Larry, while we work out what the hell we're going to tell Frank."

CHAPTER FORTY-ONE

Bentine pulled his hire car over to the side of the road in order to read the incoming text. He read it, smiled, and then sent a reply. He was on his way to try to find a country pub on the outskirts of the city. The traditional Sunday roast was one thing that he did miss from old Blighty.

He'd saved ten grand not paying his 'London contact', re the driver Gerry, but would need that to pay for the shooters instead. He knew better than to mess about with those types. Plus, he didn't know when he would need their services again. No, his London contact had outgrown his use, and his cheek on the phone the other day had sealed it. His last task had been to arrange the driver, and that done, his services were over. Net cost the same, but with a problem removed.

The driver Gerry had better live up to the mark as well, he thought. Though, in fairness, all he had to do was drive, and now with no links back to the guy who'd hired him, he'd be expendable as soon as the job was over.

Bentine had never been arrested, and he intended to keep it that way; cutting all unnecessary loose ends once a job was done was just plain common sense. How morons like Jonny Moon kept ahead of the law was a surprise to him. Just showed how thick the northern plod must be, he thought.

Before he'd cut his London man loose, he'd managed to get the details from him of the man on the ship. The one with the satellite phone. He'd even got him to ring Captain Pugwash – as he'd started to refer to him as – so he'd expect calls from Bentine from thereon in. The idiot in London had bought the ruse that as Bentine was now in Southampton, he'd need direct contact with Pugwash as the ship docked. "Cut out the middle man", he'd said to him. Once London had agreed that, he did indeed cut out the middleman; he had no further use of him. Giving that element of control up had been a schoolboy error, Bentine thought. He'd signed his own death warrant.

He then made his first call to Pugwash to introduce himself, to back up London's earlier call to reference him. Apparently, there were no problems and the ship was on schedule to arrive on Tuesday. Happy days.

One thing still irked though; he didn't know who the buyer was. That was Moon's little secret. And as the money, and it was serious money, was coming from him, or her, there was little he could do. He hated not being in total control, but he knew even Moon wasn't thick enough to share that info with him. He would have to put up with the tiresome Manc for a while longer.

He re-joined the traffic, which was light, as he continued his journey. He'd go and enjoy a leisurely lunch and then sus out this driver Gerry at three. Then he'd ring Moon up, just to keep on his case.

***

Burrows ended his call and swivelled around to face Jane, as Steele walked out of the service station towards them.

"What did Frank say?" she asked.

Burrows didn't answer, but waited the few seconds until Steele had jumped into the back seats. "He wobbled a bit, at first, but I could only say 'two unexpected have had to be removed'. He relaxed when I said we'd cleaned the area."

"Shit," Steele added.

Then, Burrows and Jane between them filled Steele in as to what had just happened.

"What now then?" Steele asked.

"Frank wants us back at Pimlico straight away, for a debrief."

"Did you mention this Tony and his phone?" Steele asked.

"I just said we had new digits for the man above Jonny, said I'd text them to him so he can have it looked at whilst we are en route back to the office."

And with that, Steele grabbed the Insignia key from Jane, which was parked behind them and said he'd take that. Jane said she would text Frank as Burrows drove, and all three set off back towards London.

Forty-five minutes later, all three were warming a brew around the oak table in the subterranean briefing room, whilst Burrows thought about what he'd say to Briers, when Frank walked in with his usual bluster and businesslike gait. He sat with them and Burrows waited until the steel door shut before he spoke.

"I've no idea who the two we took out were, but certainly one of them looked ex-military," Burrows started.

Briers stayed silent, inviting Burrows to continue, which he did. "They were just about to execute the man who Larry had just met at the services, so we had no option, but to act."

"Relax," Briers said, as if sensing Burrows' unease. "Remember this is the Special Projects Unit, and we have the PM's remit to operate outside the law. The reason you three were selected, is that we trust you to make these decisions without the fear of continually having to justify yourselves, or worse, finding yourself before a judge and jury."

The tension in the room lifted, and Jane and Steele then joined in. Between them, they brought Briers fully up-to-date. When they'd all finished, Briers checked a manila file he had in front of him, before answering.

"That's fine, and by the sounds of it, you've managed to cover your tracks well. We are covertly monitoring the Met's airwaves, and they are en route to the scene of the fire, which has spread a little, but won't be a problem according to the senior fire officer on the scene. The bodies haven't been discovered yet, but that's only a matter of time. As for the number you texted me, it's a non-registered pay-as-you-go."

"We reckoned as much," Jane said.

"Though we are arranging a live cell site analysis, so as long as it's still turned on, we should be able to pinpoint and follow it," Briers added.

"Unless this Tony guy bins the SIM card," Steele said.

"Always a ray of sunshine, aren't you, Larry?" Jane interjected, grinning.

"On a more positive note the facial recognition cameras are up and running on all routes into Southampton, so hopefully we will pick up Moon, either today or tomorrow on his way in," Briers said.

"Brill," Burrows said.

"We have to remember our prime objective is to secure the safe release of Susan Crabtree, before we sort these bastards out," Briers said.

Burrows was always slightly surprised when Briers swore. In all the years he had known and worked with him, on the Serious and Organised Crime Agency, as was, and the National Crime Squad before that, he could count on two hands the number of times he'd heard Frank Briers profane. It just wasn't his way. An indication, Burrows realised, of what he thought of Moon and his associates' strategy of randomly kidnapping people to browbeat the forces of good.

Going forward, Briers agreed that it was too good a chance not to let Larry deploy as 'Gerry' the driver and make the three o'clock meeting with Tony in Southampton. Though, this obviously came with its own risks after the events of this morning. In order to reduce those risks, Briers said he wanted Jane to accompany Steele to the meeting.

"Might that not spook Tony?" Steele asked.

"Don't mind if it does," Briers answered, "just remember the job is in two days' time, and Tony *thinks* he has just eliminated his London based contact – albeit a little prematurely for my liking – so, that should be to our advantage. Don't forget, Larry, would you 'as a bent lorry driver', just go and meet someone propping a job to you, blind?"

"Fair point," Steele answered.

"And if he doesn't like it, tough. You just say you are a two-person team, and you're surprised your contact didn't mention this. After all, he won't be able to speak to his contact, as far as he's concerned."

"What if he walks away from us?" Jane asked.

"No matter, because you'll have put this on him," Briers said, before placing a small black round plastic counter on the table. It was about half the size of a casino chip, but thicker.

Burrows knew straight away it was a tracking device, and he knew the others would realise too.

"Those things are getting smaller and smaller," Steele observed.

"Never mind that, Larry – or Gerry, as I should start calling you – but how do we manage to get that onto Tony unseen?" Jane asked.

Briers leaned back into his chair, smiling. "That's a tactical issue, Jane, I'm sure you'll find a way."

They then sorted out some admin before Briers stood to leave. "But don't forget, as soon as we get a hit on Moon from the cameras, he remains the primary objective; find him and free Susan."

Burrows and the other two all nodded as Briers made his way out of the room.

CHAPTER FORTY-TWO

Moon drove through the gap in the fence and around the rear of the cluster of trees. It was as Phil had described: a wide entrance at the rear leading into a clearing in the centre. Not overlooked for miles.

Having backed his car in, he killed the lights, and told Phil to wait at the junction for his brother to arrive. As soon as Phil left, Moon further manoeuvred his vehicle to allow room for the caravan and Land Rover combo. There would be just enough room. Ideal for wasting the daylight hours. He still intended to travel through the night and find somewhere outside Southampton to use as a forward base, whilst the job was finalised. He couldn't risk leaving Bill and Crabtree's wife here now; he'd need to keep them close to hand after what had taken place.

He wasn't bothered what happened to Susan Crabtree. He realised as soon as her husband was off his leash he would come after them big time. That didn't worry Moon, as after he'd been cashed up he'd be long gone. But, until then he had to keep him on his lead, which was why he needed to protect his wife from that moron Bill for a little longer. In fact, as soon as they'd had some sleep, he'd let Susan ring her husband to confirm she was OK and that it'll soon be over, just so long as he kept to his side of the bargain.

He was roused from his thoughts by the sound of a diesel engine approaching. Moon reached into his inside jacket pocket to feel the reassuring contours of his Glock handgun. Then he relaxed, as the Land Rover and caravan drove head first into the clearing, coming to a stop by his driver's side. He'd have to take a deep breath before he spoke to that idiot Bill. He wasn't known for his ability to control himself, but he knew he would have to, for a while longer anyway.

Thirty minutes later, he'd eased the atmosphere between a contrite Bill and himself, and he'd spoken to Susan Crabtree to reassure her. She almost, seemed pleased to see Moon. He spoke to her on his own, telling Bill and Phil to wait outside the van.

"I'm sorry for what that twat has put you through," he could see the terror still etched on Susan Crabtree's face as he spoke. Deep lines in her brow that he'd not noticed before accompanied by dark patches under eyes that almost looked like black eyes. He paused, and then added. "That moron's not touched or harmed you in any way, has he?"

She sighed before she spoke, "No, but I was very, very scared. He's a monster, look; there really is no need…" Susan started, before Moon put his hand up.

"I wouldn't let anything happen to you now; it'll all be over in a day or so. I'll even let you speak to your husband tomorrow," Moon said, noticing relief on her face, "just get some kip for now."

The woman just nodded a reply, and Moon got out the caravan. He then spoke to Bill and Phil, and arranged shifts, so that one of them was awake at all times. He told Phil to kip in the caravan, and Bill to kip in the Land Rover whilst he took the first watch in the hire car. Things were back under control.

Moon didn't sleep too well, and as soon as the sun was up, he was wide awake. It was gone eight and in any event he needed a piss. It was a beautiful autumn morning, the sun was shining and there was a heavy dew all around, steaming in the sunshine. Once this job was over, it would be sunny mornings every day for him, but warmer and without the dew. But he was grateful for the mild warmth coming through; it had been a cold night. Both Phil and Bill were up and wandering about. He asked Phil how the Crabtree woman was doing, and he said she was still asleep. He then told both of them to take his car and to go find some food and drink. Told them to drive to the next town, wherever that was, so as not to be seen too close to where they were. Two thickset Mancs wouldn't be the most common sight around here.

Once they were gone, he went into the caravan to rouse Susan Crabtree. She was curled up on the settee at the front of the van under the window, her shallow breathing accentuated by the widening of her nostrils as she inhaled. Moon studied her for a moment. Although, she looked haggard and her clothes and hair were becoming unkempt, he could understand Bill's infatuation with the woman. Undoubtedly, she would be a looker under normal circumstances.

Having gently awoken her, he let her collect herself and gave her a drink of water. He needed her calm and compliant now. Sitting up she thanked him for the water and then asked to use the bathroom.

Ten minutes later, she was as straightened up as she could be, given her surroundings, and looked fully awake. Moon told her to sit back where she had been sleeping, and pulled a mobile phone out of his pocket. He took the back from it and changed the SIM card, before putting the phone back together and turning it on.

"I'm going to let you ring hubby in a minute which will serve us both. Reassuring him that you are fine will keep him to our agreement," Moon said.

"What agreement?" Susan asked.

"That we would release you safe and sound when the job's over, if he keeps off our backs until then."

"OK, but what can I say to him?"

"Don't try and be smart, just say you're OK and it'll be over in a couple of days."

She just nodded as Moon took a slip of paper from his wallet and dialled the number written on it. He heard Nigel Crabtree's voice answer 'DI Crabtree here', then he spoke. "Say nothing pig. Just listen. I have you-know-who with me and I'll put her on the phone in a minute. But remember our agreement, so no funny business. Don't try to trace this call as we won't be on long enough, and the SIM will be ditched straight after the call. You got that?"

"Yes, Moon, I've got that," came the resigned reply.

He handed the phone to Susan, who snatched it from his hand.

"Oh, Nigel, darling, it's me… yeah, I'm fine, there is no need to worry… I've no idea where we are, just by some old wood—"

"Careful," Moon warned.

Susan nodded, before continuing. "We are on the move and I've no idea where we are, so don't ask, please. I just want to hear your voice for a moment. We'll no doubt be at the back of some other old wood, by tomorrow, and I'll probably whine when we get there. Anyway, how are the kids?"

A long pause followed, which Moon didn't like, so he took the phone back from Susan, and on putting the handset to his ear, he heard Nigel Crabtree's voice once more.

"Look, I hear what you say, but don't really understand, but tell Moon I'll keep to our agreement."

"You better had," Moon said, sensing the surprise at the other end as he continued, "all you need to know is that she stays safe, so long as you stay away." Moon then cut the connection before Nigel Crabtree could reply. He then turned the phone off and changed the SIM cards back again, before turning back to face Susan.

"What did you mean, 'we'll no doubt be at the back of some other old wood, by tomorrow'?" The phrase jarred with him, but he wasn't sure why.

"Just trying to put him off by saying that we're on the move, honest."

"Yeah, well, he now knows we're somewhere rural. I told you no funny stuff." Moon could feel his anger rising, and was considering giving her a slap.

"Yeah, but that hardly narrows things down, and I said we are on the move anyway. Look, I'm sorry, I don't know what I'm saying," Susan said, before starting to cry.

Moon realised that she was right, no real harm done, and his temper eased. He could hardly slap her after he'd told Bill to behave around her. It might give that thick twat the green light in his small mind. And, in any event, he didn't know when he might need her to speak to her husband again. He kept himself calm.

"OK, ease up, no harm done, but you'd better not start whining either; that will drive me mad. And stop bloody crying."

She did, and then apologised again. Moon just grunted.

As soon as Phil and his brother were back, they'd eat and he'd put the brothers on alternative guard, in case any nosy bastard farmers came their way. Fortunately, it'd be dark by five, and they could get moving to Southampton, which would take them through the New Forest; there should be plenty of places to hole up down there, and be in pissing distance of the port.

CHAPTER FORTY-THREE

Burrows looked across the table at Steele who was reading from the manila folder that Briers had left behind.

"Good old Frank doesn't hang about, does he?" Steele said, as if reading his thoughts.

"What do you mean?" Jane asked.

"Well, my false identity when I was a police U/C operating as Larry the bent lorry driver, was Larry Hewson, I had all sorts of the usual documents to back it up."

"Driving licence, bank cards, passport etcetera?" Jane added.

"Yeah, all the usual. Well in here is a new set; but all in the name *Gerry* Hewson, so as to fit in with what Scrawny Man told Tony."

"Impressive," Jane said.

"That sounds like Frank; always ahead of the game," Burrows added.

"There is also a second set of docs in here," Steele said, turning to face Jane. "Or should I call you, love? Mrs Jane Hewson," Steele finished, as he slid the file across the table to Jane.

"Yeah, that sounds like Frank again," Burrows said once more.

Burrows then poured all three a fresh brew whilst Mr and Mrs Hewson studied their respective back-stories, which someone had obviously thrown together whilst they had been en route back from the services. They each questioned one another over the details of their new-shared history, and once satisfied, they fed the binder through the crosshead shredder under the coffee table.

Burrows told Jane and Steele to kit up and then take the Insignia and he'd meet them at Rownham's services on the M27, which was on the outskirts of Southampton. He said to RV there at 2 p.m., and as the journey would take them an hour and twenty, or so, they had all better get a move on.

In the secure underground garage, they each moved their weapons and ballistic vests between the cars and Burrows put his gun into his shoulder holster. Jane had already said that she and Steele would leave their guns in the Insignia's boot safe for now, just in case Tony searched them when they landed. It would be an understandable precaution on his part. She also suggested that Burrows remain outside, but nearby; he could monitor the conversations and come in if it all went to rat shit. He agreed, but told her not to wear a wire for the same reasons as the gun, but if she adjusted her phone to its covert setting, it would give a live feed, which he could monitor in his motor.

All that agreed they would meet up at the services for a final talk-through, before moving to the meeting.

"Pity we can't just sort this Tony out whilst we have him in our sights?" Jane said, as he was shutting the car's boot lid.

"I know," Burrows said, "but we are stymied until we locate and free Susan."

"I know, just hope the facial recognition kit does its job," Jane finished, as they headed to their respective motors.

***

It was gone ten when Phil and Bill arrived back with food and drink. Apparently, they couldn't find anywhere open, so all they could do was grab some pre-packed food from a filling station's grocery shop. God, Moon hated the country. But at least he'd had some time on his own to think, after letting Susan ring her hubby.

Bentine had previously been pushing him to try to find out who Moon's buyer was. As if he'd share that little gem with him. Jack Jones' identity was his insurance against Bentine trying anything dirty; God, he hated Scousers – even more than the country. It was no doubt for the same reasons that Bentine seemed reluctant to tell him who the driver was. Nevertheless, once that cargo was clear of the port, Moon needed to be on it, there was no way he'd simply trust Bentine to tell his man to drive to the rendezvous for the exchange. At the very least, he'd want Phil on the wagon with Bentine's driver, just to keep everyone happy; they didn't need any foul-ups at this late stage. If Jack Jones smelled any trouble, he'd just walk away, Moon knew that.

Moon had made a loose arrangement to meet up with Bentine tomorrow, which was why he intended to wait out Sunday here and then travel through the night to the outskirts of Southampton. He also knew that Bentine was to meet the driver before the ship docked on Tuesday. Then it hit him; how convenient for Bentine that Moon was out of the way until Monday. The twat was probably going to meet him today, and then come up with some old fanny when Moon landed, saying he had to bring the meet forward but there were no problems or whatever.

He wasn't sure if he was being paranoid, but he needed to be at Bentine's meet with his driver, and the more he thought about it, the surer he was that it would take place today, and not Monday. He pulled his phone from his pocket and dialled Bentine's number.

"Can't a man finish his breakfast in peace, without interruptions?" Bentine said on answering.

"I'll ignore that remark; seeing I've just eaten shite from a garage," Moon said.

"Well, we all need to know our place in life. As for me, I couldn't eat another thing."

"Look, cut the wind-ups, I need a word."

"I sorted of gathered that," Bentine said.

This guy was really starting to get under Moon's skin, he was trying his best not to show it, but it was getting more and more difficult. "Look, I know you're meeting your driver today, not tomorrow; and I want to be there, just to keep everything sweet."

"How could you know that?"

"It's obvious."

"Sounds like you don't trust me, Jonny."

Moon was nearing the limit of his restraint; the wanker knew better that to use names when talking on this thing, now with the job being so near. He was clearly doing it on purpose. Moon, paused, calmed, before replying, "I trust you, as much as you trust me, *Tony*," he started, grinning to himself. He knew it was childish to compound on Bentine's lack of professionalism, but he couldn't help himself. He continued, "I want one of my guys with your man for the duration, just to keep everyone cool, so I want to be at the meeting. The one you are having today."

"Look, no problems OK? You need to relax, but if you insist, come to my hotel, and for fuck's sake don't say its name out loud—" Bentine started to say, before he was interrupted.

"You started it," Moon said.

"OK, OK, let's stay clear headed here, I can get my man here today if it keeps you happy," Bentine said.

"Like you haven't already, but go on."

"As I was saying, I'll bring it forward. Come to my place for four o'clock."

"How do you know your man's available today, seeing you are bringing the meet forward?" Moon asked in almost a singsong way, just not quite that obviously.

"Look, you've got what you want. OK, the driver will be here at four, so see you then," Bentine finished and then cut the connection, without any end-of-conversation pleasantries.

Moon still didn't trust him, but he'd have to make sure he was there by four, at the latest. And considering they had to get down there, find somewhere to hide the van and Land Rover, and for him to get into Southampton, all before 4p.m., they had better get going. At least it would be easier than waiting out the whole day stuck in this field; he then went to speak to the others.

CHAPTER FORTY-FOUR

Burrows arrived at the rendezvous first, but was closely followed by Steele and Jane. They had a quick bite to eat, and then ran through the job again quickly. Jane suggested if Tony wasn't happy at her being there, then they would just say they were a team; take it or leave it.

Steele said he was happy that Tony would have to take it at this late stage, and added that he would back her up by saying what an asset she had proved to be in the past. If – God forbid – they got a pull from some motorway traffic cop, she was adept at fluttering her eyelids etc.

Everything agreed, they set off for Southampton proper, which was only a few miles away. Burrows had been here before on the squad, but never stayed. His visits had all been a case of following a certain wagon as it left the dock and then surveilling it to its destination.

By two forty-five p.m., he had circled the plot several times, in the motor and on foot, and was happy that there were no lookouts. He hadn't expected any; after all, this wasn't some drug deal going down on a 1960s built council estate in south Manchester, but it always paid to play it safe. Jane had tested her phone's covert settings, and Burrows told her he could hear her perfectly, even when she'd put it in her handbag, which would make it less obvious. Even though nowadays everyone carried a phone, it was always good the less attention one drew to anything with technical kit in, even if it was well hidden.

On this theme, back at the services, they had discussed whether Jane should wear a body radio set, and earpiece under her long hair. At least that way she would be able to hear Burrows. The phone's covert setting was a one-way street; providing a live feed to him only. But after discussion, they decided not to take the risk. After all, the live feed was only so Burrows could hear if they needed back up.

Having found a comfortable position on a public car park, opposite the entrance to the hotel – which was a standard example of the large hotel chain bearing its logo – Burrows told Steele and Jane it was safe to deploy. They had also parked on the car park, but at the other side, and Burrows watched as 'Gerry and Jane Hewson' made their way across the car park. The clouds were gathering and it was starting to spit. This would make Burrows position even less noticeable; not just because of rain obscuring the car's windows, but people seemed generally less observant when it rained.

Burrows checked his watch; it was 2.55 p.m. as Steele and Jane entered the hotel lobby, he saw the glass double doors swing shut, before they were gone from view. Then his mobile rang; it was Frank Briers. Taking the call, he said, "I was just about to ring you, Frank," he lied to keep the old man happy, "there are no worries this end, and our two assets have just been deployed into the target premises."

"I'm not that needy, John, I don't require constant updating, you should know that of all people."

"Sorry, Frank, I do, it was just with you calling I thought…"

Filling his pause, Briers continued, "The reason I'm ringing is that it's game on. Moon has just passed through a facial recognition camera on the A27 at Romsey. I'm afraid you'll have to leave Jane and Steele to their own wits. Don't forget; Susan Crabtree is the priority here."

Shit, Burrows thought, as Briers went on to explain. He'd had the facial recognition cameras placed in lines of three on the approach routes to Southampton as he'd previously briefed them. But in addition, he'd had one speculative camera placed further out on the A27 to try to give some advance warning. They had picked the A27 at Romsey, simply as it was north of the port and a best guess as to which road Moon would approach from, bearing in mind he was coming from Manchester.

"Was the one camera good enough, to confirm it's Moon, or is it just a possible at this stage?" Burrows asked, half hoping, it was just a possible; he was loathed to leave Jane and Steele with no back up.

"We got lucky, John; he was facing straight towards the camera when it snapped him. And here's the thing; travelling right behind him was a Land Rover and caravan combo…"

Briers let his sentence tail off, the tacit suggestion about the caravan obvious.

"How far away?" Burrows asked.

"Best guess, about twenty to twenty-five minutes, tops."

"Shit," he said aloud. "OK, Frank, I'm on it."

He'd no way of warning the others, but he'd no choice as he fired up the car engine. He knew the covert live feed from Jane's phone was a microwave radio link, and not via the mobile phone's network, so it only had a limited range; but he'd monitor it as best he could until he was out of reach. Not that he could do anything, he just hoped the meet with Tony went smoothly, and to be honest, even though they were going in blind; with no prior knowledge on this Tony guy, there was no reason to think it shouldn't go OK.

Quickly, checking his sat nav Burrows realised the only single point that Moon would pass was too far out for him to get there in time. There were potentially two routes he could come into Southampton from, having passed through Romsey. The most obvious one was to jump on the short stretch of Motorway – the M271 – which ended at a roundabout junction with the A33. It was the way they had come from the services so he knew the route. It was also only three or four miles away, so he'd be there in a few minutes. It was the safest bet, so he accelerated hard towards the A33, which would take him back past the Western Docks.

No sooner had he set off, he heard the live feed burst into life. Steele and Jane were introducing themselves to Tony. There was background noise; he reckoned they were in the lobby or other public place within the hotel. Then he heard Tony's voice for the first time. A Scouser, saying, "Who the fuck's the Judy?"

Burrows listened to Steele start to reply, as per the script, when Tony interrupted them. "Look, we can't talk here; you'd better follow me to my room."

Then Jane's voice, "I just need to powder my nose, I'll be with you in a tick, which room is it?"

Good girl, Burrows thought, she's trying to get the room number over the air for him to hear. Then Tony again, "Not a chance, I want you both where I can see you, until we've spoken properly. You can take a piss in my room."

Not so good, though not totally unexpected, for all Tony knew Jane could be a cop, or a grass or anything. But nice try.

He didn't expect her to say the room number as they approached, it would be too obvious, but she might get the chance whilst in the bathroom.

He could hear the sound of lift doors opening, the automated voice, and the ping of a bell, but he couldn't hear clearly. There was a crackle as they entered the lift, then nothing. The signal was gone.

Two minutes later, Burrows parked on Parkside Avenue, with a good view up the A33 towards the motorway. Traffic was light, and Briers rang him back with the full registered number of the vehicle Moon was in, though it should be easy enough to see if it still had the Land Rover and caravan behind it.

"Anything on the vehicle?" Burrows asked.

"No intel, John, but PNC confirms it's a hire car from Preston. Hired two days ago from a local bloke who's not known to us. Probably, just one of Moon's lackeys."

"Thanks, Frank," Burrows said, ending the call. He then positioned his car right up to the junction, along the kerb following its curvature, which led onto the main road. He had his bonnet up to give him a reason for parking so close to the junction, and to give him a reason to be out on foot. Looking into the engine area, he had a good advance view up the road. The A33 here was a long straight urban dual carriageway, and the rain had stopped, for which he was now grateful. Checking his watch, Moon should be here in five to ten minutes.

He wondered how Jane and Steele were getting on.

CHAPTER FORTY-FIVE

As soon as Jane and Steele entered the hotel lobby, Jane could see a set of easy chairs at the side of the main reception counter. In one of them sat a man in is forties, he appeared of average height and build with grey hair, and showed the evidence of too many lunches around his midriff; made to look worse by being seated. He was wearing blue jeans and a white casual shirt. Jane spotted him for two reasons: he was tanned in a way that only the hot sun from the Mediterranean or Americas can do, and he was staring at them. Then, he checked his wristwatch.

Jane nudged Steele, who nodded ever so slightly, but without looking at her; he'd clearly seen him too. Jane could also see two young women in their early twenties behind the reception desk; both were occupied dealing with an elderly couple.

Steele spoke first, "You look like you're waiting for someone? I'm Gerry."

The man answered, "The wagon driver?" in a slight Liverpool accent.

"Yes, that's right, you must be Tony?"

"Must I?" the man said, getting to his feet. "Who the fuck's the Judy?"

Before she could answer, Steele did, as per the script. He was supposed to be the main man, she'd let him talk. She'd sensed a few nerves from Steele as they had approached the hotel. She guessed he wanted to impress, it was his first time acting properly undercover since he'd joined them.

It was clear Tony wouldn't talk in the lobby, but Jane was taken aback when he said they should go to his room. She tried to get the room number so Burrows could hear, but Tony was having none of it. He was obviously a pro, and a careful one. The toilet excuse hadn't worked, no matter, she'd relay the room number once she used Tony's bathroom. She followed both men to the lifts and nothing more was said until they reached his room, which she noted was on the fourth floor, room 412.

Tony used his key card to unlock the door and then held it open as they both entered; it was a large room with a double bed, table and chairs as well as a desk. A short corridor to what she took to be the bathroom, and a large curtain, which covered the outside wall. She thought it a little strange that it was closed. Tony flicked the lights on and waited until the door swung closed.

As it clicked shut, Jane spoke, pointing down the corridor. "May I use your bathroom now?"

Tony turned to face them as they stood in the centre of the room, he had his back to the door. "No, you fucking well may not," he said, as he produced a large black semi-automatic handgun, and pointed it at both of them.

Instinctively, Jane started to edge away from Steele, to divide the targets so to speak, make it more difficult. As she did so, she spoke in a loud voice: "Put the gun down you nutter, God knows what you're thinking." 'God knows' was the emergency signal she and Steele had agreed with Burrows. "I'm only forty- one and you're acting like you're two," she added. Trying to say 412, without being too obvious.

They had agreed if she and Steele needed help, there were two courses of action open to Burrows. He could come in all guns blazing, in which case there was no need for guarded speech – but the job, or that part of it, would be blown; or he could come in as an associate, hired back up, muscle. That way they could stay in character and try to rescue the situation. Managing the risks without blowing the job, Burrows called it. Covert rescue rather than an overt rescue, unless it really went tits up.

"I don't know what you're saying, but if you open your sweet mouth again, I'll put this fucking gun in it. That goes for you too, Gerry, now stand back close together," Tony said, whilst skilfully screwing a silencer onto the end of his gun, and still keeping it pointed it at them. He then threw a pair of handcuffs at Steele, who instinctively caught them, and told him to cuff himself one-handed to the steel curtain pole. Steele did as he was told.

This was starting to go tits up, Jane thought.

He then snatched Jane's bag from her shoulder and emptied the contents onto the floor. Makeup, her false driving licence and her phone hit the deck. Tony picked up the driving licence before he stamped his heel on the phone smashing it.

Shit, she thought, should have called for an overt rescue whilst they had the chance.

All they could do now was stay in character, remembering they were small-time crooks, drivers of knock-off goods, not big-time villains.

"I get this, I so get this," Steele said.

"Get what?" Jane asked.

"This numb nut isn't going to off us, right here in his hotel where he's been staying. He's just being cautious, if not a little rude. At least we know one thing for sure."

"What's that?" She asked.

"The job's obviously legit. He's certainly no cop."

This was good, Jane thought, very good.

"I'm no fucking cop," Tony said with shocked offence, "I'm just making sure you two clowns aren't."

"Well hurry up, search us, ask your questions or whatever, because another five minutes of this and you can stick the job up your Mersey Tunnel."

"And, if we do do it, the price just went up to twelve large ones," Jane added. She was starting to enjoy this; glad she's only asked Burrows for covert help, there would soon be a knock at the door, and they could just say he was briefed to follow them and come after them if they hadn't rung him to say everything was cool.

Five minutes came and went, and there was still no knock at the door. However, Tony had calmed down, he'd searched them both and seen the documents from both of them with their names on, and realising they weren't a threat he gave Steele the handcuff key, and put the gun down. He still had it in his hand, but at least he wasn't pointing it at them.

But no knock at the door. Jane was half-pleased, as it was starting to seem as if they were going to be OK, but half-worried that John hadn't come in after them. Perhaps the live feed had failed: she knew from her time with MI5 just how unreliable covert kit could be sometimes; not like in the movies. It must be down to the latter.

Another five minutes in and they'd been there twenty minutes or so now, and the atmosphere had completely changed. Tony apologised for the affront, he said that he'd never been nicked, and he wanted it to stay that way. Jane noticed Steele showed just the right amount of indignation, but didn't push it too far. Tony even agreed to up their fee to the twelve grand as suggested, so Jane knew they were in. Tony also seemed to like the script about Jane sweet-talking any cops that might pull them.

"But what if the traffic pig is a female? They do have 'em nowadays, you know," Tony asked playfully.

"No probs," Jane answered, "I reckon all the tarts in the filth are probably lezzas anyhow, so I'll give it my best butch voice," Jane answered, and they all laughed.

After thirty minutes, it was all sorted; Tony told Steele where to go the following day to collect the wagon and handed over a set of Volvo keys to him. The ship was due in at the Western Docks around three p.m. They exchanged telephone numbers and Tony told him to be ready with the wagon from two onwards and he'd call him in once the container was ready to be loaded onto the wagon.

"I've just got to ask two questions, Tony," Steele said.

"Go on."

"Where am I driving to, and what's the load? I think it's only fair I know what risks we're taking."

Tony had checked his watch for the second time in quick succession, and Jane got the impression that he wanted the meeting over. She wasn't sure why that would be; she shrugged it off for the moment as he answered Steele.

"You'll be driving up north, that's all you need to know for now. Even I don't know where exactly, which pisses me off a little, but that's nothing for you to worry about. And, as regards the cargo; it's better you don't know. Just suffice to say if it's worth twelve large ones, it ain't fucking toilet rolls."

Jane watched Steele open his mouth to reply, then pause, agog. She didn't know if he was going to push it. She hoped not; not now they'd been accepted. Tony had even apologised for smashing her phone. Had even given her £1,000 to get another one, which was way too much. The only trouble was when she'd picked up her bag and phone bits, underneath in several pieces was the remains of a small round black disc. So, that was the end of that. She just scooped up all the bits together. Maybe Steele had seen this, and that was why he was asking the questions. Then he closed his mouth, and said no more. She breathed a sigh of relief. They had what they needed, no point in spoiling it.

Tony gave Steele a slight nod, almost imperceptible, almost like it was involuntary, as if he was thanking Steele for not pushing it. Then he checked his watch again and stood up. Jane checked hers, 3.40 p.m.; Tony definitely wanted this meeting over. They said their goodbyes and left Tony in his room as they headed to the lifts.

CHAPTER FORTY-SIX

Jonny Moon's sat nav took him straight to the hotel in the centre of Southampton. Fortunately, there was a car park opposite; that would save him time. He hated pissing about finding car parks, but knew he couldn't just abandon his motor; he didn't want to draw attention. He knew if he just parked on a yellow line, as if he was in Manchester, then some twat would be waiting to stick a ticket on it. It wasn't a problem back home. Anyway, he was glad to park up and pay his fee; it would mean he got to see Bentine even quicker; he wanted to get to him well before 4p.m.

They had made good time, but after a bit of mooching about in the New Forest, he'd left Phil to find somewhere secure for him, his brother and the woman to park up. He'd link in with them later. He'd also left Phil with strict instructions to stay with his numb-nutted brother at all times.

He checked his watch as he walked across the car park; it was just leaving twenty to four. He stood at the kerb waiting to cross and saw a man and a woman walk out of the hotel. He only caught a glimpse, but the woman looked familiar. Then a bus pulled up in front of the hotel. Moon couldn't cross due to traffic on his side of the road. Then the bus pulled away, and the couple were gone.

He realised the woman looked similar to that bitch 'Bonnie' who came after him in Manchester, the one he never heard back from after her boyfriend escaped. But the bloke he'd just seen definitely wasn't 'Clyde'.

Those couple of bastards still needed sorting for what they'd done previously. When on their quest to find Moon's mate, Shonbo Cabilla, they had killed two of his men, not to mentioned Bonnie shooting him through his right palm.

What he wouldn't give to get his hands on that bitch. Immediately, the gnarled scar tissue in the centre of his right hand started to itch, sometimes the bastard thing drove him nuts. It wasn't helping his temper any.

As he finished crossing, he realised he must have made a mistake; the bloke was definitely not Clyde; he was even surer about that, and though he only got a glimpse of the woman, he was starting to think it wasn't her either. Just similar. The itching started to ease.

He'd never actually met Tony Bentine, and wondered what he looked like, as he banged on the door of room 412. He'd always imagined him as a skinny snake-like individual. Smarmy like most Scousers, but he got a surprise as a man answered the door, though he recognised him at once by his voice, and his pleasant demeanour.

"You're early, Moon. You are Moon I take it?"

Bentine looked older than he sounded and appeared too well fed to be snake-like, but his swarthy, tanned skin redressed the balance a little.

"We need to set the agenda before your driver arrives, and you can call me Jonny if you like," he said with mock affection.

"Moon will do fine, and you're too late, the meeting's been done."

Moon pushed past Bentine and looked around the room, there was no one else there. He turned to face Bentine as the door closed. He was about to lay into him, when he spoke.

"Look, let's not get off on the wrong foot, the guy arrived early, and then had to get off sharpish, like. I wanted him to hang on but he couldn't."

"What the fuck is this?" Moon said. He was getting a real bad feeling about this.

But over the next ten minutes or so, Bentine spoke to him with more respect than he'd previously shown which initially just made him more suspicious. But he heard him out, and when Moon demanded Phil ride on the wagon with them, Bentine agreed without any whinging. Moon was starting to calm now he had that insurance in place. He was still annoyed that Bentine had met the driver without him, and was sure the bastard had done it on purpose, but no worries. He would have Phil on board watching over things, and in any event, he had other plans afoot. He would have the last laugh.

Having both relaxed a little with each other, Moon thought he'd stick around a bit. Take the Scouser for a beer, be nice for a change. After all, he might be able to find out a bit more about the in-bound ship. He knew it was due to dock at 3p.m. on Tuesday – the day after tomorrow – at the Western docks, but so were zillions of others. He told Bentine he couldn't hang around all night, as he would have to check on his team, which was true. The next couple of hours would be enough. Bentine, who'd agreed to go for a beer looked relieved. Moon took a leak in Bentine's bathroom, just because he could, and then they both headed out.

***

"Bloody hell, that was close," Jane said to Steele as they both settled into their seats.

"What was close? And where the hell are we going?" Steele replied.

Jane didn't answer as she noticed a passenger walking towards the front of the bus; it was clearly approaching a further stop. "Tell you in a minute," she said as she got up dragging Steele with her. They walked back in a circulatory route, to approach the car park from its rear. She'd not had time to explain fully, but she was certain the man waiting to cross the road was Jonny Moon. And, he appeared to be looking straight at her. She rang Burrows as they quickly walked, conscious that Moon could leave at any time and they would have lost him, she also needed to warn Burrows to stay hidden, albeit with a visual on the front of the hotel, as Moon knew Burrows as well as he knew her.

During the call with Burrows, she spoke loudly so Steele could hear her half of the conversation; it would save repeating herself. At the conclusion, she swore as she ended the call.

"I've got the gist, but what's up?" Steele asked.

"Burrows is miles away, that's what's up. Come on let's run."

It only took a couple of minutes to reach the car park and they were able to reposition their vehicle to get a good view of the hotel. They weren't looking straight at it, but parked with a side-on view, but with a full-on view of the whole car park, which was all on one ground floor level. They should see Moon easily as he left the hotel, but without being seen themselves. And once he was on the car park, Jane could hunker down out of view, whilst Steele watched him to a vehicle. They could cautiously follow him away.

Burrows was heading back towards them, and would take up a position further down the road. When Moon left, there was only one way he could go, thanks to a central reservation in the main road outside the hotel. At least that was a help. Steele got back in

241

the car, having obtained a further ticket. He'd noticed a parking attendant mulling about. He closed the door, and then spoke.

"How sure are you it was Moon?"

"Sure."

"How sure are you that he saw you?"

"Fifty-fifty; might have got away with it. Thanks to the timely arrival of that bus."

Jane went on to explain what Burrows had briefly told her about Moon 'pinging' the outer-facial recognition camera.

"Must have taken a different route in," Steele said.

"No matter, now we're on him, piece of luck at last. We'll just have to be careful, as he knows two out of three of us."

"Unless Bentine decides to go for a nice little ride with him," Steele added.

"Sweetness and light, Larry. You're all sweetness and light," Jane answered, hoping he was wrong.

CHAPTER FORTY-SEVEN

Bentine was happy with Gerry and his bird; they seemed straight up guys. Cops would have acted differently, and he trusted his intuition. After all, he'd never been caught. He'd searched them both and they weren't carrying weapons or wires. He'd felt a bit tight at smashing Jane's phone, but he'd more than recompensed her for it. Then the banging at the door broke his thoughts. He wasn't surprised to find the Manc on the other side. He half expected him to turn up early, which was why he wanted shut of Gerry and Jane, once business was sorted. He'd only just managed it too; they probably passed in the lobby.

After he'd calmed Moon down, he knew he would have to placate him. It was more than a constant irritation that he still didn't know whom he was dealing with. Who was the buyer? No matter, he'd find out soon enough, whether the irritating Manc liked it or not. But he knew he had little choice when Moon asked to put his man on the wagon. In any event, it would only be for a few hours. The rendezvous was somewhere in the north, that much he did know. That much, Moon had let slip. So when the Manc suggested they go for a beer, as unpleasant as he found his company, he knew it was a good opportunity. The more he could find out now, the better.

He wasn't too sure what to expect on first seeing Moon, but it was a shock when he saw him. The guy had a small build, weedy-looking even, and had all the physical menace of a choirboy. He looked like Jesus' nicer brother, he thought with a grin.

"What's so funny?" Moon asked, as they walked through the lobby to the hotel bar.

"Nothing, mate," then changing the subject, "anyway, what do you want to drink?"

Moon answered, and having bought them both a lager, they settled down at a corner table away from the bar. The place was empty but for a couple stood at the bar. Over the next ten minutes or so, the Manc was hardly subtle. All his conversation was about the boat. Could he trust the guy on board? And who else had the satellite phone number? Etc. etc. Bentine just kept his answers vague, so it appeared as if he was being cooperative, but without actually telling Moon anything. He'd let him witter on for a bit, before he'd have his go. Once he knew who the end buyer was, he could bypass Moon, hopefully on this job, but definitely with future ones. But one thing was for sure, whichever way it went; he couldn't stand the thought of working with this idiot for much longer. There may only be thirty-odd miles between Liverpool and Manchester, but the differences were huge. It was more than sibling rivalry, far more. It was a complete cultural difference, inbred and ingrained deep into one's marrow.

Bentine's phone rang which brought a blessed relief from Moon's Manc drawl. Looking at the screen it just said 'call', as if the number was withheld, or like an incoming from abroad. Captain Pugwash – satellite man?

"Yeah," Bentine said.

"It's me, Boss," the caller said. He recognised the voice – it was Pugwash.

"Everything OK?"

"No worries, man. Just thought you'd like to know we have made even better time. One of the crew is unwell. Not enough to warrant an airlift, but with being so close the captain's put his foot down. Our rescheduled docking time is twelve noon—"

"That's no problem, it's only three hours difference, but thanks for—" Bentine interrupted, before the man cut back in.

"No man, twelve noon tomorrow. We're now docking Monday, a full day early. Look, I've got to go," and the line went dead.

Bentine put his phone down and turned to Moon who was staring at him.

***

Moon was on the phone as he walked briskly through the lobby. After Bentine told him what the man on the boat had said, he made his excuses and left. This would put pressure on his plans. He'd watched the Scouser put his phone back in his pocket with longing eyes, but knowing the man on the boat's details were not as critical now. Though, he would still love to know who. And from whom Bentine had arranged the shipment in the first place?

The road was clear outside the hotel so he ran across the road to his car and was soon on the main road heading northwest. He'd forced his way into the traffic receiving a tirade of angry car horns, but he had no time to lose, he needed to make the final arrangements with Phil. As he accelerated on the urban dual carriageway, he saw a wagon struggling with its load and quickly pulled into the outside lane to pass, right in front of some Sunday driver who lent on his car horns and then stamped on his brakes, in what Moon thought was an exaggerated move. The driver in the car behind him would no doubt agree with Moon as he ploughed into the rear of the Sunday driver. Checking his mirrors and smiling, Moon sped away leaving the blocked road behind him. That would serve the arsey twat right, he thought. He then headed for the M271, the route he'd come in on.

Twenty minutes later, he was in a deserted picnic area off the main road out of Romsey; Nightingale Wood, according to the sat nav. It looped back on itself hidden from view by a high privet hedge. They'd had to bust the padlock keeping the wooden gate shut, which was perfect; put back in place the gate still looked secured. No doubt, this was a busy spot in the warmer months, but kept padlocked to keep the pervs out in winter – doggers or cottagers, or whatever they were. Moon never understood the difference. These open spaces used to be ideal for drug deals during the winter evenings, until all these fresh air fuckers spoiled it, he thought.

Before he'd left the hotel, Bentine gave him the location of where the wagon would be parked prior to entering the port. It was up to him if he wanted Phil to jump on board on its way in, or on its way out. Obviously once it had cleared the port the risks were considerably less, but it was his call. Notwithstanding this, he said he wanted Phil on board from the off, he'd have him meet up with Gerry from eleven-ish. Bentine said that it might look a bit sus, but Moon didn't care; he didn't trust the Scouser one bit.

He briefed both Phil and his retard of a brother on Plan A; Phil would jump on board with the wagon, and Bill would drive the Land Rover and caravan twenty or thirty minutes behind. He asked how their guest was behaving, and Phil said there were no problems.

"Well, if it helps, you can tell her we'll be releasing her a day early now. By this time tomorrow, she'll be free, give or take an hour or so. That should keep her happy," Moon said.

"Will do, boss," Phil replied.

"Bentine's going to follow me in his hire car," Moon said, before he pulled Phil to one side, and added. "Now I'll tell you plan B."

CHAPTER FORTY-EIGHT

Jane had got her breath back, and had a good view of Moon's black Nissan. According to Briers, it was a hire car from Preston, rented with a driving licence reported stolen some months ago. She glanced at Steele, and although she was getting used to working with him, something back in Bentine's hotel room bothered her. Steele had agreed in being handcuffed to the curtain pole a little too quickly; his compliance came too easily.

Whilst they were waiting for Moon to finish his meeting with Bentine, she thought it as good a time as any to raise it. "Mind if I ask you a question?" she started. Then she elaborated. Steele's answer reassured and embarrassed her in equal measure.

"I took the cuffs quickly so I could control them. They were never locked shut. I put them around my wrist but let them hang unfastened. I turned the back of my hand away from the room to cover it."

Jane could sense an irritation in his voice. "Sorry, Larry, I feel such a jerk for asking."

"Forget it," Steele said, in his normal diction, followed by, "Shit, here he comes."

Jane looked in the direction Steele was facing and saw Moon, having crossed the road, heading towards the Nissan. She slid down in her seat as she pressed the radio transmit button.

"Contact, contact, contact. Bravo has eyes on the target, who is towards his vehicle. Alpha confirm?"

Burrows replied that he was ahead and ready, as Moon entered his vehicle, fired up the engine and headed towards the exit. The dual carriageway meant he would have to turn left. As soon as he exited the car park Steele drove swiftly to the exit give-way and paused, which Moon obviously hadn't done judging by the numerous blasts of cars' horns. "He looks in a hurry," Jane said, as Steele was clearly concentrating on joining the line of traffic, and did so without receiving a similar response from the other motorists. They needed to make ground, fast, but without any undue attention.

She could see the Nissan a hundred metres up ahead steaming towards the rear of a slow moving lorry. She also saw him pull out in front of two cars already in the process of overtaking the wagon. Moon made it past, but the two cars behind didn't. One ran up the back of the other, hit the wagon's offside, and they all came to a stop, blocking the road.

"Bastard," Steele said. "Do you think he sussed us?"

"No, he was just in a hurry, for some reason. A big hurry."

It was clear they weren't going anywhere fast, as they had stationary traffic nose-to-tail behind as well now. Jane shouted Burrows over the air, and he said he would try to take up the follow. Then one of Steele's phones rang and as he pulled it out of his pocket, he looked at it as if bemused.

"This was my U/C phone; it's either Tony or London."

Jane quickly switched off the radio loudspeaker and listened on via her earpiece, as Steele took his call.

"Yep, no probs. We can do that... yeah OK... laters," she heard him say.

Turning to face Jane, Steele said, "Well, we know why Moon was in such a rush."

"Why?"

"It was Tony ringing. The boat's making good time. It's now due to dock at twelve noon tomorrow."

Jane told Burrows over the radio, and then asked if he'd managed to get on Moon's tail?

"Not a chance. He came past me too fast. And in any event I was baulked by other cars." The loudspeaker replied, as Jane switched it back on.

Burrows said it was pointless trying to catch him on his own. Even if he got onto him, he was only one car. It would look like a pursuit rather than surveillance, and if Moon thought someone was after him, it might prove fatal for Susan Crabtree. They couldn't take that risk. Jane agreed, they'd get their chance again, and if he did leave town early, then the facial recognition cameras would surely pick him up. They only had to read his car number plate now they knew its details, which would be a lot easier than reading a face. Burrows said he would head back to the car park to see if Tony went anywhere. Steele suggested they go and check out the lorry.

All that agreed Jane got out of the car to walk back towards the hotel. She would keep a long distance eyeball on the hotel in case Tony left before Burrows arrived. She couldn't follow him, but she may be able to identify what vehicle, if any, he was using. But she wouldn't get too close and risk him seeing her. She crossed over so she was on the same side as the hotel.

Ten minutes passed before Burrows rang to say he was on the car park with a visual on the hotel. She acknowledged and walked further up the road, just in time to see Steele approaching. She jumped in and they drove the short distance to the address of the overnight-stay commercial park where the wagon was. It was a flat concrete park on one level full of heavy goods vehicles, some were tractor units with empty trailers, and some had containers on.

They eventually found their vehicle; it was a white Volvo tractor unit with a long trailer and container attached. Steele said it looked like a forty-four footer. After parking alongside, Steele said he would check the vehicle over and then familiarise himself with the controls. He said it had been a while since he'd last driven an artic but was confident he would quickly get back into it. Said the longest job he'd done was to drive a wagon full of cannabis from southern Spain back to the UK, so he obviously had experience to draw from.

"Were you a wagon driver before you joined the cops?" Jane asked.

"No, it was just after I passed my Level One Undercover training and I was looking around for a specialism – a lot of U/Cs become pretend drug dealers, but I fancied something different – and the bosses offered me a Class One HGV course, so I jumped at the chance. Thought it would come in handy when I left the cops," Steele said.

"Well it has," Jane finished.

"I guess that's true."

He then went on to explain that one problem being an undercover wagon driver, was that you didn't drive every day like you purported to, so you had to be careful, not to show yourself up in front of the villains.

Jane said they should go for a quick spin so he could familiarise himself again; he looked relieved at this. But first, she would attach the electronic tracking devices, whilst he checked over the vehicle.

"How long will they last?" Steele asked.

"They each have a seven day battery attached, so should be no probs."

Steele said he was glad she knew what she was doing, as he wouldn't. He'd been on plenty of surveillances, which had involved trackers, but knew little about how they were deployed; he said that SOCA always used a specialised team to deploy the devices.

"We did too, normally, in the secret services. But unlike the cops, field operatives needed to know the basics of deploying technical kit," Jane said. She went on to explain if she was operating somewhere remote with little support, then sometimes one had to be a jack of all trades. Especially, if you were abroad. She recalled being overseas on one job undercover and it had taken her weeks to get near to their subject; and she knew her exposure to him would be for several minutes at most. So, when the opportunity came, she knew she would only have moments to fit a device to his car.

"Did you manage it OK?" Steele asked.

"Just," Jane replied, "but fastening a limpet tracker to the underside of a limo whilst wearing high heels and an evening dress wasn't easy."

"Wow, what a gal."

"Cut the crap and go and play with your dipstick, whilst I do the real work," she answered.

Steele laughed as he got out of the car, but Jane could see he was impressed. She thought she saw something else within his grin, but cast it off as she made her way to the car boot to grab the kit.

CHAPTER FORTY-NINE

Jane was impressed watching Steele as he laboured the artic tractor unit around local roads for the thirty or forty minutes that they were away from the lorry park. He said he was happy enough with the vehicle and its controls, but it would be a different thing of course, once they were pulling a loaded trailer.

"Why do you think Tony has bothered to attach an empty container? Wouldn't it have been easier to have the tractor unit parked up without," Jane asked.

"Probably, but it may have stood out. He's obviously had someone else bring this rig here, and a tractor unit and empty trailer, may have looked odd after a while. Remember, we don't know how long it's been here."

"I guess that makes sense, but why did he need your contact 'London' to find another driver?"

"I can only imagine that this is his operational security. You know, breaks the chain."

"I get you," Jane said, "the guy who brings the rig here has no idea what it's going to be used for."

"Exactly, it may even be the driver's own rig; I don't see any company logo painted on the doors or anywhere. The empty container is unmarked too."

Steele finished by saying he would just disconnect the trailer when they left, which was easy enough to do, Tony no doubt had an empty trailer somewhere for them to use; he'd ask him about it later.

Jane watched as he expertly brought the combination back to its original parking space. He'd just pulled up when his phone rang again. And by its ringtone, Jane knew it was Steele's old undercover phone, she nodded to his pocket to indicate she understood this with a serious look, and kept quiet as he took the call.

"Hi Tony," Steele answered, as he glanced at Jane, clearly letting her know who was calling.

"Yeah, I'm at the yard now." A pause, then, "No probs, the rig's good, I've just taken it for a test spin, and it's fully fuelled up as well, but where's the empty trailer?"

There was silence for three or four minutes, whilst Steele nodded a couple of times before he said, "OK, I've no dramas with that," before he ended the call and turned to face Jane.

"That was interesting; he's sending us a chaperone in the morning, but it's clearly one he doesn't trust."

He then went on to explain that Tony was sending 'another Manc idiot' to ride with them once it was game on. Said his Manchester colleague had insisted on it.

"Moon?" Jane suggested.

"I reckon so," Steele said. Then continued to explain that as far as Tony knew, the rendezvous for the handover of the goods was still somewhere up north, but to be prepared to be directed elsewhere. But not to go anywhere, other than where he sent them.

"What do you make of that?" Jane asked.

"Wait, there's more," Steele said. Continuing, he explained that Tony wanted Steele to try to find out from the chaperone 'Phil', where the RV was as soon as he could. That he should not push this Phil, or make him suspicious, but if he could find out where it was in advance, he was to let Tony know straight away, and there would be a nice bonus in it for them.

"Right," Jane said, "sounds like all's not well between Moon and Tony?"

"Defo," Steele answered, "he stressed that if we found out the location of the RV, we were to let him know without Phil realising."

Jane rang Burrows and put her phone on loudspeaker so they could have a three-way conversation. She briefed John on events, and then they discussed the implications.

"We'll have to be on our guard here; it sounds like good old Tony is planning to stiff Moon," Burrows said.

"Well he's not all bad then," Steele added.

"And, at least he's trusting us now," Jane said.

"Yeah, but if Tony does cut Moon out, the fact that you are trusted, or that you are still with the wagon is secondary," Burrows said.

Jane looked at Steele and could see the implications hitting him about the same time as they struck her. Their primary brief was to find and release Susan Crabtree, and then deal with Moon and his criminal associates, 'removing their continuing threat to society', as Frank Briers was fond of saying. But their only link to Susan was through Moon; and if Moon was cut out of the loop, their route to her was lost.

Initially, they were all clear that as long as they had control of the wagon, they had Moon, and that would lead them to Susan.

"What about Moon's vehicle details?" Jane asked, remembering the ANPR and facial recognition cameras they had set up. "Won't we pick him up that way?"

"Not if Tony is planning to cut Moon off permanently," Burrows said, adding. "And although that sort of does part of our job for us, Susan's safe release is the priority, we have to remember this."

"On the plus side, we will still have this Phil character with us," Steele said.

"Granted, Larry, but there's no guarantee he'll tell us where Susan is. He might not even know," Burrows replied.

In conclusion, they were all agreed that this was an unhealthy development, and one which could take the control away from them. Burrows agreed that Steele and Jane should do all they could to get the RV details from Phil, if possible, but not to pass them on as instructed. Even if that forced Tony's hand to try an ambush on Moon.

"That could work out quite well," Steele had said, explaining that if Tony did try something, then they could 'appear' to side with Phil and deal with Tony – three against one – and Phil would lead them to the RV and Moon, and therefore Susan.

Jane was impressed; this could work out very well. There was little doubt that Phil would know where the RV was; that was why Moon wanted him on the vehicle. To protect his investment. So, he would no doubt know where Moon was, and probably Susan too. Burrows reminded them that they were all on their own, as the Special Projects Unit did not officially exist. They were off the radar, with no armed back-up. She knew this of course, but Burrows was right to remind them, she guessed.

Before they'd ended their conference call, Burrows had asked how the trackers were working.

"Fine, John, if you tune your sat nav into its covert mode, you should see us."

Jane knew that in the old days, surveillance teams using electronic tracking devices had to hump around large receiving equipment, which if seen, could compromise the job. Even though such receiving teams were always a good distance behind the surveillance team, let alone the target, the top villains often had 'spotters' who would follow their masters around and generally get in the way. Nowadays, nearly everyone had a sat nav on view, so they had been equipped with special ones, which had a dual function; a normal mode, and a covert mode for following their surveillance trackers.

It was agreed they should grab some rest at separate locations – she and Steele together as they were very much in character now – and Burrows would find an out of town hotel somewhere, one where he could monitor the lorry's tracker overnight. Just in case things changed. And then he could follow them as required.

"Will the sat nav work indoors?" Steele had asked, after the phone call was over. Jane explained that it would be left 'live' in Burrows' car, and when there was any movement on the lorry, the sat nav would alert John via his mobile phone. She could see Steele was impressed with this new kit, but she'd been using this stuff in the security services for years.

Using the side of the container for cover, they each drew their weapons from the car boot-safe, but left their ballistic vests behind. Steele had suggested it might increase their risks if this Phil character was switched on and clocked them wearing them. Jane had to agree, it might look a bit policey.

"Come on, let's go and find the nearest hotel, it looks like we're in for a long day tomorrow," Steele said.

Jane just nodded as they both climbed into the car, as she tried to hide her disquiet. She was very aware how this job could go tits up. Steele seemed a little over enthusiastic to her, but that was probably born out of a little naivety through lack of experience. She'd have felt better if Burrows was with her and Steele was following, but then felt guilty at thinking such. It was just that she'd worked with Burrows longer and in dangerous situations. She decided she wasn't being fair and shook it off.

CHAPTER FIFTY

Bentine relaxed in his room, having just cut the connection to Gerry. He was happy with the way things were starting to progress. It felt like he had more control again. He had always been a control fan; it was what kept him one-step ahead. He was glad to have received the call from Captain Pugwash bringing the job forward: the less time he had to stay in the UK the better. And it would give Moon less time to mess about.

Gerry seemed a trustworthy guy; he'd had no problems when Bentine gave him his last instructions re the RV and Phil. He'd keep his details for future reference. That was always one of the biggest problems in this line of work; staff. Either he'd end up with unreliable and cheeky bastards like his London contact, or worse; end up working with disrespectful idiots like Moon who thought they were the top man.

He couldn't wait to see the look on his face. Then he'd find out who the buyer was, if his man in Manchester hadn't already. Time to give him a ring, he thought, reaching for his phone again. "Did the usual arrive in the usual?" Bentine started, referring to the last ten grand he'd wired to the man.

"Yes thanks, boss, it's shown on-line as due to land tomorrow, when the working day starts," the man answered. "Look, get to a box and bell me back so we can talk, will you?"

"Give me five," the man said, before ending the call.

Bentine made himself a brew and had just eased himself back onto his bed when his phone rang; it was his man in Manchester.

"That's better, look; the job's been brought forward. The ship lands at twelve noon tomorrow," Bentine started.

"Everything OK?"

"Yes, it's for the better as I want to remove that irritating cretin Moon from both our hairs."

"Good, it'll save us a lot of work afterwards going after him, and the taxpayer a fortune."

"How's Crabtree behaving?"

"No worries there. Like I told you, he's no heart in finding the toe-cutter; in fact he's gone off sick over the weekend."

"What's up with him?" Bentine's suspicions, piquing.

"Period pain? Stress? Who knows? But don't worry; when I saw him on Friday afternoon he looked a broken man. Whatever you've got hanging over him is clearly working," the man answered.

"Good," Bentine said, "look, I'm obviously going to need you close from tomorrow now."

"No problems, I'm off all this coming week, just tell me what you want me to do."

"I will, but you'll need to make a start now."

"I'll be packing my overnighter as soon as the phone goes down. Look, boss, just out of interest, can you tell me how you've managed to crush Crabtree so effectively?"

"His wife."

"Wife? You mean the lovely Susan?"

Bentine then went on to explain what Moon had done. How it initially had pissed him off, but might have worked out for the better. Especially after what his man had said about Crabtree being crushed. He clearly wasn't going to start being a problem whilst his wife was at risk.

"And if we sort Moon out, like you're saying, boss, it'll keep Crabtree busy chasing shadows that no longer exist."

"Dead right," Bentine answered, "even though I'll be out of the country sharpish, it'll create a suitable break in the chain. What about you?"

"More than covered, boss. There is absolutely no link whatsoever between us. Even the bank account I'm using is in a false name, so no worries there."

Bentine knew this, and trusted his man, but also knew he would be the only link left after he'd sorted out Moon. "What's your cover story whilst you're away?"

"I've booked into a hotel in the Lake District. I have all my hiking and bivouac kit with me. I'll go out walking – tomorrow now, rather than Tuesday – and tell the landlady I may camp overnight for a day or two, so won't be in my room or need breakfast until I'm back. Around the corner is a train station where I'll jump a rattler down to Lancaster and then hire a car."

Bentine said he was impressed, and he was. He'd hate to have to cut this loose end off, as he'd always been so reliable. No need, all was good. He ended the call, and decided to head back to hotel bar, at least this time he could enjoy a drink without that Manc wittering in his ear.

***

Burrows ended his call to Jane and then dialled Frank Briers' number, "Zulu, this is Alpha," Burrows said as the call was answered. Whenever he spoke to Briers, he had to remember that Frank did exist, and could be with anyone when he took his calls.

"OK, John, you can speak freely. How's it going down there?"

Burrows then filled Briers in with the events of the day, including Tony's brief to Steele re the RV and Phil.

"A pity Moon got away from the hotel. But that's not a criticism; I know there are only three of you."

"Yeah, I know, but hopefully it'll work round to our advantage."

"How do you mean?"

"Well, we will have Phil now as our guest, so apart from gathering the RV intel from him, it saves us the trouble of knowing who else to locate and remove, after we've found Susan."

"True." Briers said. "Any issues?"

"We have to be careful about our identities," Burrows started to say, and continued before Briers asked the obvious. "Moon knows what Jane and I look like, and Phil also knows me, albeit not as well."

"Solution?" Briers asked.

"Well, Jane successfully changed her appearance before when I was lifted in Salford, Moon never recognised her, though he didn't get too long to study her. But she is going to change her appearance again, and before you ask, obviously a different look from Salford."

"Granted, she's a resourceful character. But what about you?"

"I'll try, but it isn't as easy for blokes as you know, but I won't be as near to it as Jane obviously is. Also, as they managed to deploy the tracker, I can follow the rig from an even safer distance. The only time Moon is likely to see me up close, is if it all kicks off, and if that happens, recognising me will be the last thing on Moon's mind. Hopefully, literally."

"That's what I used to like about you when we worked for SOCA; your confidence. Or should I say arrogance," Briers answered, with a laugh in his voice.

"You wouldn't have it any other way, Frank. That's why you hired me again."

"We'll see," Briers said, "but what about Moon and Tony? They won't be far away from that lorry."

"I suspect they will be close by, but now the tracker's deployed that helps a lot. I can hang well back like I said, and only need to make ground when things liven up."

"Keep your eye on the primary objective, John. Though I know you will."

Burrows reassured Briers, and told him he had stressed as much when speaking to Jane a few minutes ago. "I almost sounded like you, Frank. Now that's a worry."

Burrows asked if there was any intel on what the commodity might be. They assumed drugs, probably heroin, but didn't know. Briers said, he was remotely monitoring all chatter, but nothing was jumping out.

"Can you do anything now we know the exact time the ship is to dock?" Burrows asked.

"We came up with nothing on the earlier details you gave me, but we'll try. Now it's been brought forward a day from Monday, it might show up more obviously, but we are only able to monitor the Western Docks' publically accessible systems. We could do with a man inside."

"Is it worth trying to get a local police intelligence unit to deploy someone?" Burrows asked.

"It's crossed my mind, John, but I'm worried we may leave a footprint, even if we route the request through obvious firewalls. We don't know what you'll have to leave behind which could link back."

Burrows realised that his old crime squad governor was right, once again. Such a request would be fairly innocuous but they couldn't yet know how things would pan out, once they'd freed Susan, and dealt with Moon. Ideally, they would be able to clear up any mess, but if not, the container could be left on offer, with a body or two linked to it. That link could zoom straight back to any inquiry related to the ship it came off. "Good point, Frank, you're right again of course."

"I'll take that as a massive compliment coming from you," Briers said.

"And I'll take that as the opposite," Burrows answered. They both laughed, and then said their goodbyes.

Burrows then checked the sat nav tracker in its covert mode and could see it was working perfectly. By now, Steele and Jane would be headed for somewhere to stay the night. Burrows couldn't help but feel a tinge of jealousy. He recalled fondly, how on the last job; their first job, when tracing Shonbo Cabilla, they had sort of ended up in the sack at Jane's flat.

He knew they had agreed to park things until after the job was over, which made good operational sense. But that was several weeks ago now, and she'd not, so far, shown any interest in getting jiggy again. Burrows felt guilty at thinking physically about Jane, she was far more than an attractive woman. He was very fond of her, and in their line of work, relationships would be even harder than they had been when he was a police detective. But then again, he was supposed to be the team leader, her supervisor; though he thought of things as more of a partnership. He would only force an issue if he had to, and up until now, he hadn't had to, which was another reason why he was fond of her. Maybe he'd wait until this job was over and then have a chat, make a play, a proper play; and show her she meant more to him than just the best sex he'd ever had.

Burrows then stopped himself; here they were about to conclude a dangerous operation with innocent lives at stake, and he was musing inappropriate thoughts.

Allowing his big brain to kick back in, taking control back from his little brain, he pulled out of the layby he'd been in and headed out of town to find a hotel for the night. He reckoned tomorrow was going to be interesting, to put it mildly.

CHAPTER FIFTY-ONE

Susan Crabtree caught a glimpse of herself in the caravan's side window and shuddered inwardly. She had always thought she wasn't bad looking, in a non-arrogant way, and definitely didn't look her age. But the woman staring back at her in disbelief, looked more like early forties than thirties. Her shoulder length dark hair was matted and would probably have to be cut off and left to grow again.

She sighed, as the sun rose, and she faced the prospect of another day in hell. She prided herself, usually, on her stoic persona. Her husband Nigel always said, "God help anyone who crosses you." Well, these bastards had certainly done than, yet she felt so utterly helpless; having to seem pleasant, compliant, just to get by.

She had worked out her three captors, and categorised them accordingly. It helped to pass the time, and gave her a coping strategy. Another of Nigel's phrases was "no matter what you face, have a coping strategy."

Johnny the boss-man was all smiles and seemed to pitch himself a cut above the rest. But even if that was true, one level above the slime is still just one level above the slime. But at least he seemed able to keep the other two in check, which was when he was here. Not that he was here too much. He was a gaunt man with an angelic countenance, which Susan found disturbing.

Phil, the brother of Bill, had spent most of the last twenty-four hours with her, which was blessed relief. He was OK with her, polite even, and seemed a little uncomfortable at times. She forced herself to engage him in pleasant conversation. At first, he seemed a little suspicious; as if she was trying to trick him into giving away some vital detail about where they were, and what they were doing? This would have been nice, of course. But her main concern was keeping everything calm. She'd once seen a TV programme about Helsinki Syndrome or was it Stockholm Syndrome? She couldn't remember the exact name. About a kidnapped person who befriended their captors as a coping strategy. She also thought that the nicer she was to Phil, the more protective he may become towards her, especially from his brother Bill.

Now Bill scared her. From the off, she'd seen the way he leered at her, and the fact that he was as smart as a stunned slug made him all the more menacing. The sort of bloke who'd lick shop windows for a pastime. When he'd kidnapped her from the others the previous night, she was terrified at what he might do. Her stoic demeanour crumbled. The terror she'd felt had matched her relief when he changed his mind and took her back. Only Susan, she thought, could be kidnapped twice. And how perverse it was; her feeling relief at being taken back to the others. It amazed her how normal perceptions and values all changed under such circumstances.

She was glad that the boss-man had kept Bill away from her, but it worried her almost senseless that they felt they had to. But it was Monday morning and her spirits were high, as Phil had told her she would be released today or tomorrow at the latest.

One thing did keep niggling her though, and after Phil brought her a cup of tea, she couldn't help but ask, "You keep saying I'm going to be released unharmed."

Phil was stood close as she sipped her tea. He always stood very close when he undid her restraints.

"Yes?"

"Well, I just want you to know that irrespective of who my husband is, you've no need to worry as I won't give him any useful descriptions of you, I promise, I just won't, so—"

Interrupting her, Phil said, "Relax, we aren't going to silence you if that's what's worrying you."

Susan felt her shoulders sag with some relief, if only she could believe him; she dearly wanted to.

Filling the pause that followed, Phil continued. "Look, I can see where you're going with this, but for reasons I can't go into, the cops will know who we are anyway. So, why add a potential life stretch to everything. Not that it'll come to that."

"What do you mean?"

"We will be... let's just say, well away from here, so don't worry."

"Thank you, I won't then."

"But today is going to be a busy one, and I'm going to have to leave you with my brother for most of the day."

Susan's brief elation now came crashing down again. Similar to when she'd spoken to Nigel on the phone. Hearing his voice, and then not hearing it. Before she could speak, Phil continued.

"Look, don't panic for fuck's sake. The last thing you should do is kick off. I know he's a bit of a numpty, but he's under strict instructions."

"Stricter than before?" Susan said, trying to hide any sarcasm in her voice.

"Look, before was different," he said.

She couldn't work out why.

"I shouldn't tell you this, but we'll be headed off early afternoon, so Bill will have to drive the motor with you in the van on your todd, OK? So you'll only have to get through the morning with him, and it's as I say, he's under strict instructions. The job's nearly over so no time for fucking about, OK?"

"OK," she replied weakly. But she couldn't stave off the crushing anxiety creeping through her. She needed a new coping strategy, but she didn't have one, and her resolve was descending fast.

***

Moon checked his watch, then reached across, and leaned through the open passenger door of the hired Nissan, "COME ON, PHIL, FOR FUCK'S SAKE."

He was joined moments later as Phil jumped into the front passenger seat, "Sorry, boss, just giving Bill his final instructions."

"Good," Moon said, as he put the car into gear and navigated his way from the picnic site back onto the road, heading towards the port.

"You happy enough riding pillion with Bentine's driver?"

"Yeah, no probs, it's not forever."

"And you remember everything I've told you?"

"Yes, boss, I'm Phil, remember – not Bill."

Moon just grunted.

"What's the script with Bentine, boss?"

"Surprisingly, he's agreed to ride shotgun with me. Which amazes me. I know how much he enjoys my company. I thought the awkward bastard would insist on following me in his own motor. Which would look a bit showy; an artic rig and two cars in tow; look like a bleeding convoy."

"Well, at least it'll keep things tight, boss. I'll be careful what I say when I ring you."

"Yeah, the devious Scouser would love to know who the buyer is, so keep it tight, like you say."

Moon glared at a boy racer who cut him up, pulling in front of him and then jumping on the brakes. He swore to himself, as he in turn braked, subduing what would have been his normal response. Not today, he knew he had to keep a low profile.

"What about the copper's wife?"

"Sorted. She'll be no problem," Phil said.

"You've reassured her about your nutter of a bro. No offence." Moon looked across at Phil and saw a hard glint flash across his eyes. "Ease up big man; I'm only winding you up." Moon didn't need any dramas with him today. He needed Phil fully on side.

"I wish you wouldn't slag him off so much, boss, I know he fucked up a bit the other day, but he's been a loyal man to you over the years. I once watched him put a bloke from Salford into intensive care for slagging you off," Phil said.

Moon hadn't heard that story before, and was impressed. "Fair enough, Phil," he said.

"He knows to behave until the job is over, and that thick bitch believes everything I've told her. Stuck up cow thinks she's smarter than I am, she thinks she's befriended me. Thinks we're bessie mates now."

Moon knew Phil had done a good job keeping her sweet, "So no probs with her or Bill. That's what I like to hear." He then turned off the main road and headed eastwards. He planned to go the wrong way for a few miles and then let the sat nav route them back towards Southampton. It was game-on day today, and time to be extra careful.

After a brief pause, Phil added, "Well, until the job is done of course."

"Of course," Moon replied, adding. "Then he can do what the fuck he likes. She's in for a real treat," Moon said, grinning at Phil who was smirking back.

CHAPTER FIFTY-TWO

Susan tried to calm herself as she saw the car carrying Phil and the boss-man drive away. Bill turned towards the caravan and headed towards it. She was back on the bench seat with her right wrist handcuffed to the table leg, which was fastened to the floor. She took a deep breath as Bill entered the van, and put a smile on her face. Trying to look pleasant; but not too pleasant. Charming without allure. "Good morning," she offered.

Grinning back with that hideously fake smile of his, he answered, "It sure is," before closing the door and sitting down.

She wasn't sure what, if anything his reply meant, but no matter, it was some relief that he choose to sit on the bench under the front window, although at right angles to her, he was further away than he could have chosen. Though, she could still smell his familiar aroma of dried perspiration; she shuddered inwardly, as she sensed the coldness within him. She could feel his darkness.

Then suddenly, she was dying for a wee. She hadn't been until a minute ago. She would try to relax and it might go away. When she had to go there would be no problem of course; Bill would release the cuffs and stand close as she used the small bathroom. But, every time she'd been before, in his presence, she had the feeling he was listening at the door. It freaked her out. She'd put loads of toilet paper in the bowl before she went, to try to be as quiet as possible, but there was always some sound. And, then when she'd opened the door again, he was always stood there, right up close, in the doorway almost. Smirking.

As these memories flooded back, she wanted to go even more. She had to relax; it was going to be a long enough morning as it was.

***

"What time did Tony say this Phil chap would meet us here?" Jane asked, as Steele pulled the rig back into its space on the lorry park.

"Any time now, about eleven," Steele answered.

When he turned to reply, Jane could see him looking through her almost, as if seeing her for the first time. She took that as a compliment; she'd spent most of the morning dying her hair red. She'd tied it back, so it would look a different shape as well as a different colour since the Hope hotel in Salford. And to finish the look she had a baseball cap on and no make-up – that was the worst bit, she could put up with red hair for a bit… but no make-up; not easy. As if reading her reaction, Steele added, "I hardly recognise you; it's amazing what you've done."

"Why thank you, kind sir," Jane answered in a mock Texan drawl, but returning to her normal voice, she continued. "But let's not take chances. Phil only ever got a glimpse of me back at the Hope so I'm not too concerned about him, but if Moon drops him off – which is highly likely – I wouldn't want to put my new image to the test with him."

Steele nodded, and then said, "No point taking chances. Plus, we don't want to freak this Phil out; he's probably only expecting to meet me."

"I'll get out and wait round the back as if I've been checking something, then join you a minute or two after he's arrived."

That agreed, she got out of the tractor unit and walked around the back. No sooner was she there that she caught a view of a saloon car driving onto the park – which in itself was unusual – but it was heading straight towards them. She hid herself behind the trailer's wheels, glimpsing the car's registration plate, as she did so. It was the car they'd tried to follow Moon in from the hotel. Then she realised, they'd dropped a huge bollock. They should have anticipated this sooner. If they had, they could have asked Burrows to plot up nearby, and he could have tried to follow the car away. Moon was their link to Susan after all. Shit.

She heard Steele get out of the artic's cab and heard two doors open and shut from the car, which had been positioned side-on, on the other side of the trailer. She assumed it was Moon and Phil. She snuck under the trailer, now Moon had got out she had to be careful. He was obviously not going to just drop Phil off and leave; he probably wanted a look at Steele.

She crawled under the trailer up against the inside of the wheels at the driver's side to try to hear the exchanges better. She heard Steele introduce himself as Gerry, and Phil and Moon reciprocated. They all moved around to the front of the cab, but she could still make most of it out. Moon seemed to be asking all the questions. It was as if Gerry had gone for a job interview. Where was he from? Whom did he know? Had he done time, and where? And who was his pad-mate? All, pretty standard stuff for a former undercover officer, and Gerry obviously knew his legend and back-story almost better than his own antecedents. One of his strengths, Jane realised, was that his persona as a bent lorry driver meant he didn't have to pretend to have some elaborate past as a top villain. Just a petty criminal who had spent the odd month inside and nothing more. Jane knew all about the hierarchies that existed in prisons. How the biggest criminals – top drug dealers, armed robbers and suchlike – would have status.

Often they would have coffee mornings held on the wing, where only the elite were invited.

This would make it easier for Steele. He could say he was in Strangeways at a time when he knew from research that a top named villain was there. Giving credibility to his legend. And, even if Moon had any doubts about 'Gerry' and rang the named villain, it wouldn't help. It would be unlikely that he remembered a petty idiot who was in for minor stuff.

Jane was enjoying listening to Steele operate; he'd obviously been an excellent asset during his time with SOCA. This was clearly one of the reasons Briers had hired him. She'd tell John when she saw him next.

Then, an idea struck her. She still had an electronic tracker in her coat pocket. She was wearing the same coat she'd had on when they'd tried to follow Moon away from his meeting with Tony. It wasn't the same type of tracker she'd fitted to the rig; they were better quality, but took longer to fit. No, she had a 'golf ball tracker'. So called, as they resembled a golf ball in size, and they bounced. They were designed to be attached to the underside of vehicles in a hurry. They had internal magnets, and one could walk past a parked vehicle, bend down to tie a shoelace – or whatever – and simply bounce the thing underneath the car, and hoped it attached itself. Had they been able to follow Moon, and he had parked somewhere and walked off, she'd have tried then. Now would be perfect, but she had to be quick. From the sound of the conversations at the front of the cab, things were ending.

She pulled the device from her pocket, primed it, and then slid as close to the edge of the trailer as she dared. She knew she would have one shot at this, and if she got it wrong, the thing would probably bounce off the car's underside and roll away. It was at times like this she wished she'd made more effort during school rounders lessons. She'd preferred baseball, but was useless at that too.

Laid flat on the ground she reached out from under the trailer and sent the tracker on its way, pulling her arm back just as she heard shoes scuffing the ground, which sounded as if someone was turning the corner of the cab, back towards the car. This was followed a split second later by a dull thump, followed by a satisfying silence. She breathed out: the tracker had stuck.

CHAPTER FIFTY-THREE

Bentine paced around his hotel room; he had time to kill, but not much. It wouldn't be long now. Peering out the window, he could see it was starting to drizzle. The sooner he was back in the sun the better. And he'd be all the richer too.

Pulling his phone from his pocket, he rang his Manchester contact, who picked up almost straight away; at least he was one person Bentine could rely on. "Are you near?"

"Near enough, boss. Everything working out at your end?"

"Yep, that nob Moon has suggested we travel in one car, so we can control things jointly, 'in harmony.'"

"Do you trust him?"

"Of course not, but I think it's more about him not trusting me. Twat's in for a shock." He laughed and his Manchester contact joined in.

"It'll make it easier," the contact said.

"Too true. And I've told him to pick me up at the hotel. The twat's late, probably on purpose. But it means I can bin the hire car, which is for the better. I watched him leave the hotel yesterday so I'll give you his car details in a mo. I've told Gerry which route to take with the wagon and that we'll be a little way behind it."

"I'm almost at the RV now so I'll have plenty of time to recce it."

Bentine grunted, and then gave his man Moon's car details. No sooner had he ended his call he received a text from Moon saying he was outside. He didn't bother replying. He picked up his holdall and made his way to reception, where he paid his bill in cash and handed the hire car keys to a spotty youth in an ill-fitting hotel uniform. The keys were wrapped in a fifty-pound note. "There's days left on the hire so there's nothing to pay. The car's in the car park opposite, so if you can sort it out? The fifty's for you."

"Well, I'm not really sup—" The youth started to say.

"Don't be a greedy twat," Bentine interrupted, and the boy nodded and grabbed the money.

Bentine took a deep breath as he approached Moon's Nissan saloon parked on the opposite side of the road, he'd only have to be nice to him for a while longer. He put his bag in the boot, which he noted was empty, and then got into the front passenger seat. He saw Moon start to open his mouth, but spoke first. "Let's play nice."

"What do you mean?"

"I mean, we have often rubbed each other up the wrong way, probably because we come from different ends of the East Lancs Road. But it's game-on day, so let's get it sorted with no dramas."

Moon, just nodded, and pulled the car away from the kerb.

"Any problems dropping your man Phil off?" Bentine asked.

"No. I had a quick chat with your man Gerry, and he seems OK, so should be no problems," Moon replied.

Bentine noticed Moon had made no mention of Gerry's wife, Jane, so he said nothing. He hadn't told Moon about her, so he just reckoned Gerry was doing the intros in stages. He liked his style – good tradecraft.

Moon suggested they park up somewhere near to the Western Docks, where they could take up a following position once the lorry had cleared customs. Even though it was a million-to-one chance that their container would get a tug, what with the thousands that passed through the port every day, but the next hour would be a tense one nevertheless.

"Have you heard from your man on the boat?" Moon asked.

"Spoke to Pugwash a while ago as they left the Solent and entered the estuary. No worries," Bentine answered.

Neither spoke for a while and Bentine couldn't help but notice a tension surrounding Moon. He smiled inwardly. If the idiot was tense now, he'd soon be fossilized.

***

Jane listened as Moon's car drove away from the lorry. Then she carefully rolled out from under the trailer and made her way quickly around to the rear, where she would be out of mirror range. She stretched, and waited. She'd decided to give Phil a couple of minutes to get more used to Steele – or Gerry, as she would have to start thinking of him now – before she surprised him with her presence. It was obvious from the part conversations she had overheard that Tony hadn't mentioned that Gerry had his missus with him.

She checked her watch: it was now eleven fifteen a.m. Not long now. She made her way to the front passenger door. She opened it and started to climb in. "Budge up," she said to a startled Phil.

"That was a long piss," Gerry said. "I was just telling Phil about you. Apparently, Tony hadn't mentioned you."

"It's going to be cosy, that's for fucking sure," Phil offered.

"Don't worry. I'm Jane by the way, us women can have our uses on jobs like these. You'd be amazed at how disarming I can be."

"Suppose, it just looks a bit top-heavy," Phil said.

But it seemed to Jane that Phil wasn't too bothered. She caught Gerry's eye, and he dropped his eyebrows, as if to say, 'that's gone OK'. She nodded back.

Gerry then started the engine and turned to face her and Phil. "We may as well get port side now," and then he jumped from the cab and started to separate the tractor unit from the trailer and empty container. She explained to Phil, that they had been parked up appearing to be a full rig so as not to arouse attention. "Apparently, you only tend to see tractor units with empty trailers a day before they are due to collect their load, or so Tony had reckoned."

"It seems like a lot of hassle, if you ask me."

"I get the impression that Tony is a cautious man," Jane finished, as Gerry jumped back into the drivers' seat. He then drove the unit to the other side of the lorry park where an empty trailer with no container was situated. All ready with the same rear number plate attached as was on their tractor unit. Gerry quickly coupled the rig and they set off for Western Docks.

CHAPTER FIFTY-FOUR

John Burrows had just finished his McDonald's bacon and egg McMuffin, when he received Jane's text. She was at the rear of the trailer and confirmed Moon's presence and which vehicle he was in, together with the deployment of a golf ball tracker. Brilliant, he thought.

He reached for the sat nav on his dashboard and turned it to covert mode. He could see the wagon – identified as Tango-one – manoeuvring around the lorry park. He then switched channel and could see Golf-one appear on screen. It was mobile and headed towards Western Docks. Then the cursor stopped. Looking at the road position, he guessed it was outside Tony's hotel. Excellent; much easier if those two are together. He knew he couldn't follow both trackers at the same time, which was a bit of a pain; he'd have to keep switching. But for now, he'd monitor Golf-one, as he knew the lorry was going to the docks. He'd keep tabs until it was loaded and away. But for now he'd stay on Moon and Tony, after all, they'd want to be close to the lorry, and once in convoy he could sit behind both vehicles. But he needed to check something with Briers.

He rang him and quickly gave him a situation report, and then asked, "Keeping our eye on the squirrel, Frank, we first thought that by staying with Moon, it would lead us to Susan, but I'm not so sure now."

"I see what you mean; it looks like Moon and Tony are set to follow the lorry to the exchange now. There might be no further need for Moon to go to wherever he has Susan. On the plus side, if Moon's goon Phil is now with our two, then that probably only leaves his brother to overcome when you do find Susan."

Burrows paused for thought, then said, "What if Jane and Steele can open Phil up to talk about family. He might innocently talk of his brother Bill, and he might give us an idea where he is, without realising the implications."

"Worth a try, I suppose. After all, Jane and 'Gerry' couldn't know about Susan, as far as Phil is concerned. I'll text them, but for now stay on it. If it comes to it, you may have to intercept Moon and use more basic ways of extracting Susan's location from him. Remember, John, we are playing by their rules now."

They ended their call just as Golf-one started to move, it was headed in the general direction of the Western Docks. He checked channel one, and Tango-one was headed the same way, albeit a way back. He pulled out of the layby and drove towards the docks.

***

"I don't want to drop any surprises on you, Jonny, during our new found detente," Bentine started.

"Uh?"

"But, I've told Phil that once the lorry is clear of Southampton, to pull over so we can check everything is OK. OK?" Bentine finished.

"Where exactly?" Moon asked.

"Nowhere specific, just a layby or somewhere similar," Bentine lied.

"No worries, makes sense. That's why I've told Gerry to do the same," Moon replied.

Bentine didn't believe him, but no matter. Then his satellite phone trilled in his jacket pocket. This got Moon's attention as he answered it. "Yes?"

"We are anchored at the dock; the Cuzzies have just come aboard. No problems, they're starting to unload," the caller said.

Bentine recognised Pugwash's voice, and asked, "How long?"

"Your container is in the first batch to be offed. It'll be stacked on the dock, and then a crane will load them onto the queue of waiting lorries. Just make sure your rig is booked in and at the right place in the queue. Miss your slot and you'll have a long wait."

"Brilliant. Look, keep this phone and I'll give you a call in a day or so, we can do more business," Bentine said, as he glanced at Moon. He could see the envy in his eyes.

"Will do," Pugwash answered.

"Make sure you do, I know you've been sorted already, but there'll be a nice little bonus in it for you."

"Thanks, boss, gotta go," Pugwash answered before cutting the connection. It was the first time Pugwash had called him boss, he noted. Amazing at what the thought of extra cash did to people's attitudes.

He filled Moon in, who rang his man. As he did so, Bentine rang Gerry who told him that they were already in the Western Docks with the paperwork Bentine had given them; checking in, and getting their allocated slot. All good news.

He then asked Moon how things were going with the copper's wife. "No problems" came the reply. When he pushed him, Moon said he had a man with her in a caravan nearby.

"Afterwards?" Bentine asked.

"All sorted. There'll be no problems," Moon answered.

"Better not be. I hate loose ends."

***

Burrows glanced at his watch, yet again. It was a minute later than when he'd last looked at it, twelve fifteen p.m. Then his phone rang, it was Briers. "Yes, Frank?"

"Some good news. Our two are now only three or four lorries away from their turn. Jane has snuck down in the back of the cab in the sleeping quarters out of view at Phil's request. He say's it'll look less showy. Which is giving her chance to text me unobtrusively," Briers started.

"Go on, boss," Burrows said.

"They all seem to be getting on rather well and Phil has opened up a bit. When Jane asked him which hotel he was staying in, he said he wasn't. Said he was sharing a caravan with his brother, somewhere out in the sticks."

"That's a very good start."

"They naturally asked him why he'd gone to all that trouble. Why hadn't he just booked into a hotel?"

"Fair question; what did he say to that?"

"Just came out with some old baloney about his brother having a caravan in the area, which he needed to bring back to the northwest, so they thought they'd kill two birds, so to speak."

"If that's true, I mean that they're going to move the caravan, then hopefully your ring of steel of the ANPR and facial recognition cameras should pick them up. That would be great."

"It would, John, but don't discount the possibility that they could – God forbid – dispose of Susan before they move the van. After all, we are in the New Forest," Briers added.

There was a pause as this sunk in. Burrows' initial elation was over. Trust Frank to see the pitfalls of anything before anyone else.

Briers broke the silence. "Could be better, but it could be worse. We still have eyes on Moon, and he knows where Susan is."

Burrows agreed with Frank and then ended the call. He checked the trackers, both were stationary. Tango-one in the docks, and Golf-one outside nearby.

He pulled his SIG Sauer from his shoulder holster and checked it, again. All working correctly. He knew it was as he'd checked it properly in the hotel before he left, oiled it, checked the magazine springs etc. Weapons only jammed when used by idiots, and he had a feeling he was going to need his before the day was out. Plan B was a definite now. And he'd do whatever it took to get Susan's location out of Moon.

CHAPTER FIFTY-FIVE

Susan flushed the toilet, washed her face with cold water, and then took a moment to steady herself before opening the narrow bathroom door. As expected, Bill was right there, in the way, with that unhinged smile on his face. He looked dumb enough when he wasn't grinning, but when he was, what little intelligence his countenance displayed disappeared altogether. She tensed as she pushed her way past him, noticing that he leaned against her as she passed. She hurried back to her bench seat and quickly snapped the handcuff around her left wrist. So Bill wouldn't have to.

She watched out of the corner of her eye as Bill ambled back to his bench seat under the caravan's front window. She glanced at her watch, it was nearing noon. How much longer before they got going? At least then he'd be in the car driving, and she'd be alone in the van.

"You don't like me, do you?" Bill suddenly asked.

This took Susan by surprise. He'd hardly spoke for the last hour, just sat leering at her. "It's not that I don't like you, I just don't like the way you look at me," she answered as spritely as she dare.

"Can't a man appreciate a pretty woman? 'Cause you sure is pretty."

"I don't mean to offend you in any way, and I thank you for your compliment," Sue lied, continuing, "but you scared me the other night when you just took off with me." It was the first time she'd referred to that since, and didn't want to provoke him, but needed to show some mettle. She was sick of being a victim. It was time to start coping. Coping, that would be her 'coping strategy'.

"I figured you didn't like me," Bill said, as he inched along his bench towards her side.

"Look, I just want to get through this, as I'm sure you do. As I told your brother, I won't say a word once this is over. I'll have a complete memory loss; I won't give the police your descriptions or anything. I swear."

"When this is over, you'll have no memory of it. I'm sure about that."

Unnerved by Bill's reply, Susan pushed the darker connotation of his words from her mind, and then ventured, "So you trust me to say nothing? Is that what you mean?" She knew he wasn't the most literate of people.

"Yeah," was all he said in reply. Then he started grinning again.

***

Burrows flipped his sat nav back to channel one just as Tango-one slowly started to move again. Golf-one had been stationary as he flipped frequencies. It was now headed towards the perimeter. Then his phone bleeped. A text from Jane. It simply read 'A'. They had agreed a number of coded messages prior to today. A blank message – the easiest to send – would mean that immediate assistance was needed; come in loud and proud. 'A' however, would mean that they'd collected the load and were preparing to leave the docks with no problems. Excellent.

He pulled away from the kerb and drove slowly towards the dock entrance. He changed back to channel two to find that Golf-one was still stationary, so he pulled over. Once he had confirmed that the lorry had left the docks proper, he would stay on Golf-one's tail. Safer that way. He could flip back occasionally to ensure that Golf-one was still following the lorry (Tracker-one), but couldn't imagine why that would change.

Ten minutes later, and the convoy was settled. The lorry was on the main road heading towards the motorway, Moon and Tony were in the Nissan – Golf-one – a few hundred metres behind, and Burrows was about a further half mile behind that. He reckoned if Tony was going to pull a stunt, it would be before they hit the motorway. They were on the A33 headed towards the M271, which was a short link motorway that fed onto the M27, which in turn would lead to the M3 towards London and all points from there. There was an outside chance they could go across country on local roads to the M4. That would lead onto the M5 at Bristol from where they could head up to the M6 and north. But, bearing in mind that they were driving an artic and trailer, Burrows reasoned they would use the motorways whenever possible, even if it made the journey longer.

Then the tracker, Golf-one, came to a stop on the A33. Burrows couldn't see any major junctions nearby on the sat nav's map, so they must be at the side of the road, or in a layby. He pulled over and checked channel one. Tango-one was also stationary, right in front of Golf-one. He checked his mobile; there were no new messages or texts. He knew Jane's phone was OK, so had to stand steady. He was dying to drive past to see what was going on, but that would have been the sort of thing a rookie operative did. A lot of surveillance work, he knew, was all about being patient and sticking to the brief. If Jane needed help, she'd have sent the empty text.

They were probably just checking the load. It made sense. It was what most villains would do, as soon as they were clear of the port. In which case, they'd be off again soon. This probably meant they were going to use the M271 after all.

***

Susan needed a wee again. Christ she hated her weak bladder; it had only been half an hour or so since she'd last gone. She'd hang on a while longer, but she'd have to go before they set off. "Any idea how much longer it will be before we get going?" she asked.

"Dunno, shouldn't be too long. Why?"

"I'm sorry, but I'm going to need the loo again, well, before we set off."

"You seem worse than normal for the bog. You're not nervous or nothing, are you?"

"No, no," Susan answered briskly, "must be that coffee from earlier on. It's gone right through me."

Bill stood up and grunted something as he stepped towards her. She didn't hear him clearly, as he'd muttered, but it sounded like 'lucky coffee'. She shook it off; she must have misheard. No point in getting all paranoid. She turned her face away from Bill's rancid breath as he unfastened the handcuffs. She wasn't sure which was more offensive; his breath or his body odour. Probably a dead heat.

She hurried her way to the bathroom, instinctively putting her hands behind her to try to cover her rear. A defensive act, which she knew was of little use, but it made her feel less exposed.

She locked the door and for the few brief moments she would be inside the bathroom, she felt a little more secure. Even though she knew the flimsy lock and door was no match for a brute like Bill. But the sound of the lock clicking into place brought some small solace, if only for a short time.

Then she jumped at the sound of a phone ringing. Bill's, she listened at the door, straining to hear as clearly as she could.

"Yeah, boss. No dramas here," Bill said, followed by a pause. Then, "Yeah, she's been as good as…" A further pause, then, "Are you sure? No, I know that, you two split it. Yeah, tell Phil I'll bell him would you please, and thanks again, boss." Then she heard the sound of the call ending.

She jumped again as Bill banged on the door.

"Hurry up in there."

"Just coming," Susan answered as she flushed the toilet and quickly washed her hands. Feeling euphoric now, she didn't understand all she'd heard, but it sounded as if they were about to get going. It wouldn't be long now, and at least she wouldn't have to spend any more time in Bill's company.

She unlocked the door, and opened it to find Bill stood near the doorway, with his usual stock grimace. But as she made her way to squeeze past him, he blocked her path. She looked up at him, unsure. Then repulsion hit her as Bill spoke.

"It's over. But not for you. Now it's fun time."

CHAPTER FIFTY-SIX

Bentine finished a call from Gerry, and before Moon could ask him anything, Moon's phone started ringing. Bentine guessed it would be Phil telling Moon the same as Gerry had just told him. All clear. Waved through by the Cuzzies – thick twats – and the lorry was now headed towards the dock entrance.

He couldn't hear much, if any of Moon's conversation, but it didn't matter now. He had texted Gerry earlier directing him to a layby just prior to where the M271 begins. That's where his man would be waiting. That's where he would finally get rid of the annoying Mancunian sat next to him.

He'd also given his Manchester man Gerry's phone number, so they could speak to each other if needed. He'd told Gerry that if his Manchester man had reason to call Gerry direct, he was to pretend to be taking a call from him, Bentine. Thick Phil would be none the wiser.

"Was that your man Phil?" Bentine asked Moon, as he started the Nissan's engine up.

"I'm guessing that was your man, Gerry, with the same good news," Moon answered with his own question.

Awkward twat, Bentine thought, too much trouble just to simply say yes. No matter, he just grunted, before saying, "THERE IT IS," pointing through the windscreen.

A hundred metres ahead, the rig driven by Gerry pulled out through the main gates to Western Docks and headed northwest along the A33 away from the city. Moon pulled into the roadway and mirrored the wagon's slowly increasing speed.

"Not too close," Bentine said.

"I fucking know that," Moon spat.

Bentine ignored him as they continued tailing the wagon. There were several cars between them, filling the gap nicely.

Ten minutes later, the wagon started to slow and showed a nearside indicator as it passed a sign telling of a layby up ahead. But it was too early. It was the wrong layby. As he was trying to compute what was happening Moon broke the silence.

"I told Phil before, when you were talking to Gerry, to find a layby and pull over so we can check the load. You know, as we agreed."

"Yeah, yeah that's right," Bentine answered. It was still the wrong layby, but he obviously couldn't say as much.

"It's just that you look slightly surprised?" Moon asked.

Restoring his composure, Bentine answered, "No, not at all, it's just that I thought they'd have gone further away from the port before pulling over," he lied.

He started to relax, the last thing he wanted to do was pique Moon's suspicion. For whatever reasons there must have been a change of plan.

His Manchester man must have rung or texted Gerry with new instructions. He'd have recced the original layby shortly after he'd last spoken to him. He'd said he was nearly there; there must have been an issue with it. As he reasoned the change through his mind, Moon pulled into the layby and stopped a few feet behind the lorry. It was empty otherwise and was set back well away from the actual roadway with a kerbed area between the layby and the road itself. This made it more secluded. He could see why his Manchester man would have preferred this as the place for an ambush.

He strained to look down the nearside of the wagon. As soon as his man broke cover from the privet hedge at the side of the layby, or from wherever he was hidden, and approached the artic's cab, he'd pull his gun on Moon.

"I'm not sure what you're expecting to see down there dick head. But if I was you…" Moon started to say.

Bentine, hearing Moon started to turn towards him. He'd soon make the Mancunian pay for that lack of respect. But as he turned fully to his right, he faced a grinning Moon who was pointing a large calibre handgun directly at his groin.

"What the—" Bentine started to say before Moon launched a straight left to the side of his head, knocking his face forward.

"Shut up and keep looking that way. Then slowly pull out your gun using your forefinger and thumb of your left hand. Try anything, and I'll gladly blow your bollocks off," Moon said.

He knew enough about Moon not to try anything whilst in this position. He'd no doubt that Moon would carry out his threat with relish, given the chance.

If he took his time though, slowed things down as much as he could, then once his Manchester man and Gerry had secured the cab, then Moon would be outmanned, and outgunned. Then they'd see who got their bollocks removed.

CHAPTER FIFTY-SEVEN

Susan realised this was never going to end well. In a flash, she faced the uncomfortable truth her conscious mind had refused to admit. She should have confronted this before now, or certainly, after this monster had half abducted her away from the others the previous day. The fact that none of them was bothered about hiding their faces from her, the weak excuse given to her by Phil. If only she had woken up to the signs, or at least admitted them to herself, she could have planned something at a time of her choosing. So much for playing the compliance game. But this had given her one advantage; she was sure that Bill thought of her as some weak and timid woman; it probably gave the repulsive worm a bigger hard-on.

In the split-second in which all this reason raced through her mind, she found her spirit. These bastards had nearly terrorised it out of her, but it was back. She lunged at Bill, pushing him backwards until his back slammed against the caravan wall. She saw the look of amazement on his face. She knew this advantage wouldn't last long. She stepped back into the open bathroom doorway to give herself some space, grabbed the sides of the door jamb with both hands, and whilst pushing against this support will all the strength she could command, she kicked out with her right foot.

The look of surprise on Bill's face grew as her pointed right shoe connected fast with his groin. He screamed as he bent double, both his hands instinctively going to his injured genitals. The sound of his pain gave Susan a primeval thrill mixed with a rush of confidence. Her desire to flee that instant was overbearing, but she knew she had to maximise her advantage, whilst Bill was temporarily incapacitated. His head was bent forward and she placed her left hand firmly on the back of his skull locking her elbow into a straight arm. As she pushed with the left, she forced the sharply nailed fingers of her right hand up into his face hoping to find his eyes to cause the most damage.

A brutal act, which would make her sick if she witnessed it as a third party, but she was driven on by instinct to survive, powered by adrenalin. She knew she had one chance to disable Bill, and had to make it count, if she was to have any chance. God help her now if she failed.

Dashing past him as both his hands covered his eyes, she could see blood running down his cheeks as he howled in added agony. Arriving at the caravan door moments later, she knew it had a Yale type lock and so would open from the inside. It did, and she was out in seconds.

She took in her surroundings in the mere instant she dared allow herself. A car was rigged up to the front of the van, as she already knew, and a high hedge covered both. This much she had previously seen from looking through the van's front window. But, now she had a new view to take in. They were in a grassed clearing with wooden picnic tables dotted around. The clearing itself was boarded by trees. She desperately wanted to head for the hedge; for she was sure, the road must lay beyond it. But she couldn't see an opening. There must be one, but in the short time she had to hesitate, she couldn't see it.

The trees were only about ten metres away and appeared dense. These would give her quicker cover, so she bolted for them, just as she heard movement behind from within the van, no time to waste. She dared not look back, not even for a second, and was soon into the trees. She ran with energy and pace she never knew she had. She could hear Bill behind her, but the noises sounded slow, as if he was lumbering. Then she heard his voice.

"I'M GOING TO RAPE YOU AND KILL YOU FOR THAT, OR PERHAPS I'LL DO IT THE OTHER WAY ROUND."

She kept going, even faster, spurred on by the horror of his words. Then she heard a gunshot.

She realised what the noise was about the same time as bark exploded from a tree to her left. Debris flew in front of her in a sawdust mist, caught by the autumn sun as it shone in rays between the trees. Shit, that was close, she thought, but a miss is a miss. She was sure she was fitter than Bill, but as fear spurred her forward, she was under no illusion that anger and pain would do the same for Bill.

The trees were all two to three feet apart, some narrower and some wider. Hopefully, this would aid her but hinder Bill. Then she heard the sound of heavy footfalls behind her, and they sounded closer that she'd have hoped.

CHAPTER FIFTY-EIGHT

Jane breathed out loudly and started to relax, as they pulled out of Western Docks onto the A33. Collecting the container and leaving the port had been easy. And even though they were the good guys, when acting in character it was amazing at how you felt like the criminal you were not. She was surprised at how big and busy the port was. It was little wonder that Customs had little chance of success, unless they were acting from intelligence.

Steele had rung Tony, and Phil had spoken to Moon. They were parked up nearby and preparing to follow them as they made their way out of Southampton. As to what happened next, Jane wasn't too sure. She knew Steele had taken a call earlier, where he just listened before ending the call. Phil had seemed suspicious, but Steele waved him off, saying it was just Tony checking everything was OK. This had seemed to placate Phil, as he'd taken a couple of similar calls from Moon, but there was something about Steele's body language as he took the call. She hadn't known him long, but long enough. His shoulders seemed tense. And then soon after he'd finished the call, she caught his eyes in the rear view mirror. It was an alert of some kind. It must be to do with Tony and their summation that he was going to pull a stunt on Moon. She'd just have to wait and see, but from now on, she would stay fully alert. Phil told her to join them in the front and moved over to the passenger door so she could sit next to her 'husband'.

They had only been gone a matter of minutes when Phil pointed up the road ahead and said, "There's a layby coming up, pull over so we can check the goods."

When Steele answered, Jane found his response curious.

"Aren't we a bit close? We've only just cleared the docks."

"Nah, it'll be all right," Phil answered.

"But I know there's a layby just before the motorway, wouldn't it make more sense to—" Steele started to say, but stopped mid-sentence looking stunned. He was staring past Jane towards Phil.

She turned to look at Phil, who had produced a silenced handgun and was pointing it directly at her.

"Do as you're fucking told or I'll blow your wife's tits all over you. And you stay perfectly still with your hands on your lap," Phil finished off, aiming his latter remarks at her.

She hadn't seen this coming. It was supposed to be Tony ripping off Moon, not the other way round.

"Easy," Steele said. "Remember, mate, we're just hired hands. Whatever is going on here is nothing to do with us, and our bung ain't big enough for this kind of shit."

"Glad to hear it," Phil said. "Just behave and you'll spend some time trussed up whilst we fuck off with the wagon, end of. Get it?"

"No worries," Steele answered.

"You?" Phil said, aiming his question at Jane now.

"Good as gold, honest," she replied.

Jane quickly took in all that was happening as Steele started to slow and make his way into the large layby. Remembering what he'd said to Phil, she was certain that he knew something, from the earlier call. This was the wrong layby.

Steele pulled over and she saw him glance in his door mirror, someone must be behind them. She wished it was Burrows but knew it would be Moon and Tony, though Burrows would realise from the trackers that they'd stopped.

"I'm going to put my hand in a pocket, and pull out a couple of pairs of handcuffs, which you will each put on, OK?"

Jane nodded, and glanced back at Steele and mouthed the word, 'now'. He winked back his understanding. Jane turned back towards Phil, who had started to put his left hand into his outside coat pocket, whilst still training the gun in her general direction. She saw Phil's eyes squint, as the autumn sun shone through the windscreen.

At the same moment, Jane thrust both her hands at Phil's gun arm. Her left gripped above the elbow, her right below. She pushed as hard as she could with her back pressed back against the seat rest. This caused two things to happen. Firstly, it pushed Phil's aim away from her and Steele, and secondly, it created a channel of clear space between the two men.

Phil's gun went off, making a loud phutt type noise and a small hole appeared in the lorry's windscreen. She instinctively gripped his arm even harder, to try to compensate for any recoil. Notwithstanding that she could only keep hold a few seconds longer, she realised she wouldn't have to.

A second gunshot roared from her right, drilling a hole through the centre of Phil's face. The passenger window exploded taking a mixture of skull and brain fragments, with surprisingly little blood, out with glass splinters into the Hampshire air.

"I told him I could be disarming," Jane said, in a state of mock humoured shock.

"Now what do we do?" Steele asked.

"I've no idea, but we'd better think quickly; Moon and Tony must have heard that."

***

"Did you hear that?" Moon asked.

"Of course I did. Look, what's happening here?" Bentine said.

"That'll be the sound of my man Phil, explaining a few things to your man Gerry, as planned. So, unless you want the same fate, start talking. I want Pugwash's details, and I want the name of your supplier, the man who arranged for the goods to come over here in the first place," Moon demanded.

"That sound could have been my man, Gerry, giving your arsehole Phil the good news, just as easy?" Bentine said.

Moving his gun to the side of Bentine's head, he pushed the muzzle into contact with the man's temple, before saying, "Well, we'll soon find out, someone's coming." But Moon could also see that the approaching man was coming from the driver's side of the artic. Shit. He pushed the gun harder into Bentine's head, as he knew he would have realised this too, and assume it was his man Gerry.

But, as the man neared, head bowed, hood up, it looked like Phil's jacket. He quickly thought back to when he met Gerry at the lorry park. What kind of jacket did he have on? Did it have a hood? He wasn't sure. But, he knew Phil's coat did have a hood, irrespective of the fact the approaching man was coming from the driver's side. It was Phil, it must be.

As the man drew closer, he turned his head back towards the lorry, as he carried on. What was he looking at? And what had Phil done with the girl? Arriving at the Nissan's driver's door, Moon saw 'Phil' turn to face him in the driving seat. But as he did so, he raised his hand to reveal a silenced gun in it. Moon recognised it as Phil's gun. He relaxed. Then the glass window exploded next to him, as the butt of the weapon smashed its way through and onto the side of Moon's head. Stunned, he felt hands on his own gun arm, and a voice.

"Drop the weapon," the man he thought was Phil said.

But he realised it wasn't Phil; it was Gerry, with Phil's gun and coat.

"Now, or you're dead," Gerry commanded.

But there was no need; the Scouse twat next to him had already twisted the gun from his hand.

"Nice work, Gerry," he heard Bentine say. Now he was really in trouble.

CHAPTER FIFTY-NINE

John Burrows kept checking his watch as the minutes ticked past. He was starting to become fractious. It was taking too long. Both trackers remained stationary, and he'd moved as close as he dare: into a side road off the A33, probably no more than a few hundred metres away from where the wagon and the Nissan were parked. Then his phone rang. The screen read, 'Bravo calling'. It was Jane.

"Hi, John," she started, "we've had a situation here, but it's under control, well for now."

Jane went on to explain what had happened, adding that they had tied and gagged Moon and put him into the rear of the container along with Phil's cadaver.

"Where's Tony now?" Burrows asked.

"He's in the back of the wagon trying to get Moon to tell him where the handover RV is? And who the end-user is? He's desperate to know who Moon's buyer is, that's why I'm ringing you quickly."

"What do you want me to do?"

"Tony's Manchester man, whoever he is, is now on his way from the layby near the motorway. This is where Tony had originally planned to ambush Moon, before Moon tried it on first. Can you get as close as you can, to try to cover his arrival. I'm suspecting he'll take Tony with him. Also, Tony's surname is Bentine. I've heard Moon use it."

"Good work, I'll start some checks. Tony and his Manchester man will probably take Moon with them if they don't get what they want," Burrows said, adding, "Anyway, I'm on it," before ending the call.

He quickly checked the map, there was a side road junction just west of the layby, and as the road was a dual carriageway, there was only one way they could go. He'd drive past at normal speed, park, and then try to get nearer on foot behind any foliage.

Guessing, he reckoned the side road was only a hundred metres past the layby. Hopefully, he could get in a good position to see the arrival of the Manchester man, and be able to get back to his motor in time to take up any mobile surveillance as they left.

**

Bentine couldn't believe his luck, when he realised it was Gerry who had prevailed. For a horrible moment, he thought it was that twat Phil. No matter now. He was in the back of the wagon, where he'd quickly checked the commodity, well, found the suitcase anyway. He'd check it properly later.

Once his Manchester contact arrived, they could take off with it. They didn't need the wagon now. That had all just been for cover; an ideal way to hide the commodity and get it into the country. The container was full of crappy Chinese made furniture, with just a few feet of space by the doors, which was where Moon now lay. The suitcase had been hidden in a wardrobe a couple of rows in, he'd found it easily enough.

He knew there was far less risk involved in using freight as a means of transport, rather than passenger airlines or private boats or planes. Ports like Southampton were simply huge. The bigger the haystack, the smaller the needle, as he liked to think of it and it had worked well so far. Apart from Moon's pre-emptive strike.

He didn't need Gerry or his wife Jane, now, he'd tell them to take the lorry and Nissan away somewhere and burn them. He'd be in touch with a hefty bonus. They'd both earned it. As for Moon, he doubted he'd get the information he needed out of him now; but get it he would. Then he'd make him pay.

He pulled the gag off his mouth, and then used the butt of his gun to remove one of Moon's front teeth. "That's just for starters, Moon. If you tell what I want to know I promise, I'll make it quick. You do realise, you're going to die don't you?"

Moon, spat out the broken end of a tooth, which gave Bentine much pleasure, before replying, "Without me, you've got fuck all. If you want the money, we'll have to do a deal. Granted, a different one to that which I was expecting, but a deal nonetheless. Otherwise, just shoot me now. I'd rather take it to the grave than just gift you two million pounds."

"Brave words from a toothless wonder," Bentine said, before laughing at his own joke. Then he jumped at the banging on the container's door. He walked towards it and pushed it open, to reveal his Manchester contact.

"This wasn't exactly as you'd planned it, boss, but all's well and all that shit, I suppose."

"You could say that. I have the suitcase so no probs; it's just behind the door. I've also got that twat Moon here, but I've haven't had too long with him, so we'll probably have to take him with us."

"Give me five minutes will you? I've waited a long time to meet this little shit."

"OK, I need a quick word with Gerry and Jane, tell them what's going to happen," and with that Bentine jumped down from the trailer and walked the few feet to where Gerry and Jane were stood. He heard the sound of his Manchester man climbing into the container and the squeak of the hinges as he pulled the door to behind him.

He'd just finished briefing Gerry and Jane when a muffled scream came from the container. It was higher in pitch than anything Bentine had ever heard before. He walked back towards the lorry but halted outside as he heard a crunching noise, followed by a similar sounding screech. He never knew his Manchester man had it in him. The sounds were lost as the traffic on the A33 flashed past. As if on cue, a large goods vehicle or fast car would speed past masking each scream.

Bentine counted to five, before it stopped. He listened at the door, which was ajar an inch or so. He heard Moon's nasal vowels pant, "OK, I'll tell you, but leave me the other one for fuck's sake."

Opening the door wide enough to allow him room to climb in, he could see his Manchester man's handiwork before him. Moon was propped up against the furniture, a bolt cutter lay on the floor and blood was running everywhere. Moon was speaking in ragged breaths whilst looking at his left hand, disbelief and terror in his eyes. Bentine could see the fingerless stump and shuddered. He only caught the end of what Moon was saying.

"…And the Crabtree woman is in a caravan at a disused picnic site with Bill," he paused to vomit, caught his breath and said the location.

"I missed the first bit," Bentine said, "Has he given us the RV?"

"Oh yes," the Manchester man said.

"Why do you give a fuck about the Crabtree woman?" Moon panted.

"We don't," Bentine answered for his man. "We just don't like loose ends," He said as he pulled his own gun from his coat pocket. "You've had your fun, now it's my turn."

**

Burrows drove past the layby and strained to use his peripheral vision to glimpse the scene. He could see the wagon and the car behind it, and a group of people in between. Three probably, at least two. And he recognised Jane, just.

He quickly found the side road and parked his car facing back towards the A33 ready for the off. He made his way behind an established privet hedge, trying not to get his feet bogged down. The field behind the hedge was grazing land, but it sloped off towards the hedge. Also, the grass was short and muddy; it made the going difficult. He tried to get a view through the hedge, but it wasn't easy. He pushed in as far as he could, but it was dense. He had a broken view, but could see little more than the wagon. He was about to give up and make his way back to his car, when he heard the unmistakable sound of a gunshot going off in a confined space. Inside the container. Then he heard a second.

He was as sure as he could be that Jane and Steele were OK, he saw figures roughly where he had seen them when he had driven past. Their shapes were the same, and one was definitely a woman. But he needed to get back to the motor as quick as he could and ran as fast as the heavy ground would allow.

CHAPTER SIXTY

As Burrows scrambled back onto the side road, he saw a blue car flash past on the A33 heading west. It caught his attention as the engine was revving as the vehicle was under hard acceleration. But more than that, he couldn't see. Then his phone started to ring. He slew to a halt by the driver's door of his car and took the call; it was Jane.

"Did you clock the blue Vauxhall?" She started.

"I think so, but only just. Two on board, both males, but that's it, I'm afraid. Are you two OK?"

"No worries, but Moon's been stiffed."

"Yeah, I heard the gunshots. Hang on a sec; I'm going after the Vauxhall." Burrows then got into his car and started the engine, before continuing. "Any idea on the reg number?" he asked, then threw his phone onto the passenger seat as the car's Bluetooth kicked in, piping Jane's voice through the door speakers.

"Better than that," her voice boomed, "I've stuck a golf ball tracker on it."

"You beaut," Burrows shouted, as he switched on his sat nav, and turned to a third covert channel. A dot flashed up as 'Tracker-two' and then disappeared. They were obviously making some serious ground, and he had lost the signal. Burrows turned onto the A33 and floored the accelerator pedal.

***

Jane flinched on hearing the gunshot. But at least Moon was out of whatever misery he had just been put through. Not, that a scumbag like him deserved much sympathy, but they were civilised, compared to Tony and his mate. His fate may have been the same at their hands, but it would have been less brutal, she was sure of that. God knows what Tony's man had done to him, but the sounds of his high-pitched wails would stay with her for a long time.

As soon as Tony had joined the party in the container, Jane pulled out her last golf ball tracker and stuck it on Manchester Man's blue Vauxhall Astra.

She briefed Burrows, and gave him the Manchester Man's description – white male, mid to late forties, well built, short grey hair, with a certain presence about him, possibly ex-military, not that she wanted to stereotype him. He had a clear Manchester accent, but the vowels were softer, almost posh, or 'northern posh' as Steele had said.

Anyway, John had gone after the Vauxhall, and as much as she and Steele wanted to join in the chase, they had a bit of a scene here to sort out. Burrows asked her to ring Frank Briers in London, to fill him in and request a clearance team. She knew from her days with the security services, that a clearance team was always on stand-by somewhere. Usually, to clear up 'situations' caused by foreign intelligence agencies operating on British soil. Sometimes they were allies, and sometimes they were not, but certain protocols existed – not that they were always adhered to – but she'd made similar messes herself whilst operating abroad. Not that the current chaos was caused by official agents of the state, but the clearance team wouldn't know that.

Briers quickly rang her back and said a team from the Bristol Office of MI5 was en route to them. She suggested to Steele that one of them should back Burrows up; it didn't need both of them to babysit the scene. Steele agreed, and to her relief volunteered to stay. He said he never seen a clearance team before so would find it interesting, plus if they needed the wagon moving, he would be needed for that. Afterwards, he would get the clearance team to drop him at the nearest car hire outlet, probably, back in Southampton, and he would catch up with them when he could.

Jane quickly rang Briers back, and then ended the call before addressing Steele's last point. "No need, I've just asked Frank to sort a motor for you, he said he'd get the clearance team to pick one up en route for you. They should be here within the hour."

"They can do that, so quickly?"

"You'd be surprised at what they can do, Larry. As for motors, no worries, they've got them stashed all over the place," Jane said, as she enjoyed the look of surprise on Steele's face. "Anyway, I'd better get going," she finished, as she headed towards the Nissan.

***

Susan Crabtree could feel the burn in her legs as she negotiated the dense woodland. Shards of light seemed to jump out from behind tree trunks temporarily blinding her as her pupils struggled to constantly change from half-light to bright sunshine.

In such a moment, she misjudged her way and crashed into a tree with her left shoulder. Ignoring the pain as she bounced off it, she powered forward once more. The temporary easing in her pace gave her legs a much-needed respite from the exertion, if only for an instant. But the delay came at a cost. The heavy footfalls behind were closer now. Much closer.

Up ahead, perhaps twenty or thirty metres, the forest seemed to clear. But into what? She couldn't see. She prayed it wasn't just a field; she wasn't sure how much longer she could keep going. She was surprised at how Bill had kept pace.

Ten metres to go, and her heart raced as euphoria flooded her system. She saw a car flash past the opening to the clearing up ahead. It wasn't a field; it was a road. Bill must have seen it too. He'd know that once there, she'd be free. Emphasising this, a further car shot past the opening. Five metres to go.

Then, the sound of gunfire as pain sliced through the outside of her right thigh. She screamed as she fell. She went down hard, felt dizzy with shock. Looked up to see that the clearing was a few feet away. Another car zoomed past. Then darkness.

CHAPTER SIXTY-ONE

Susan was running through autumn fields, and she was happy and carefree. Could this be so? Then she realised she was about eight years old. Then she wondered if she was dead? Or was this just a dream? She couldn't tell, but she felt content.

Wasn't that what was supposed to happen, at the end? Dreamy contentment as the memories filed past. Then the pain returned. A numb throbbing pierced with a deep-rooted stabbing at its centre. It hurt like hell.

Slowly, she awoke to the horror of realisation that the dream was just that. The sense of contentment dissipated as her vision cleared. She was back in the caravan; her heart sank, her spirit felt crushed. She sat up on the bench seat and clasped her right thigh where the pain was. It was crudely bandaged with white knickers secured in place with a pink bra. Her underwear. The recognition brought vomit into her mouth. She spat it out, as she focused on Bill stood in the centre of the van. Hoping, but knowing her acidic breath wouldn't stop this vile monster. He was grinning again.

"You can thank me later."

"For what? Shooting me in the leg?" Susan said, with as much distaste as she could muster. What did she have to lose now?

"For stopping the bleeding. And don't be ungrateful, you're lucky I'm a good shot; it's only a flesh wound."

Her memories flooded back, she had been so close to the road and freedom. That was the last thing she remembered before she must have passed out.

"I couldn't let you get away, could I?" the monster said.

She almost wished the bullet had done its worst. At least she'd have been spared whatever misery this perverted bastard had in mind. Maybe she could make another break for it. After all, he hadn't put the handcuffs back on her. But she realised why as she tried to moved her leg. Jolts of agony raked through her as she attempted to stand. Falling back onto the bench, she knew escape was futile. But, perhaps she could buy some time.

"Look, I know what you want, and I know I'm in no position to resist you," Susan started. She ignored the enhanced leer in Bill's eyes as she spoke. "But, as you can see I'm in a lot of pain at the mo. If you can give me a day to recover, I won't fight you. In fact, I'll make it extra nice for you," she lied. Her own words sickened her nearly as much as the sight of drool now spilling from the sub-human's mouth in front of her.

"How do I know it isn't some trick?"

"Look at me, I'm in agony, if you start humping me I'll be screaming the place down. If you agree to what I ask, then I'll go with the flow," Susan answered, praying she was saying the right thing. It flashed across her mind that the twisted creature that Bill surely was, might find her agony and screaming a joyful extra.

Her fear abated slightly, as he answered.

"You think I'm thick, but I'm not. I can see that. I'll give you some painkillers and a few hours. But, if you don't make it extra nice for me then you will pay. And if you think you're in agony now…" Bill said, leaving his sentence unfinished.

Susan dug deep as she thanked him with fake gratitude, and layback down whilst her tormentor headed to the kitchenette.

***

Burrows hurtled along the A33 as fast as he dare, trying not to draw too much attention from other drivers. It was a balance between making ground after Bentine and his assistant, and not showing out by suddenly happening on them. The tracker should stop the latter, but only if it had stayed in place. The golf ball style was a great design for quick deployment, but not as secure as other types that took longer to fit. He hoped it was still secured.

He'd rang Briers quickly, and given him the blue Astra's registration number to upload onto the ANPR network, but Briers had said the chances of a hit were low, until the vehicle headed towards a more built up area. He'd also said that Tony's surname – Bentine – had failed to throw up any hits on the systems, but he'd keep checking.

Burrows thought he caught a faint glimpse of Tracker-two flashing up on the sat nav's covert channel three, but it was gone before he could be sure. The sat nav itself might map using satellites, but Burrows knew the system was only as good as the radio signal between the golf ball tracker itself, and the receiving antenna in his sat nav. And the range was never good, worse in built up areas. But as he headed into the New Forest, the rural landscape should help the signal reach farther, or so he hoped.

He was approaching the start of the M271 so a decision had to be made. The obvious route would be for Bentine to join the motorway network. Apart from speed of journey, the motorways were safer by far; less chance of a random pull by the cops. But Jane had told him that she heard some of the interrogation of Moon; asking about the RV, and where "that copper's woman" was being held.

Working on the guess that Moon would have the woman nearby, Burrows chose to ignore the motorway and head north on the A36 which would take him into the woodland areas proper. He just hoped he was right.

The other thing that confused him was the commodity, whatever it was, had been taken away in a Samsonite type suitcase, hard and silver. So what was the wagon all about? Jane said Steele would search the rest of the load as best he could before the clearance team arrived. She also said she was backing him up in the Nissan. It crossed his mind whether to ask Jane to take the motorway; cover both options. But on quick reflection, he decided that if he caught them up he would need her to equalise the odds.

Decision made, right or wrong, he drove on, ringing Jane to give her his instructions. Minutes flew past and the traffic was quiet now he'd passed the start of the M271. The road was still a dual carriageway, but the central reservation was just a narrow grass divide with no barriers, he could easily do a U-turn if needed. His only dilemma now was exactly which way to go? Up ahead he'd pass under the M27 and according to the sat nav map, he could either go due north on Romsey Road, or carry on the A36 headed northwest. The first would eventually provide access to the M3, whereas the latter went deeper into the forest towards Salisbury. He pulled over onto the grass verge to gather his thoughts.

Then his sat nav blipped again, before disappearing. It was close to where the roads parted, but it looked as if Tony and his man were headed towards the M3 on Romsey Road. It was time they had a piece of luck, he thought. A woman's life was at stake here. Irrespective of any danger she was already in, Tony Bentine's decision to pay her a visit en route to the RV didn't bode well. He couldn't begin to image what terror was coursing through her, or how crushed her husband Nigel must be feeling. After all, Bentine had no further need for her.

He rang Jane to tell her, and she said she was only a few minutes behind him now, he put the Mondeo into first gear and pulled back onto the road.

CHAPTER SIXTY-TWO

"Nice work back there," Bentine said, with genuine admiration. "I never knew you had such a dark side. And I've know you for a few years now."

"Only when pushed, boss, and I've hated that bastard Moon for a long time."

"Clearly," Bentine said, before asking his man what Moon had told him.

"He gave me the RV details and the location of Susan Crabtree; she's in a caravan with Phil's brother Bill."

Bentine then asked him for the specifics, which he gave him. He mulled over about the woman Susan for a minute or two before he spoke. "I know you're aware of my policy on loose ends, but this may prove a little difficult for you, having met her before, so I'll sort it when we get there."

"Cheers for that, boss. But what do we do if Bungalow Bill has already done one with her?"

"Moon spoke to him earlier to tell him it was nearly over, but gave him strict instructions not to move until nightfall. Saying it would be safer then."

"That was handy."

"I think Moon just wanted to be well away before Bill made a move."

"Talking about Moon how are we going to play the RV without him?"

"Yeah, I've been thinking about that. Perhaps, we should have kept him alive and brought him with us to the exchange," Bentine said.

"That wouldn't have been easy."

"You're right, he'd have been a liability. We'll just have to charm the buyer instead. The fact that we know where the RV is can only have come from Moon, so that should go some way to allaying any fears. Plus, in the end, the bloke wants what we have. And he must know he'll not be the only one. Nah, he'll deal with us without Moon, he'll have no choice. We'll just have to be on our toes in case he tries to rubber dick us. Anyway, to the first matter in hand, do you know where you're going?"

"Well, according to the sat nav, there are two Romsey Roads, I think they loop around and eventually connect. We missed the first one as it was near to the docks, and by the time we had got going it was too late, so I'll take the second. The hard bit will be finding the exact location of the site."

Bentine just nodded, as he drew his Glock handgun and checked it over.

***

The pain in Susan's leg was easing as the painkillers started to kick in. It was still severe, but the analgesics Bill had given her had taken the edge off it. She could move around now, albeit slowly. But still couldn't put her weight on her right foot, but she could use it to keep her balance. She was relieved to find this out when she went to the bathroom; the last thing she wanted was that monster helping her.

Then it occurred to her, whilst in the bathroom, she didn't want to appear too well too soon, or the vile bastard outside would be after collecting what he believed he was owed. No, she would have to have a relapse on the way back to the bench seat. First, though, she would change the bandage, not because it wasn't working, but she couldn't bear to look at her underwear on display for a second longer, not when she knew who had put it there.

Having taken it off her leg, it gave her a chance to look at the wound, and fortunately, it didn't seem too severe, and had stopped bleeding. Which slightly surprised her measured against how much it had hurt so far. Perhaps she was being a bit of a wuss, but she knew she'd have to keep it going for as long as she could. She pushed some tissue into the wound before wrapping a hand towel around her leg. She knew the tissue would stick in the wound but only God knew where the towel had been.

She was desperate to rinse her mouth out, as she could still taste the acrid remains of her stomach's earlier reflux, but she resisted the temptation. If that monster was going to rape her, then she knew there was little she could do stop him, but, she was determined he wouldn't kiss her. The thought of his mouth on hers seemed worse to her in some ways, and if her rancid breath stopped him doing that, then that would be a small victory. No, it would be a huge victory, she decided. She needed something positive to hang onto, and this was a start.

She flushed the WC and washed her hands before hobbling back to her seat, markedly with less ease than before.

"You've changed the dressing," Bill said.

"Yes, it was full of blood," Susan answered, as matter-of-factly as she could.

"Can I have them?" Bill said, with his trademark leer back in place.

"Oh God," she thought, it just gets worse. She didn't answer, she wouldn't dignify his remark, and in any event, the question was entirely rhetorical.

After a pause, he continued, as she eased herself back onto the bench.

"You've had long enough now, and I can't wait any longer."

It was then she realised she was sat on a hard base. Looking around she could see the other two benches were without their cushions, all three pushed together in the centre of the caravan's floor making a makeshift mattress.

Panic surged through her as her resolve fled leaving naked terror in its wake. Surging through her as if her blood had frozen in her veins, she started to scream, "HELP, HELP!" repeatedly, she knew she was out of control. "HELP!" she continued, brought to an abrupt stop by the stinging across her right cheek as Bill slapped her hard. Stunned to an impasse, she stared into his loathsome eyes, as he undid his trouser belt and let his pants fall to the floor.

CHAPTER SIXTY-THREE

Burrows had slowed down as he cruised along Romsey Road. Jane was behind him now, and he knew they were close. The signal – Tracker-two – had reappeared on his sat nav. This time it was bright and stable, as the signal strength had improved. It was stationary. It glowed on the mapping, and seemed to be on a parallel route to the actual road. Parked in a layby or other similar off-road place.

Driving at twenty miles an hour, with all the windows down, he could hear nothing except the rustling of the leaves in the trees as a slight breeze picked up. He could see a layby up ahead, which was empty. He pulled over and put his hand out of the window to signal Jane to do the same. Looking at the sat nav, the blimp was only a short distance in front of them. Time to approach on foot.

He put his gun in his shoulder holster and grabbed a couple of spare magazines from the car's boot safe, as Jane did similar.

"It can only be just down the road to our left, somewhere behind the hedge, so let's approach slowly," Burrows whispered.

Jane nodded, and then said, "After you."

Burrows stayed close to the privet hedge, which bordered the roadway. There was no pavement, just a narrow grassy verge. After only a few metres Burrows could see a break in the hedge up ahead: an entrance? He pointed it out to Jane and they continued.

Then he heard a car engine firing up, somewhere off to his left, coming from the field behind the hedge. Then he saw the front of a car appear at the opening and stop. He threw himself into the hedge, as did Jane, before the passenger compartment came fully into view. The car hesitated, and turned away from them, before accelerating along Romsey Road. It was Bentine's car, and there were only two people in it. Bentine as a front seat passenger with another male driving. Burrows didn't get a good view of the driver. He was too busy looking into the rear of the car, which appeared empty.

"Tony and his mate from Manchester," Jane said.

"And the back seat was clear – no Susan," Burrows said.

"Unless they've got her in the boot?"

Jane had a point, they couldn't be sure. Burrows quickly gave Jane his car keys and took hers in return. "You go after them with the tracker and I'll check the field."

Jane nodded, and was gone.

Replacing stealth with speed, Burrows ran to the entrance, stopped and looked around. He could see what looked like a picnic area, with wooden trestle tables dotted around in a glade, which was backed by a copse of trees.

To one side was a caravan coupled up to a Land Rover. The car appeared empty and there seemed to be a light on in the caravan, even though it was daylight, which was strange as it was still bright outside.

He slowly entered the area and could see that the caravan's door was wide open. Then he heard something. Like a crackling sound from within the van. Then he realised where the illumination was coming from – the caravan was on fire.

Burrows rushed over to the van, and as he passed the motor, he noticed a small fire on the driver's seat in there too. He confirmed that the vehicle was empty as he passed and slid to a halt at the caravan's door. Peering in, it appeared empty. The source of the fire came from three bench seats piled up in the centre of the space. It hadn't been lit long.

Burrows jumped into the van and checked the bathroom, which was empty. Shit, they must have grabbed Susan and taken her with them, probably in the boot as Jane had said. But at least she's not lying in there dead, he thought.

Burrows jumped back onto the grass and started to feel around for his phone, he'd give Jane a quick update before going after her.

Then he heard a noise coming from the back of the van. A rustling sound. Was it the breeze? Didn't sound natural. Then a groan. No, more of a humph type noise, denoting exertion of some kind or other.

He quickly drew his weapon and slowly made his way towards the rear of the van. He paused; the noises were definitely man made; of that, he was sure. A rustle and a humph; it sounded like someone dragging something heavy.

Tensed and ready, he jumped around the corner, his gun pointed straight in front of him in a two-handed pose. Susan Crabtree was being pulled from under the van by a man with his back to him. She was clearly alive. She turned to look at him.

"Don't shoot, please," Susan pleaded. Burrows realised at once that although he knew what Susan looked like, she didn't know him. But before he could reassure her, he had to deal with the threat. The man let go of her forearms and stood up as he turned to face Burrows.

Burrows' right index finger tightened on the trigger of his gun taking up the slack, as the man faced him proper.

"For God's sake, John, put that thing down," he said, followed by a short pause. "And, what the hell are you doing here anyway?"

Burrows dropped his arms, and stood there momentarily stunned. "I could ask you the same thing," he replied to detective inspector Nigel Crabtree, who then turned back to help his wife from under the caravan.

"We'd better get out of here quickly. That fire's taking hold and is going to attract some attention fairly soon," Burrows said.

"Sure thing, John. But where's the nutter? Is he still in the caravan, or have the others taken his body away?"

"Body, what body?"

"The maniac who had Susan hostage. He was just about to attack her when I arrived. And I mean attack her in the worst possible way. Then as we were leaving, the others arrived so we hid."

"I'm getting the picture; but don't fret if you've had to er, deal with him," Burrows said, rushing around to the caravan's entrance again. He could see that the fire was taking hold now, and as such, the three bench cushions at its seat had fallen apart. Underneath them, he saw an arm jutting out.

CHAPTER SIXTY-FOUR

"That's not exactly what I was expecting to find. Bill dead and the woman gone," Bentine said, as his Manchester man accelerated hard along Romsey Road, and away from the picnic area. "Don't get me wrong," he continued, "Bungalow Bill is no loss to society, and with his brother Phil gone too, it sort of works out OK."

"What about the woman?" the Manchester man asked.

"I'm not too fussed either way, the filth know who's taken her, i.e. Moon and his gang, and nothing has changed. Nothing back there is linked to me or you."

"True," the Manchester man answered, adding, "and by the time your mate Gerry has got rid of the wagon and the bodies, the cops will be chasing shadows for a long time."

"I told Gerry to burn the lot, so even if they do identify the bodies from bone DNA or whatever, once they realise who it is, that'll be the end of it."

"There's only one thing though," the Manchester man said.

"What?"

"Well, you probably noticed yourself, but when I started the fire back there, it was obvious that Bill had been shot. So does that mean someone else is involved?"

"How can there be? No, I reckon whilst she was entertaining the idiot she must have got hold of his gun somehow. He got what he deserved for dropping his guard along with his pants."

"Fair point, his strides were around his ankles when we found him."

Both men laughed, before Bentine turned his mind onto the matter in hand. They now knew where the RV was, and they knew what time. What they didn't know was how to contact the buyer on arrival, or even what his name was. He'd mull it over, as they made their way north, they had a few hours yet within which to sort out a plan.

***

Burrows ushered Susan and Nigel Crabtree to his car as quickly as he could. He could tell that Susan had had a hard time, by the look of relief on her face, which was matched only by the adoring gaze she gave her husband. As they reached Burrows' car, Nigel said that his motor was parked around the corner on a parallel road, the other side of the copse of trees.

"I don't believe it," Susan said, as they closed the car doors. She then explained her bolt for freedom, and how her leg had become injured. She was literally feet away from where Nigel had parked his car.

"How did you find her?" Burrows asked.

"Well, this clever one here," he started to say as he smiled at Susan, "gave it away. Moon's mistake was allowing her to call me. Ostensibly, I guess to reassure me that she was still alive, and therefore keep me at arm's length."

"And me compliant," Susan added.

"Well," Nigel continued, "Susan made some remarks about her being at the 'back of another old wood' and that she'd probably 'whine' when she got there."

"I wasn't sure you'd get it," Susan interjected, "you were never as good as me at cryptic crosswords."

"Help me, please, someone?" Burrows said.

"Well, 'back of another old wood' I eventually took to mean 'new forest'; back of old, being new. So new wood meant new forest; as in *The* New Forest," Nigel said, before pausing.

"Ah," Burrows jumped in, "so whine was wine; as in port—"

"—As in Southampton," Nigel finished.

Nigel then explained he had thrown a sickie giving all the hallmarks of a beaten man: he was still unsure who Moon had working for him, but knew he had the inside track on too much. Stuff that could only have come from within. Then he set up a back door cell-siting with a mate who worked at BT, hired a car and headed for Southampton. Then he got lucky.

Moon or whomever must have used the phone again, whilst he was driving down, and that had given him the remote location near Romsey, where the phone signal had pinged a local mast.

Once in the area, realising how rural it was, he figured they were hidden in a field, old farmhouse or suchlike. A second pinging confirmed this, and he'd spent the last twelve hours or more scouring the area, until he found the caravan.

It was quite a story, and sounded as if Nigel had arrived just in time. He then became a bit vague on how Bill became wasted. Not that that would be a problem, he knew, but Nigel wouldn't; he was still playing by the good-guys rules. Most pressing was the fact that Burrows was now compromised, but they had planned for this, as they were always going to have to explain something to Susan when they found her.

Before he dropped them off at Nigel's car, he put a quick call into Frank Briers and gave him the updates. Frank confirmed the cover story to use, but before Burrows did, he asked to speak to Nigel and Susan direct. When the phone came back to him, Briers confirmed that he had put them both on a 'need to know policy'. He then offered Burrows the services of the clearance team that was still in the area, having recently finished their first task. But Burrows declined; he said the whole scene was well alight when they left, and as if on cue, he could hear the sound of sirens approaching. Time to go.

He cut the connection and prepared to leave the Crabtrees at their car, he'd then have to wring everything out of his car's engine that it had on offer. Jane was apparently on the M3 now and heading northeast towards the M25. Briers had also told him that Steele was clear of Southampton, as of a few minutes ago, and was about to pick up an MI5 fleet car, and head north too.

Burrows suspected, whatever happened next would take all three of them, and still, they didn't know what was in that briefcase.

He was just about to say his goodbyes, when Nigel spoke first.

"There is just one thing I haven't told you yet."

"Go on Nigel, but be quick, it sounds like Trumpton are almost upon us."

"Well, as I said when the other two arrived I only just managed to get Susan and myself under the caravan, before they found Bill and started the fires."

Burrows knew this, and although the descriptions were very limited, he knew they were Bentine and his associate, though he obviously kept this to himself. "Yeah?"

"Well, I know who one of them is. We both do."

"What? How?" Burrows was surprised, he hadn't expected this.

"We recognised his voice, a hundred per cent. It was my boss, Detective Chief Superintendent Gary Ray. And *he* kept calling the one with the tan, boss."

CHAPTER SIXTY-FIVE

"Let's get out of here," Nigel said, as he started the car engine, adding. "Do you believe Burrows' explanation as to why he was here and involved in all this?"

"Not sure, what do you think?" Susan said, as she watched her husband at the wheel.

"Not sure either, but I guess we'll have to accept it and respect Frank Briers' instructions. After all, we are on the same side."

Susan wasn't sure she believed any of it, but no matter as far as she was concerned. It was over. Bill the monster had received summary justice, which he more than deserved, her husband's involvement would be kept a secret, and that bent bastard Ray would be 'dealt with' according to Burrows. She wasn't sure exactly what that meant, nor did she care. She just couldn't believe it when she heard his distinctive clipped tones. He'd been a guest at their home many times; he'd even been to both her children's christenings. She was flabbergasted. But after what those maniacs had put her through, not to mention her family, Ray deserved the same fate as Bill as far as she was concerned. She just wanted to get the next stage over and done with so they could go home.

The man on the phone – Frank – had told her that they couldn't hide the caravan or the body in it. So, in order to protect Nigel he gave her a list of clear instructions.

She was to tell it as it was, only to say that in the end, it was Phil who returned, and got into an argument with Bill over her, which culminated in Phil killing his brother before setting the caravan alight, whilst she was tied with rope to a table or similar. She managed to escape and ring the police from the first phone box she found, which is where Nigel was driving her to now. Nigel was then to disappear until he received the happy news from the local police.

Nigel said that the hardest bit would be wasting the few hours it would take him to 'drive' down from Manchester, where he would purportedly be when he received the call. He just wanted to take his wife home to her family.

"What about that Ray, I can't believe he was the mole," Nigel said, as he slowed on the approach to a telephone box.

"I somehow think he is the one with problems now, and whatever they do with him is fine by me."

"And me," Nigel added.

Susan got out of the car and checked that the phone was working before nodding back at Nigel and blowing him a kiss. She turned to face the phone as she heard him drive away, took a deep breath and dialled 999.

***

Burrows was still reeling from the shocking news from Nigel, as he made his way out of the area. The sound of the approaching fire engines had become quite loud before he left; he'd got away without much time to lose. As he drove along Romsey Road, he was conscious of not driving too fast until he was clear of the area. He didn't want to attract the attention of any incoming patrol car making to the scene of the fire. 'Always remain the grey man', his National Crime Squad surveillance trainer used to say. It was good advice, and he'd always tried to stick to it.

But back to his thoughts on Gary Ray; he hadn't even known his first name. Senior officers never seemed to have them, and a detective chief superintendent was a very senior rank. Thinking back, Ray had been at the briefings before and after the failed covert entry in Southport when the locksmith had been taken. And everywhere Nigel Crabtree went, Ray never seemed far behind, which was normal, as he was the senior officer and Nigel's boss. But talk about being the grey man, Ray had certainly been that. As far as Burrows was concerned, he'd had his doubts about the DS called Henry, but that was only because he'd questioned what Burrows was doing up there in the first place, which on reflection was a fair point.

Having caught his breath, he knew he would have to give Briers the bad news, as he joined the M3. At least now he was clear and could put his foot down. He wanted to catch Jane before she hit the northwest. That was if the northwest was their destination, they could be going anywhere; things change. Thank God she'd managed to deploy the tracker in time.

He ended his call to Briers who had gone very quiet when he told him about Ray. Frank and Ray apparently went back a long way and it was clearly quite a shock for Frank when Burrows told him.

Briers said he would ring him back shortly, so Burrows used the time to ring Jane and Steele to update them. He didn't stop on the line, just gave them the bad news and said he'd speak again after Frank's return call.

Thirty-five minutes later, Frank did ring back.

"I've just brought the Home Sec up to speed and as you can imagine, he is less than ecstatic about the news about Ray. He has in turn spoken to the other two members of the Special Projects

Unit executive – the DPP Sue Jones, and the head of the National Crime Agency, George Reed – you can imagine their reactions, but in particular, that of Reed. After all, Ray is one of Reed's senior officers, and he is now raking his memory as to what if anything he might have said to Ray."

"What, you mean Reed might have told Ray of our existence?"

"No, John, don't panic, he's not that stupid. But he's reflecting on what asides he might have said, quite appropriately when dealing with one of his senior staff. Now re-visiting those conversations through the fresh knowledge that he was talking to a bent copper."

"Yeah, yeah, I get that," Burrows said.

"Anyway, to business. The main objective has thankfully, been achieved, and the executive have ratified the secondary objective to remove all of Moon's criminal empire. But in addition, the prime minister has agreed an addendum, which is why I'm a little late in getting back to you."

"Go on, boss."

"In addition to Bentine and whoever it is he is RV-ing with. Detective Chief Superintendent Gary Ray is to be removed; permanently: clear?"

"Oh yes, loud and clear."

CHAPTER SIXTY-SIX

Bentine liked Gary Ray, he'd always been a hundred per cent; both trustworthy-wise, and in the work he had done for him. Which, until now had manly consisted of passing him intel on what the Crime Agency were up to. He knew from this that he'd never been on their radar, but people he had to deal with often were. Occupational hazard, and Moon was a prize example, but he'd had no choice in working with the Manc.

However, it still puzzled him how a thug such as Moon had managed to come up with a buyer for the goods – the merchandise being such an unusual commodity on today's black market. But, Bentine could see that changing in today's climate. His chance meeting with that Serb back in Hanioti had led him to the seller; and the seller had said there was more where this current lot came from. All he had to do was romance whoever Moon's buyer was and this could prove to be a very lucrative partnership.

Sure, he'd thought about retiring after this 'one off', but things change, and this new distribution route, from the Serb – through himself – could be an absolute gold mine. And, with Gary on board, he was confident he could manage the risks. He already had the transportation means with Captain Pugwash – or whatever his real name was – and the new guy Gerry had already proved his worth. No, things were looking good.

As they had driven away from the Romsey area, and both laughed at Bungalow Bill's demise, Gary proved his worth once more.

"Here you are, boss," he'd said, as he fumbled around in his coat pocket, "a little present for you. I managed to liberate this from Moon before you off-ed him."

He'd then thrown Moon's mobile phone into his lap. Bentine spent some of the journey time researching it. It was a pay-as-you-go, as he would have expected, and its number was the one that Bentine had for Moon; so it was his operational phone for this job. In fact, it only had a handful of numbers in it. Two he realised were Bill and Phil as they appeared next to texts, which made it obvious. But one number had been rung at roughly the same time each day over the last week. It had no incoming call from it, but did have one text conversation exchanged shortly after the lorry had cleared the port saying, "Cargo clear and en route. Should be at Charnock on time, will advise if any delays." The single answer simply read, "Yes." Bentine didn't know what 'Charnock' meant. He turned to face Gary. "I thought Moon told you that the RV was at the Forton services on the M6 in Lancashire?"

"He did, and I'd convinced him he'd live if he told me straight. Why?"

Bentine, then repeated the texts to Gary, and said. "What the fuck is Charnock then?"

"Charnock?" Gary said quizzically, before pausing. Then, "Got it. The little twat. He'd said the exchange was to take place at motorway services, which made sense. He's just given us the wrong ones. Forton is near Lancaster, whereas Charnock Richard services are near Chorley."

"Brilliant, Gary. Let me know when we're thirty minutes away and I'll give this number a ring. It'll take some of the surprise away for the buyer, should help the exchange to go more smoothly."

"What if it freaks him out?"

"Well, the trouble with a motorway services, is he could be anywhere. He will have to show himself to us, so without a warning it could all go to rat shit. I'd rather ring him first and smooth out any concerns he has at Moon's absence. End of the day, the guy wants to buy, and what we're selling isn't something that's easy to get your hands on. He'll know that. He's bound to be wary, but we can reduce that with a call. It also shows an act of good faith; ringing him in advance."

"You're the boss, and yes, I can see what you're saying."

"That's why I'm the boss. Anyway, how far away are we?"

"About an hour, give or take. Anyway, what'll you tell him about Moon?"

"I'll tell him that we discovered Moon's plan was to rip us both off. How he was going to take the money and keep the goods, how but for us, he was about to be ambushed. That we are doing him a favour, because I know – as the supplier – that there are more deals available for the future. If he's anything like the businessman we think he is, that should reassure him, and feed his greed."

"Sounds good to me, boss."

"Fuck it, I'll ring him know."

Ten minutes later, Bentine closed down Moon's phone and turned to face Gary once more. "Did you catch most of that?"

"Your half, yes, it sounded sweet enough by the end."

"Yeah, he was a bit sus at first, but then opened up a little. Said, he'd always had some reservations about Moon. He's dealt with him before, but only on 'far less sensitive commodities', which I took to mean drugs. Said, he was surprised what was on offer when Moon first approached him to see if he could find a buyer for our stuff."

"So, this guy, our buyer, is obviously not the end-user then."

"Obviously not. But I guess that's not uncommon. Though he does say he is passing it on directly to the end-user, so then the chain as good as ends with him."

"So, he's happy enough then?"

"He was by the end, though, I think the prospect of future deals whet his greed, and sealed any doubts. He's given me his motor's details and told me where on the car parks he'll be."

"Happy days, boss."

"Happy days indeed, Detective Chief Superintendent Ray. Happy days indeed."

***

Jane had calmed down now. She'd nearly lost Bentine and the bent cop – Gary Ray, Burrows said his name was – on the M25. She had hit the pre-rush hour traffic. And judging by the tracker's signal, Bentine must have just missed it. The signal kept greying out on the sat nav's covert channel, but she had just kept on its limit with some creative driving. She'd ignored the cacophony of horns from other drivers, who must have thought that some of her manoeuvres were crazy. The hard shoulder undertakes were some of the trickiest stunts, which always brought a response. She just hoped that no one rang the cops with her number plate, but she couldn't risk losing the signal fully; everything rested on her keeping the eyeball – albeit, a technical one.

She'd rung Briers who said he would have the relevant police radio channels monitored and warn her if her number plate, or that of the others, was mentioned. She did have a set of ghost plates in the boot, same make and model, from a car in Inverness, but if she had to stop to change them, she'd surely lose the tracker signal. She pressed on, hopeful.

Burrows had kept in touch and seemed to be making good ground. He reckoned he was only ten to fifteen minutes behind her, and as soon as she had settled down behind the targets, at a normal speed, he'd close the gap even faster. Steele, on the other hand was further away, but apparently 'ringing the balls' out of the MI5 pool car, God knows what state they'd get that back in.

According to the tracker, Bentine and Ray, had stayed on the M6 and not used the toll road at Birmingham. Their route was longer and slower as a result, probably wanted to avoid any CCTV cameras that might be present at the paying booths. She passed this onto the others and knew they would all make up some ground on the toll road, which was always quiet. Indeed, by the time she had reached Staffordshire, Jane reckoned she was only ten miles behind the targets. By the time she entered Cheshire, she had slowed down to a steady seventy miles an hour, a mile or so behind the targets.

They were probably the only two cars doing seventy, most other flashed past at around eighty, but clearly Bentine wasn't taking any chances; the last thing he'd want would be a pull for speeding.

As she mused on this fact, Jane realised she hadn't seen a police car since the M25, when she'd had to brake like hell, and then safely crawl past it. They seemed to delight in driving at sixty-five miles an hour, for no apparent reason. But at least this meant that none of the drivers she'd pissed off had bothered reporting her. She hoped Burrows and Steele had the same luck.

Fifty minutes later, the targets' signal suddenly started slowing. She looked at her watch, it was nearly five – supported by the steady increase in traffic over the last hour – and it was pulling away from the blue line on her screen. They were leaving the motorway.

She put her foot down in the hope she might get a glimpse of their car on the exit slip road, but knew there was little chance. After a few minutes, she entered the exit lane, leading to Charnock Richard services, near Chorley in Lancashire. There was no sign of the target vehicle, but at least she was in a stream of traffic giving her good cover, just in case they were monitoring which vehicles followed them off the motorway. After all, Ray was a cop. Jane didn't know if he was surveillance trained in any form, but he would no doubt be vigilant.

The exit lane went uphill to the services, so nothing came into view until she actually entered the site. There was a large car park ahead of her, which she headed for, whilst she took in her environment. The signal on the sat nav was still moving, albeit, slowly. She pulled up behind a large 4 x 4 to give herself some cover, while she scrutinised the screen.

The tracker dot seemed to be behind her, and then stopped. She jumped out of her vehicle to look. Ahead of her were the services buildings with signs for petrol and the exit back onto the motorway beyond that. Looking behind her, the way she'd come, she could see the exit slip road and then a hotel or lodge set back. Parallel to the motorway, but hidden behind trees. In front of it was an access road, which led past car parks in front of the motel buildings. She also noticed a road that bridged the motorway. Looking across, she could see the services at the other side, on the southbound carriageway.

She jumped back into her car just in time to see the tracker dot crossing the motorway bridge. Shit, they'd left the services. She quickly, manoeuvred her car and went after them.

CHAPTER SIXTY-SEVEN

Jane was about to enter the access road that led from the services to the lodge, and beyond, when she saw a police 4 x 4 pull into the lodge car parks from the road that crossed the bridge, and park up. Shit. She quickly swerved back onto the services road and returned to the main car park. She knew if she tried to leave the way Bentine had, she would surely get a pull from the cops. It was illegal to leave the motorway this way, though she was sure many motorists did, which was probably why the cop car had parked where he had. Right in front of the lodge, covering the exit onto the road bridge with a view of anything that came off the main service area.

She had no jurisdiction, and the last thing she wanted was to attract the attention of the local law: she'd have to go on foot. If they did stop her, she could say she'd hitched a ride and had been dropped off. They couldn't prevent a pedestrian from leaving this way. Hopefully, they wouldn't stop her, presumably knowing this; but it was the only option. She quickly put her ballistic vest on under her puffa jacket and checked her Glock handgun. It was loaded with a full magazine and she had a spare in her pocket. She parked the car on the main car park, pulled up her hood and set off on foot.

She walked with purpose, as if it was a journey she did regularly. She avoided looking at the parked patrol car, and due to her hood, wasn't able to use her peripheral vision. A small price to pay as it covered her face; the less the cops saw, the less they would recall.

She continued to walk purposefully, being 'overt to be covert' as her surveillance trainer had once told her. Being obvious in plain view, but with a reason for being there, meant people often saw you, but without noticing you.

She pulled her phone out as she walked. Props were always good to help you blend in, but she needed to update Burrows anyway.

He told her to be careful, he was hammering it as fast as he could, and was only minutes away. He said he'd get Briers to put a bogus call into the local police to get rid of the motorway patrol. It would not come quick enough for her, but at least he'd be with her sooner.

She walked straight past the front of the police car as she chatted on the phone. She was half expecting an 'excuse me', but none came. She ended the call, as she turned left onto a narrow footpath that bordered the road across the bridge. She blew out a sigh.

As she reached halfway across the bridge, the other side came more into view. The bridge and roadway, which traversed the motorway, were arched, and it was only at the midway point when she could see the other side clearly. It looked similar in design to the northbound, but with no lodge. She also saw the access road to the services from the roadway, which was where Bentine's motor had gone a few minutes earlier.

Then she realised something else; she was alone. She felt a shudder of anxiety go through her. She'd often operated for Five or Six having spent months in the field alone. But this was different. At least with the security services she was always confident in her cover. The fact that her legend was meticulously prepared, and would stand any scrutiny, but this was far cruder. This was confrontation. And as much as she had enjoyed her short time with the Special Projects Unit, virtually all her work had been with Burrows or latterly with Steele. This time she was alone, and things could go loud and proud. It gave her a newfound empathy towards cops; after all, they dealt with confrontation every day, often in life threatening circumstances. They were not like other public servants, whatever the politicians might think.

Neither was she certain of her next steps, it all depended on what she found when she got to the other side. She'd have to find Bentine's car first and then find Bentine and Ray. Presumably, they would be doing the exchange with whomever. She decided to try and simply observe for starters. She couldn't take them all on. If she could see enough of the buyer and what vehicle he might be in, then they could go after him later. Her focus had to be on Bentine and Ray. Once she found them, she'd wait until after any meet had finished before challenging them. This would also give Burrows a little extra time to arrive.

She turned left from the bridge road, and headed down the access road to the southbound services. It ran downhill and curved in the middle, which cut off her view. Now out of sight of the police car on the other side, she ran down the road.

She also realised something else; the success of this job now firmly rested with her. She shook off her trepidations, crystallised her emotions, and felt her confidence returning. No time for pre-op nerves. It was time to go tactical.

CHAPTER SIXTY-EIGHT

Bentine kept his eyes fixed on his door mirror as Gary drove down the access road to the southbound services. He watched as the patrol car crossed over the road bridge. "Did you clock that?"

"Yeah, he never saw us thankfully. He's either just passing or heading to the other side. Either way he'll be out of our view."

"True, but we'd better keep a look out for the bastard in case they serve better doughnuts on this side."

Gary just smiled back at him as he manoeuvred the car onto the edge of the main car park and pulled up. Taking in his surroundings, Bentine gave himself a start. The layout was similar to the other side without the lodge. However, right in front of them, adjacent with the end of the access road was a small standalone single-storey building with the word 'POLICE' above it. But it looked empty.

"Don't panic," Gary said, as if seeing his surprise. "It's derelict now, cuts and all that."

Bentine relaxed, he could now see the windows were covered with metal mesh and the paint was peeling from the window frames. It had obviously been unoccupied for some time. He texted the buyer to say they were here, and no sooner had he pressed the send button, his phone gave him his second start as it vibrated and rang to life. He answered it without speaking.

"Tony?" said the buyer's voice.

"Yeah I'm here, but you have me at a disadvantage, I don't know your first name."

"Just call me Mr Jones," came the reply.

Arrogant twat, Bentine thought before speaking further. "Where are you?"

"I'm in the disused police post. Moon suggested it, and for all his Scouse wit, it's the perfect place. We're in a busy environment, yet this is private with no chance of being disturbed."

"Granted."

"But the sooner we conclude business the better, if you'd like to come via the front door which is closed but unlocked, bringing the commodity. And come in alone. Do it now." The line went dead.

"I don't know who the fuck he thinks he's talking too," Bentine started, and then relayed the conversation to Ray, who then started the car engine and parked behind a HGV cutting off their view of the police post.

"What are you doing?" Bentine asked.

"Well, this Jones bloke doesn't know what we look like, but he'll no doubt be watching out the front of the police post. He's told you to go in alone, but doesn't actually know if you're on your own or not. So, why don't I go in with the case? Pretend to be you, it'll be safer. I won't have to say much, and we don't sound too dissimilar anyway."

Bentine never ceased to be impressed by Gary. What he was saying was true.

"If it's a trap, I'll sort it without you having to put yourself at risk. And if it goes sweet, you can bell him later to sort out future business or whatever," Gary added.

"Nice one Gary, I'll let you take it in then. There'll be a bonus in it for you." Bentine then watched Gary check his gun, refit a

339

silencer to it and shove it inside the pocket of his jacket. He then got out of the car, collected the Samsonite briefcase from the boot, and set off around the HGV towards the police post.

***

Jane rounded the bend and slowed down as she walked the last few metres down the access road. At the junction with the services road, she could see a large car park in front of her with a large HGV directly in front blocking off most of the view. On her right was a disused looking single-storey building. There was a row of unoccupied cars parked in a row to her left. As she crossed onto the car park, she saw a man leaving on foot carrying a silver case. She quickly ducked down behind a parked car and watched as the man approached the disused building, which she could now see was an old police post. This must be it. The man entered via the front door, which closed behind him.

As quickly, but as stealthily as she could Jane scoped out the immediate area of the car park. She soon found Bentine's car parked on the other side of the HGV, with Bentine in the front passenger seat. The man carrying the case must have been Gary Ray.

She quickly rang Burrows to tell him exactly where the meet was going down.

"Cheeky bastards," he started, then, "is there any way you can get a view?"

She said she'd try, and he finished, saying he was close now.

Jane had been trained by the military in the art of rural Surveillance which to the lay man simply meant she could set herself up as an OP – Obs Point – be it in a field, or in a flower bed in a busy shopping arcade. And part of her training had included how to conduct a CTR – Close Target Reconnaissance.

As furtively as she could, she made her way from the main car park staying out of view of both Bentine and the front aspect of the police post. The building itself backed straight onto a high privet hedge, which would make her job easier and quicker.

Once hidden behind the bush, she made to the rear of the building where there was a single window, which was covered with a steel mesh. It was also partly overgrown, which helped.

Within minutes, she was crouched down behind the rear-facing window with a view into the room. She'd blacked her face with some earth to stop any light reflecting off her skin. Hardly a classy facemask, but it would do the job. She also put her sunglasses on to cover her eyes. The light was fading quickly now, which only helped conceal her presence.

Inside the darkened room, she saw a man stood with his back to her. He appeared white from his hands, was over six feet tall and well built. At his side was a large black briefcase. Stood in front of him was the man she'd seen moments earlier – Ray – and the silver case was at his side. She couldn't make out the conversation but both men exchanged cases, and each looked inside. She couldn't see the contents, but both seemed pleased with what they'd seen; each nodded.

Then in a flash, Ray pulled a silenced handgun from his jacket and shot the other man twice.

He'd been standing to one side as he did so, and the first round came out the back of the man's head at a right angle, taking a large part of his skull with it. Closely followed by a liquefied grey sludge. It looked like porridge.

The second shot went straight through the man's neck and narrowly missed the window. It must have hit a main artery as a pressure washer jet of blood covered the glass and obscured Jane's view.

CHAPTER SIXTY-NINE

Bentine's phone started to ring. It was Gary. He looked at his watch; he'd only been gone four minutes; that was quick.

"Everything OK?"

"Yes, it all went sweet. Though Mr Jones knows, I'm not you. He saw us arrive apparently, and said I sound different." Gary said.

"Problem?"

"No, he understands security, though he's alone. No, we have done the exchange; he'd just like you to come in."

"No worries, I'll be in in a minute," Bentine said, and then ended the call. This guy was sharp, that was for sure, but that could only bold well. He was sick of having to deal with dickheads. He got out of the car and headed towards the police post.

***

Jane heard the body fall but couldn't see through the glass. A moment passed, she could hear a voice, Ray's, and he didn't sound as if he was going anywhere, obviously, on the phone. Then the blood on the window started to thin as it ran down the pane. She got a glimpse of a shadow moving towards the door.

When she'd first looked inside, she'd realised that this was a rear room with a door to the front part of building. It looked as if Ray was now leaving. She rushed around the side of the building, but without showing herself at the front. She would get a clear view if Ray left. But he didn't.

She used the brief impasse to ring Burrows and whisper her update; he told her he was approaching the services now, and she should only watch until he arrived.

She closed the phone, frustrated. There had been no noises coming from the front of the building so she risked a quick look around its corner, keeping her head low. Nothing.

A couple of minutes passed, still nothing. She went back to the rear window, but still couldn't see clearly through the blood; what was left on the glass was starting to thicken as it clotted, making visibility bad again. She was as sure as she could be that no one was standing.

She darted around to the front again and a peek provided nothing. She decided to run to the main car park to get a view of the front of the building. She did so, using a nearby advertisement hording to mask her route.

"What are they doing in there? They've been ages now" Jane wondered. She made her way to the HGV, which was still unoccupied, and rolled underneath the trailer. At least from here she could see the front of the police post, and if she turned the other way, Bentine's car.

She turned the other way. Bentine's car had gone.

CHAPTER SEVENTY

Bentine walked into the front room of the police post, closing the door behind him. Standing in front was Gary Ray, with a black briefcase in his left hand. He was dying to see all the cash in it, but didn't want to appear crass in front of Jones; he could play with it later. "Where's Jones?" he asked.

"In here," Gary said, gesturing to an inner door with his head, "but there has been a slight problem. Didn't want to say too much on the phone. No need anyway with you only being outside."

Bentine was puzzled, but just nodded a response as he followed Gary into a rear room.

"What the fuck—" he started to say, before ending his own sentence prematurely, whilst he stared at a man's cadaver oozing gore and brains over the threadbare carpet. Then his thought process kicked back in. Jones must have tried to rip them after all. Gary had really done well. He heard the door close behind him and turned to face Gary. "You really are due a bonus—" he started to say. But he paused on seeing Gary's silenced handgun pointing straight at him. He continued. "What are you pointing that at me for?"

"You've always thought that you were so fucking clever," Gary started.

"What?"

"Shut up and just listen for a change. I've been dangling from the end of your string for years now, like some yoyo. You yank my rope and I come running. Living off your scraps, whilst you live it up in Greece or wherever it is you bore the shit out of the locals with your condescending arrogance."

"Look Gary, I don't know where all this angst is suddenly coming from, but fuck me, there's plenty in the case for both of us. And, as Jones tried to rob us and you brilliantly dealt with him, we can double our money with a new buyer."

"It's no good trying to blow smoke up my jacksie. This, pal, is all mine," Gary said, tipping his head to floor where both cases now stood together. "And you're staying here."

"I'll find you."

"No, you won't."

***

Jane rolled from under the wagon. Christ, she must look a treat, mud all over her face and dirt all over her clothes. This was hardly the time to worry about her appearance, but the thought flashed through her mind nonetheless.

She ran over to the police post, and pulled her Glock out, just in case. Glancing around her, she saw no one. Gingerly she entered, cringing as the hinge squealed its resistance. She listened, no noise they'd both obviously gone, but she knew she couldn't be too careful. The inner door was closed and she burst through it with her firearm outstretched in a two-handed grip.

She immediately saw the body of the man shot earlier over by the window. Then as she took in her environs, she saw a second one. Tony Bentine. Minus most of his face; where several rounds had obviously destroyed it.

She checked for a pulse on both men, knowing it was a futile move. Nothing. Then she searched them, nothing on either body. No wallets, keys, or phones; Ray had been thorough. She rushed outside just as Burrows pulled up. His car engine was issuing a strange assortment of metallic tinkling sounds.

He jumped out, and she said, "It's OK. I'm OK."

"Have they gone?"

"Well, Ray has. He's got the money and the goods."

Jane quickly explained all to Burrows who first rang Steele, and then Briers. She heard him update them both, as they got into Burrows' car. He set off back up the access road, as he turned to face her.

"I've told Steele to stay on the M6, whilst we jump in your car. Hopefully, the tracker will still be active."

"What did Briers say?"

"Said he'd turn out a clearance team from the Manchester field office to clear up the mess. Even though there is probably good evidence to put Ray on trial now, we couldn't do so without compromising us or the Special Projects Unit."

"Or Nigel Crabtree," Jane added.

"Plus, the bastard would no doubt make it sound like he was there to arrest the bad guys and claim self-defence. Before 'having some sort of breakdown,' which he'd no doubt claim as his reason why he'd legged from the scene. End up being a hero."

Jane nodded.

"Anyway, Briers reaffirmed our orders. Nothing has changed."

CHAPTER SEVENTY-ONE

Burrows was thankful that the cops had gone as he powered his motor past the lodge onto the main northbound car park. He pulled up next to the other car and they both got in. The sat nav was still connected, which was good, it would save them some precious moments; but he needed to confirm which way Ray had gone. He could have stayed on the local roads for all they knew. Shit. The dot on the screen wasn't moving, it was still showing the car as being on the southbound services. It wasn't greyed out, as it would be if they were out of signal range, it was glowing red. He didn't know what that meant.

Jane reached across from the passenger side, shortly after he swore. "Shit," she joined in.

"What?" Burrows asked.

"Red means the battery on the golf-ball transmitter is down."

She quickly explained that the golf-ball trackers were only supposed to be used as a temporary measure, until a more substantial device could be deployed.

He had Steele powering north, so Burrows was about to set off south, then decided to ring Briers first. He came off the phone a couple of minutes later, and turned to face Jane. "All is not lost. Briers said that the sat nav we're using is experimental, and has another use," he saw Jane raise one of her eyebrows, which always looked cute, then carried on. "The new version of golf-ball trackers are designed to monitor all mobile telephone signals within six feet."

"What, record conversations?" Jane asked.

"No, they're not that good, but they do record the mobile phone numbers. It's supposed to capture phone use within the car, and then transmit the data to the sat nav."

"That's impressive, I feel out of date already and I only left the security services six months ago."

"Me too; nothing stands still. Anyway, Briers suggested we sit tight. He's transferring the stored data from our sat nav, and working with it in conjunction with the live cell-siting facility he's got on the go. Said he'll ring us back in five."

Jane nodded, and they both sat in silence, which surprisingly became an awkward gridlock between them. There was something he'd been meaning to ask Jane, and it might as well be now. On the last job, they had ended up in bed at her flat. He wasn't quite sure how, but he knew his feelings for her were deepening; it was more than physical.

They had agreed to park their feelings until after that job, and consequently had done nothing about it since. He was sure she felt similar; he'd seen the side-glances when she thought he wasn't looking. Here goes.

"When this job is over, how about you and me... you know?"

"'You and me... you know', what?"

Burrows wasn't sure if Jane was pretending to seem obtuse, or just toying with him. "You know we said we'd 'park our feelings until after the job', well that job finished, and so nearly, has this. I know they came pretty much one after the other, I just thought I'd ask if you—" Burrows started to say, until his damn phone started to ring. Looking at the screen, it was Briers. He'd have to take the call.

"Good news, John. We've isolated one number that was predominately used from within the car; it called an outside number a couple of times, and most tellingly, around the time of the meet, give or take. I reckon that must have been the buyer. It also took an incoming from another number at the same site. That could have been interplay between Bentine and Ray; and the number we are attributing to Ray has come up on the cell-siting. As long as he keeps it switched on, we're on him."

"That's absolutely superb, boss. Is he heading back towards Manchester?" Which Burrows had fancied all along.

"No, he's M6 north, just entering Cumbria."

Burrows had no idea why Ray would be going up there. Briers finished by saying that the ANPR was limited to none existent north of Lancaster, away from the most populated areas, so it was down to them to get on him whilst they still had his signal on the cell-siting.

Burrows ended the call, and quickly brought Jane up to speed as he headed for the exit lane. Their previous conversation would have to wait, again. Jane said she'd ring Steele whilst he concentrated on driving like an idiot.

CHAPTER SEVENTY-TWO

Fifty-five minutes later, after some serious driving, Burrows and Jane arrived on the outskirts of Windermere, a small town in south Cumbria, near the lake of the same name. Burrows knew it was one of England's largest lakes at twenty-odd miles long, but what was Gary doing here? Or more accurately, his phone. He just hoped the two were still together, and this wasn't some elaborate ruse; with Ray's phone on the back of some flat-back, minus its owner. They had to remember they were dealing with a National Crime Agency detective, and a senior one at that.

After Preston, the traffic had thinned markedly, and it was now dark, which was a blessing and a hindrance. Hard to see, hard to be seen; but he'd take the darkness any day.

In a further call, Briers said the cell-siting had the phone static in the centre of this quaint hilly town. But that's about as accurate as he could be. Said they were lucky to have that much; it was only due to a nearby mast atop a foothill. There were no real mountains here; they came further north into the national park proper.

But, it would do, the town wasn't that big. He started to traverse the area starting from the outskirts working his way in. Jane rang Steele, who said he'd been here five minutes already.

Then Steele rang back a moment later, and Jane put the phone on the loudspeaker. Burrows could hear his hushed tones. He'd found Ray's car.

"It's stationary on a small car park next to a bed and breakfast," he said, and then gave them the address. It was just down the road in neighbouring Bowness.

Burrows' phone rang whilst Steele was still talking. It was Briers; he put the receiver to his ear and whispered, "Be quick, Frank. Steele's on the other line. He's found the car."

"Don't lose him, the signal's gone. He must have turned his phone off."

Burrows quickly relayed this to Jane and Steele.

"Contact, contact, contact," Steele said down his phone, "confirming Gary is out of the guest house side-door and towards his vehicle. I'm going to engage," then Steele's line went dead.

Burrows knew Steele was right. They'd lost the signal, and the chances of maintaining a physical eyeball on mountainous country lanes at this time of the evening would be difficult.

Jane had already tapped the address into the sat nav, and five minutes later, he braked hard as the B & B came into view. Next to the grey slate building was a small car park, Burrows drove into it to see only two vehicles in it. Steele's and Ray's.

Steele's was parked across the back of Ray's, at a right angle preventing it from reversing out of its space. Though, it looked as if there might have been a coming together. The car park was dark, benefiting only from ambient light from streetlights down the road.

Burrows stopped his car halfway into the car park's only entrance. His headlights illuminated the scene. Burrows and Jane were both out of their motor in an instant; both had weapons drawn. Burrows could see that the car park was empty. And, so it appeared, were both the cars. He ran to Ray's as Jane ran to

Steele's. As he arrived, he could see that the car was indeed empty, with its driver's door open. Then he heard Jane.

"JOHN, OVER HERE. QUICK. LARRY'S BEEN SHOT."

Burrows arrived at Jane's side a moment later to see Steele, slumped down in the driver's seat, blood oozing from his side.

"In and out," Steele panted, caught his breath, and continued. "Bastard got the jump on me. Might have done a rib or two as well. He went that way," Steele pointed towards the lake.

Burrows told Jane to stay with Steele, and shushed him when he said there was no need. He checked Ray's car, no keys left behind, not that he expected there to be any. He shut the door and shot out one of the rear tyres with his silenced handgun.

Turning to Jane, Burrow's said, "Get Larry and his car out of here, I'll go after Ray."

"I've had a quick look at Larry's side," she said, continuing, "and I think he'll be OK so long as there's no serious internal damage, but I've got to stop the bleeding. This is an MI5 pool car, so there should be a first aid kit hidden in the boot somewhere. As soon as I've moved him and sorted out the bleeding I'll head after you."

"Agreed," Burrows said, before turning and heading for the lake.

CHAPTER SEVENTY-THREE

Burrows pondered whether Ray would have a boat moored or not. He wasn't even sure whether this lake led to a river or not. But, it was so vast; a boat to the other side would be enough to secure his escape. For now anyhow. He'd no idea why Ray had come here, but he can't have expected to be attacked. In fact, Steele said he made some remark when he shot him, 'Go join your boss' or suchlike. He probably thought Steele was the buyer's man come after him.

The side road that led to the B & B had been on the flat, traversing the hill that the town appeared to be built on. He soon reached its T-junction with the main drag, which went downhill towards the lake, or uphill towards the main A-road which by-passed the town on its journey north.

He hesitated. Which way to go? He looked both ways; nothing. Downhill would be the easiest option looking at the road's severe gradient, and Steele had said 'towards the lake', but how could he know? He rang Jane quickly, and asked the question. The reply impressed him. Steele told her that when Gary ran off, he crossed over to the other side of the road, which indicated he would be headed downhill when he reached the junction. Clever lad, Burrows thought, as he set off downhill as fast as he could.

Burrows was confident in catching Ray, as Steele had passed on another gem. Ray was carrying two briefcases: one silver and one black.

Five minutes later, Burrows slowed as the lake came into view at the bottom of the hill. Or one end of it did. He could see a road, which crossed its end, with fields to its southern edge and moorings to its north. Some of the boats tied up were impressive, and the bigger ones had lights on. He'd have to be careful.

In front of him was the eastern edge of the lake, with the town behind him. The grass verge disappeared out of view, presumably to the water's edge. This side didn't appear to be as grand a mooring place, indeed the few boats there looked like rowing boats. They looked like pleasure craft.

He stood still as he scoped the area. In the centre of the green was a small building, which Burrows soon realised was the start of a short pier. Lighting was sparse here, and shadows were long. Then Burrows saw one lengthen behind the pier head building. He ran across the grass and slowed as he made his way around the other side of the structure.

Five metres in front of him he could see Ray in the gloom at the water's edge. His back facing him, as he undid one of the rowing boats. It had a brightly painted number '13' on its side.

Ray placed both cases into the boat and was about to join them.

"Ahem," Burrows said, in a mock clearing of his throat.

Ray spun around, and even in the half-light, Burrows could see the look of incredulity on his face.

Burrows was pointing his handgun directly at Ray now, aiming for his central body mass. Both of Ray's hands were free, but Burrows knew his gun wouldn't be far away.

"You?" Ray said.

"Yes me, now keep both your hands were I can see them."

"Were you working for Jones all along?"

Guessing Jones must be the buyer, Burrows answered, "Don't insult me. And don't judge everything through your own shattered view of the world."

Burrows had made a rudimentary error. The insult had angered him, and his reply was turning into a rant. A rant, which was the distraction Ray had clearly been after.

He cut himself off as he saw Ray pull a silenced gun from behind his waistband, followed by a small flash of light from the end of its muzzle.

He felt warm air accompany a whizzing noise as the round flew past his left ear.

He fired back, as a second round from Ray's gun found its target, slicing its way through his left upper-arm. He hit the ground, but saw his shot explode through Ray's stomach, taking him into the water.

Burrows caught his breath, and tried to forget the pain. He was urged on by the belief it was only a flesh wound, and by the adrenaline rush that had started to numb the agony. He pulled himself up and went to the water's edge. He could see Ray floating, his open and empty eyes reporting his passing.

With his good arm, Burrows grabbed Ray's trouser leg before he drifted off. Pulling him back, and ignoring his own pain accentuated by the effort, he heaved Ray's body into the rowing boat.

He caught his breath and then rang Jane. "I need a bit of help. I'm down by the lake. Are you any good at rowing?"

"What?" Jane replied.

He ignored her question. "And bring that first aid box with you."

EPILOGUE

Burrows walked into the subterranean briefing room at Pimlico with his left arm in a sling. He had been wearing it for the past two weeks, and should really have ditched it by now, but he was hoping to incite more sympathy from Jane.

He'd initially, been taken to the same military hospital as he had after the last job, when he'd been shot through the other arm. Surprisingly, the same doctor and nurse had attended to him. "Making a bit of a habit of this," the doctor had said.

"Now you've done both arms, will you start on the legs next?" the nurse had added, "just so we can prepare things in advance."

Funny, everyone was a comedian these days, he'd thought.

He let the thoughts pass as he grabbed a coffee and sat next to Jane.

As they waited for Briers to arrive he recalled how he'd seen Jane twice over the last fortnight, she'd been up to his home in Thame from her Milbank flat to see how he was. But each time she had headed home at the end of the day. Consequently, he had not finished the conversation he'd started with her at Charnock services.

The steel door opened and Briers came into the room with his usual business-like manner, grabbed a coffee and joined them.

"How's the arm, John?" Briers asked.

"Fine thanks, I'll have matching scars now, which will be nice."

"How is Larry? Jane asked. "I've been to see him a couple of times and he seems to be making progress."

He mashed up his insides a bit, but will make a full recovery, in time. Bit more severe than your little nick, John."

Even Briers was getting in on the act, and he wasn't known for his one-liners.

"How is he up there though?" Jane pushed, pointing to her head.

Burrows had also noticed that Larry had seemed down when he'd been to see him.

"Let's just say, he's considering his future. It was his first mission with the SPU and he came off worst. Well, worst out of you three," Briers added.

"I wondered if he might," Jane said.

"I've told him to take his time, there is no rush. And in any event, it'll be a while before he's fully fit, so he can use that time to ponder," Briers added.

Burrows already knew there were no issues from the operation; Jane had helped him get Ray's body to the centre of the lake, before weighing it down with stones they'd gathered from the shore. To make certain, Briers had sent the Special Boat Service in to find the body and weigh it down properly. The lake is vast and deep, it had taken them a couple of days to find him. Fish food now.

They had left Ray's car, and the room he had in the B & B, untouched (apart from having to change the flat tyre). It would just look like a disappearance, or so they hoped. Apparently, he'd told his landlady a day previous he was off overnight walking and camping in the hills. The resulting search by the mountain rescue and RAF teams had been called off a week later.

The clearance teams had sorted out the police post, and made the comment that they didn't know what the hell had been going on over the last twenty-four hours, but they hoped that was the end of it." Briers' contact at Five had reassured them.

"What about the Crabtrees?" Jane asked.

"They swallowed the story John gave them. That he'd been hired as a one-off to help find Susan, whilst her husband and his team were on hold. As he'd retired, neither the cops nor the baddies would know about him."

"Not too far away from the truth," Jane said, adding. "And what about that phone box in London that Moon had been ringing? The one which Steele was sent to watch?"

"No idea," Briers said. "Could have been any number of things. I don't think it was connected."

"Anyway, Frank," Burrows said, turning to face Briers. "We're still waiting to find out what was in the cases. What all this has been about."

"Well, as you know the black case was full of cash from Jones – Jack Jones – to give him his full name, a known criminal, a middle-man. But the silver Samsonite case was a bit trickier."

"How do you mean?" Jane asked.

"Well the locks were coded, which took GCHQ until yesterday to crack. We tried x-raying it and scanning it, but it was lined with lead."

"That explains the weight," Burrows interjected, "no wonder it slowed Ray down on his way to the lake."

Briers carried on. "We were bothered it was something nuclear or chemical as a result, so it had to be opened under laboratory conditions at Porton Down."

"Is that the government's military science place in Wiltshire?"

"Yes," answered Jane.

"Well, we needn't have worried, as it was neither of the two," Briers said, continuing, "It was diamonds; blood diamonds to be correct. Or conflict diamonds as they are often known as."

Burrows had seen documentaries about these. They were illegally mined rough diamonds sold on the open markets to fund African armed conflicts.

"I've read about these," Jane said, "but wasn't there an agreement reached in South Africa with all of the diamond producing countries to stop the sale of these stones?"

"There was," Briers answered. "It was called the Kimberley Process, named after the town where the agreements were made. They brought in a certification process to prevent the sale of these diamonds on normal markets. Which, I guess opened the floodgates for criminals to try to develop. Countries such as The Ivory Coast are still accused of transferring diamonds of dubious source out of the country across her borders."

"Well, I'd have not guessed this was all about stones," Jane said.

"Nor me," Burrows added.

"Well, I'll just wrap this up, and say thanks for a top job. Had these idiots got away with this, word would have spread, and the thieving classes would have been snatching cops and suchlike off the streets whenever they felt the heat getting too near. I'm paraphrasing the prime minister's words here, but I wholeheartedly agree."

Burrows nodded, as did Jane.

"I suggest you grab some down time whilst you can; you never know when the executive of the SPU will reconvene. Come on, lunch is on me."

THE END